'Murray Middleton deftly [illegible] propulsive new novel. He [illegible] origins hark back to *Blackboa*[illegible] long been mired in journalisti[illegible] and in hand-wringing sentimentality, and he makes it fresh, troubling and compelling. The structure is cinematic, but the real strength is in the operatic assuredness of the writing. The chorus of voices have real bite, real sting and real tenderness and truth. It sounds like real life.'

CHRISTOS TSIOLKAS

'I don't know if Murray Middleton is the bravest writer in Australia or the stupidest. What I do know is that *No Church in the Wild* is amazing; a novel of wisdom and assurance and audacity. The fact that this book exists is a triumph. The fact that it works – and that it's so good – is a miracle.'

MILES ALLINSON

'A fierce, urgent, necessary book.'

JAMES BRADLEY

Murray Middleton is a Melbourne-based writer who spent eight years working in the city's education system. His first collection of stories, *When There's Nowhere Else to Run*, won *The Australian*/Vogel Literary Award and was shortlisted for the New South Wales Premier's Literary Awards. He is also a winner of *The Age* Short Story Award. In 2016, Murray was named *Sydney Morning Herald*'s Best Young Australian Novelist. He currently restrings tennis racquets for a living.

Also by Murray Middleton

When There's Nowhere Else to Run

NO CHURCH IN THE WILD

MURRAY MIDDLETON

PICADOR
Pan Macmillan Australia

Pan Macmillan acknowledges the Traditional Custodians of Country throughout Australia and their connections to lands, waters and communities. We pay our respect to Elders past and present and extend that respect to all Aboriginal and Torres Strait Islander peoples today. We honour more than sixty thousand years of storytelling, art and culture.

First published 2024 in Picador by Pan Macmillan Australia Pty Ltd
1 Market Street, Sydney, New South Wales, Australia, 2000

A catalogue record for this book is available from the National Library of Australia

Typeset in 12.2/17 pt Adobe Garamond Pro by Post Pre-press Group

Printed by IVE

For our bub, Leonard,
who brings us bursts of joy
and wonder
every day of our lives

A NIGHT OF FIRE AND NOISE

ALI

You can already hear the screaming. Ali and Funda bolt through the moonlit park, towards the red and blue lights that're bouncing off the high-rises. Ali's chest is full of electricity. The cops have been hanging around the flats for months, doing slow circles of the car park in unmarked Holdens, getting Afros to empty their pockets on the half-court, wanting this to happen.

People are pouring out of the towers, surrounding the police cars that're parked in the middle of Holland Court. Cops in shiny yellow vests keep forcing their way through the crowd, trying to get to the action. Other cops have got a crew of mostly young kids pinned on the concrete, knees digging into their spines.

'Is that Walid?' asks Funda, clutching Ali's arm.

Through the crush of bodies, he recognises his grade six friend, facedown on the road.

'You can't do this!' cries Walid's older brother, Hassan, wriggling and weeping as the cops cuff him.

Ali hears a woman wailing and follows the animal-like sound until he sees Walid's mum pleading, 'Please, please stop!'

More police cars rock up. They start loading the kids into the back of divvy vans. Walid's eyes are frozen with concentration, like they always are when he's trying not to cry.

A muscly female cop gets off her radio and begs everyone to calm down, but it only makes the crowd go more crazy.

Another one of Ali's friends, Musa, shows up and pushes past them, ripping off his LeBron singlet. 'What the fuck are you doing?' he yells, putting on a deep, adult voice.

The muscly cop tries to talk to him, but Musa dodges her and sprints towards the group of cops who've got Walid pinned.

'Get back!' they yell.

He starts throwing roundhouses and gets blasted with capsicum spray. Orange blobs splatter his flesh. The cops wrestle Musa to the road. He keeps struggling and spitting at them, even though his eyes and mouth are covered in goo.

Walid's mum lets out a squeal and collapses, her body getting swallowed by the people around her.

Musa's neck is totally locked off, cheek kissing the concrete.

A plastic bottle gets hurled from behind Ali, just missing one of the cops' heads.

Even more police cars roll up, their lights going mental, sweeping over the fishnets on the balconies of the walk-ups. An orange mist's blanketing everyone. Ali's face feels like it's on fire as his throat starts to tighten.

'What happened?' he hears Funda ask someone.

'They're saying Hassan threw a rock at the pigs, but he didn't do nothing.'

'So who started it?'

'The pigs,' says Jai, who Ali used to play hide-and-seek with when he lived in the Victoria Street walk-ups. 'Hassan was chilling with his bro and they started calling him a black cunt, and this and that, wanting him to arc up.'

Musa's in cuffs now, gunk dripping off his chin, getting dragged towards the divvy van. His legs are limp, like he's been shot. Jai starts yelling, 'Racist pigs!'

'RACIST FUCKING PIGS!' croaks someone else deep in the crowd.

Soon everyone's yelling it out, even Funda.

'Take it easy!' the muscly cop's saying, edging towards the crowd, trying to make sure no one else steps up to them. 'Please,' she yells, raising her hands. 'Get outta here. Go home!'

'Why should we?' yells Ali. 'We *live* here.'

SUMMER RENEWAL

ANNA

'How was the PD?' asks Zoe.

'You would've hated it,' says Anna, straining her voice to be heard over the racket coming from the communal tables behind them. 'It had a real cultish vibe. Some of the other teachers actually looked like they were swallowing it.'

'God.'

A slim, psychotically efficient waitress drops off their laksas and scans the restaurant to see if there are any tables she can guilt into leaving before the seven-thirty turnover.

'They had this absurd colour wheel of emotions that we all supposedly pass through over the course of our lives. I felt like putting up my hand and asking how asylum seekers stranded on Manus Island are supposed to pass through the stage of *inspiration and renewal*.'

'You should've.'

'I don't think it would've gone down too well.'

'Who cares?'

Anna slurps a spoonful of her broth and is disappointed by the lack of chilli.

'They gave us this survey – it had thirty yes or no questions – and if you answered *yes* fifteen to seventeen times, it meant you have leadership potential. And of course the new principal was smack bang in the middle with sixteen yeses, which, as far as I could tell, was the point of the whole exercise.'

'How many yeses did you have?'

'I've got no idea. Maybe ten. I wasn't taking it seriously,' says Anna, noticing Zoe's phone pulsing on the table. 'It's fine, you can answer it.'

'Nah, it's not important.'

'Please don't feel like you've got to choose my bitching over the Cannes Film Festival.'

'Very funny.'

A voicemail alert flashes across the screen and Zoe flips her phone facedown on the table.

'What's happening with your Kokoda trip?' she asks.

'I haven't decided whether I'm going yet.'

'Are you serious?'

'Yeah, I'm still weighing everything up,' says Anna. 'It's just . . . sleeping in a tent full of creepy-crawlies and getting mozzie bites that'll probably become infected and turn into malaria . . . to be honest, it kinda freaks me out, Zo.'

'If you don't fucking go, I will.'

She can picture Zoe over there, leaping out of her sleeping bag at the crack of dawn, no aches in her spine, scaling mountains and filming it all on a GoPro.

'You know fifty people a year get airlifted off the trail?'

'Stop being such a misery guts,' says Zoe. 'Just go. It'll be great for you.'

Anna prods at her rubbery egg noodles, feeling her appetite vanishing as she repeats Zoe's condescending words in her own head. *Great for you.* Sooner or later it always comes up, sucking the air out of any good time she might be having.

'Sorry, babe,' says Zoe. 'That's not how I meant it.'

'I know.'

The loud hum inside the restaurant is deafening. It's hard to figure out why there's a line stretching out the front every night. There are so many other amazing Asian places in Flemington where you can eat without sounding like you've had a tracheostomy the next day.

'Wanna talk about it?' asks Zoe.

'Not really.'

All talking about it will do is bring everything back to the surface. The waitress paces over and glances at their lukewarm laksas, unable to hide her contempt for their slow progress.

'I hate that I'm still thinking about him,' says Anna.

'Babe, you're entitled to think about him,' says Zoe, taking hold of Anna's bony wrists. 'You've just gotta give it time.'

'Isn't six months enough time?'

'Obviously not.'

'You know, I literally have no memory of volunteering to go on the trip. It's like the whole thing was set in motion during some kind of trauma-induced psychosis.'

Out the window, Anna sees a year eleven boy emerge from the underpass of Newmarket Station, clutching a giant Slurpee and dribbling a soccer ball, blindly, across the road. It feels like only yesterday that the boy, Musa, was a chubby year seven student begging her to let him go home early from school camp.

'You okay?' asks Zoe, squeezing her wrists.

'I'm just tired,' says Anna.

She already knows she'll have a terrible sleep. The night before classes start is always the same. Even if she does manage to pass out before midnight, she'll only wake up, heart fluttering with anxiety, and end up monitoring the time on her phone until she bites the bullet and showers before it gets light outside, her sole objective to survive a day of perfect exhaustion.

ALI

'Guess who I just saw at Laksa King,' says Musa as Ali's lining up the nine ball.

'Nicki Minaj?' says Ali.

'I wish, man!' says Musa. 'Seriously. Miss Kelly and some smoking hottie. They were sitting in the restaurant, holding hands, looking in love and shit.'

'Miss Kelly doesn't like women that way.'

'How do you know?'

Ali will never forget the choking sounds echoing from the English teachers' office as he was leaving detention last winter. All the words that spilled out of her mouth after he knocked and asked if she was okay. Her apologising every ten seconds, between sobs.

'She just doesn't.'

'Whatever,' says Musa. 'I bet those two are gonna go back to Miss Kelly's crib and screw each other's titties off all night.'

He puts the pool cue between his legs and thrusts it at Ali and Walid, making loud women's moaning noises. Some of the young'uns at the table tennis table start giggling.

'Who're you laughing at, fresh boy?' yells Musa, getting in the face of a new kid with wavy tribal scars on his forehead.

'No one,' says the kid.

Musa raises the cue behind his ears and the kid flinches. 'Far out, I'm only playing you,' he says. 'You don't have to shit your pants.'

The kid looks like maybe he has shat his pants.

Ali's already seen him a few times this summer, hanging at the half-court, wanting to join in, but not having the courage.

'Leave him alone, Musa,' says Walid.

They go back to playing the game where everyone has five balls on the table to protect. Musa gets on a roll, sinking three in a row, celebrating each time by flexing his flabby biceps.

'I thought of a banging MC name,' whispers Ali to Walid.

'Yeah, what?'

'Sediment.'

Walid squints at the red cloth of the pool table, the skin tightening into a V between his eyebrows. 'I don't really get it.'

'It means, like, I'm the dirt that's sunk to the bottom of the towers . . . you feel me?'

'Maybe you need something more positive?'

'Nah, that's not how –'

'It's your turn, Prince Ali!' yells Musa.

'See!' hisses Ali. 'I'm sick of that name. It's too obvious.'

He grabs the cue and slams the white ball as hard as he can, accidentally knocking Walid's last ball into the middle pocket.

'Sorry, man.'

Walid goes over to the couches where Ali's cousin, Funda, and Kylie are poking at their Nokias and starts airing out his Chelsea top in front of the fan. Ali busts Tyler standing above Funda, pretending to read a *Naruto* comic while looking down her singlet. The way young'uns at movie nights and on the Youth Bus have started checking out Funda this summer is disgusting. Not being able to stop what's happening in their imaginations does Ali's head in.

'Nah, no chance,' says Musa as Ali aims at his second-last ball, feeling his wrists shake with anger. The ball wobbles off a hole in the cloth, changing its path just enough to make it rim out of the far pocket.

'This table's rigged!' says Ali.

In year seven, he thought life would be perfect when they were old enough to boss the pool tables at the Community Centre, but now that they're almost adults, and they can kick kids off the tables whenever they want, life doesn't feel so perfect. The cloth is faded and ripped, and no one ever does anything about it. The main chick who supervises them is always reminding them that they should be grateful for everything they've got, as if it's wrong to want more, even though 'more' isn't even close to equality.

'FUCKING BITCH!' yells Jai, cracking his bat on the table tennis table and chipping a piece of wood off the handle.

The supervisor races over and snatches the bat out of Jai's hand. She leads him past the couches where Tyler's still perving on Funda to the back door, and tries to calm him down outside.

The new kid with tribal scars is too afraid to pick up the broken bat and play. Musa grins at him and starts humming 'Lemon Tree', the song he and Walid learnt at the Language Centre. Most of the young'uns join in. The new kid looks seriously weirded out. Hearing the chorus, Ali gets this crazy feeling: like even though he was born in this country and his two best friends weren't, and even if things have happened to them that should never happen to any kid, the song is one thing they have that he never will. And maybe that's why Musa's smiling while he sings it.

Traffic rumbles above Ali, Musa and Walid as they sink under the concrete ribcage of CityLink. Soon the rumbling gets drowned out by the fruit bats screeching to each other, sucking the juice out of eucalyptus trees, slowly turning them into giant, twisted pips. Heat pulses from the concrete, stinging Ali's eyes. It's way too hot to go home, even if he wanted to. Families are hanging around the play equipment out the front of the towers, still deciding if they're going to sleep in the park tonight.

Every summer a different journalist comes from one of the important newspapers to take photos of residents looking hot – last year they brought a thermometer for kids to pose with – but nothing ever changes once the articles get published.

A rhyme slices into Ali's mind:

Makin prizners bake nights
Sizzlin from them scrape heights

As they climb Racecourse Road, he hums the new lines to the loop that's been popping in his head all January – phat beat, ride cymbal, glitchy string sample on the first kick of every bar – working out where to put the emphasis on each syllable. Hacking into '*bake* nights' and '*scrape* heights' from the back of his throat, so there's a harsh rhyme and a soft rhyme.

He can feel the track making the back of his neck tingle, like it does whenever he hears 'Changes' by Pac. Always as the beat drops over the piano. This crazy feeling, as if Tupac knew he'd be dead by the time everyone was hearing it.

Familiar faces fill the tables of Bulsho Café and Deli Afro: *Xanjo*, *Bidar*, *Genay* – cheeky nicknames Walid has explained – plus Ali's dad, sitting by the window in his wrinkly grey shirt. He hardly even nods back when he recognises Ali. Still, it's perfect having a place where Dad and all the cleaners, security guards and taxi drivers can eat *bajeya*, *bur* and *sambusas*, pulling slippery lamb bones out of their soup, before starting their shifts every night.

The problem is that it's so close to where the important horserace happens. That's why skippies who wear suits and put dead birds in their hair at the races want this land. You can tell because cafés keep opening and every time there's an auction in F-Town, the street is packed. Million-dollar houses across the road from blocks of graffitied low-rises, like Funda's crib, crawling with rats and cockroaches, both sides always seeing each other as a threat. The skippies regret letting the people from the towers have somewhere so expensive to enjoy their cultures, even though none of them ever say it from their own mouth.

Someday soon the government will demolish the four towers, because the real estate prices are going to be too good to let anyone stay. It's already started happening with the walk-ups in Carlton, where Ali used to rap battle Viet crews back in the day, before they all got dumped in suburbs with no train lines. The government will build hundreds of shiny apartments on the site of his, Musa and Walid's homes, so the fancy houses from when this area was rich with gold will be worth even more money.

'I can't believe school's starting already,' says Ali, splitting open his Snack Box and letting the steam rush out.

'Wanna wag tomorrow?' asks Musa.

'Yeah, maybe.'

'How bout you, Walid?'

'The first day's important,' says Walid.

'Bullshit!' says Musa. 'It's just a boring-arse speech by the principal and then we watch some white people movies.'

'The school's got a new name,' says Walid.

'A new name doesn't mean *shit*.'

'It means they wanna get rid of Somali pirates like you!' says Ali, pegging a half-eaten chicken nugget at Musa.

'YO, PICK THAT UP!' yells Jasmine from the counter.

Ali finds the soggy nugget on the floor and slots it into the bin. He hears Jasmine rapping 'My World' to Najima, putting on Iggy Azalea's fake American accent. Her flow's pretty tight, carving the lyrics with her left hand as she holds an imaginary mic in her right.

A single-carriage 57 tram screeches to a stop out the window. Three inspectors step off to bust a hottie from Kensington Community for not having a ticket.

'I was hanging with my cousin on Sydney Road last week and they had this new sexy tram,' says Musa, pausing to slurp his Coke until there are only ice cubes rattling inside his cup. 'There were, like, four or five carriages and extra space for people with handicaps. The pillows were all nice and soft, like this . . .' he says, patting his own tummy and purring like a happy cat.

'That's fucked up, man,' says Ali, over the top of Musa's meowing. 'They always give us the stinky old trams.'

'Your bro was in Brunswick, too,' says Musa to Walid. 'He was chilling in the shisha lounge, watching Arsenal–Man U. I nearly didn't recognise him.'

'I know,' says Walid. He stares at his fat-stained chip packet, eyes elsewhere, like they always are whenever anyone mentions Hassan, expecting him to have answers.

'Look at these ugly fucking pigs,' says Musa, pointing at two cops who're walking towards the entrance.

Ali recognises one of them. Her name's Athena, like the Greek goddess. She comes to the school sometimes to let students try on her bulletproof vest while she craps on about making the 'right choices' in life.

'I smell bacon!' hisses Musa as the police wait for Jasmine to get their food. Neither of them bothers to look at him. 'Fucking rats,' he says, under his breath.

'Jazzy told me they get free KFC,' says Ali.

'Yeah, right,' says Walid.

'Did you see them pay?'

'I wasn't watching.'

'There you go. It's the same at Macca's and everywhere.'

'Far out,' says Musa. 'That's corruption!'

'You should become a policeman, Musa, so you can get free chips.'

'True that!'

Musa starts sniffing, pretending there's a bad smell.

'Careful,' says Ali. 'They'll fuck you up like they fucked up that G from Footscray.'

'Seriously, why would they do that?' says Walid.

'What do you mean, *why*?' says Musa. 'He was, like, in their custody and because he kept talking smack to them, they beat the shit outta him and dumped him in the river.'

'You can't just kill someone and get away with it in this country,' says Walid.

'*We* can't,' says Musa. 'But they can.'

Hopefully Jasmine or Najima spits in the cops' Zinger Burgers.

'Should we bounce?' asks Musa.

'For sure,' says Walid.

Ali catches his own finger scraping off skin around his thumbnail at the thought of going back to his stuffy, empty flat, while Dad drives wasted strangers in and out of the city all night.

'You have a good night, officers,' says Musa on his way past the police, still sniffing.

Athena smiles, but the other cop – a solid guy Ali hasn't seen before – stares Musa down. He looks like the task force officers on steroids who get sent in whenever they want to pretend to clean up the towers. The beasts who don't have to obey any laws.

Hot air whistles through the gaps in the pebbles on the thirteenth floor, fighting the smell of cigarettes and stale urine. Abandoned shopping trolleys, stuffed rubbish chutes, stinky shoe racks, paint chipping off the pipes, the rusty wire over the windows; walking in these unloved corridors every day, having to step over syringes and red and blue–topped vials and avoid kids in hoodies weighing up in the laundry every morning, it's obvious to Ali what politicians think of him, no matter what they say in front of TV cameras.

Walid's mum has got the security lock on again. He knocks softly so he doesn't startle her. She drags her mattress away from the door and opens it, kissing Walid on the cheek and smiling sleepily at Ali. The whole flat has the after-smell of garlic and slow-cooked meat. Picturing the purple-flowered basil that Walid's mum sizzles in butter to give her stews their special flavour makes Ali long for their primary school days, when he used to get invited over for iftar.

Hassan's sprawled on the couch, topless, fidgeting with the PlayStation controller. He doesn't bother to say anything to Ali or Walid when they sit down. Flesh glistens on his round stomach. It looks like he's starting to grow breasts. From staring at him, you'd never think he used to be able to dunk a basketball.

'You wanna play?' asks Walid.

'I'm good,' says Ali.

Without talking, Hassan saves his game of *FIFA* and hands Walid the spare controller. Walid picks Chelsea and Hassan picks his favourite team, Liverpool. Before home games, back in the Rafa Benítez days, he'd always sing 'You'll Never Walk Alone' with the crowd at Anfield, red scarf stretched in his hands, belting the lyrics out in his throaty, tone-deaf voice.

Soon the score is 6–0 to Liverpool. But Hassan has no mercy. 7–0. 8–0. 9–0. Walid sits deep in his box and defends, only hoping to score on the counterattack. Loose fittings rattle inside Hassan's controller. Ali can feel the intensity of Hassan's silence underneath the English commentator who keeps saying nice things about his goals, and the thousands of imaginary Liverpool fans, singing songs that stop his brain from getting too busy at night.

Sweat stings the corners of Ali's eyes. There's no way he'll be able to sleep tonight, even in his own flat, ten levels lower down. He stares out the window at the grid of lights that blanket the factories and shipping containers of the western suburbs. Endless electricity. This is the thing about living in the sky. Everyone pretends you're invisible, but you get the best view in the city. *Towerz to tha Throne* would be a sick name for an EP. The cover art could be the One Tweezy tower dissolving into a throne with Ali sitting on it.

He cocks his hand and plays with the rhyme from earlier:

Makin prizners ***bake nights***
Sizzlin from them ***scrape heights***
Dah-dah dah-dah ***fake light*** *. . .*

Whispering the syllables, he works out how he can have a lit finish to the first verse of the EP:

We talkin white flight
I'll give u my sight
Take a long fight
Ta make this city wake right
Makin prizners bake nights
Sizzlin from them scrape heights
Hate ta break ya fake light
I never seen a day bright (uh!)

A wave of applause rises from the TV, building to a roar of excitement. The bright colours of the screen swim across Hassan's eyeballs, like police lights. Ali remembers the first time he ran into Walid and Hassan after the police had dragged them into their van in front of everyone. Five years ago now. Even though it was only the morning after they'd been arrested, he could see something was different in Hassan's eyes. It wasn't just that there was still blood in them.

TYLER

'I'm sorry, Binh,' says Tyler.

The little Vietnamese nerd looks up from his laptop, taking the bait perfectly. 'For what?'

'I'm sorry you have such a small penis,' says Tyler. He raises his little finger and wiggles it at Funda and Kylie, who scream and swerve out of the way.

Binh goes back to work, but Tyler can tell he's mad. He thinks he's so much better than everyone else. Selling rotten fruit at the Vic Market with your tight-arsed parents who can't even speak English isn't something to be proud of.

Tyler wiggles his finger at the girls again until Mr Hunter finally builds up the balls to tell him to stop.

'What's the matter, sir?' asks Tyler. 'Have you got a little one too?'

Ali and Musa crack up laughing. The stupid dicks, always carving *Flem Boyz* and *Thug Life* into school tables, believing crazy conspiracy theories about Tupac.

'Shush!' says Mr Hunter, trying to act all tough.

Tyler lets it slide because it's the first day back. Mr Hunter's such a pussy, with his stale coffee breath and dandruff sprinkled all over his shoulders. He probably goes home every night, puts on some weird jazz music and cries himself to sleep after he jerks off over his students.

The class settle down and start typing on their new laptops. Tyler doesn't even have his yet. All the kids look like private school yuppies in the uniforms that they're being forced to wear by the fat-arsed new principal. Tyler's glad he hasn't got one. Wearing fugly shirts and uncomfortable pants to help the school pretend it's something it's not is lame as. Everyone knows it's full of refugees who're going to give jack shit back to the country and it's going to get shut down by the government in a year or two.

'Hey, Jai,' whispers Tyler, noticing Jai drawing Nazi symbols on the European settlers in his textbook. 'Let us borrow a pen.'

'Sorry, man, this is my only one.'

'That looks sick.'

Jai adds a Hitler moustache to one of the settlers who's buying a possum skin from a crew of Indigenous people. At least Jai's people were born here and actually contributed something back in the day, unlike Musa, Walid and all the other African bludgers in the flats.

Tyler puts his arm around Funda, but she shrugs it off.

'What's your problem?' he says. 'I was just asking for a pen.'

'No you weren't,' says Funda.

Ali's staring daggers at them from the back row, thinking he's some tough as Turkish gangster.

'Why're you still wearing that?' asks Tyler, pointing at the faded orange wristband Funda has from some lame music festival she must've gone to over the holidays.

'Because I feel like it.'

'Whatever,' he says, stealing a pen from her pencil case,

which has *Bruno Mars* written all over it. Girls are pathetic, actually thinking they have a chance with celebrities. 'What're we sposed to be doing, anyway?'

Funda rolls her eyes.

Tyler sees Mr Hunter look up at him and he stares him down, like a boxer at a weigh-in.

'You're so annoying,' whispers Funda, checking if Ali's still watching, then smiling. 'We're writing about our favourite history event.'

'You know you love me.'

'As if!' she says, rolling her eyes again. Tyler can tell she wants him. He takes one last peek at her tits pressing against her school dress, so he can memorise what they look like for when he's in bed later.

He hunches over his piece of paper. Everyone's being quiet and boring. He can't think of what to write about. History's the worst subject. The only good parts are when America gets seriously pissed off and starts nuking its enemies. Remembering how to write words is tiring. Teachers are always bitching about how he puts the letters in the wrong order, circling his mistakes and telling him how he should've spelt the words. But they don't really give a shit, and neither does he. You don't need to be able to spell to aim a semi-automatic at a camel fucker out in the desert and let them have it.

Small groups of losers are chilling on the benches around the court – *Minecraft* geeks, drama weirdos and goths, listening to slit-your-wrists music – passing time until they don't have to be at this povo school anymore. The yard's dead these days, unlike when Tyler was in year seven, when there were hundreds of kids running around in jeans and NBA singlets, stirring up all kinds of hectic shit. You didn't even talk to people who weren't in the same year as you. Now kids from every year get to play soccer, just so there can be a game.

Ali and Musa keep doing fancy step-overs, trying to look like pros, without ever actually going anywhere. Tyler hardly runs because he hasn't got deodorant on and he doesn't want to reek of BO for the rest of the day. The smell of fried food from the canteen's driving him crazy. He'd kill for a dim sim with soy sauce – or anything for lunch – but there's no way he's asking anyone for money.

He recognises a few new kids from Flemington Primary watching the game, so he goes up to them. Year sevens look young as these days. They're pretty much asking for a beating.

'Hey, do you guys wanna play?'

The kids look at each other, too scared to say yes. He bets their parents are yuppies with heaps of ugly paintings and boring books in their houses, probably in those massive terraces right near the police station.

'It's cool,' says Tyler, putting on his friendly voice.

Eventually the two pussies stand up and follow him over to the court.

'I'm Tyler,' he says, shaking their limp, fishy hands. 'If anyone gives you shit, let me know.'

The boys join in, but no one passes to them.

Tyler lays a sick shoulder check on Binh and apologises by slapping him on the back as hard as he can. He catches Binh's eye and wiggles his little finger.

A few minutes later, the ball gets kicked up his end and he sees Binh sprinting after it down the sideline. Tyler knows it's the perfect moment. He bolts towards Binh and clips him on the ankle just as he's trying to accelerate by, sending him flying to the asphalt, hands first.

Binh starts bawling straight away, like the bitch that he is. There's a chunk of skin missing from his knee and his palms are all cut up. He charges at Tyler. Tyler's ready for it, so he swerves out of the way, catching Binh with a jab in the ribs.

A crowd quickly forms around them. Binh goes lower this time and tackles Tyler, but Tyler manages to roll him so that when they hit the asphalt, Binh takes most of the impact. As they're grappling, Binh lands an arsey elbow on Tyler's jaw, which means it's time for shit to get real. Tyler pins him down and goes all out, pummelling Binh's sternum and slipping his head into a chokehold, ready to strangle the little nerd.

'What're you gonna do, huh?' pants Tyler.

Someone grabs the back of his t-shirt and tries to drag him off Binh.

'FUCKING LET ME GO!' screams Tyler, swinging one last punch.

'No way,' says a familiar-sounding teacher.

'Alright, alright!' says Tyler, holding up his hands and allowing himself to get pulled away from the crowd. 'You can let go now.'

'Sorry, not yet.'

He twists his neck and sees that Ms Kelly's the person scrunching his t-shirt. Her hands are shivering. Teachers aren't allowed to lay a finger on students. He could easily arc up and get her fired, but he decides to let it slide as she drags him towards the office. It's better if he grins while everyone's watching, so they think he's properly crazy.

'So, tell me what happened,' says Ms Costello, lowering her glasses like she always does when she wants you to tell the truth.

'Binh had the ball and I slide-tackled him, but I accidentally tripped him,' says Tyler, making sure he looks her in the eye, 'then he got up and was all pissed off and in my face, so I had to defend myself. I can't just let someone beat the shit outta me.'

'Are you sure, Tyler?'

'Yeah, he totally flipped out. I don't know why. All I did was tackle him, which is in the rules.'

'The rules,' she says, snorting as she shakes her head.

'What, did he dog on me?'

'Sorry?'

'You know, *dog*. We're all wolves, miss, but only a dog takes the side of man over its own kind.'

'I'm not sure I follow.'

He can imagine Binh sitting on this couch fifteen minutes ago, crying pathetically as he snitched.

'Am I suspended or what?' asks Tyler, noticing a splotch of blood on the shoulder of his t-shirt.

'I'd rather not have to suspend you on your first day back,' says Ms Costello. 'The first thing you're going to do when you leave this office is walk into the sickbay and apologise to Binh.'

'Fuck that, suspend me then!'

'Luckily, I know you don't mean that.'

'Whatever.'

It makes fuck-all difference whether he gets suspended now or later. Everyone knows how it's going to end. They just pretend they don't, so they can sleep at night.

'While I've got you,' says Ms Costello, putting on her caring mother's voice, 'I can't help but notice that you're not in uniform today.'

'Everyone looks gay.'

'Unfortunately, Tyler, you don't have a say in whether or not you wear the uniform. It's compulsory.'

He glances at the clock on her wall and calculates that he's already missed half of General Maths.

'I don't get why the school's pretending it's rich now.'

'Believe it or not,' she says, smiling at him for some stupid reason, 'I didn't invite you into my office to debate the school's new marketing strategy.' She adjusts her glasses. 'Do you have any idea why your mum hasn't registered for our assistance package?'

'Nah,' he mumbles.

Ms Costello's been annoying as ever since the meeting with Mum's social worker last year, always asking if he's happy living at home and if he's getting enough food, thinking she's an expert at being *his* mum. Her own kids probably hate her.

'I have to drop by Highpoint after school,' she says. 'Would you mind if I picked up a shirt and some extra pairs of shorts and socks while I'm there?'

'Do what you have to do,' says Tyler.

He doesn't give a fuck either way. Mum and him don't need sympathy from anyone. Sympathy is what makes you weak.

*

PAUL

'Great stuff, mate!' yells Paul as a little tacker from Debney Meadows handballs the footy, lace out, to him.

Paul sends it skimming along the dry grass and watches the next kid paddle the pigskin in circles, scuffing up dust, running round like a headless chook.

Few of the detectives from Moonee Ponds are volunteering today as well, letting the kids take hangers over them on the tackling bags. That's one drill the youngsters never get sick of.

A smart-arse in AJ's group boots the footy at his head, spinning like a bloody helicopter.

'Come here a sec,' yells AJ.

He shows the kid how to hold a drop punt: seam upright, guiding the ball onto his laces and kicking through it. Problem is, most of these flats youngsters kick like goalkeepers, slicing their leg across a soccer ball.

Smart-arse grabs the ball and roosts a torp near the entrance to the Community Centre. AJ's already shaking his head.

'When can we have a match?' asks one of Paul's kids.

He remembers what it's like, cracking the sads at all the boring drills the adults make you do. Just wanting to get out there and play a game. Figure the rest out for yourself.

'I don't know,' says Paul, enjoying playing it straight. 'What do you reckon, AJ?'

'They haven't been very well behaved, have they?'

'Nah, mate, not today.'

'*Pleeeeeeeeease!*' begs the kid who proposed the match – feisty bugger – trying to prod the footy out of Paul's hands.

'Maybe a quick game?' says AJ.

The kids all cheer and pump their fists. Easy crowd.

Paul and AJ start laying out the cones. Beautiful new patch, this. Nothing like the quiet, concrete courts of display homes in the old patch. Gum trees everywhere here. Young couples walking staffies through the park, flinging slobbery tennis balls with that plastic launcher the hipsters all seem to have. Old-timers resting on benches, walking sticks glued to their laps as kids rattle by on scooters. Mum in a hijab teaching her son to ride a bike, hovering over him as he wobbles along the path, picking up speed.

'POLICE DOGS!' yells a topless bloke in trackie pants who's cutting across the oval. Tattooed, arms glistening. Elbows must be on fire the way he's thrashing them about.

'Mind walking around next time?' yells AJ, completing the boundary cones.

Bloke starts barking. A few of the kids join in.

'Old mate reckons we've got it in for him.'

'Why's that?' asks Paul.

'A while back, one of our police ops caught him trafficking crystal meth up there,' says AJ, pointing to the northwest block of flats, where the bloke's heading. 'Typical set-up, people coming and going at all hours. Everyone within cooee knew what he was up to.'

Bloke's still barking as he turns at the half-court.

'The prick copped the plea and ended up on an eighteen-month community order. Got evicted. But at VCAT, his lawyer found some bloody loophole. She was a real piece of work – young, idealistic, daughter of a QC – reckon you already know the type.'

'My brother just started dating one,' says Paul.

'Honestly, the way this muppet's lawyer was carrying on, you'd have sworn he'd done nothing wrong in the first place. They decided that because he was only dealing in the doorway, handing it around his screen door, instead of inside the actual flat, he could keep his grubby home.'

Paul grabs the goalposts as the detectives start dividing the kids into teams and handing out bibs.

'*Common ground*, that's what the prick's lawyer called it,' says AJ, gnawing at a loose tissue of skin on his lip. 'Never mind that there's a family of five living next door to a drug den. Somehow *his* rights have been infringed.'

'Unbelievable,' says Paul, noticing the sunlight melting into the pebbles of the high-rises. 'So it's more meth than heroin over here?'

'Maybe fifty–fifty these days,' says AJ. 'The issue we've got round here is the number of chefs there are in the western suburbs – it started out as Macedonians and Middle Eastern fuckers – buying pseudoephedrine, cooking battery acid and wholesaling it. A lot of it ends up leaching into these high-rises.'

'Sounds like one hell of a shit fight.'

'I'm ten years deep, mate. After all the gangland stuff, when we locked up most of the blokes with presses who were flooding the market with cheap pills and speed, the game changed. Suddenly there wasn't as much muscle around. Now every scumbag reckons he can cook up a batch of hillbilly shit and make an easy profit.'

'And if it goes pear-shaped, he'll at least get a Channel Nine show written about him.'

'That too,' says AJ. He finally bites off the fleck of skin and starts nibbling on it. 'I miss heroin, to tell you the truth.

I don't mean that how it sounds. The old-school crooks, at least they knew their role in the game. They were just drowsy. These new punks, all jacked up on amphetamines, are unpredictable. You never know what they're gonna do next.'

They walk towards the kids, dwarfed by the rectangular shadows that have already swallowed half the oval.

'Old mate will slip up sooner or later,' says AJ, looking back at the flats as if they're one giant organism. 'Whoever thought it was a clever idea to whack four thousand people on top of each other was dead-set kidding themselves.'

Everything's good to go for the match.

'You want the reins, Knowlesy?' asks AJ, offering Paul his crusty whistle.

'See how we go.'

'Where are all the defenders?' yells AJ, his tone instantly brightening.

'Let's start!' screams feisty bugger.

Paul hurls the pigskin into the air. Kids in red and blue bibs chase it in every direction, misjudging the bobble off the rock-hard turf. Feisty bugger gathers the ball and tucks it under his wing, charging towards the goals, forgetting to bounce. Should've known a whistle wasn't going to stop him.

* * *

Rebecca J. • 26 January, 9:04pm
These African kids are literally laughing at our policing

> **Swagman** ⮫ **Rebecca J.** • 26 January, 9:05pm
> *Taking. The. Piss.*

Swagman • 26 January, 9:05pm
Happy Australia Day btw, not that we're allowed to celebrate it any more

Concerned Mother • 27 January, 8:51am
As a taxpayer I'm fed up with thugs every night committing crimes, spitting in the face of OUR culture

Mayday Malone • 28 January, 5:33pm
Honestly lock em up throw away the key not complicated

> **Swagman ⮫ Mayday Malone** • 28 January, 5:34pm
> *Or deport*
>
> **Jesse ⮫ Swagman** • 28 January, 7:18pm
> *Where r the parents?!?!?*

* * *

Paul spots the mother up front in black, clutching her friend's arm, sitting a few metres from the Commissioner. So much of the bleeding-hearts horseshit starts with the family; how hysterically they want to play it for the cameras. They sweep all the stuff about their kid being in custody in the first place right under the carpet. Suddenly he was a loving, talented teenager who had the world at his feet.

Easy to pick the journos from the left-wing rags sniffing around in the crowd, pestering old folks and plugging notes into their phones. You don't need to be Einstein to figure out what spin they're going to put on tonight, no matter how it plays out. The worst part is that it empowers the crackpots on the VicPol blog who're always running with the 'taxpayer' line, as if they personally pay every cent of coppers' wages. These days any keyboard warrior can throw in their two cents and feel good about themselves in their cosy echo chamber. Never mind the facts. He'd like to see them have to make split-second decisions under pressure, instead of sitting in front of their laptops, sipping chai lattes and thinking they've got the answers to all the world's problems.

You can't win. If you take a softly-softly approach, the fruit loops on the right will say kids are laughing in your face. But if you go any harder, you end up in a stifling hall like this, with a couple of hundred people baying for your blood.

The murmuring inside the Community Centre trails off as the Commissioner shuffles his notes, finally ready to get the ball rolling.

'We understand the community's interest in this case,' he says, nice and slow, making sure everything hits the mark, 'and we understand why there might be a perception that justice has not been served. Someone's son has died. A young man. To have a young life taken away is a tragedy. I'm sure we can all agree on that . . .'

The mother's face is already buried in her hands.

'I have complete confidence in our local detectives, as well as the Homicide Squad . . .' says the Commissioner, rabbiting on about ethical standards and the OPI, not that he's appeasing anyone.

Someone else is sobbing in the front row. Impossible to tell if it's a man or a woman. Within seconds, the sobbing erupts into a blood-curdling wail, echoing off the vaulted ceiling.

'I can assure you all that the investigation has been very thorough . . .' the Commissioner's saying.

Seems heartless for him to keep reading, pretending he can't hear the grief gushing out – no doubt that's what everyone's thinking – but if he stops every time the family starts blubbering, he'll be here until midnight.

'We haven't found any evidence to indicate that a murder took place,' he says, looking up from his notes and doing a stern Union Jack of the audience. Journos are going berserk. 'There is also no evidence to suggest that the police were involved, in any way, in what took place.'

The murmuring starts again.

Hands are shooting up left, right and centre. The poor bugger's got to pick them out one at a time without any idea who got in first. Might as well have skipped the verbal foreplay and cut straight to the part where his cojones get sliced and diced. He greets every tag he's given – 'liar', 'corrupt', 'gangster' – with that famous steely gaze of his. One bloke comes straight out and says the coppers drowned the kid, as if he hasn't heard a single word all night.

Mum up front rises to her feet, cheekbones wet and taut, making sure the Commissioner can see her clapping.

Paul can feel his own blood boiling; same as the previous Commissioner – *Glass Jaw*'s – used to whenever he was getting grilled. The precious prick could never hide it. If Paul's ever going to climb the chain of command, keep his paws clean, and wear the red crowns on his shoulders, he's got to find a way of swallowing it, just like the Commissioner. Cool as a cucumber. Knows he's still got hours to go up there without grub or a piss break. You want to start handing out Academy Awards, look no further.

ANNA

'*Hello, puppies!*' chirps Anna, clinking her knuckles against the giant bay window of Hardimans. Pippa looks adorable, curled up next to Banjo in the dusty morning light. Anna wishes she could race inside the pub and wrap her arms around Pippa, crushing the life right out of her.

'*Who's-a-good-boy?*' she blurts, feeling her teeth grind as she turns her attention to Banjo. His buttony schnauzer eyes finally open, searching through the glass. As always, he starts going off his head. '*Who's. A. Good. Booooooy?*'

So cute. The problem is that it only makes her miss her parents' kelpie, Sam, even more. Sam Boy. The best dog in the whole world. As the pressure on her molars increases, Anna fights the familiar urge to call the Lost Dogs' Home and keep a secret from her landlord, knowing it'd be the final step on the path to permanent singledom. Spending the summer watching dog compilation clips on YouTube every night has been alarming enough.

'*Easy there, Banjo!*' she says, seeing the publican wander in to check on the commotion, which is her cue to smile sheepishly and make a run for it.

She cuts through sloping backstreets, past renovated

workers' cottages – rows of beautiful Victorians that she'll never be able to afford on a teacher's wage – and follows a bluestone cattle route towards the old saleyards, weaving by rickety-looking stock pens. She's missed this walk. Decades-old ghost signs above shopfronts on Racecourse Road. Squashed pink petals outside heaving cafés. Suited-up public servants bustling towards train platforms, sipping from KeepCups that smell of toasted spices. It's impossible to imagine this suburb ever reeking of abattoirs, tanneries and glue factories, being considered the bowels of the city.

Her backpack vibrates against her lower spine. She can't think of any friends who'd be messaging her this early in the morning. The possibility that it's *him*, finally touching base – finally apologising – brings on a flash of heat and a sharp, stabbing pain in her intestines.

She yanks out her phone:

Thoughts on Easter? xxx

Mum again. If only the invisible knives, set free, would stop slicing at her organs.

Too early to think about it

She knows she let her parents down by not going back to the farm over the holidays and lending a hand for a couple of weeks, and enduring the annual family piss-up on Christmas Day, patriarchal roles on full display. Coming up with an excuse was an ordeal. Not that anyone believed it.

Everything else ok?

The endless pity; the way everyone who knows what he did looks at her, and treats her like she's lost a limb.

It's the last thing she wants to be thinking about as she catches sight of the hideous concrete façade of the school. Zoe promised she'd get over it. 'Give it time,' were her exact words. This *is* time and nothing's even close to being fixed. The thing that still eats away at her is how she could be so unobservant. So complacent in her own life. You think you know someone inside out. You sleep next to them every night, you smell them, you confide in them, you argue, you laugh, you feel their pubic hair grinding against yours as you scrutinise each other from point-blank range . . .

After seven years, how can you still not have an inkling of what's going on inside your partner's head? And even if the crime is theirs, what does it say about *you*?

Linda's already in the new principal's ear as he plucks his third lamington finger, no doubt spruiking her credentials as a leading teacher. Patches of freckled skin are visible on his scalp through what's left of his thin grey hair. He looks a bit old to be starting from scratch. Even though he keeps preaching a digital education scheme and student-centred curriculum for the school in his briefings, it's hard to shake the suspicion that he'll go through the motions for a couple of years – new name, new uniform, put the literacy program out of its misery – before landing some cushy advisory job with the Department of Education to see him through to retirement.

Anna's already sick of him waffling on about attracting 'aspirational families'. What a ludicrous expression. If he really wants to increase enrolments and retain more VCE students, he'd be better off reviving the applied learning program. But she knows he doesn't care about the kids from the flats. For all the uproar that comes with flagrant racism, often it's the unspoken, embedded biases that are a million times more sinister.

Jenny Costello clacks into the staffroom in her heels, looking as trim and officious as ever, still glowing from her 6am spin class.

'I just had the pleasure of being sworn at by Tyler Peirce in the corridor,' she says, squeezing Anna's forearm. 'One of these days I'm going to throttle him.'

'I'll give you an alibi.'

'You're such a darl,' says Jenny, cheekbones rising like clenched fists. She surveys the uninspiring spread, wincing at the party pies, and settles on a carrot stick. 'The scary thing is, I doubt the mother would even notice Tyler was missing.'

'What's *her* story?'

'Four kids, three different dads.'

'Impressive!'

'You know, I genuinely think the world would be a better place if people had to seek my permission before they started breeding,' says Jenny, lashing out on another carrot stick. 'Mind you, it'd be a disaster for enrolments.'

She squeezes Anna's arm again and excuses herself, hurrying over to save Van from Rob Hunter, who's practically slobbering over her.

Anna piles fruit onto her damp serviette, avoiding the

pineapple, which has already started to turn brown. So much for doing big shops this year, slow-cooking curries and having delicious leftovers for lunch. All the New Year's resolutions she made – cook more, join a book club, try Zumba, read three political articles from *The Guardian* every day – require effort that's exhausting just to think about.

Van's nodding and smiling at Jenny, pretending she can't see the bouquet of farewell tulips behind her back.

Anna threads her way over to the sink and starts wiping it down with the mould-infested cloth, hoping to occupy herself until the speeches start. She'd kill to be on yard duty. Something about the fight she broke up yesterday still feels strange; the way Tyler was so wound up one minute and then able to make small talk with her the next. And how all the old chalk-and-talk teachers in her office, like Linda, were so quick to say he should've been expelled years ago.

'Hi there!' says the new principal, shovelling Moccona into his *Best Dad in the Galaxy* mug, unknowingly joining the conga line of *Star Wars* freaks to avoid at every morning tea. 'Apologies, we haven't had the chance to properly chat. I'm Peter,' he says, pointing at a dark splotch on his mug. 'Your new Sith Lord.'

'Anna Kelly.'

'I'm told you'll be tackling the Kokoda Trail this year.'

'Maybe,' she says, pretending she hasn't spent months scanning blogs and fixating on electrolytes, salt tablets and hourly calorie counts.

'In my younger, more robust days, my wife and I walked the trail,' he says, glancing down at his own paunch. 'I know it might be a little difficult to believe.'

'What was the worst thing that happened?'

'The *worst* thing,' he says, watching boiling water dissolve brown crystals. 'Why do you want to know the worst thing?'

'So I can start mentally preparing myself.'

Cutlery's clinking against glass. Jenny raises a spoon and waits for the cacophony of pleasantries to die down, reserving an extra special *are you done?* glare for the Neanderthals in the science department.

'Can I pop an article about your trip on the site?' whispers Peter, cheeks melting into a salesman's smile.

'Only if you don't fire me next,' says Anna, watching the insult wash away his smile.

'Yo, miss!' yells Musa as Anna's plugging her laptop into the new interactive whiteboard. 'Miss, miss!'

'Yes, Musa,' she says. 'Can we please reduce the decibel level?'

'How come you get a MacBook and we get stuck with this shit?' he says, grazing his knuckles over his Lenovo.

'Because we treat our belongings with more love.'

'*More love*,' says Musa, drumming on the lid of his laptop. 'I can give you more love, miss, if that's what you need. Are you free tonight?'

'Believe it or not, teachers have lives too.'

'What're you doing tonight, miss?'

'None of your business.'

'Do you have a hot date?' asks Musa, his eyebrows twitching with glee. 'You do, yeah?'

'No comment.'

'You should tell them you're sick and come to Red Rooster with me.' His drumming on the laptop's getting even more frenetic. 'I promise I'll share my *cock* with you.'

Musa starts chanting, '*Cock-a, cock-a!*'

Anna glances around the room to confirm that there are no integration aides present.

'You know what they say in the teaching fraternity,' she says, trying to hold back a smile. 'Once you go black, you get the sack.'

'Damn!' yells Musa, forcing Walid to hook thumbs with him. 'You just played me, miss.'

She's relieved by his response. There's a line she knows she's crossing by permitting his banter, but engaging with it feels more instructive – and more enjoyable – than condemning it.

'*Wallah, wallah!*' says Musa, rocking back on his chair to repeat the line to Jasmine and Najima. Najima covers her lips as she giggles. The gossiping in Arabic starts. Anna picks up a few words she's learnt over the years, and remembers why she loves this job: there's no other setting in her life where she feels even remotely funny.

The only girl not giggling is Kadra, one of the two new students. She's sitting at the front with her head bowed, her black hijab swallowing her shoulders.

Finally, the interactive whiteboard fires up.

'Alright, eee-nough!' yells Anna, feeling a stab in the back of her throat.

She clicks the link to ABC iView, ignoring the chorus of groans, and tries to play the most recent episode of *Q&A*, but it takes an eternity to load. If the IT department weren't so creepy and useless, huddled in their stuffy nerd cave, she might actually be able to embrace the twenty-first century and teach engagingly.

'It depends, man,' Musa's saying to the other new student, Yassin, who most of the flats kids seem to be avoiding. 'Are there gonna be fit chicks?'

'Always,' says Yassin.

Walid's sitting next to them, looking expectantly at the screen with that stern face of his: probing eyes, gaunt features, hair already receding. He catches her staring at him.

'Walid,' says Anna, pretending it was deliberate, 'I see you've applied to go to Kokoda this year.'

'That's right, miss.'

'Are you excited?'

'Yeah, I mean, if I get in.'

He'll be the first to get in. The Police Commissioner's already phoned Jenny to make sure enough 'kids of colour' are going.

'I'm excited, too,' she lies.

His gaze searches beyond her to the revolving arrow on the screen. For every disruptive kid with the attention span of a five-year-old she has to put up with, there's a nagging guilt about not making the most of a student like Walid. It's just that there's always been something about him – some sort of silent distrust – that makes her feel as if her overtures aren't entirely welcome.

Eventually the episode buffers enough to start. The panellists debate the ethics of hitting a child. As a nervous, middle-aged audience member explains why smacking should be banned in Australia, all the kids except Kadra burst into hysterics.

'This lady's got no swag!' yells Musa.

Someone in the corridor thumps on the windows of the classroom, cutting across the laughter. Tyler's face appears above the sill, grinning.

'SHUT THE FUCK UP!' yells Yassin.

'Make me!' yells Tyler, launching his palm into the glass again. It's a miracle he doesn't break it.

'Fucking snowflake!'

'Yeah, whatever.'

Tyler keeps walking, rattling the windows of the next room.

A few minutes later, Yassin yawns and calls out, 'This show's boring. Can I go to the toilet?'

'Once the episode finishes.'

'Who cares if these stuck-up white cunts don't wanna smack their kids? That's not *my* problem.'

'It's what we'll be writing about on our language analysis SAC this term,' says Anna, hating the whiny sound of her own voice, 'so it might become your problem.'

Yassin leans back and slips his giant headphones over his ears. Anna decides to leave him alone. She can already tell she's got to pick her fights with him. He's hardened in a way that no seventeen-year-old ever should be, but that many of her students over the years have been. You always know from the eyes.

ALI

Musa keeps spreading his eyes into slits behind the tutor's back, pretending he's Asian, on the beanbags at homework club.

'Can you explain that again?' asks Ali.

The tutor runs the lid of her pen along the parabola she's just drawn, showing him and Walid how the X and Y intercepts are decided by the input and output columns.

'Try drawing one yourselves,' she says in her squeaky, American-sounding accent, pointing at the next equation:

$$y = x + 3$$

Ali glances over at Walid's graph paper as he rules a line that cuts through the dots on his grid. Maths has got crazy complicated in between year ten and year eleven. Like a totally different subject. There's no way any of this stuff will ever be useful in life.

'Excellent,' says the tutor, ticking Walid's work.

A horrible eggy smell drifts into their corner of the room. Slowly, the kids and volunteers start to notice it. Musa's flapping the air around him with a pillow.

'Far out, Musa!' yells Ali, covering his nose. 'Something's seriously wrong with your arse.'

'It wasn't me!' says Musa, even though the stink is exactly the same as all his other deep-fried, KFC farts.

Walid's breathing wheezily out of his mouth as he dots the line to the next equation.

'How're *you* going, Ali?' asks the tutor.

'Yeah, good.'

He knows she's trying to ignore the smell. Hopefully she doesn't think it's him, because she's cute in a shy, geeky sort of way. She definitely wouldn't go to university parties.

'Can I ask a question that isn't about maths?'

Walid flicks him a look that's been happening whenever

he's trying to be smooth with girls lately, as if even *that's* against their faith.

'I guess so,' says the tutor.

'What's it like at university?'

'Really hard,' she says, her pupils expanding behind her glasses like girls' eyes always do when they're into someone. 'You get super stressed – the end of semester's full-on – and my parents expect me to get an H-one in every subject.'

'What are they?' asks Walid.

'They're like, the highest mark you can get. It's the same as an A-plus at high school.'

'Lit!' says Ali.

She's crazy for complaining about her parents caring too much. Imagining Dad caring about the grades he gets in school, or even if he turns up, is basically impossible.

'Next week's O-Week,' says the tutor, smiling girlishly at Ali. If he was eighteen and more experienced, she could be his girlfriend. Especially once she heard him freestyle. 'Our campus is pretty cool. You boys should come along and check it out.'

'Maybe we will,' says Ali, nodding his chin at her.

Again, Walid gives him the angry look before shifting his attention to the wrinkly textbook they share.

'Think about it,' says Musa, joining his fat fingers into a pretend gun, 'Pac gets whacked in the middle of Las Vegas – in front of hundreds of people – and no one ever gets busted for it. He was always, like, refusing to give a fuck about his lyrics, saying whatever he wanted about Biggie, stirring up that whole

East Coast–West Coast beef, and the Illuminati knew they couldn't control him like they control Jay-Z and Pharrell now, so they had no choice.'

Musa fires four imaginary shots into Walid's chest and makes the Illuminati triangle with his fingers.

'Isn't Tupac still alive?' asks Funda, smiling at Ali as she sinks into the beanbag next to him.

'Those pictures aren't real,' says Walid.

Ali sees their tutor packing away her graphic calculator, getting ready to leave for the night. He knows they'll have to go too in ten or fifteen minutes, even though none of them wants to leave this comfy, air-conditioned room.

'Really?' says Funda, punching his arm. 'You're into *her*?'

'Kind of.'

'What do you like about her?'

'I don't know . . . she's like, mature.'

'Pff! She'll leave at the end of term. You watch. People from the uni only volunteer at homework club so they can put it on their résumé and get a better job.'

'That gives me ten weeks to make a move,' says Ali. 'I'll write a song for her.'

He'll have to get a job to pay for a session at the studio where Musa's cousin recorded his demo. But once he plays the track to the tutor, it'll totally be worth it.

'She's five years older than you,' says Funda, getting full-on and annoying, like she does sometimes out of nowhere. 'You should be attracted to people your own age.'

Ali watches Kylie pose in front of one of the desktops, taking selfies with butterflies all around her head.

Musa grabs a copy of the *Herald Sun* from the bookshelf and turns to the sport section. It's obvious he's trying to read soccer articles – the January transfer window's about to close and clubs with oil money are going crazy – but Musa can't concentrate for more than thirty seconds without getting fidgety.

'That newspaper's old,' says Walid.

'How do you know?'

'It says the date on every page, you dumb-arse,' says Ali, pointing at the top of the paper. 'Plus, look at the cover. *Special Australia Day Edition*.'

'Man, fuck that day!' says Musa.

'Why?' asks Kylie.

'Because Miss Kelly's relatives invaded this country and started killing Jai's relatives on that day,' says Musa, waving to the tutor out the window. 'And now all the skippies have a barbeque every year to celebrate.'

The tutor's already on her phone, hopefully calling her parents, not some nerdy gamer boyfriend.

'I mean a *bah-bee*!' says Musa, copying how bogans talk, straight out of their nose to make the 'ah' sound.

It gives Funda the giggles. She's laughing the same way she used to when Ali and her were in primary school, before she started worrying about her body all the time.

'Alright, shut up, are you ready?' asks Musa, spreading open the paper. '*The Great Aussie Sports Quiz*.'

Love hearts are floating above Kylie's grainy reflection.

'Question one: you have three lifelines,' says Musa, pretending to be the pink-faced host off *Millionaire Hot Seat*. 'Jockey Bobby Lewis shares the record for the most Melbourne Cup victories. How many wins did he get?'

'Six,' says Funda.

'Eighteen!' yells Ali.

Walid doesn't bother to guess.

'Four,' reads Musa. 'He also liked to have sexy times with horses. Question two: which player scored Australia's first goal against Japan at the 2006 World Cup?'

Ali gives Funda a chance to answer. He can remember the goal as if it happened yesterday, and he knows Walid does, too. Because it was a special occasion, Hassan let them go with him to the hookah lounge on Racecourse Road, where all the night workers were deliberately forgetting about their shifts. None of the East African countries had a team in the World Cup, so people cared about the Socceroos and wanted them to go far in the tournament. For most of the game Japan was winning, and life was hopeless, but then Australia scored three goals in the final ten minutes. Grown men were jumping on leather couches, smiling with missing teeth, and yelling the craziest things – really just random words – at the TV screen.

Ali, Walid and Hassan walked home way after midnight, their hoodies stinking of sweat and shisha. Car horns kept beeping and yellow and green scarves were hanging out of windows. It was like a war had just ended. You could hear the happy cries rippling in and out of the city, like dominoes twisting backwards and forwards. For once, everyone was on the same team, wanting the exact same thing. And it felt so nice to be part of it.

'Black and Yellow' is blasting out of surround-sound speakers, and Yassin's crew are partying like Wiz Khalifa – shirtless, showing off their sixpacks – in the vacant walk-up they've taken over. Jasmine and Najima's friends from Kensington Community are digging their vibe, busting out moves in the kitchen, which makes Ali psyched that he hurried home to change into his vintage Sixers singlet.

He squeezes onto a foamy couch in the living room, next to Walid and Musa, who's graffing all over the wall, giggling to himself because there are no consequences.

'Give me that,' says Ali, snatching the permanent marker.

He writes SEDIMENT the way he's been practising in class, getting this crazy feeling that he's pressed his fingers against the uneven glue beneath the wallpaper before.

Musa grabs the marker and puts two lines through the $, so it makes a dollar sign.

'Yeah, boy!'

If Ali can afford for his EP to sound half as slick as 'Black and Yellow', it'll go platinum for sure. The production's so clean coming from these speakers. Every note is like glass, showering down on their bodies from the cracked ceiling.

Musa screams the chorus, wrapping his slippery arms around Ali and Walid. 'This party's where it's at, I swear. Fuck the Community Centre!'

Yassin's unloading strips of foil from a backpack at the kitchen table with two cocky MCs from Footscray City – the school he got expelled from last year – wearing saggy jeans, Timberlands and a brand-new Lakers cap.

'Imagine if the pigs raided this crib right now,' says Musa.

'Talking of pigs,' says Ali to Walid, 'how do I apply to go on that trip with you and them?'

'*You* wanna go?'

'Fuck it, why not!'

Saying he's going overseas – to the jungle – would be the perfect way to impress the tutor from homework club.

'If you're serious, I can help,' says Walid.

'Of course I'm serious.'

'Man, why would you fools choose to hang out with the pigs?' asks Musa.

'It's a free holiday,' says Ali.

'Yeah, they beat the shit out of us and then they offer some suckers a free holiday every year to say sorry,' says Musa, trying to punch through the ugly green wallpaper, 'but they never wanna actually *say* sorry. I don't get it. Saying sorry is heaps cheaper.'

'Not necessarily,' says Walid.

'What's up with that trial, or whatever, against the cops?' asks Ali, realising they haven't talked about it in ages.

'It's a civil case,' says Walid. 'We've got new lawyers now. People that only do important cases. They have this massive office in the city.' He stares at the plaster that's showing through the knuckle holes in the wall. 'It's like, all glass.'

'Is Hassan down with it?'

'Not really, anymore.'

The night Hassan was dragged away by the police, Ali could tell people thought he was weak for crying; like it made him not a man or something.

'He never even says hi to me.'

'Me either,' says Musa.

The Footscray City boys are passing around jays in the kitchen to anyone who wants to hit them, not even asking for them back.

'When Hassan left the case,' says Walid, 'the main lawyer

took me and him to this expensive restaurant in the city where all the other lawyers and, like, corporate people go on their lunch breaks.' He coughs and waves a cloud of smoke away from his face. 'Even though she couldn't make Hassan change his mind, she still wanted to say thank you, you know, to help him keep his dignity. She said when people think they've lost their dignity, that's when they lose hope.'

'Why didn't *I* get an expensive lunch then?' says Musa.

'Because you left too soon,' says Walid.

'Yeah, coz nothing was happening. If you guys get a million bucks in court, I expect free footlongs from Subway for life, you hear me?'

'Yonkers' is playing now. You can't hate on this track, with its catchy synth slicing into the beat and the schizo clip where the guy swallows a cockroach before hanging himself.

'I'm gonna go say hi to Jazzy,' says Ali.

Jasmine, Najima and one of their cute friends are chilling on the kitchen bench. He clears the Vodka Cruiser bottles and the mouse shit around them and jumps up so his legs are dangling over the edge like theirs. Again, his brain gives him this whacked signal that he's done this exact thing – rested his hands on this same sticky bench – before.

'Did you hear Kendrick's new track?'

'Uh-huh,' says Jasmine.

'What did you think?'

She shrugs, watching her Air Jordan 3s kick against the cupboard door below them.

'Come on, it's a banger.'

'His voice is just . . . I don't know,' says Jasmine. 'It's too high-pitched or something.'

'Like a chipmunk,' says Najima.

'Nah, you don't get it. Kendrick has heaps of different voices that he raps in,' says Ali, checking out their friend, who's in full Vans get-up. 'That's what makes him so lit.'

'Yo, Jazzy!' yells Musa, leaning against the bench. 'What's that stuff they put on the chips at KFC called?'

'Chicken salt.'

'Yeah, yeah, chicken salt,' says Musa, grinning at Jasmine and Najima's friend. 'African people *love* chicken salt, trust me. You just sprinkle a bit like this . . .' he says, pinching his fingers above the water-stained lino, 'and all the Africans come running out of their houses.'

'What houses?' says Jasmine.

Najima's hand shoots up to cover her crooked teeth as she laughs.

'Far out, I feel high just from breathing,' says Musa.

Without even looking, Ali can sense how angry Walid is that they're all accidentally blazing.

'I know you, yeah?' says Ali, leaning over to chat with the chick Musa's been riffing with.

'What?'

'You got busted by inspectors two nights ago, outside KFC.'

'Oh my God, you saw that?'

'Yeah, they totally dogged you.'

Najima rolls her eyes at him.

'The ticket machine wasn't working,' says the chick, pausing to wet her glossy lips. 'Those inspectors *hated* me.'

'Probably because you're hot.'

Her vibe is slick and sexy, like a backup dancer in a Lady

Gaga clip. If he could hook up with her, right before the tutor, he'd figure out exactly how women like to be stroked.

'Do you wanna come to Highpoint with me some time?'

She smiles and kind of avoids his eyes.

'What's so funny?'

'Nothing,' she says. 'You're just . . . confident.'

'You don't have to say yes or nothing.'

The music suddenly expands in Ali's ears. Big bass notes make his brain feel like it's vibrating inside his skull. Jasmine and Najima start to dougie to New Boyz, popping their shoulders and twisting from side to side on the soles of their sneakers. Ali hops down from the bench to boogie with them.

'Watch this!' yells Musa, busting out some of his unco b-boy moves.

The chick Ali's been tuning dodges Musa's wild, twisting legs. She's got actual moves, swaying her tummy and her hips to the beat in half-time. Her sweat smells like all the sweet celebrity perfumes that Funda's into.

'Can I at least get your number?' asks Ali.

'I don't know.'

'Ali, man!' yells Jasmine, shoving him in the chest. 'Give her some space!'

'Fine!'

He goes and dances alone near the kitchen table, pretending he's cool with whatever just went down.

'You didn't have to go psycho,' he yells back at Jasmine.

'Nice singlet,' croaks Yassin, nodding to the bass.

'It's authentic,' says Ali, pointing at the stitching on the logo of his Sixers singlet. 'You like NBA?'

'For sure,' says Yassin as he tips dozens of balls of foil, and a pocket scale, into his backpack.

'Who do you go for?' asks Ali.

'I don't have a team,' says Yassin, handing the backpack to a young'un in a G-Unit tee from the North Melbourne towers.

Seeing the stick-and-poke tat on Yassin's forearm, which looks like a faded squiggle of the continent of Africa, the stories Musa has about Yassin's past definitely seem possible.

'Here!' says Yassin, turfing Ali one of the small pieces of foil. 'Take this, fam.'

Ali checks to see if Walid's watching, but he isn't hanging on the couch anymore, or anywhere in the flat that Ali can see, so he slips the bud into his pocket.

'YEAH MOTHERFUCKER!' yells Musa as he boots the cupboard below the kitchen sink.

He lines up another kick and caves the door in, cackling at the uneven splinters of wood that're framing the pipes. Musa keeps going until the door's hanging off its hinges.

'Stop!' yells Ali.

It's only now that the strange feeling he's had all night is starting to make sense.

'Why?' asks Musa, still cackling.

'I'm not, like, one hundred per cent . . . but I think this is where I used to live,' says Ali.

'Bullshit?'

'Nah, I'm pretty sure.'

Ali takes in the kitchen: the bottles and the twisted joint butts – ash smeared everywhere – and the huge gap where a fridge is supposed to be. The flat feels the same as where he lived until he was four years old; when he had a whole family.

Before Mum packed her dresses into a purple wheelie bag, as quickly as she could, and disappeared. And before Dad turned silent, acting like he no longer cared about a single thing in the world.

TYLER

As Tyler's eyes adjust to the hazy morning light, he sees the new rashes in the folds of his elbows. They itch like crazy, but he knows not to start, otherwise he won't be able to stop. It's another grey, smoky day out the window because of the bushfires that've been blazing through redneck towns in the country. There's no sun, and the grass in the park below is all yellow, with tiny human ants scurrying across it. Flemington's got this weird layer of smog hanging over the trees and the rusty iron rooftops, like it's one of those movies where the world's about to end. Not that he gives a fuck if it does.

Ciggie smoke's drifting under his door. He might as well go to school now that Barney's going to be on the couch all day, cackling away at the telly and stinking out the whole flat. The stupid fuck. All he had to do was sit on his dopey arse with his deadshit mates and unload a truck every few hours, but he couldn't even hold it together working the cruisiest job in the world. Mum deserves a million times better.

Tyler counts fifty-two push-ups under his breath without stopping. One more than yesterday. On the army's website, they say it's important for cadets to arrive with a good 'base fitness', which he's pretty much got already. He tucks his feet under his mattress and does sit-ups until his abs burn and his back feels like it's about to split. Then he changes to the kind of sit-ups that his half-brother, Shannon, taught him over the holidays, where you lock your legs together and tone one side of your stomach at a time by twisting and jerking. He can see it's working by the little ridges just above his hips. By the middle of the year, he's going to be totally ripped – like an MMA fighter – with no fat anywhere on his body.

He slips into the bathroom, avoiding Mum and Barney, and stares at himself in the mirror, studying the shiny veins along his biceps. They're definitely poking out more. He tries to figure out the exact spot on his arm where he'll get the tattoo of Mum's face. When she sees it, she'll go mental with happiness. Then he'll rock up at school in a singlet, instead of his lame uniform, to show off his new ink and say 'fuck you' to the new principal and Ms Costello, for thinking she could change him.

She's the only teacher who's ever mentioned Dad, doing that annoying thing where she lowers her glasses, expecting him to talk about it with her. Lying to her – letting her think they're friends – is always funny as.

Tyler runs his hand across his smooth jawline in the mirror. Dad never had a beard or anything before the pigs broke in and took him away. Just a bit of brown hair coming out the top of his sweaty singlet. Always wet and matted, with this kind of salty smell. No one's ever smelt more like a man, or acted more like a man, than Dad. Once he gets released, whenever that is, he'll move back in and wipe the floor with Barney.

*

Tyler waits near the gym mats and tells everyone on his team to let the other team have all the balls, so they can try to catch them out. Ali hurls his ball at Tyler, but he weaves out of the way.

'Freestyle about *that*!' yells Tyler.

Musa struts in late from recess and joins Ali and Walid's team, which makes it totally unfair.

'Sir!' yells Tyler. 'We should get Musa.'

Mr Hunter's getting all stressed, counting the players on each team, not understanding that all the sporty people, except Tyler, are playing together.

'Oh my God, you're *so* cooked!' snaps Tyler.

Ms Costello walks into the gym in her loud, ugly shoes and asks to speak to Tyler. Ali and Musa make animal noises as he follows her to the foyer. He smirks so they know he doesn't give a fuck about what's coming.

'Sorry to interrupt your physical education,' she says.

'Mister Hunter's the worst ref ever.'

'He's taking a spare, Tyler, so I trust you've been on your best behaviour,' says Ms Costello, smiling, even though nothing's funny. 'I just wanted to remind you to drop by my office at lunch to pick up your sparkling new uniform.'

'Whatever,' he mumbles.

It's annoying how Ms Costello tries to turn everything into a joke. Her daughters must be so over it. From the pictures of them on her desk, the older one looks kind of hot, but she's probably all snobby and into politics.

'I know you'll hate me for saying this, but from now on there are no excuses if you turn up in casual attire.'

'Yeah, I get it.'

She keeps staring at him, expecting a thank you. There's no way he's going to say it. He never asked her for anything.

'I've gotta bounce, miss.'

'Sure,' she says, squeezing his arm. He flinches and looks around to see if anyone in the gym noticed. Luckily, no one's watching.

Most of his team are already out of the game. Tyler gets hold of a ball and sprints towards the half-court line. The first person he sees is Najima. He pegs the ball at her, clocking her right on the head. She goes down like a sack of shit. Mr Hunter blows his whistle and everyone crowds around Najima. She's such an attention seeker. They're soft balls. If this was war, she'd get up straight away.

'Hey, I'm sorry,' says Tyler, crouching and patting her on the shoulder. 'I didn't mean to throw it that hard.'

Najima shoves his hand away from her headscarf, trying to get as much sympathy as she can. There isn't even a mark on her face.

Eventually she stops having a sook and Mr Hunter lets them continue the game. Tyler's team keeps losing players until it's just him, Binh and Kylie left. Kylie has no strategy, squealing whenever a ball gets pegged at her. For a maths nerd, Binh isn't that bad. Funda tries to hit Tyler, but she can't even throw the ball far enough for him to catch it.

'You throw like a grandma!' he yells, and she pretends to be pissed off. He can see her tits wobbling as she runs. They're so massive that her nipples are poking into the fabric of her PE uniform . . .

A ball smacks into his head.

When he gets his balance, he sees Walid pumping his fist near the half-court line.

'Suck shit!' yells Funda.

Tyler pretends he hasn't been hit and hurls the ball back at Walid, but Mr Hunter makes him sit with the rest of his unco team.

'Stop being a pussy, Binh!' he yells. 'Catch it!'

He wedges himself on the end of the bench so he can be the first person into the game if Binh or Kylie catch someone out. Screw the others. The only way they can win is if he gets back onto the court.

Tyler sees Yassin sneak into the foyer of the gym and start unzipping people's backpacks, boosting their stuff, thinking he's invincible because he's been to juvie. And because he's got muscle. Tyler isn't scared. Yassin and his try-hard gangsters can come at him whenever they want. He decides not to snitch about what's happening in the foyer. At least not right now. There are always other things he can get from it.

'One, two, three . . .' he mouths to Jai, hearing the creepy nasal sounds coming from the art room.

They burst in and see a dozen Muslim weirdos, kneeling on vomity rugs in their socks, eyes closed, looking like they're waiting to take it up the arse. Jai flicks the switch on and off until they stop praying.

'Man, have some respect,' says Ali.

'Who for?' asks Tyler. 'Some camel fucker that doesn't even exist?'

'Just let us finish,' says Walid.

'I'd rather jerk off five times a day than pretend I'm gonna get, like, a hundred virgins when I die.'

'Punk-arse bitch gonna die soon, anyway,' says Musa, leaping up from his rug.

'It's bullshit how you get to hang in this room every day,' says Jai, pointing at the *Stolen* badge on his backpack. 'They never give *us* anywhere to chill.'

'Coz you're all fucked in the head,' says Musa.

'What did you say?'

'You heard.'

'Please!' says Walid. 'We didn't do anything to you.'

'Except for blow up our buildings,' says Tyler.

He's seen the footage of the aeroplanes flying into those two skyscrapers in New York – there are some sick slow-motion angles on YouTube – and all the pictures of camel fuckers holding AK-47s, wanting to take away people's freedom.

'Fucking terrorists!' says Jai.

'What was that?' says Ali, bouncing round like the yuppie rappers he worships. Musa and him rush towards them, forcing them up against a rack of paintings.

'What're you gonna do, take us hostage?'

Ali shoves him into the rack, making the plastic rattle against the back of his skull.

Jai's already got his fists up.

'Do it again!' says Tyler, laughing.

'Povo cunt!' yells Ali, getting right in his face with his rank Chiko Roll breath.

'Your cousin digs me.'

'You better not fucking touch –'

'Please, please!' screams Walid, wedging himself between them and holding out his hands. 'No fighting!'

'*No fighting!*' says Tyler, putting on a girly voice. It's fun as getting revenge for Walid's arsey throw at dodgeball. 'What a massive pussy!'

There's a knock on the glass. Mr Hunter's lurking in the corridor, too scared to be a man and break it up. Ali and Musa back off, and all the excited energy starts draining from Tyler's body. Stomping on those dumb-arses' feet – crushing their toes while their shoes were off – would've been the perfect way to win the fight.

'TY, TY!' someone's yelling. 'Over here, bud.'

He turns around and sees Barney waving at him from the other side of the fence.

'How's school going?'

'Pretty shit.'

Barney runs his hand through his greying hair as he paces up and down on the footpath. Clumps of stubble and dried shaving cream line his bony jaw.

'What the fuck do you want?' asks Tyler.

'Easy there, bud. Your mum and me just need to borrow a couple of bucks to tide us over til Thursday. Got much on ya?'

'I haven't got –'

'Hi,' says Ms Kelly, clutching a walkie-talkie as she glares through the fence at Barney. 'Everything alright here?'

'Yeah, all good,' says Tyler.

'I'm the boy's stepdad,' says Barney, extending his hand for a shake and pretending to laugh when he can't fit it through the twisted wire.

'He's not my stepdad.'

'Don't be like that, bud. Me and your mum are getting married in a couple of months.'

Everyone knows it's never going to happen.

'I was just asking the boy for a couple of bucks to run up to Woolies,' says Barney, showing the gaps between his teeth like it makes him all sincere, the stupid fuck.

'I haven't got *shit* for you,' says Tyler.

He could probably take on Barney with all the push-ups he's been doing lately.

'I'm sorry,' says Ms Kelly, leaning back from the fence to avoid Barney's rotten breath, 'but you're not allowed to speak to students on school grounds.'

'Okay, missy, no problems here,' says Barney, raising his hands and showing the gaps between his teeth again. 'See ya tonight, bud.'

He hobbles down the hill, all high-elbowed and twitchy on the footpath, trying to figure out his next dodgy plan.

'Was that really what he wanted?' asks Ms Kelly.

'Yeah, he's a tripper.'

Her laugh is embarrassing as. 'He's not supposed to be here, even if money *is* tight.'

'We've got money,' says Tyler.

He runs back to the basketball court before she can stick her big nose into any more of his business.

No one's really trying at soccer anymore. Fat flies buzz around his ears and his nostrils, and the rashes on his arms and legs sting from sweat. He remembers he's meant to get his uniform off Ms Costello, but he can't be arsed. It'll be better if she comes and gets him out of whatever boring class he's got after lunch.

Yassin wriggles through a hole in the fence at the back of the oval. He stretches his long legs out on the grass, listening to tunes as he eats Red Rooster.

Tyler sneaks up behind him and pinches a few chips.

'What're you doing?' asks Yassin, in his fake, husky voice.

'Give us another one,' says Tyler, trying to swallow the lump of potato that's stuck in his throat.

'As if, snowflake.'

'I'd rather be white than Somalian, any day.'

Yassin stares him down, adjusting his wireless Dre headphones. A slow, electronic beat is crackling out. 'I'll fucking shank you, man.'

'Go on then,' says Tyler, lifting up his t-shirt and pointing to where he wants it. 'Give me a hundred bucks first.'

'You're a crazy bitch.'

Tyler clears his throat and slides the gluggy potato to the inside of his cheek. 'How much did you get in the gym?'

'Huh?'

'I said: *how much money did you steal in the gym*, you dumb African fuck?'

'I didn't steal nothing,' says Yassin, cocking his head.

'Fine, then you won't mind me telling Ms Costello who took everyone's stuff.'

'Fucking snitch!'

'What if I am?' says Tyler, smirking.

He lunges for another chip, but Yassin pulls the soggy cardboard away just in time.

'She won't believe you.'

'Maybe not,' says Tyler. 'If I get Jai to say *he* saw you do it, maybe she'll believe him?'

'Fuck you, dog!'

'Give me a hundred bucks and I'll keep my mouth shut.'

'You're tripping, man. Fifty?'

'Whatever,' says Tyler, acting bored.

As he pretends to zip his lips shut, he finally manages to get the lump of potato down, making sure he looks Yassin right back in the eye. Fifty bucks will be enough to help Mum do what she needs to do.

PAUL

'How's the new patch?' asks Mum.

'I haven't found any Outback Jacks in the city yet,' says Paul, eyeing his blackened barramundi. Pity he didn't order the steak, like last year. 'Sauce, Davey?'

He slides the bottle towards the little bastard.

'Are you having any issues with the local . . . youths?'

'She means the black kids,' says the old man, rolling his half-shut eyes.

'It's like serving over in Fallujah, Dad,' says Paul, winking at him. 'Life or death stuff, every single shift.'

'Oh, stop it!' says Mum.

'So far the kids don't seem too bad. Just a bit cheeky. To be honest, I'm enjoying being a role model. Especially now that Davey here no longer wants my guidance.'

Davey finally finishes drowning his chips in the red sea.

'You right there, mate?' asks Paul.

Gets doughnuts back.

'There was an article last week about a group of children taking the Flemington police to the Federal –'

'Don't read the papers, Mum.'

'Just be careful, is all I'm saying.'

Feels like everyone's always walking on eggshells at the station. Even after a few knock-off pints, no one wants to say boo about the case.

'How're *you* travelling, Davey?' asks Paul, figuring it's time to change the subject. 'Still seeing that muso, or whatever she is?'

'Astrid's a singer.'

'Would I know any of her songs off the radio?'

'Get stuffed!' says Davey, reaching over and cracking him on the arm. Not a bad punch for a lightweight.

'You should've invited her along tonight. She eats dead animals, right?' asks Paul, glancing up at the giant croc that's suspended above them, all chompers.

'Leave your brother alone,' says Mum. 'We just saw one of Astrid's gigs. She's got a beautiful voice, doesn't she?'

'Voice of an angel,' says the old man, hand over heart.

'You're both dreadful,' says Mum. Even Davey's having a good grin. 'Astrid's lovely. You'll have to meet her soon.'

'Sure.'

Truth is, he doesn't really have to. He knows the type: arts degree, hospo job, probably loves yoga and lentil burgers, always crapping on about refugees and carbon emissions in her own little echo chamber.

'You got a missus?' asks Davey.

'No time,' says Paul. 'You got a job?'

'Easy, you two,' says the old man.

Seems like only yesterday that he was at Paul's graduation at the barracks in Glen Waverley, proud as punch, Mum bawling her eyes out once the bagpipes kicked in. He was always so set on Paul joining the force. Why he started going soft on Davey a few years back is anyone's guess. Now the little bastard and his Steiner-school girlfriend are still mooching off the folks in their mid-twenties, not that anyone else seems to give two shits.

'Happy birthday anyway, Mum,' says Paul, planting a kiss on her cushiony cheek. New perfume she's got on makes her smell like she's from the ragtime era. 'How old are you now: twenty-five, twenty-six?'

'I bloody wish,' grumbles the old man.

'Why didn't you tell your folks?' asks Athena, taking a nip from her 7-Eleven coffee as she stops the divisional van at the lights on Flemington Road.

'I figured I'd wait and see if I got in,' says Paul. 'No point rocking the boat, is there?'

'Depends if your folks give a shit.'

She hacks out a cough and surveys the straggler swaying at the window of the Kebab Box.

'Where'd you tell them you were going?'

'I said I was going camping for a few weeks,' says Paul, 'which, strictly speaking, was true.'

Instead of giving him a laugh, she starts picking away at an imaginary goatee below her lips, easing her foot onto the accelerator. Always risky mentioning the Special Forces.

'The jungle shouldn't be much of a problem for you then, should it?'

'Don't know about that,' says Paul, taking in the endless

darkness of the parklands on their left. 'I had a bit more of a death wish back then.'

'Ever have nightmares about it?'

Before he can answer, the dispatcher crackles:

'Reporting, they've just observed up to ten African males with sticks and other weapons in the car park . . .'

'Here we go again,' says Athena, flicking on the sirens.

As she wrenches the wheel to swing a U-turn over the tram tracks, adrenaline starts to surge through Paul's chest. First decent piece of action he's had since changing patches. Sure as hell beats signing stat decs back at the station.

'Roger that, reports are coming in that they're armed with baseball bats and are doing damage. I've had another call now saying they're hitting cars . . .'

Athena runs a red light and swings into the service lane, flying towards the flats.

'The two five six unit's out on foot, chasing one through the low-rises . . .'

'They usually vanish in the rat maze,' says Athena.

She pulls up outside the Community Centre and they hop out of the van, ready to cut off anyone trying to escape through the park.

'I've lost him. I think he had a crowbar in his hand . . .'

No movement on the oval. A breeze is whistling in, rattling the leaves on the trees and finally taking the smoky sting out of the night. The hum of traffic echoes from the tollway. Distant horns. Paul feels a pang of disappointment that it might all amount to nothing.

'See that?' whispers Athena.

Darkness looks like it's contorting somehow – gleaming

little somersaults – right where they run the footy clinics. She shines her torch. Three or four figures snap their heads sideways, towards the light.

'STOP RIGHT THERE!' yells Athena, sprinting over as she marks them out.

A group of teenagers are wearing similar get-up to the boy who drowned in Footscray last year. No crowbars or baseball bats. Paul makes a quick mental note of each of them: fluffy hair, fat boy, black basketball singlet. The kid at the front of the group – fluffy hair – is acting the shiftiest, eyes glued to the grass.

'Did you bring us Krispy Kremes?' says fat boy. Looks like he's already gobbled his fair share. Paul recognises him from KFC a few nights ago. The punk who was giving them lip.

'What are you boys up to tonight?'

'Is he your new boyfriend?' asks the kid in the basketball singlet with the word *SIXERS* splashed across his chest.

'You could do heaps better,' says fat boy.

Zero chance Athena's taking the bait.

'I'll ask again,' says Paul. 'What're you boys up to?'

'Just hanging out,' says basketball singlet.

'You know, like white people do,' says fat boy.

'No need for that sort of talk, mate.'

'You've got nothing on us, you dumb-arse pig!'

'Give it a rest, Musa!' says Athena, mirroring his sour-faced expression. 'Any of you boys got ID?'

'You already know who we are.'

'We've received information that there's a group of kids in the area causing trouble,' says Athena, pausing to scan fluffy hair's Keypass. 'We just wanna know where you boys are coming from.'

'Nowhere.'

'Where's nowhere?'

'I don't have to answer you.'

'We came from 7-Eleven,' blurts fluffy hair. He's got no problem looking Athena in the eye.

'Why'd you *say* that?' hisses basketball singlet.

Put these three clowns on a desert island and it wouldn't take long for them to turn on each other.

'You're all gonna be searched,' says Athena.

Musa groans as he raises his arms. The other two seem to know the drill, dropping to the grass, hands in their laps.

'I'll get you to spread your feet, mate,' says Paul.

'Careful of my shoes,' says Musa, shuffling his feet in line with his elbows. 'Adidas Originals, man. You step on them, you pay!'

He and fluffy hair aren't carrying anything.

'Every fucking day,' moans basketball singlet, under his breath.

Paul eases him up, inhaling the mix of sweat and Lynx as he starts patting him down. Definitely works out. There's a little lump at the back of his button-ups. Paul digs a crinkled ball of foil out from his jocks. Looks like a mini meteorite.

'You planted that on me.'

Paul passes the foil to Athena and she gives it a quick sniff. 'What're you trying to do to yourself, Ali?'

'Nothing.'

Red and blue shadows are twitching against the Holland Court high-rises.

'Don't fucking shake your head at me,' says Ali, getting stuck into fluffy hair as Paul sits him back down. 'I swear, man, it isn't even mine.'

'Boys!' says Athena, having to raise her voice above their bickering. 'I tell you what, drop and give me twenty and you can all move on.'

'Nah, it's a trick,' says Musa.

'I don't play tricks. Here, you can have this poison back,' she says, tossing the foil to Ali. 'I'm buggered if I want it. Now give me twenty of your best.'

Ali flips onto his chest, pressing his palms into the grass, and starts counting each push-up out loud.

'No way, that one doesn't count,' says Musa.

He sledges his mate through every exertion, forgetting whatever beef he has with Paul and Athena, but fluffy hair stays silent the whole time, refusing to have a bar of the fun.

PAUL

Athena yawns, staring at the buzzing overhead tubes as she waits on her third caffeine hit of the shift. Grills and fryers hiss in the kitchen. A bunch of paramedics are getting stuck into the all-day brekkie burger: pickles, lettuce, beetroot, bacon, bun full of sugar, eggs hanging out the side like tongues lined with gangrene. Salt city. Clogging their arteries, one stubbly mouthful at a time.

'This place not your cuppa tea?' says Athena.

'Each to their own.'

'You'll come round,' she says, wry smile.

Not to the brekkie burger, he won't.

Light's finally poking through the giant black slate of sky out the window, spreading over the taxi-lined street that slopes towards the rail siding. Paul finds himself having a good yawn. Almost time to do a quick shop, head home and catch up on a bit of shut-eye. Last thing he wants is to get a call to a domestic – some whiny, public housing couple playing out their drama after another night on the turps – that'd drag the shift out an extra hour or two.

'How well do you know those three smart-arses from the park last night?' he asks.

'Pretty well,' says Athena. 'I've known them since before they had the testicles to make doughnut jokes.'

He eyes the crusty sauce bottles that're bunched up along the counter, trying to figure out if this is the invitation he's been waiting for.

'Mind if I ask about the Flemington stuff?'

'Sounds to me like you just did.'

'I know it's none of my –'

'I'm pulling your leg, Knowlesy,' she says. 'Knock yourself out.'

'What's your take on it all?'

'A bit of support from above would've been nice. We've done a lot of time for a few bad apples.'

'They gone now?'

'Yep, plus some good police,' she says, watching a group of clubbers wander in. Flares, glowsticks, probably coming from some doof down on the docks. 'That's the thing in this job. You never know when it'll be your turn to take the fall, like those poor coppers up in Mildura a few years back. Once they play the race card, it automatically makes us the bad guys.'

'You reckon this racial profiling stuff's got legs?'

'I'd say so. They've lawyered up. Got some fancy firm working pro bono for them. That can't hurt. Plus the hoo-ha about that kid in Footscray isn't doing us any favours, is it?'

'Guess not.'

There's one allegation, going back a fair while, that feels too risky to run by her; something about the Flemington coppers apprehending a kid, driving him out to an old warehouse in the western suburbs, beating him up, then dumping him on the side of the Ring Road.

'Just quietly,' says Athena, voice hushing, 'we're already a couple of million in the hole.'

'That much?'

'Yep.'

'Jesus!'

The curly-haired woman behind the counter's trying to stay patient with the clubbers, who're standing around, chewing their cheeks out, still deciding what they want.

'Wait til the taxpayers get wind of it,' says Athena, winking at a girl with purple dreadlocks, who ducks outside for a smoke.

'How many kids are there?' asks Paul.

'Most of them aren't kids anymore.' She seems like his kind of copper, so he hopes he hasn't hit a nerve. 'Last I heard, there were maybe seven or eight left. Half of them have dropped out over the years. The ones that're left aren't going anywhere. Probably smell blood.'

Athena squeezes past the clubbers to get her takeaway.

'They've got all the power now,' she says. 'You saw how it was last night. If we even come close to putting our foot in it, they'll go straight to the press. Or their lawyers will.'

Purple dreads is puffing away at one of the scungy tables out front. Easy to see in her eyes what she's been up to. Why anyone would actually want to put that filth in their blood is beyond Paul. He wonders whether Davey and his new missus ever get on the gear. Bet he'd be one of those peaceful pricks who ends up staring at his own fingers for hours, mouth wide open, crapping on about how much he loves everyone.

'I almost forgot to tell you,' says Athena, lugging her legs back into the divisional van. 'Guess who's decided to tag along to Kokoda with us.'

'No idea.'

'Think North West Metro, back in the day.'

'Not the bloody Commissioner?'

'Bingo!'

'Jeez!' says Paul, getting a whiff of burnt milk, 'he must be shitting bricks.'

* * *

bananas ✓
eggs ✓
milk ✓
yoghurt ✓
muesli bars ✓
lean cuisine ✓
protein powder ✓
body wash

Paul starts his second lap of the personal care aisle, squinting at yellow labels in search of the good brand of cocoa butter body wash. Fatigue's finally kicking in. Panels of light glint off the vinyl flooring, disappearing the second his eyes try to catch up with them. He gets out his phone to double-check that no messages have pinged through overnight. There's that familiar plunge of emptiness in his chest when he sees the vacant green bubble in the top left-hand corner of his screen, as if the rich geeks in Silicon Valley have bottled the feeling in the rooms after losing a footy grand final.

'Excuse me,' squeaks a short woman, similar age to him, pointing at the top shelf. 'Could you please grab a pack of those for me?'

Doesn't want to say 'toilet paper'.

'Sure,' says Paul, setting his basket down behind him so she can't see the Lean Cuisine packets. 'These bad boys?'

'No, the one with the frog on it.' Might as well wipe her arse with sandpaper. 'It's so annoying. God knows why there're none on the middle shelf.'

'There you go,' he says, brushing her hand as he passes her the twelve-pack.

No ring.

'Thanks.'

'I'm Paul, by the way.'

'Hi,' is all she says back.

Sun-bleached hair. Must be an outdoorsy type. Maybe a physio or a personal trainer. Great figure. A real pocket rocket.

'Don't spose *you*'ve got a name?'

'I'm not really comfortable telling you.'

Takes a second or two for his brain to compute.

'No worries,' chirps Paul. 'I'll leave you to it.'

He picks up his basket, pretending he wasn't playing at anything, and heads straight for the checkout. The body wash can wait. Probably does look a bit wired after pulling an all-night shift.

ANNA

There's something so depressing about the library – or the 'resource centre', as they're supposed to call it now – after school: the lumpy grey carpet, the drab magazine racks, the wooden tables that look like relics from the corporal punishment era, mixed in with the new-age educational buzzwords that've been photocopied, laminated and splashed all over the walls:

create + connect + imagine + inquire = ***inspire!***

No doubt Peter's already got a picture of this equation up on the website, below the hideous logo he paid some consultancy company five figures to come up with.

He clicks between PowerPoint slides as he explains the digital guidelines of the school's new growth strategy, somehow managing to stay immersed in the dry details. It's much more fun when students are huddled around the old PCs, trying to play *Counter-Strike* and *Call of Duty* without the librarians – the resource centre-arians – catching them. Half the time, Anna would rather be playing first-person shooter games than slogging her way through the books that the kids have been assigned.

'My students hardly ever bring their laptops to class,' complains Rob Hunter, 'and when they do, they spend the whole time watching YouTube.'

'I wonder why,' whispers Jenny.

Anna swallows a laugh.

'Can't the computer techs block the website?' asks Rob, looking as though he's on the brink of a breakdown.

'Let's hold off on totalitarian measures,' says Peter, with the hint of a wry smile. 'We need to learn to trust our students, so that they can trust us.'

He eventually manages to steer the discussion away from the perils of technology, towards his next item: Kadra and her two sisters.

'The middle one!' interrupts Tracy, purple-cheeked, as usual. 'What's her name again?'

'Hamdi,' says Jenny.

'She stands up and walks out whenever I play a pop song to the class. I can't even reason with her. Just up, and out! And she refuses to communicate with any of the male integration aides.'

'It's the same in my class,' says Linda, resolute in her current affairs, stop-the-boats blinkers.

'What am I meant to do?' asks Tracy. 'I can't exit her, because she's already, technically, exited herself. But I can't let her stand outside, unsupervised, for fifty minutes.'

'Kadra seems lovely,' Anna finds herself saying, feeling her colleagues' eyes suck straight to her. 'I mean . . . so far we haven't had any issues.'

The silence that follows is mortifying.

'In education these days,' says Peter, finally putting an end to her torture, 'one size doesn't fit all. We can't pretend like it does anymore.' You'd swear he came up with the philosophy himself. 'So let's make the Mohamed sisters feel welcome at every opportunity, and try to bear in mind what they might've had to deal with before they came to this country . . .'

The audacity of him; preaching tolerance towards the same people his growth strategy is designed to weed out.

Peter guides his gaze around the room as he gives his sermon, without ever seeming to fix on anyone in particular, clasping his puffy hands on top of his belly. Even his paunch seems like an indispensable part of his bubble of charisma.

*

'Do you mind if I have a quick chat?' asks Anna as Peter emerges from the library with Linda in tow.

'Not at all,' he says.

Linda flicks Anna a deathly glare before plodding around the corner to their office.

Anna follows Peter along the corridor that's decorated with vertical banners sporting the school's new house names, each with their own tacky Greek mythological insignia.

'I was looking through the Kokoda applications last night and I noticed we've only got six so far,' she says.

'I'm sure there are plenty of other students interested.'

Anna waits for him to elaborate, but soon realises that he isn't going to.

'I wanted to run this by you before I suggested it to him,' she says, wishing she'd prepared some lame, light side–dark side analogy. 'I've been thinking of encouraging Tyler Peirce to fill out an application. I'm confident the experience would have a positive effect on him.'

Peter spreads the poached-egg flesh of his cheeks.

'It's a lot to take on,' he says. 'I'm sure you're aware of some of the incidents he's been involved in.'

'That's *why* I'm asking. Isn't the program supposed to be about the police reconnecting with disengaged youth?'

'Ah, you've done your homework.'

The way he delivers his condescending words; it's as if he's still performing at the afternoon briefing. She wishes he'd drop the act and stop indulging an imaginary audience.

They walk on in silence down the empty corridor, past the year twelve lockers and the common room where she busted Kylie getting fingered on muck-up day. Within the heavy silence, Anna can feel herself compromising her chances of landing the leading teacher position that's just been advertised.

'Whatever happens,' she blurts out, 'it's on me.'

'That's beside the point,' says Peter, slowing his waddle as they near his office. He spreads his fleshy cheeks again when he notices the school cleaner emerging from the sickbay. 'All I'm trying to do is make sure you don't have any added stress while you're over there, or along the way, for that matter. It's best to be realistic.'

'I *am* being realistic.'

He sighs, releasing a waft of his sour, late-afternoon breath. 'I trust you know about the family?'

Anna nods, assuming he's alluding to Jenny's 'favourite' mother, or the bumbling junkie she met at the school fence yesterday. 'So, do you mind if I have a chat with Tyler?'

'I just want what's best for my staff,' says Peter, absolving himself with another phoney smile as he lingers at the door to his office. The muffled whir of a vacuum cleaner starts up inside the conference room. 'Now go home, or go to a trendy wine bar, or whatever it is that the young do these days.'

The young, that's a stretch.

On her way out, Anna stops in the foyer and studies the photos of old students on the walls. Ten years ago there were over fifty year twelves, mostly Vietnamese kids, with a handful of Africans. Last year only thirteen kids graduated. There are so many familiar faces from when she was a grad teacher. One face, in particular, leaps out at her. Hassan Dahir. Walid's older brother. He had the same probing eyes as Walid, always fixed on her in class, as if he was trying to suck the knowledge straight out of her head. But he had a bit more 'swag', as the kids say, and he knew how to take a joke.

The craziest memory of Hassan pops into her head. It must've been six or seven years ago, at the swimming carnival in Queens Park. His best mate, Mukhtar, probably dared him to do it. During a break between races, he sprinted to the deep end of the pool and did a bomb, fully clothed, drenching Anna and spraying the teachers around her. The schedule on her clipboard was reduced to an illegible grey paste. Hassan got in huge trouble. She remembers him sitting next to the old principal in his sopping clothes, grinning at his mates, and the realisation that it all might've been a ploy to see her nipples, which, at the time, carried with it a tingle of gratification.

A shitfaced uni student crashes into Anna, spilling beer down the front of her denim jacket.

'Sorry-bou-thah,' he slurs, quickly re-joining his mates, who're bouncing around near the stage, belting out cock rock covers with their arms draped over each other.

Dancing to the driving snare beat soon becomes tedious, so Anna decides to take a break. She needs to cool down. The pub's starting to feel warped. Bright jets of colour are shooting out from the bottles of spirits behind the bar and looping into each other, messing with her depth perception.

Zoe's on a stool in the front bar, showing off her yoga-perfect posture as she chats to a bartender with a cute bushranger beard.

'One more drink,' Anna hears herself say, feeling a sloppy

smile spread across her cheeks. She gets out her purse and orders three vodka and pineapple juices.

'What time is it?' she asks.

Zoe checks her phone. 'Almost twelve thirty.'

'That's early.'

Anna rips a drink from the bushranger's paw and slams it down, her mouth dry and chalky. It's impossible to even taste the alcohol. Zoe only sips hers.

'Drink faster!' says Anna.

'Maybe you should drink slower?'

The cover band have finally finished their set and the jocks are chanting for an encore.

'How're you feeling?' asks Zoe.

'Fine.'

'Any new hunks at work?'

'Nope, I think I'm just going to become one of those crazy cat or dog ladies.'

'*I* think it's time to start putting yourself out there.'

'Great!' says Anna, noticing how damp her jacket is. She hangs it on the back of the barstool. 'I don't suppose I get a say in any of this.'

'Of course you do,' says Zoe. 'It might be fun.'

'Fun, yeah right.'

She's so sick of people giving her advice, as if they know what it's like to suffer through every paralysing emotion she's had in the past six months.

'Did you ever find out anything about *her*?'

Not now. Any time, but now.

'I assumed she was one of his breezy customers,' says Anna, realising, from her aching molars, that she's been clenching her teeth. 'I didn't really want to ask. Is that stupid?'

'Nah, I get it. I wouldn't ask, either.'

It'd never happen to Zoe in the first place. She wouldn't allow herself to be so invested. So vulnerable. Anna finds her eyelids sealing as she remembers hearing Zoe have sex with a random while she was crashing on her couch after a traffic light party at uni. She could tell Zoe was on top. The drunk, nasal moans got louder, absorbing the dark share house, until Anna had no choice but to envisage the arch of her friend's spine, and the way it collapsed as she contracted and shuddered.

'Maybe this is dumb,' says Anna, prising her eyes back open, 'but one time I randomly asked if he watched porn and he said: *Yeah, sometimes*, without bothering to look at me. It wasn't even that he did; just that he seemed so casual about it. As if it should've been obvious to me, even though he never watched it when I was around. Don't you think that's weird?'

'Not really.'

'Seriously?'

'Yeah, most people watch porn.'

'So you're basically saying I'm a prude?'

'You know that's not –'

'I don't care. It's more that there are all these memories now that feel like clues I missed,' says Anna, her mouth already dry again. 'Let me ask you this then, and you've got to be honest with me: when you found out, were you surprised?'

'Babe!'

'I won't get mad, I promise.'

'I'm the wrong person to ask,' says Zoe. 'I don't expect much from men.'

As the bushranger's pouring a jug of beer for one of the jocks, he exchanges glances with Zoe, clearly desperate to take her back to Stringybark Creek for the night.

Kate finally appears, her cheeks carefully contoured, and puts her arm around Anna.

'Where've *you* been?' yells Anna.

'Just letting Ryan know I'm safe,' says Kate.

'I got you a drink,' says Anna, prodding the lowball glass towards Kate, leaving an oily puddle on the bar.

'I'm good for now.'

'Fine then,' says Anna, knocking back the vodka and pineapple juice. Her wrists are starting to tingle. She notices that her foot's tapping along to the DJ's beat, but she can't figure out which nineties song it's a remix of.

'Come on!' she says, grabbing Zoe's hand and hauling her away from the bar. She looks back at Kate. 'You coming?'

'I'm happy here,' says Kate, getting out her phone.

There's heaps more space on the dance floor now. Anna closes her eyes, lets the deep bass notes reverberate up from the floorboards and spread along her limbs. Bodies brush against hers, warm and full of static, dissolving into the darkness. She runs her hands through her hair, feeling the electronic sequences in the tips of her fingers. Even though she usually knows nothing about music, she can miraculously anticipate whichever note's coming next.

'Wanna know a secret?' asks Zoe, her sweet pineapple breath right up against Anna's ear.

'Alright.'

'Ryan's gonna propose.'

'What!' says Anna, opening her eyes and copping the full force of Zoe's smile. 'How do you know?'

'I had to help him find a fucking ring.'

'That's amazing!' says Anna. She strains her jaw and her cheekbones to try to reciprocate Zoe's smile. 'And you managed to actually *do* that?'

'I'm sure Katie will let us know if the ring isn't to her satisfaction.'

'God, they didn't muck around.'

'eHarmony love,' says Zoe, smirking, her face drenched in violet light. 'It sounds like a bad eighties sci-fi movie.'

Another uni student – northside hipster haircut – shuffles over to them and starts dancing next to Anna. He can't be much older than her year eleven kids. Chewing gum, eyes about to pop right out of their sockets. Zoe eases back a few metres. Anna tries to dance like she was before, but his presence makes her feel self-conscious, even with her eyes closed. She opens them again and sees him sleazily nodding to the beat, watching her.

'You're hot!' he yells.

'Thanks.'

She can't help but laugh. He's probably still living with his parents, reaping the rewards of the magic washing basket.

'What's your name?'

'Anna.'

'I'm Joe.'

He holds out his hand and wraps it around hers, refusing to let go. It's all moist and icky. She can feel herself constricting inside.

'What's the matter?' he asks.

'I can't see my friend.'

'What?'

'My friend, Zoe.'

'Don't worry about her,' he says, stroking her hand and looking at her with devil's eyes. 'I can take care of you.'

It's so cringeworthy. The fact that he honestly thinks she'd want to go home with him, or that he thinks it's acceptable to reduce her to prey. She gives a light tug, but he won't release her hand, so she yanks it free and runs away from the dance floor, crashing into a group of smoky-smelling strangers.

'Hey, where're you going?' calls Joe.

Kate isn't in the front bar. Heat starts coursing through Anna's veins, triggering a familiar fluttering inside her chest.

'ZOEEEE!' she yells, bursting into the toilets.

No one answers. She presses her forehead against the mirror, concentrating on breathing through her diaphragm to ease the palpitations, imagining her lungs filling with air, before slowly releasing it.

Her heart starts hammering again the second she steps back out into the pub. She can feel him watching. A group of older men at the pool tables are staring at her. Bald freaks. The bushranger probably knows where Zoe is – if not, he'll have to help protect her – but he's serving people, and they'll think she's nuts if she barges in and starts blabbering about some creep on the dance floor.

She runs for the exit and stumbles out onto Racecourse Road. The night air instantly cools her face and the exposed skin on her arms. Denim jacket. There's no way she's going back in. Hopefully Zoe or Kate find it, wherever they are. She tries to text them, but the pulsating screen of her phone – blurry letters, trapped beneath twisting grids – is impossible to focus on.

Someone's clomping along right behind her, so she cuts across the road, struggling to figure out which direction cars are coming from amid the mosaic of lights. A horn blares and there's a warm gust of wind, followed by a rip of shouting. Everything's happening way too fast. She manages to make it over to the other side of the road and stands on the corner outside Subway with her keys wedged between her knuckles, ready to be attacked. She looks up at the commission flats. The windows are all smudging together, melting the cement and burning like a giant inferno in the night.

'Are you okay?'

She can't tell where the voice is coming from. A person shifts into her line of sight, but everything except their jaw is obscured by a dark hoodie.

'It's Tyler, miss.'

'Tyler, what're you doing here?'

'Coming back from my brother's place.'

'I'm trying to get a taxi,' she says, swallowing the keys into her palm.

Tyler glances over his shoulder at the dark street behind them. Anna finally manages to form the words *Crusty Demons* on his hoodie.

'I'll wait with you until a taxi comes,' he says. 'You don't wanna be out here alone.'

ANNA

She races to the bathroom, desperately trying to hold in the bile that's surging up her oesophagus. Chunks of prawn and calamari form small clots in the rusty-tasting liquid that slops into the toilet, like canned soup. She moans as she kneels over the bowl between retches, daylight drilling into her temple, just wanting everything to be over.

* * *

U ok babe???

Just got home cab u font my jacket?

She can't even remember texting Zoe. The one-and-a-half-minute voicemail from Mum can wait.

Any luck with Ned Kelly?

Ha!

Maybe

As if she isn't jealous enough already.

You realise he's probably in love with you?

Unlikely

Now that her stomach's finally stopped churning, eating itself from the inside, there's the ordeal of figuring out what to do with the rest of her Saturday. She isn't in the right headspace to write about her 'leadership capacity' – and it's too early in the weekend to start planning – but the thought of walking up to the strip and sitting in a café on her own, nursing a smoothie and being surrounded by children screeching in prams is equally depressing.

Kids are probably out of the question now. By the time she meets someone, and tries to hold it together for long enough to convince them she's stable, she'll be in her mid-thirties, lacking the energy that all the fun mums in vibrant post-partum dresses around Kensington magically seem to have. They've got no idea how lucky they are. So much of it is chance; who you invest in at what time. And how much you invest. She invested everything. Maybe it's because she grew up in the country and her head's never been filled with the entitlements of the city. No one in the city is content. That's the nature of a city.

She flicks open her laptop and finds the YouTube clip that Ali's been nagging her to watch of him rapping in the scrub under Flemington Bridge Station, arms wide in his puffer jacket, gesturing to the concrete pillars that loom above him.

The vision's pixelated and his words sound gravelly and wind-affected as they echo from the speakers of her laptop:

Blazin with my g
Waleeeed
In tha back bits
Lazin on them weeeeds
Underneath
Where tha trax split . . .

Funda, who must be filming it, lets out a cheer as Ali gulps for breath. Even though he slips in and out of time as he finishes the first verse, what's undeniable is his belief in the glory that this world has to offer him.

71 views.

Another hour dissolves in bed as she flicks through memes of accidental Chinese hipsters and watches updates of the two English girls whose rendition of 'Super Bass' went viral last year. The emptiness she feels after each clip – how un-profound her own life is – only compels her to click on the next one.

Game of thrones tonight?

Got a screening in city

Want 2 come?

Don't think I can face the world

Would rather look @ Jon Snow trust me

Anna digs out the personalised cookbook she was given for her twenty-fifth birthday. It's been almost a year since she's used any of the recipes. Zoe's 'recipe' is typical Zoe. No words, just two pictures: one of her at Tiba's on Sydney Road, handing a twenty-dollar note over the counter, and another of a Lebanese platter with lamb skewers, bread, dips, falafels and tabouli.

Mum's beef cannelloni.

Kate's gluten-free rhubarb and raspberry muffins . . .

She remembers *his* impersonation of Kate. Always with a posh English accent, placing square upon square of toilet paper over an imaginary public toilet seat, neatening each fold so neurotically that he/she never actually sat down to go.

'*Now, Katie,*' says Anna out loud, trying to reprise his over-the-top accent, '*deary me, not yet, that square's a little crooked. How about . . . now? Much better!*'

'I'm not taking the piss out of her,' he once protested, after Anna pretended to disapprove of the impersonation. 'The piss never comes out!' Smiling sadistically at what he'd just come up with.

This time last year they were going to open inspections most weekends, walking through townhouses in Braybrook and Sunshine, as she tried to picture their life in a few years' time with kids, dogs and all that wonderful mayhem, before racing home to see how the local primary schools ranked on the Better Education website. She assumed they were in it together. What was he thinking every time she waffled on about how much she'd love a walk-in wardrobe or a sunken living room? Why didn't he just tell her there was someone else and save them both a shitload of time? How else did he imagine it was going to end?

And to find out via text was like a cruel joke: *There's no way I'll ever be able to do this face to face . . .*

Do this? It was already done. Seven years of feelings – a quarter of her life – razed in a single text, every moment of joy and tenderness between them suddenly lost.

The blue stickers on his belongings, littered throughout the house in the surreal days afterwards, so the removalists would know what to collect. Imagining him calmly putting them on, room by room, just about killed her.

Maybe Zoe's right. There's nothing wrong with having a bit of 'fun' to remember what it feels like.

Or just to feel something at all.

ALI

Tents with blue and white balloons are set up along the South Lawn, packed with showbags with the University of Melbourne's weird angel logo on them. Onion smoke's drifting over, making Ali's mouth froth with saliva. Students are holding leaflets, trying to convince people to sign up to their special clubs, and writing angry messages about politics on the brick footpath:

Hate Muslims = vote Liberal
NO PRIDE IN GENOCIDE
Face up to climate change

Ali watches the hectic movements of the students around them, feeling his thigh muscles go tense. Everyone must be so smart just to be on this campus. They're full of confidence. Not like at the towers, where people only pretend to have it so they don't get rolled in the lift.

'I'm starving,' he says to Walid. 'Let's get some free food before they run out.'

The Christian Union, the Science Students Society, the Wine Society, the Socialist Alternative; fuck knows what half of these things even mean. Walid stares inside every tent as they walk past, expecting the young people sitting at the tables to try to get his attention, or to offer him a showbag, but they all just pretend he's invisible.

Ali and Walid line up at a sausage sizzle – authentic 'Aussie' food – near the stage where a horn band is playing.

'Man, this Pitbull motherfucker's got the dumbest lyrics ever,' says Ali. 'I can't believe these chicks are dancing.'

Walid nods, barely checking out the wasted girls on the grass who're all shaking their butts the same way, thinking they're being sexy or something.

'Seriously, look at them!'

'I did!'

Ali can feel the unspoken tension between them – Walid's silent rage – because of the tiny bit of bud the cops found in his underpants.

'Are these sausages halal?' asks Ali, when they reach the front of the line.

'What's that?' squeaks the girl holding the tongs.

'You know, *halal*?'

She scrunches her freckly nose.

'Can you ask someone?' says Walid.

The girl whispers something to the dude next to her: a

sporty-looking guy in a University of Melbourne t-shirt with disgustingly hairy biceps.

'Sorry, boys,' he says, talking like he's twenty years older than them, 'I've got no idea if these're halal.'

'Forget it!' says Ali, storming off.

They buy a packet of Doritos from the food court and keep exploring. Every building is different. There are so many epic gardens and sports fields that the uni has all to itself. It must be someone's job to make sure every blade of grass is kept perfect, because every blade *is* perfect.

In the middle of the campus there's a massive square that looks like something out of those boring old English movies, where people wear silly clothes and talk in pretend voices. A sign on the sandstones says the square was built in 1856. Walid stares at a crane that rises above the castle-like walls. Watching it hang in the sky, Ali realises what the university is trying to be: a perfect balance between history and the future – like when MCs give shout-outs to OG rappers like Nas and Chuck D while laying down new flows – moving backwards and forwards at the same time, never staying still.

'We should find that Malaysian hottie from homework club,' says Ali. 'Where do you think she's at?'

'I think we should leave her alone.'

'Nah, man, I wanna get her number.'

'Let's keep checking this place out.'

'Fuck that!' says Ali. 'I know where she'll be.'

He leads them through the sliding doors of the library, past rows of computers, desks where people are standing instead of sitting, reading rooms and project rooms, all the way up the spiral staircase to the top level, where there are shelves full of encyclopaedias and faded hardcovers. Ali's never seen so many books. It must be ten times the size of the library in F-Town.

'Can we chill for a minute?' he asks when they reach the silent study area.

He searches the spines of the students who're hunched at wooden desks, trying to see if the tutor is around in one of her nerdy cardigans, working on a crazy-smart essay.

She isn't.

They hang at a creaky desk by the window, overlooking the South Lawn. Hundreds of students are relaxing on the grass behind the tents, sitting in small groups and lying on their backs, trying to get sunburnt.

'Why'd you wear your school shirt?' asks Ali.

'Out of respect.'

'Respect for who?'

'The university.'

'Man, the university's not an actual person,' says Ali. 'It's not gonna say: *Since you wore a cheap-arse shirt, Walid Dahir, you can be one of my students.*'

'I didn't want anyone to see me in my Chelsea top. They might think I'm not serious.'

Two girls in skirts are doing cartwheels on the lawn while their friends laugh without sound. Even just from their postures, Ali can tell they've had easy lives.

'You really wanna come here, hey?'

'Yeah,' says Walid.

'That's cool,' says Ali. It's kind of nice to imagine Walid on this campus in two years' time, being surrounded by all these smart, confident people, wearing a University of Melbourne t-shirt with the angel wings on his chest. 'So what do you think I should do, if my career doesn't take off soon?'

'You could come here, too.'

'Yeah, right.'

'I'm serious.'

'No way, man. There's probably some secret rule, like they only let one kid from the towers in every year. So if I come, then you *definitely* won't be allowed to.'

Walid ignores his joke, staring at a giant gum tree out the window.

'Are you pissed at me or something?' asks Ali.

'Nah,' says Walid.

'Then what the fuck's up?'

Walid squints at the tree, the skin at the top of his nose stiffening into its normal V shape.

'Do you still pray?' asks Walid. 'When you're at home, I mean.'

'Not really.'

'Faith can't be flexible, you know.'

'I feel you,' says Ali, relieved that Walid's finally talking to him properly. 'My head's been full of this shit since Yassin's party at my old crib, yeah. It's like . . . after my mum flipped out or whatever, and she didn't come back, my dad stopped making me pray. Religion isn't really part of our lives now. Not how it is to you.'

Walid nods, still squinting. Chunks of bark are starting to peel away from the tree's pale trunk.

'Plus, it freaks me out when we have to empty our heads at lunchtime,' says Ali. 'I need my head to stay busy.'

A geek with a laptop and a huge stack of books coughs aggressively at them from one of the nearby desks.

'Anyway, stuff this Malaysian honey,' whispers Ali, his thigh muscles aching with tension. 'I feel like I can't even breathe here, man. I wanna hoop with *you* in your sexy shirt.'

On their way out, he stops at a spare computer and types in the link to the Sediment clip he loaded onto his YouTube channel last week. He mutes the clip, presses play and gives it an extra 'like'.

Everyone's amped because Jasmine's balling, trash-talking all the boys as she busts out post moves, shoving them off balance with her big bootie. It's a beautiful time of day. The park is the most packed it's been since Eid last winter, when it was full of men in *kanzus* and women in their favourite *dirac*s. The sky is like a big, split-open peach. Even the towers look nice, pebbles orange and glowing in the late-afternoon sun. If it weren't for the ugly sound barriers of the tollway, it could all easily be on a postcard.

The only annoying thing is that Musa keeps messing around on offence, trying fadeaways and floaters that hardly ever touch the ring. He's the biggest ball hog. Ali takes over playing point guard, dribbling between his legs, weaving in and out of traffic and pump-faking kids who watch his body instead of the ball. Walid's the only one who doesn't fall for it.

Musa randomly stops playing D, letting Binh score a piss-easy lay-up.

'YO, HASSAN!' he yells.

Ali sees Hassan walking along the path in his Magic Hand Carwash uniform, his shoulders slumped as he concentrates on his black Zooms.

'Hassan!' yells Walid.

This time, his brother looks up.

'Come hoop with us,' says Ali.

Hassan's zombie expression doesn't change. It's like he's staring *through* Ali or something. He slowly makes his way over to the half-court, airing out his shirt with the puffy blue man and his magic bucket on it. Walid passes the ball to him. He catches it and twists it in his hands as if he's hypnotised, spreading his fingers over the seams.

'You down or not?' snaps Jasmine.

'Okay,' says Hassan, eventually.

He tightens his kicks and asks to play on Walid's team. Trying to shoot over him – seeing him standing, instead of slouched on a couch – Ali remembers how tall he is. Basically two metres. The game's too easy for him. It's like he always knows what's about to happen next. He owns the paint, boxing out Musa and getting pretty much every rebound, but he isn't interested in scoring. Instead, he keeps dishing the ball off, trying to include Binh, Walid and Jasmine in the game.

Some of the young'uns from the Community Centre rock up and dump their BMXs around the bench, sucking on Zooper Doopers. They soon start shouting 'LeBron!' whenever Hassan has the ball.

'Have you scored yet, bitch?' gasps Jasmine, nudging Ali in the ribs so she can shake his D.

'Easy, girl!'

'I ain't *your* girl.'

Hassan grabs another board and looks around. One of the young'uns – whose voice is still squeaky – yells, 'DUNK IT!'

Ali glances over to the bench and spots the kid with tribal

scars on his face, mouth open, next to the boy who was looking after Yassin's stash at the party.

Hassan flicks a pass out to Walid, who hits a long-range J that would probably be a three-pointer if the markings weren't faded off the court.

'Concentrate, Musa!' yells Ali.

When their team gets the ball back, Musa tries a skyhook that sails over the top of the backboard and rolls towards the car park. He's too puffed to run after it.

'Can you get me a job at KFC?' Ali asks Jasmine as they wait for Musa.

She frowns sideways at him, like he's joking.

'I'm fucking serious.'

'In the kitchen, or what?'

'Anywhere,' he says. 'I'm saving for studio time.'

'I can ask my boss.'

'Lit!' says Ali, offering to bump fists with her. 'We should lay down a track together . . . *Sediment featuring Jazzy Flow*, or some shit.'

'Only if you pay me, like, Beyoncé money.'

Musa hurls the ball back and the game continues. Usually Walid would be doing homework by this time on the weekend, but Ali can tell that he's pushing it to the back of his mind so he can keep hooping with his brother, brushing palms after every basket. It's easier for them than words.

Hassan rolls off a screen from Binh and cocks the ball in his hand. He leaps for the rim, still just able to jump high enough, and throws down a dunk.

The young'uns go crazy, high-fiving and screaming 'THE KING!' with their rainbow tongues.

'This cunt should be playing N-B-A!' brags Musa, 'taking on KD and shit, I swear.'

For once, Walid joins in Musa's wild laughter.

Ali's eyes meet Walid's. He reaches into his button-ups and removes the bud that Yassin gave him, feeling a wave of relief wash through his chest as he pegs it onto the grass.

There's a nice wind finally rolling in from the Docklands. Birds and insects are singing. Red and yellow swirls of peach are bleeding together, slowly draining into the horizon. It's one of those days when you wish the sun would never go down.

AUTUMN

NO CHURCH IN THE WILD

ALI

'A smidge to the left,' says the photographer.

The principal shuffles towards Ali and puts his palm flat on the desk, so close now that Ali can smell his cologne. It's like a leather chair's been dipped in a pot of sweet spices.

'I don't think I was cut out for the runway,' whispers the principal, showing Ali the folds of skin around his lips.

He's put new red, black and grey couches in the resource centre just for this photograph, and he's taken out the librarian's desk, leaving a strip of fresh-smelling carpet.

The photographer stares through his camera, rubbing his stubble as he thinks about what else has to happen for the photo to be perfect. He starts playing with his shiny reflector, leaning it in different directions, even though it's impossible to see what changes it makes.

This is a sick rehearsal for Ali's EP publicity shoot. Once he saves up enough money working at KFC, he'll get some artsy photographer to shoot him crouching in the communal garden where Walid's mum grows her chilli vines, cucumber wire blurred in the foreground, as he looks right into the lens, like Dre when he was in full-on beast mode in N.W.A.

'You!' says the photographer, pointing at Kylie. 'Can you pop your screen up?'

Kylie tilts her laptop and makes sure that her straightened hair's flopping where she wants it to flop. There's a crazy amount of powder over the pimples that're normally on her cheeks.

'Why do you keep staring at me?' she says to Ali.

'You're tripping, girl.'

It's whacked they even chose her and him for this photo over Walid, who's in the student leadership team.

Ali can feel the photographer watching him. He pretends to concentrate on his screen. Knowing this photo's going to be in the newspaper is lit. Maybe Mum will see it – wherever she is – and come find him, and apologise for all the ways she's done his head in these last twelve years . . .

'Relax,' says the principal. 'It's all a bit of fun.'

He makes this creepy smiling face at the camera, putting all his weight through his hand on the desk.

'Fingers on your keyboards,' says the photographer as he gets in the zone for the shot. 'Just pretend you're doing what you normally do.'

Ali can't think how he normally sits at a laptop. Usually he isn't hunched like this. He doesn't want anyone to think he's a geek or something, so he leans back to look more casual.

'Hold still, champ!' barks the photographer.

Instead of two or three clicks – like when they take your school photo – these ticking noises keep coming from inside his special camera. Every few seconds a big flash goes off, blinding everyone, the same as Will Smith does in *Men in Black*.

'Excellent!' says the photographer, drawing imaginary

circles with his spare hand. His fingers have the same yellowish tobacco stains as Ali's dad's. 'Now, can you kids pretend you're *really* interested in what's on your screens? You're enjoying this . . . you're having loads of fun.'

Kylie yawns.

Ali can't really be arsed doing the fake smile. He catches the principal staring down at him with a blood-red face he's never had at assembly, no longer making a joke out of everything. In a weird way, the principal's eyes look just like Dre's.

'Seriously, I don't know any of this shit,' says Ali, flicking through Walid's Legal Studies textbook on the grass of the school oval.

Musa's jiggling his shoulders, humming 'Roll Up'.

'Alright, answer this one,' says Ali. 'Rachel has a criminal trial in the County Court of Victoria. Has she been charged with a summary offence or a . . .'

He shows Walid the textbook, pointing at the word.

'Indictable offence.'

'Yeah, whatever that is.'

'The second one, I think.'

'When did we learn that?'

'Probably while you were clicking on your own dumb-arse song, like, every single class,' says Musa.

'You know what,' says Ali, 'when I'm getting a Grammy off Kendrick, and you're still bumming in the towers, I'll remember you said that.'

'Man, I bet you a million bucks that never –'

'Can you guys be quiet for *one* second?' hisses Walid.

He's still pissed about the principal choosing Ali for the photograph. Walid rips the textbook off him and starts drawing a chart with the different courts on it, so he can burn everything into his memory before the test.

'Which one of those are you having your trial with the pigs in?' asks Ali.

'The Federal Court,' says Walid, without looking up.

'Yo, check it out!' yells Musa, pointing at the delivery truck that's parked behind the canteen. Yassin's jumped into the back of it and he's stealing a whole box of soft drinks.

'Far out,' says Ali. 'What a crazy cunt!'

Walid's writing frantically – the same as Ali when he's just had a banging idea for a track – knowing the recess bell's going to ring any second.

'You thirsty, fam?' croaks Yassin, walking towards them with the cardboard box balanced in his hands.

'For sure!' says Ali, ripping the top open and grabbing a bottle of Coke. 'That shit was smooth, man.'

Musa takes a Coke, too.

'How bout you?' says Yassin, staring Walid down.

'Nah, I'm good.'

'I'll have his,' says Musa.

Yassin shakes his head and tilts the box towards Walid, not giving a fuck if the truck driver busts him.

Walid concentrates on his notes, mouthing the names of the courts: *magistrates court* → *county court* → *supreme court*

'What's your fucking problem?'

civil trial, burden of proof → *probability*

'HEY, I'M TALKING TO YOU!' yells Yassin, dumping the box and pulling out a Coke.

'Answer him, Walid,' pleads Ali.

There's a pop of fizz, followed by the slap of liquid across Walid's face. As he rubs his eyes like he's got chlorine in them, Yassin pours the rest of the Coke over his chart. When Walid can finally see again, he tries to check out his notes, but they've already become a river of ink, flooding his whole exercise book into brown wrinkles.

TYLER

Everyone in Ali and Walid's class is being boring, so Tyler ducks down outside the sliding door and yells, 'THUG LIFE!'

'Shh!' says Ms Lee, thinking someone in the room said it.

Tyler stays silent for a minute then yells, 'TUPAC SHA-KUR!' in a totally different voice, waiting for the laughter.

Fucking squares.

He can't be bothered going to Psychology, so he keeps cruising along the corridors, rattling on windows. No one really pays attention. He walks to the top of the stairs, near the rooftop where the depressed teachers smoke at recess, and rolls up his sleeves to check out his biceps. As he's flexing by the window, the rash on his left knee starts burning like hell. He twists the blotchy skin, scraping at it with his nails, until goo spills out and this weird shiver passes through his whole body.

When the bell finally rings, he bolts down to the lockers to see who's kicking about. It reeks of Lynx Africa.

'Hi!' he says to Binh, all friendly, just to mess with him.

Ali's bitching to Kylie outside the computer room about

how 'impossible' some test they just did was. The top button of her dress is undone, so everyone can see her pale cleavage.

Kadra and her two sisters are whispering in the corridor, probably planning a terrorist attack at the next assembly.

'Sup, man?' says Jai when he spots Tyler, winding up for a brother boy handshake, bumping shoulders.

'Got any deodorant?'

'Yeah,' says Jai, reaching into his locker and pulling out a can of cheap shit that smells worse than mosquito spray. 'Did you hear about Yassin?'

'Nah, what?'

'He robbed the drinks truck at recess when the man was in the canteen. He boosted, like, a whole box of Cokes and he was giving them to everyone.'

'Robbing a truck's not that bad-arse,' says Tyler, passing the deodorant back. 'Did you take one?'

'Yeah, it was free.'

'That's dumb as.'

'Why, man?'

'Now you owe him.'

'He was giving them to everyone.'

'Exactly!' says Tyler. It's a good strategy by Yassin. 'Hey, what class have we got?'

'PE.'

'Fuck that!' PE's all about how your body works now – with long science words that don't even mean anything – instead of being about sport. 'I'll catch you at lunch.'

'Sweet,' says Jai.

Tyler's gut rumbles for food. At least hunger helps his abs stay flat. As he checks his locker for old muesli bars, he hears the principal's voice coming up the stairs. He turns around and catches the fat-arse giving some dick with a notepad a tour of the school, pretending he's tight with every kid that passes by.

'What's most important,' he's saying, 'is that the school becomes a place for the community to be proud –'

'Hi, sir!' says Tyler, putting on his friendly voice.

'Good afternoon, Tyler,' says the principal. He turns to the dick with the notepad and says, 'Tyler's one of our more, ah, *colourful* students.'

'This school's really dope,' says Tyler, grinning like a student support kid as he sticks up his thumbs. Stupid fucks. They don't even get that he's being sarcastic. He waits until the principal starts crapping on about the new science labs. 'Just so you know, sir,' he interrupts, 'I busted Yassin robbing the drinks truck this morning. He probably needs to get in shit for it, don't you think?'

The yuppy dick with the notepad smiles and the principal pretends to smile with him, but Tyler can tell he's seriously pissed off. It's funny as getting people mad when they're not allowed to show it. Hopefully it makes the school close down, so all the principal's bullshit will have been for nothing.

Ms Kelly keeps talking shit about the documentary she's forcing the group to watch, saying how it's important to appreciate the soldiers that died on the Kokoda Trail and the old farts who sook in wheelchairs every Anzac Day, which is cool, because there's always a day off school for it. Walid's scribbling notes as she talks, acting like he's better than everyone else, even though there are brown stains all over his shirt. Probably shit stains. It doesn't matter what he thinks he's going to become. He's just going to end up unemployed and addicted to meth, like every other deadshit from the flats.

Skateboards keep cracking against the concrete outside. Some year twelves are playing three-on-three, trash-talking each other. Having to stay back after school sucks balls. If Tyler had known this was part of the deal, he'd never have agreed to go on this stupid trip. But at least Ms Costello's walking Yassin towards her office, hopefully about to suspend him.

Someone's written *I ❤ Chris Brown 4eva* on the table. It's messed up how anyone could think that after what he did to his girlfriend. Raising your hand against a woman is the one thing you never do. That coward should've got the death penalty.

Funda's sitting right in front of Tyler, between Kylie and her cousin. It's crazy how different she is whenever Ali's around, hardly looking at Tyler and acting all disgusted by him. He'll have to become mates with Ali while they're training to go to this povo country, and pretend that his lame hip-hop tracks are interesting, so Ali can put in a good word for him.

Staring at Funda's thick, curly hair, all he can think is how badly he wants to lose his virginity to her. It's hard to work out where it's going to happen. Barney and Mum barely leave the flat anymore and Jai reckons Funda's dad will put a proper beatdown on anyone who goes near her, so her place would be risky as. It'll have to be at a party. Tyler imagines them hurrying into one of the messy bedrooms at Kylie's grandma's flat and barricading the door. Quickly stripping down.

Him on top of her, rubbing her clit, then sticking his cock in as far as it will go, and her making these soft little moaning noises every time he thrusts. Squeezing her big tits and sucking on them, licking her nipples, until he takes his cock out and blows all over her.

The lights flick off. Ms Kelly comes and sits down right next to him. It's weird how she practically filled out his Kokoda application form for him, but whatever. At least it'll help him stay in shape. Cadets have to sleep in a tent during their first two weeks of training, so the trip will be the perfect practice for when he enlists later this year.

The documentary's boring as at the start because most of it's in black and white, but then they get to the fighting in World War II and it suddenly becomes interesting. Tyler never even knew that Japan bombed the shit out of Darwin, killing hundreds of innocent Aussies, or that they snuck submarines into Sydney Harbour. Those little fuckers got seriously close to taking over the mainland. It's insane how no one ever mentions that they used to be on the same side as the Nazis.

Jungle warfare is sick. On the screen, they show overhead maps of the different attack routes and the Japanese flanking movements. There's a crazy amount of strategy in war. Occupying airfields. Stretching enemy supply lines. Foxholes and fallback positions. It's funny how all the Aussie soldiers have names like Smoky, Snowy, Rusty and Bluey. Now the survivors are just old men with wobbly cheeks, patchy eyebrows and shaky voices, telling the camera how they were sick and scared most of the time. There's no way Tyler would be scared. Dying for your country's freedom is the biggest honour there is.

A few Japanese soldiers get interviewed, too. Their faces are heaps different – rocks that've been chiselled until they're extra sharp – and their voices are all throaty and evil. They keep smiling, for some reason, and crapping on about fighting to the death for the Emperor, even though *they* obviously didn't do it. Knowing you're going to die would make you invincible in a way, like Tony Montana at the end of *Scarface*, when he drops his M16 and lets his enemies blast him all the way to hell.

'What did you think of the documentary?' asks Ms Kelly, catching up to him at the school gate.

'It was okay,' says Tyler. 'War's pretty cool.'

'I'm not so sure about that,' she says, chuckling, thinking he's being sarcastic. 'So many innocent people lose their lives in a war and even the people who *do* survive often bear the scars for the rest of their lives.'

'Yeah, I guess.'

She's nowhere near as interesting as she thinks.

'A girlfriend of mine used to date this man who'd served in East Timor . . .' says Ms Kelly. It's dumb how chicks call their female friends 'girlfriends', deliberately trying to make you think they're lesbians. 'She once woke up in the middle of the night in a chokehold, and the scary thing was that her boyfriend didn't even know he was doing it. He was fast asleep.'

'That's pretty messed up.'

Funda, Kylie and Ali cruise by, giggling. Funda's arse looks kind of fat in her school dress, which gives Tyler this weird feeling of shame and pleasure, mixed together.

'Japanese people are evil,' he says, looking Ms Kelly in the eye, so she knows he means it.

'Why do you say that?'

'Eating dead Aussie soldiers once they ran out of rice was fucked up, miss. There's no way our soldiers would've done that to them.'

'You never know.'

'I do.'

'Well, *I* went to Tokyo four years ago and the locals were the most courteous people I've ever met.'

'Yeah, probably because we bombed the shit outta them and put them in their place.'

'Tyler!' she says, exhaling, to try to stop herself getting all pissy at him. 'You can't hate an entire country for something that happened over seventy years ago.'

'Whatever,' he says, shrugging.

They walk on in silence, past massive old terraces that're owned by yuppies who'll live there until they keel over in their boring gardens. If Tyler were loaded, this'd be the last place in the world he'd live, right next to the scum of the flats.

'Are you confident about walking the trail?' she asks.

'Yeah, I'll smash it,' he says, feeling tired from having to answer all her stupid questions. 'I wish there was still a war going on over there, so I could shell some more nips.'

That shuts her up.

A grey-haired woman's coming towards them with a black staffy on a leash. Tyler crouches down and lets it slobber all over his knuckles before rubbing its belly. Ms Kelly tickles its ear and starts having a lame as conversation with the owner. The staffy has nice, strong tummy muscles. As Tyler's patting its ribs, he busts Ms Kelly checking out the scab on his leg, so he stands up and walks off.

'You like dogs?' she pants, all surprised, as she catches up to him.

'They're pretty cool. My brother's got a greyhound.'

'I *love* greyhounds.'

Ali's stopped ahead of them, sticking up his middle finger at the bricks of the police station. Kylie and Funda laugh, before they all keep walking.

'If I were allowed to have pets in my apartment,' says Ms Kelly, acting like her and Tyler are friends, 'I'd get a pug.'

'Pugs are okay.'

He's got no idea why she's telling him all this. If she thinks he gives a stuff, she's wrong.

'What's that thing up there?' she asks, pointing to the big cloud on the roof of the Holland Court flats. 'I've been living here almost eight months and I still don't have a clue what it's supposed to mean.'

Kylie looks back at them and whispers something to Funda, whose shoulders start wobbling.

'Tyler?'

'Huh?'

Funda, Kylie and Ali disappear into Macca's.

'Sorry, miss, I've gotta go,' he says, shaking her smooth-skinned hand. 'I'll catch you later.'

'It was nice chatting.'

Tyler hurries towards Macca's. Before opening the door, he checks his pockets to see if he's got enough money to buy a soft-serve cone. Luckily, he finds the ten- and twenty-cent coins that he scooped out of the ticket machine at the train station this morning.

Fluffs of Tyler's hair float to the concrete around his feet. The clippers are making his neck go all twitchy and the blades keep getting stuck, ripping at his scalp. But it'll be totally worth it. His upper body's going to look jacked with a shaved head.

'How's Mum?' asks Shannon.

'Good.'

'She still with that cockhead?'

'Barney, yeah.'

'You should do something about that.'

Marley prances up and stretches his skinny body over the hair on the concrete. Tyler strokes him with his foot.

'I got this cocky African dick in shit today,' he says. 'It was funny as.'

'Nice,' says Shannon, not sounding that impressed. He starts shaving around Tyler's ears, going all the way back to the skin. 'You know what we call them out here?'

'Nah.'

'Obamas.'

Tyler makes sure he keeps his head still as he laughs. The backyard is sick, letting him peer out over the big wooden beams of the neighbour's new extension. Unlike at the flats, you actually get space, and air to breathe, in West Footscray.

Shannon switches off the clippers and admires his work, nodding. 'You look sketchy as, bro,' he says.

They feed Marley on the decking. Watching him slide his long, skinny tongue around his bowl, Tyler feels his pec muscles relax for the first time since he woke up. Greyhounds aren't like humans. Once they know you, they only have friendly feelings to give you.

Shannon shows him this American thing on YouTube, where some dude in Florida gets his mates to pay to watch bare-knuckle fights in his backyard while he films it.

'Check this fight out,' says Shannon, turning the volume as loud as it will go on his laptop.

One dude with a martial arts background is up against a cocky dude whose style is all street. The cocky dude's wearing a bandana over his mouth, trying to be a gangster, which is dumb as because it blocks his breathing.

'Look at him wiggling and jiggling,' says Shannon. 'You should never fight like that, bro. You're asking to be hit.'

'What about Muhammad Ali versus Foreman?'

'Nah, that was totally different. Ali trained for that. You can tell this Obama doesn't train. He just rolls up and expects to win.'

The dude with the bandana over his mouth keeps trying to avoid a proper fight, skipping around the dead grass, dodging punches, wanting to drain the energy from his opponent. But all he's doing is making himself tired.

'Watch how heavy his legs are,' says Shannon, covering the top half of the laptop with his arm.

The people sitting by the ring are going mental, bitching to the ref that they're not getting their money's worth. Eventually the martial arts dude finds an opening and sends the try-hard gangster to the turf with a brutal right hook, his eyes rolling back in his head.

'See what happens!'

Shannon rips off his singlet and starts working away on the punching bag, showing Tyler how he would've fought the martial arts dude. Lots of body shots. His punches are quick and hard. He makes these sharp breathing noises – '*hoo, hoo, hoo!*' – every time he sinks his knuckles into the bag, before ducking and dodging imaginary punches.

'You got your dick wet yet?' asks Shannon.

'There's one chick I'm kinda into.'

'So why aren't you fucking her?'

'I think she's a bit frigid.'

Shannon throws three jabs into the guts of the bag. 'Just stick your tongue down her throat, bro.'

'What if she isn't into it?'

'Easy, then you find one who is.'

They chill on the decking, eating leftover Domino's and staring into the barrel drum fire. Marley nestles against Tyler's foot and falls asleep. Tyler shivers, feeling the cold breeze on his skull. Shannon chucks him a grey Holden hoodie that's covered in dog hairs. The inside of it smells like dry sweat.

'Keep it if you want,' says Shannon.

'Thanks.'

It's nice how Shannon's always giving him clothes. None of his other half-brothers act like he even exists.

'You crashing here tonight?'

'Yeah, sweet,' says Tyler.

Shannon packs his homemade bong and rips a cone. He holds the smoke in his lungs for ages before blowing it out. It smells wet and mouldy, just like the carpet at Jai's place. Shannon rips three more cones and starts pissing himself.

'You look like such a tough cunt,' he mumbles.

Tyler rubs his head. He can't wait to check himself out in the mirror. Hopefully Funda digs it. Shannon nudges the old Powerade bottle of dirty water towards him.

'It's cool,' says Tyler. 'I've gotta stay in shape for this stupid Kokoda thing.'

'Look at *me*,' says Shannon, flexing. 'Am I in shape or what?'

The chopped-up bud in the mixing bowl seems harmless, but Tyler doesn't want any hydro stuff in his blood. Drugs make people go all clumsy and stupid, and then they're fucked in the head forever.

'Just one,' says Shannon, packing a cone and pressing it with his thumb. 'All you do is laugh at shit, I promise.'

Flames spread a shield of warmth over Tyler's face. He reaches down and pats Marley, feeling his thin bones underneath his fur. It'd be perfect right now if it were just the two of them.

PAUL

'You're a cop, yeah?' says one of the public school girls as their group forms a tight semi-circle on the wing of the St. Bernard's footy oval.

'Is it *that* obvious?'

'That's really cool,' says her ditsy friend. Hint of sarcasm in her voice. If Paul ever has a daughter, there's no way she's leaving the house dressed like this: skimpy singlet, short shorts, plastered in foundation. 'Are you, like, a detective?'

'Nope, just a boring constable.'

Paul concentrates as one of the boys from St. Bernard's closes his eyes and lets himself plunge into the group's outstretched arms.

Heavy unit.

'Do you watch *Underbelly*?' asks heavy unit.

'Every now and then,' says Paul. 'The problem I've got with cop shows is the police always seem to end up doing four different people's jobs. One minute they're in the forensics lab and the next they're in the interrogation room, working over a murder suspect.'

'Have you ever killed anyone?'

'Negative,' says Paul. 'And I don't plan on it, either.'

'What about that kid the fisherman found in the river?' asks foundation mummy.

'Yeah, what about him?'

'Didn't you guys drown him or whatever?'

'I don't know what all those cop shows are teaching you lot,' says Paul, doing his best to keep his tone light-hearted, 'but we're actually the good guys.'

Silence from all three of the smart alecks.

Paul checks the car park for a sign of the Commissioner. Long shot expecting him to rock up to the first training session. He's keen to see what sort of nick the old-timer's in. Have to be in his mid-fifties, at least. It's a gutsy move tagging along. Now that the racial profiling stuff's getting some traction, he probably figures this'll make good press, especially if those hotshot lawyers Athena's always on about end up subpoenaing him.

Foundation mummy lets out a scream as she surrenders her weight to the group. 'Oh my God!' she pants, readjusting her singlet, 'that was *so* scary.'

Heavy unit's eyes are about to pop right out of his skull. Never seen so much female flesh at his Catholic private school.

Athena calls them all in to explain the next trust exercise and starts handing out blindfolds. Once Paul hears they'll be breaking into pairs, he edges closer to the only African kid in the group, making sure they're standing next to each other.

'G'day, my name's Paul,' he says, offering his hand.

Limp shake.

'I remember you.'

Paul gets a good look at the kid's face and realises that he's one of the boys they searched in the park a month or two back.

Fluffy hair. Still, he figures he might as well stick it out. If the kid doesn't like it, he can grab a new partner.

'How're you finding it?' asks Paul as they start scouting the oval for a suitable spot to begin.

'Not so bad.'

Paul has a bit of a chuckle. 'Not so bad! Mate, you sound like you're about to face the firing squad.'

Fluffy hair still won't look him in the eye. No point pushing too hard. Paul catches him admiring the classrooms on the hill overlooking the row of sporting fields.

'Bloody big school, isn't it?'

'I know.'

'We'll be doing stair climbs at the flats next week. These toffs won't have a clue what hit them.' He immediately feels like a prick for taking a pot shot at the kid's home. 'You live in the high-rises, right?'

Fluffy hair nods.

'How do you like it there?'

'It's okay.'

'Let me guess,' says Paul. 'It'd be better if us coppers left you and your mates alone.'

'We're used to it.'

Ice cold. So far most of the flats kids have either shot daggers at him or been happy enough to share a bit of banter, especially the youngsters at the footy clinics. It seems like there's almost no front with this kid. More of a 'grey man', as they used to say when he gave the Special Forces a crack.

'Spose you're expecting *me* to go first,' says Paul, figuring they've got enough space to start. 'What's your name again?'

'Walid.'

'Wah-lid, is that right?'

'That's fine.'

'It's been nice meeting you, Wah-lid,' says Paul, wrapping the blindfold around his own head. 'Now try not to let me crash into any of these clowns, okay?'

He pulls the blindfold over his eyes and sets off. Weird thing, walking without sight. You keep thinking the earth's about to drop out from underneath you. Fuzzy shapes start quivering on the back of his eyelids. The squawks of the birds sound amplified, whirring around in high circles, as if they're trying to disorientate him.

'We good, mate?'

'Yeah,' calls Walid.

Paul takes note of every turn Walid gets him to make, mapping each movement in relation to the soccer pitch that was on his right to begin with. He remembers the trick from when the directing staff yanked a balaclava over his head and bundled him into a van on the selection course, drove him every which way, and he was still able to give them intel.

'Turn left,' says Walid.

The soccer pitch is back on his right. Someone's coming from the direction of the pavilion. Short, sharp breathing. Could be AJ exhaling. Paul feels his toes dig into the squishy insoles of his runners. Squelching behind him, too, right in the back of his skull. He wishes he could stop and brace.

'Left again.'

Paul pivots in the opposite direction to the soccer pitch. The darkness is warping. Birds are going berserk. Footsteps converging.

'Quick, right!' barks Walid.

The vindictive prick's trying to make him and AJ crack noggins and split each other's heads open. Some twisted form of revenge for searching him. Not going to happen. Paul rips off the blindfold, his retinas scorched by the rush of white light.

* * *

What was that hissy fit all about?

Sorry Ath, my bad

Mate!

Yeah I know

This is supposed to be a bloody peacekeeping mission!!!

* * *

A couple of sponsors from some God-boring superannuation company call timeout halfway up the third climb. AJ flicks Paul a grin as his group overtakes them. Didn't think anyone would be this useless. Compared to the Special Forces selection course, a few quick hill climbs are nothing. Try going three weeks, doing the 'twenty-clicker' with a bag of bricks on your back, directing staff setting off firecrackers in your ear while you're asleep and getting bound, gagged and interrogated every second night. See what you're really made of.

'Don't worry, it'll get easier,' says Paul, waiting it out with the two soft, smashed-avo eaters. He might have to get up early tomorrow and go for a five-k jog before work to make up for all this piss-farting around.

The next one to throw in the towel is a teacher who looks like she could do with a decent feed. Probably a vego.

'Everything alright?' asks Paul.

'I think I'm about to pass out,' she gasps.

'You'll be right, trust me.'

'This is embarrassing.'

'Never mind that,' he says, crouching beside her. 'All we've gotta do is slow your breathing down.'

Her collarbones jut out of her pale flesh as she sucks in the big ones. She'll want to beef up before they get over to New Guinea – same strategy as going on *Survivor* – otherwise there'll be nothing left of her come the end of it.

'You don't have to wait.'

'It's fine,' says Paul. 'We're all on the same team.'

He stifles a grin as he imagines the bile the directing staff would be spouting at her right now. Even foundation mummy and some clown who's gangster rapping to her have got more gas in the tank, trudging their way towards the top.

'I reckon it's time we get back into it,' says Paul. 'We can take it as slow as you want, okay?'

Vego teacher sighs, then nods.

Something comforting about attacking the hill together, planting one foot in front of the other, dry dirt crunching under their runners as the lactic acid builds up in their legs. After a minute or two, her breathing starts to sound normal again.

'This isn't too bad, is it?' he says. She shoots him a sharp look that's somewhere between a smile and a scowl. 'Always gets easier on the other side of the pain barrier.'

'I've been hearing that a lot lately.'

Has to be a hint. Definitely got a 'single' vibe to her.

'Do you know what they call the first few hours of the Kokoda Trail?'

'No, what?'

'The death zone.'

She shakes her head, panting. 'That's not funny.'

'Who said I was joking?'

'You better fucking be!' Cups her lips straight away. 'I shouldn't swear around you, should I?'

'I'll let you off with a warning this time.'

One of her students – a skinhead straight off the set of *Romper Stomper* – whizzes by, trying to keep up with heavy unit and a bunch of his mates. The kid doesn't smell too flash. He breaks into a jog whenever the others put a bit of distance on him. Got to admire the determination.

By the time skinhead gets to the top of the hill on the fifth or sixth climb, his face is strawberry red and he's coughing up a fair bit of phlegm.

'Why don't you take a quick break?' says Athena to him.

Skinhead bursts straight past her, chasing the St. Bernard's boys back down to the footy oval.

'Sorry about him,' says the vego teacher, smiling tiredly at Athena. 'He's a work in progress.'

'I know who he is,' says Athena.

*

ANNA

'What's it like teaching that skinhead?'

'Tyler?' asks Anna.

'I didn't catch his name,' says Paul, clasping his pint of beer opposite her. 'The kid who was going hammer and tongs up your favourite hill.'

'I've never actually taught Tyler,' she says, paranoid that the wine has turned her lips black. 'From what I understand, he's been on all kinds of behaviour management plans and conduct cards over the years that've achieved nothing. He can barely read or write. Most of the teachers in my office think it's a waste of time keeping him at the school.'

'But you don't?'

'I think we've failed him.'

'Righto,' he says, pausing to take another sip, 'and why's that?'

'He just needs someone to believe in him. People at my work are terrified of putting in the time because they're too busy looking over their own shoulders.'

'Sounds grim,' says Paul.

There's something strange about the slackness of his lips when he smiles, possibly a hint of smugness, as if he could curl them back into a frown at any second.

'I had the nicest chat with Tyler yesterday,' she says. 'Deep down, he's not a terrible person.'

'Maybe not. But if school isn't his thing, wouldn't he be better off going out into the real world and getting a job?'

'It's not that simple.'

He necks the rest of his beer and grimaces. 'And you're about to tell me why not.'

'Who'd hire him?'

'I don't know . . . Red Rooster or Macca's? That's where most of them start out, isn't it?'

'Weren't you listening? I just said he can barely spell. To work at McDonald's, you still need basic literacy and numeracy skills.'

'Yeah, I know. There're other jobs.'

'Such as?'

Paul leans back on his chair and exhales like a sportsman giving a moronic post-match interview. 'It's tough when you put me on the spot,' he says, flashing his slack smile again. 'How about some sort of apprenticeship?'

'Maybe,' she says, her eyes struggling to focus on the insects flitting above the pot plants in the beer garden.

She'll show Tyler what it's like when someone believes in you. It doesn't have to be a big Hollywood ending. Maybe she'll walk past a construction site in five years' time – somewhere in the CBD – and see him in a fluoro yellow vest, holding a road sign or joking around with workmates. Talking absolute shit. He won't even have to acknowledge her. Just seeing him there, out of trouble, will be enough.

'I've gotta use the little boy's room,' says Paul. 'More Ribena?' he asks, pointing at the remnants in her wine glass.

'Only if you let me pay.'

'If you want,' he says, his brow stiff with bemusement as he accepts her debit card.

Anna follows the contours of the wooden table with her finger, completing small circuits around a tuft of mould. Her stomach's going nuts. It was a mistake proposing a drink on a whim and skipping dinner, even if she never has an appetite anymore. She wishes she were relaxing beneath her silk sheets, trying out one of the guided meditation podcasts that Zoe's been nagging her to listen to. Zoe's stomach would never sabotage her like this . . .

'So!' says Paul, jolting her back into reality. 'The troops aren't happy at school.'

'You could say that.'

'Tell me more.'

'We've got this new principal who's . . . well, *I* think he's more interested in building his own cultish brand of education than helping the school survive.'

'Chain of command, I hear you barking.'

'He's dropped literally thousands of dollars on this slick new website, and one of the icons he's put up for prospective parents is called *Busting Myths*.'

'Sounds scientific.'

'Hardly! It's a list of the ten most commonly held myths about the school,' says Anna, unable to stop herself sounding like a psychopath. 'Most of which are true, of course.'

'I'll bet.'

'My favourite *myth* is number ten. It goes something like: *At the college* – because we're obviously a college, not a secondary school – *students are known by a name, not a number.* What I want to know is: which school out there is calling their students by a number? *Morning four-o-four, how're you today?*'

Paul's smile looks sleazier every time.

'And you should've seen this article in *The Age* today. It was basically a puff piece for his regime, bragging about the influx of aspirational families. Honestly, anyone with half a brain would know what he was really saying.'

'And what's that?'

'*We hate black kids!*'

'You sure?'

'Uh-huh.'

'Sounds like you're drawing a long bow.'

'No, not really.'

He probably hates black kids, too.

'Anything interesting going on at *your* work?' asks Anna.

She can see him weighing up his response as he rips the corner of his beer coaster. 'Same old, same old.'

'Sorry, I wasn't trying to imply –'

'Nah, don't be.'

It's not going to happen tonight, even if she did want it to. At least she'll get her smooth sheets to herself.

'I'm sure your station's doing a better job these days.'

'I'd like to think we make a difference.'

Make a difference. It's the kind of phrase she'd have used when she was a student teacher. He keeps shredding his coaster into a neat little pile as they listen to an old funk vinyl pulse and crackle, building up to Curtis Mayfield's unmistakable falsetto. Anna winces down two gulps of shiraz. They're the only people left in the beer garden. Mosquitoes are ravaging the veins along her arms, but she tries to ignore the itchiness.

'One more?' she asks, draining the rest of her wine and hearing the rumble of protest from her stomach.

'You know I've gotta work tomorrow?'

'Me too.'

'If I have one more, I won't be able to drive home.'

'Stay at mine then,' she says, trying to make it sound impulsive.

*

'Nice pad,' says Paul, glancing at his own reflection in the built-in robes, pretending he's got no idea what's about to happen.

'It used to be a meat market.'

'Really?' Of course he doesn't get the joke. 'How much do you pay?'

'Fifteen hundred a month.'

'Not bad.'

He spreads his elbow across the pillow, invading Anna's side of the bed. She flicks the sheet over her pasty thighs. She'd forgotten how much she hates this part. The scrutiny you put yourself under isn't even human.

'Everything alright?' he asks.

'Yeah, fine.'

He reaches for her shoulder and starts caressing it, slowly running his fingers towards her collarbone. His nails. They're so inhumanly clean compared to a jewellery maker's nails. Seven years of disgustingly dirty fingers, prints fossilised in silver dust, and now she finds herself longing to be stroked by them again.

'I'm gonna take off my shirt, okay?'

'Uh-huh.'

He slips off his hideous French Connection polo and folds it on the bedside table. So much for a fit of passion. It's strange having a topless man in her bed again. Pecs bulging, his armpits releasing a buttery, chemical tang that makes her want to gag. He rolls onto his side so he can face her, frighteningly self-assured.

'Do you have any idea how beautiful you are?' he says, breaking into his slack sportsman's smile. She chokes out a laugh. 'I'm serious . . . do you?'

'Probably not.'

He wets his lips.

'I didn't see *this* coming when I woke up this morning.'

'Well, here we are,' she says, feeling a stab in her intestine.

There's no escape now.

'Don't stress,' he says, in a soft voice. She can't tell if he's trying to sound comforting or seductive. Either way, it isn't working.

Her stomach won't stop growling. The stabbing in her intestine's getting sharper. It feels like crystals are exploding inside her chest, fracturing into tiny shards that're probing away at her internal organs.

He leans towards her with his yeasty beer breath, closing his eyes. The first touch of their lips feels alien. Two balls of dry rubber, squished together. The pressure of his hand on the back of her head forces her body towards his. He's doing it all wrong. Palming her skull, pasting saliva around her mouth. She tries to breathe heavily through her nose to pretend she's enjoying it. He rips back the sheets and crushes their bodies together, stifling the pleas from her stomach.

'This is coming off,' he says, lifting her torso and sliding his hands beneath her dress to unhook her bra.

He eases her back down, massaging her breasts and kissing her neck way too firmly. She can feel his cock digging insistently into her hipbone. And hear the clean rip of a plastic wrapper, followed by a whispered groan.

It's happening.

ANNA

'Strong soy latte, please,' says Anna, wondering whether the young, raven-haired cashier's going to charge her for a double shot. It'll probably give her heart palpitations, but it's better than being half-asleep and having to deal with a horde of testosterone-fuelled year eights first thing in the morning.

'You work at the school, don't you?' asks the owner of the café as Anna taps her debit card.

Double shot.

'Yeah, I teach there.'

It's weird. She's been coming here every weekday for six months and the owner – a Greek woman who stopped dyeing her greys over summer – has never before tried to make conversation with her.

'Everything I'm hearing from the community at the moment is really positive. I personally think the uniform looks nice,' says the owner, placing her palm on the heart of her flowery apron. 'We can see you're all on the same page now.'

'Thanks, that's great to know.'

'And it sounds like you finally got rid of all the gangs.'

It almost makes Anna snort in her face. 'I don't think there were ever any *gangs*.'

'I'm only saying what I'm hearing.'

The owner lowers her eyes as she fastens a scoop to the steaming coffee machine. It's not the end of the world if Anna's offended the old stickybeak. This is one relationship she'll have to wean herself off as Kokoda draws nearer, to avoid caffeine withdrawal headaches as she trudges along the trail.

Traffic crawls along the street as a peak-hour train pulls into Newmarket Station. She's pretty sure she was still awake when the first train of the morning rattled by. Of course Paul's a snorer. The putrid smell of his morning breath. He'd better not have used her toothbrush. Seeing him at their next training session is going to be humiliating. Fucking Zoe. Nothing about last night was 'fun', and now everything's even more complicated than it was in the first place.

'Strong soy latte!' screeches the owner.

Anna feigns a smile as she takes the scalding cup off her.

'I had lunch with one of my dearest friends on the weekend,' says the owner, wiping her hands before grinding more coffee beans. 'Her son just started at the school. She was saying how impressed her and her husband are with the new principal, and what a lovely man he is. Very approachable. Afterwards I was thinking: I'd probably send my daughter there now, you know, if she was that age again.'

'It's still early days,' says Anna.

The cashier flicks her an apologetic smile. She's got the same black marble eyes as her mum. Perhaps there's a touch more sadness in them, or maybe the marbles go beyond sadness. Maybe she just has the scope to pick away at a dark seed that her mother never did.

*

EMPOWERING STUDENTS TO LEARN reads the banner that's just been unfurled from the school's roof. The dour slabs surrounding it remind Anna of the Stalinist architecture in Berlin, a city she'd love to visit again. Now that she's going to be renting for the rest of her life, she might as well travel. Berlin, Paris, Barcelona, anywhere along the Portuguese coast. It'll be a great way to escape the pitying looks, and to avoid going to Kate's God-awful Basilica wedding in the eastern suburbs, where she'll have to spend the entire ceremony biting her tongue.

She can imagine how her parents will take the news; the conversation they'll have the second they get off the phone with her. *Going overseas, again.* And they wonder why she never returns their calls.

It's all laughably meaningless, anyway. You save up for decades just so you can end up like Jenny Costello, with a brick fortress in the heart of Moonee Ponds and a beach house on the Peninsula, which you barely even use because you're still working sixty-hour weeks well into your fifties.

Who's it all for?

Jenny's daughter on the Climate Commission in Sydney, or the other one – the less sociopathic one – who's about to fly to Rome to volunteer for the UN?

Anna checks her phone. Five minutes until Rob replaces her on yard duty, if he remembers.

A scattering of year nines, tens and elevens are playing soccer, using the canteen wall as goals. Tyler's among them with his new prison haircut, hacking the ball along the asphalt, tackling ferociously. The younger kids are staying well out of his way. She's not afraid of him. Their rapport has already turned into another one of those eerily silent things in the staffroom, where everyone has their own opinion that they no doubt share with each other the second she's out of earshot.

Jasmine and Najima are krumping to a Rihanna song in the shade of the peppercorn trees, flaunting bumps and curves, getting cheered on by Funda and Kylie. Anna wanders over and joins them. Jasmine and Najima smile at her as they swivel on hennaed feet. She envies the belief that they have in the music, their ability to surrender themselves to lyrics and mood without questioning the artifice behind it all.

'You like to dance with us, Miss Anna?' asks Jasmine, her arse wobbling.

'No, I couldn't.'

'Please, miss,' begs Najima. 'You can do a sexy dance.'

'Yeah, a sexy dance!' shrieks Kylie.

'I'm pretty sure they'll revoke my teaching degree if I try to do that,' says Anna.

'Okay, you just watch,' says Jasmine. The beat morphs into Reggaeton and she breaks into frantic fist-pumping, her eyes narrowing, lips vibrating. It's mesmerising watching the control Jasmine has over her young body, and how she thrives on being watched.

'Shake that thing, girl!' purrs Najima.

Kadra bursts into the shade and starts yelling at Jasmine in Arabic. Jasmine unclenches her fists, listening to Kadra rant above the driving bass.

'What's she saying?' whispers Anna, kneeling on the grass next to Najima.

'She's giving her, like . . . what do you call it . . . like a lecture or whatever,' says Najima, keeping her eyes glued on Kadra.

'She says the music we're listening to is about greed and lust . . . Jazzy's like . . . having no respect for herself . . . and her religion, by listening to it . . .'

Kadra's barrelling Jasmine with her eyes as she yells. Anna can't figure out whether or not she should intervene, but since there seems to be no physical threat, she lets it continue.

'Dancing to this . . . I mean like this . . . it diseases your soul,' whispers Najima. 'It takes you away from the path of . . . when you – hold up, I think she's saying something about – men are animals with desires they, like, can't control . . . and you're asking their eyes to be on you . . . you deserve for terrible things to happen. Sorry, miss, she's cooked. I can't understand everything she's saying.'

Someone's turned the music off.

Kadra's still ranting and raving, saliva spurting out of her mouth, but Najima's stopped translating. Seeing Funda's freaked-out face makes Anna's chest burn with indignation.

'Eee-nough!' she yells, stepping between the girls.

Kadra doesn't flinch.

Anna waves her hand right in Kadra's eyes, forcing her to take notice.

'What?'

'LEAVE THEM ALONE!'

'*Kafir!*' says Kadra, spitting the word out.

'Excuse me!' says Anna, making sure she returns Kadra's deathly glare. Her calves convulse, heat hammering through her limbs. Rob's finally turned up and is watching on, dumbstruck, beside Funda and Kylie. Anna thrusts the walkie-talkie at him, stumbling away on legs made of jelly.

*

ALI

Present tense verb: Mohammad is washing the dishes
Past tense verb: Mohammad washed the dishes

'Yes, Musa,' says Ms Kelly, still not busting Ali for sneaking into her class.

'Actually, my name's *Big Moose* now,' says Musa, spreading his hands behind his ears and making a deep, grizzly sound through his nose. 'I changed it to Big Moose with the government.'

'Yes, Big Moose,' says Ms Kelly, sighing.

'None of those answers are true, miss. There's no way this Mohammad G would wash the dishes. He'd get his mum or his sisters to do them for him while he was out hustling.'

'Is that the kind of society you want to live in?'

'That's just how we roll.'

Musa makes his moose noise again. Ms Kelly finally sees Ali as he cracks up.

'What're you doing here, Ali?'

'It's cool, I've got a spare,' he says. 'I wanna get better at English for my flow.'

'As if you even *have* flow,' yells Jasmine.

'Miss, how come you never watched my clip?' asks Ali.

Ms Kelly stares him down, her left eye twitching like a total psycho. This freaky vein's poking into the rosy skin on the surface of her forehead. Just as Ali's about to get up and leave, she snaps out of it and opens her mouth.

'I want you to work in pairs,' she says, handing out sheets with some boring old story on them. 'Every time one of you sees a past tense verb, please underline –'

'What's a verb, again?' asks Musa.

'A doing word,' says Ms Kelly. 'Such as *intrude*,' she says, glaring at Ali.

'It's a free country, man.'

'Najima dear,' says Ms Kelly. 'Can you please lend Kadra a pen? She seems to have forgotten to bring anything.'

'Don't give her one,' says Jasmine.

'Sorry, miss.'

Walid slides a biro towards Kadra, but she refuses to pick it up. He starts underlining his and Musa's sheet. Ali stares out the window at the whacked new apartment buildings on the other side of the road. They're like tall zebras with 3D stripes coming out of them that wobble in the sunlight. Even if the apartments look silly from the outside, they've probably got air-conditioning that the students who live there can switch on to help them sleep in summer.

It's the kind of place where he can imagine the tutor from homework club living. No mice or cockroaches. He scribbles down lyrics for the song he'll sing to her:

Pretty girl your eyes
Is like the skies (ta me)
When our worlds unite
Be no surprise (ta me)

Her eyes aren't really the colour of the sky, but she won't care. He'll pull her aside tonight and sing it deep and soulful:

Dah-dah dah dah-dah
What our lives could be . . .

'Can we have a quick chat outside?' asks Ms Kelly, standing over Kadra. 'Otherwise I'll have to get Miss Costello.'

Kadra keeps staring at her table, pretending Ms Kelly isn't there.

'Please, Kadra!'

'*Bashal!*' says Musa, fanning his face with the worksheet.

'What's your problem, bitch?' yells Jasmine.

'Quiet!' hisses Ms Kelly. 'Kadra, I'll give you to the count of three to stand up and come outside with me.' She counts the numbers on her shaky fingers – 'One . . . two . . . three' – and hurries over to her desk to write a note.

A weird silence falls over the classroom. Musa makes his moose noise, but no one laughs this time.

'Back to work!' snaps Ms Kelly, her eye twitching again. When she's finished writing the note, she thrusts it at Ali and says, 'Can you make yourself useful and take this to the office?'

'It's too hectic in here, anyway,' he says, snatching her stupid note. She's become the biggest sook ever since he busted her crying in her office last year. 'No wonder your boyfriend cheated on you.'

He can feel, from the low 'Ooooooo!' rising behind him, that it was a messed-up thing to have said. But looking at Ms Kelly's face, it's like he said something so bad that he didn't say anything at all.

'HELLO IN THERE!' yells Musa, leaning over the counter as he tries to get the attention of the two Asian guys who're wrapping burgers in the kitchen. 'I NEED SOME ROOSTER, NOW!'

'I think you're addicted,' says Walid.

'I'm telling you, man,' says Ali. 'Any time he goes, like, two days without eating Red Rooster, he gets shaky.'

Musa isn't even concentrating on their insults. High-pitched electronic sounds keep going off, like a bomb's ticking down, about to explode. The drive-thru's so busy that they don't have anyone taking orders at the register.

'Fuck this!' says Musa. 'I thought Asians are meant to be good at shit.'

Some of the young'uns from the Community Centre roll up, talking over each other about how fit Kanye West's girlfriend is, and when he's releasing the next Air Yeezys. The kid with tribal scars is hanging with them. When he sees that no one's at the register, he hurries over to the drinks fridge.

'It's locked,' says Walid.

The kid tries to jerk the door open anyway.

'Are you deaf or something, fresh boy?' yells Musa, but this time the kid doesn't flinch.

'You know they've got cameras here?' says Walid.

'So what?' says the kid.

'Once the police know your face, they won't forget you.'

'I don't care about the pigs.'

Ali can tell he's just saying it to seem tough in front of his crew. He doesn't quite believe it yet.

'What's your name?'

'Huh?'

'Your *name*, shorty,' says Ali.

'Michael,' says the kid.

'I'm Walid. Take it easy, you hear me?'

'You're not my fam.'

When Michael joins his crew on the stools by the front window, one of them yells, 'MICHAEL GARANG!' in an Aussie accent. Walid glares at them, shaking his head.

'Forget about that fresh cunt,' says Musa. 'He's not even Somali.'

They eventually get their Spicy Burgers and sit at the table near the toilets, so Musa can shit before homework club.

'I can't believe that smack you talked to Miss Kelly,' says Musa, taking a handful of Ali's chips and swallowing them almost without chewing. 'After you left, she nearly cried.'

'I feel bad now,' says Ali.

'Nah, fuck that. Miss Kelly's always getting in people's faces about their personal shit. When I was on school camp with her, she kept asking about my *journey* to this country. Like, how me and my mum came here back in the day.'

'Same with me,' says Walid.

'I swear, being tight with us is only important for how she thinks about herself.'

The cops are no different; the way they all wanted to joke with Walid at training yesterday was crazy after what they did to him, Musa and Hassan outside the towers.

'Schizo junkie!' barks one of the young'uns as Tyler struts by, checking out his own reflection in the window.

Tyler can't hear their laughter through the glass.

Him and Funda have the weirdest vibe. Kind of ignoring each other, but always looking to see where the other one is, and who they're talking to. It's whacked that she thinks Ali doesn't notice, especially since she noticed his thing for the tutor.

'Big news,' he says, pretending Musa's Sprite is a mic. 'I'm gonna tell that smoking tutor how I feel tonight.'

'Seriously?' asks Walid.

'Yeah, I'm pretty sure she's into me. When I told her I was going to the jungle for charity, she nearly lost her shit.'

'Look at this playa!' yells Musa. He licks the mayonnaise that's smeared into the hairs above his lip. 'She can be his tutor in *other* ways, yeah, Walid?'

'To enjoy someone else's body, you need to be pure, and have commitment to them,' says Walid.

'I've got commitment,' says Ali. 'Me and that Malaysian honey are gonna have babies together, you'll see.'

As Musa groans and thrusts, ramming his guts into the table, Ali can feel Walid judging him for not wanting to keep his soul pure.

'You worry too much about the next life,' says Ali, glaring across the table at Walid. 'I want *this* life, man.'

'You can have both.'

'I can't,' says Ali. 'Maybe you can.'

The legs of a baby's highchair scrape across the floorboards near the front window. One of the young'uns jumps on top of the highchair, like a cowboy in a plastic saddle, and tries to squeeze his feet through the gaps. Michael Garang's skull rolls back as he giggles, his closed eyes facing the ceiling, and his legs kick around as if he's a happy child.

Ali's tummy churns as he watches his Air Force 1s drum on the carpet. For once, he needs to shit as bad as Musa.

She's always early.

'Take that, cunts!' screams Musa from the desktop closest to Walid, firing at the pixelated rubble of some war-torn town on his screen.

Walid's still sulking after their beef in Red Rooster, doing his homework on his own so he can get a high ATAR score like the rich kids from St. Bernard's will. They'll all probably end up at the University of Melbourne with the hot Malaysian tutor.

Ali whispers the rhymes of the love song to keep the flow ticking over in his mind:

Skies (ta me)
Surprise (ta me)
Lives could be
Highs we'll see . . .

His throat's crazy dry, just from whispering. He'll have to hurry out to the water fountain straight after homework club, so he can sing the last verse perfectly:

Aint no bigger prize (ta me)
Than when u kiss me girl
And give ya life (ta me) . . .

Still, his kicks won't stop drumming on the carpet.

He tries to distract himself by filling out one of the forms that Jasmine gave him for his KFC trial. Writing his date of birth always makes him feel this weird guilt because Musa and Walid don't even know theirs. They just kept the date they were given by the immigration officials: 1 January.

'Hey, did you hear about Walid?' asks Kylie, adjusting her push-up bra as Funda and her plop onto the beanbags.

'Nah, what?'

'He dogged Yassin,' says Funda. 'That's why Yassin got suspended.'

'How did he dog Yassin?'

'I heard he, like, told the principal about Yassin stealing all those Cokes.'

'Bullshit.'

'Everyone's saying it,' says Kylie.

'That doesn't make it true.'

Walid's hunched at his table, highlighting a textbook as Musa jams the keyboard with his thumbs.

'Ask him,' says Funda.

'I don't fucking have to,' says Ali. 'There's no way Walid would ever snitch, trust me.'

'Isn't that what he's doing, like, to the cops?'

'Nah, that's different. Don't spread lies.'

Kylie searches the pockets of her school jacket for a lighter. She's smoking pretty much every day now, boosting menthol ciggies off her grandma.

'I'll be back,' she says, holding eye contact with Ali for an extra half-second.

Funda shuffles her beanbag over until it's wedged right next to his. He wraps his arm around her. Volunteers are starting to rock up, but not the sexy tutor.

'What's going on with you and Tyler, cuz?'

'Nothing,' says Funda, her shoulder stiffening.

'I see you two, you know.'

'Honestly, there's nothing going on.'

Musa swivels on his wheelie chair as he lets off rounds at some ninja-looking enemy, spraying shells everywhere.

'I'm only asking coz you're, like, a billion times too good for him,' says Ali, tightening his grip on her shoulder. 'You know that, yeah?'

'Thanks,' says Funda, sniffling. Sometimes it's like she wants to be depressed or something.

'I'm serious, you've gotta have more confidence.'

'Where's *your* girlfriend, anyway?'

'Stuffed if I know. It's stressing me out.'

Ali checks the clock. His brain's so hectic that the hands don't even mean anything.

'Who's that?' asks Funda.

An older guy in a blue shirt's walking towards Walid's table with a laptop bag slung over his shoulder. He sits in the chair opposite Walid. They start flicking through the textbook, writing down calculations. Watching them, Ali feels a stab at the back of his eyeballs.

'I told you she'd leave,' says Funda.

'She's probably sick, or studying for a test.'

'If you say so, cuz.'

'Come on, lads!' yells a man in a cheap-arse suit as Ali approaches the carwash on his walk home.

He spots Hassan kneeling on the slick concrete with a cloth and a spray bottle, polishing the bumper of a Range Rover. There's enough parked cars to keep him and his work crew busy for hours. Vacuuming, waxing and steaming. A bearded guy in a turban climbs a small ladder and hoses down the roof of the Range Rover, pretending he doesn't notice the man in the cheap suit lingering next to them.

'Get cracking, Hassan!' bitches the man, pissed off because Hassan's nearly the same height as him working on his knees. 'We're not on Africa time.'

He grins, like they're sharing a joke. Hassan's stomach almost bulges out of his shirt as he rubs his cloth in small, fast circles, ignoring the water that's spraying into his eyes. Watching him, Ali can tell that it isn't so simple for Hassan to keep his dignity, even after that lawyer took him out to lunch when he left the court case. Maybe, in a back-to-front way, the expensive lunch was so the lawyer and her friends could feel good about themselves.

Dignity can never be as simple as one lunch. There're so many other ways that it gets taken away. Ali's seen the look that flashes across strangers' faces when there's a spare seat next to Hassan or Walid on a crowded tram. The look can last less than one second. Sometimes strangers get over it, and sometimes they don't. But it was still there, even if they *do* take the seat. It's part of who they are, and who they force others to be. Same as the man who works night shifts at 7-Eleven, watching Ali differently depending on whether he's pouring a Slurpee with Musa and Walid, or with Funda . . .

These looks happen every single day of Musa, Walid and Hassan's lives. And every time, it strips them of something that Ali – and the jocks from St. Bernard's – get to have. That's the thing the cops don't understand when they wonder why Walid won't share a joke with them.

*

Dad stubs his rollie into his coffee mug, ignoring Ali's eyes, as a qanun crackles from the crappy old radio in the kitchen. Even though the instrument would make a lit sample in a track – a shout-out to his heritage – going to his bedroom and smashing out lyrics feels hopeless now that the tutor's ghosting him.

'Did you see the photo?' asks Ali, pointing at the open newspaper he left on the table this morning.

Dad nods, eyeing it as if for the first time.

'I look kinda nerdy, yeah?'

A grunt is all he gets back, air whistling out of Dad's dimpled nostrils. His eyelids are still heavy from waking up so late in the afternoon, making his face look bloated, like it's been peeled inside out or something.

'Do you have any photos from when you were, like, my age?' asks Ali. 'I wanna see how similar we look.'

'Not anymore,' grumbles Dad.

Ali tries to see himself in the face opposite him, but other than the deep brown irises they share, there's nothing there. He stares at Dad's woollen jumper, where years of dust and tobacco smoke have settled into the faded fabric. He could swear the jumper's old enough for Mum to have knitted it.

'You think Mum saw the photo?'

The eyes they share meet quickly across the table.

'We don't talk about her.'

'Yeah, but why not?'

Again, a grunt is all he gets. This one, more aggressive. Imagining Dad ever not talking in grunts, at Bulsho Café or back when he hooked up with Mum, is basically impossible.

'Just coz she broke your heart, or whatever, that's not *your* fault, man.'

This time the look across the table isn't so quick.

'*Man*, *man*, *man*,' grumbles Dad, shaking his head. 'Who's this man?'

'No one,' says Ali. 'It's just how we talk.'

Mum's never coming back. Somehow he knows, already, that it's the truest thought he's ever had. Whatever reason she had for leaving, and doing this to him, it must've been fair.

'Is there any food, or what?' he asks.

Dad shrugs, twitching the black bristles of his moustache as he starts rustling through his tobacco pouch. Inside the fridge, a stuffed eggplant's been slopped onto an oily plate, looking more like regurgitated food.

'How old's this?'

'Eat it,' grunts Dad, with a filter between his lips.

Ali carries the plate to the table and nibbles on the cold, soggy tomatoes, waiting for flavour that never arrives. There's a familiar relief in their silence. The qanun's getting more hectic, notes tingling up and down some snowy, clear-mooned Turkish mountain in his mind. Without beats, you can't even tap your foot along to it. If this music's supposed to be a part of him, like it always has been for Dad, then something's seriously, seriously wrong.

TYLER

The burn in Tyler's chest feels sick. He's up to twenty kilos now, ten reps per set. This time next year, when he's living at the barracks, he'll be able to bench press forty kilos for sure. Proper presses. Unlike Jai, who isn't bringing the bar anywhere near his scrawny as chest.

'Those don't count,' says Tyler. 'Give us another go.'

'Can you spot me?' gasps Jai.

'Nah, sorry,' says Tyler, pulling his hands away. Jai's arms tremble as he slowly lays the bar back on the rack. 'See, I helped you be more of a man.'

'Get fucked!'

Tyler slides onto the sweaty bench. For his final set of reps, he narrows his grip on the bar and watches his triceps bulge, every muscle in his arms heavy and tingling beneath the skin.

'You wanna spar?'

'I don't trust you no more,' sooks Jai, holding his right shoulder.

'Don't be a pussy,' says Tyler. 'It was just a joke.'

He has to use his bare fists on the punching bag because the school's too povo to afford boxing gloves. Skipping around, working the bag from different angles, he pretends he's landing body shots on Yassin, cracking his ribcage. Yassin's a pussy deep down. No one's ever actually seen him come at anyone. Tyler knows he could take him. He imagines them in a backyard fight, with Shannon barking from his corner:

Elbows tucked in, protect your ribs, bro, watch the shoulders, learn his range, jab to keep your distance, get in and out, in and out, bro, sharp footwork, dominate the space, don't give him any rhythm . . .

Kylie and Funda are pretending to use the dumbbells, but Funda's really just checking him out in his singlet. He goes extra hard on the punching bag, unloading quick combinations, so she knows he can protect her if anyone ever tries to hurt her.

Punch in straight lines, punch through the cunt, don't stop your fist at his nose or his jaw, bro, cave this Obama's skull in!

Once he's finished working out, he changes back into his wrinkly school shirt and chills with the girls on the gym mats.

'Nice hitting,' says Funda.

'Thanks,' he says, relaxing his head against the mat.

'Why were you making those weird sounds?'

'That's what you're sposed to do.'

'Yeah, right.'

He can't think of anything to say. It's annoying. Usually Kylie won't shut up, but she's trying to psych him out.

'Where's Ali?' he asks.

'Being emo at home, I think,' says Funda. 'He had this lame crush on a girl who was, like, five years older than him, or whatever.'

'She isn't even interesting,' says Kylie.

Tyler notices that there are shitloads of rubber balls stuck between the panels on the ceiling. One, two, three, four, five . . .

'What's wrong with your leg?' asks Funda.

He looks down and sees that the skin's flaking away from a few of the old scabs.

'They're just cuts from soccer.'

'It looks gross,' says Kylie.

'Not as gross as your grandma's sideburns.'

Funda giggles as she shakes her head.

'You'll probably have sideburns too, Kylie, when you get older,' says Tyler, pointing to where they're going to be on her squirming face.

Funda lies down so her head's next to his, wriggling until their legs are just touching. Her hair smells all sweet and fruity.

'What do you wanna do, like, in the future?' she asks.

'I'm joining the army next year.'

'Seriously?'

'Yeah, I've gotta wait til I turn seventeen.'

There are all these tiny pimples at the top of her chest, right above her tits. Tyler can feel his cock pressing against his boxers, making them sticky.

'The only reason I'm doing this stupid Kokoda thing is to stay in shape for next year,' he says.

'Why do you wanna be in the army so badly?' asks Funda.

'So I can, like . . .' says Tyler, distracted by the warmth of her skin. 'Someone's gotta protect the fucking country.'

'Won't you have to kill people and stuff?'

'Yeah, probably.'

Her tits are slowly swelling as she breathes.

'Do you really think you could do that?'

'If I have to,' he says, shrugging.

'But you *don't* have to.'

She rolls away from him, onto her stomach. Chicks take everything you say way too seriously.

'The army's more interesting than school,' says Tyler.

Funda doesn't even say anything back.

Walid and Ms Kelly walk into the gym with their arms full of rice bags, carrying them towards the storeroom.

'Come on, slackers!' yells Ms Kelly. 'If you're not going to work on your fitness, you can at least give us a hand.'

'Do we have to?' moans Funda.

'Yes, you do.'

They follow Ms Kelly out to her girly Mazda 2 to unload the rice bags that everyone has to stash in their backpacks at the next training session. Tyler grabs six rice bags, one more than Walid, who reeks of soap, mixed with weird African spices.

'What's up, snitch?' asks Tyler.

Walid ignores him and walks back into the gym.

Ms Kelly shakes her head and slams the boot, but Tyler can tell she's laughing on the inside.

'Hey, miss, I heard you and Kadra had a cat fight yesterday.'

'I wouldn't say that, exactly.'

'Whatever, it sounded pretty funny.'

'You know, you don't always have to antagonise people, Tyler. There *are* other ways to communicate.'

'That bitch had it coming,' says Tyler, repositioning the rice bags in his arms. 'If her and her ugly sisters wanna live in *our* country, then they've gotta –'

'Tyler!' she says, closing her eyes.

'What? I'm serious.'

She's always so worried about pretending she believes in equality. No Aussies really want it. To get it, they'd have to give away heaps of nice stuff. Just because he speaks up when no one else has the guts to shouldn't make him the arsehole.

'Those towelheads can't expect –'

'Please, can you just . . .' says Ms Kelly, stopping halfway through her sentence to open her eyes. She clutches her chest, taking big, wheezy breaths. 'Sorry, I need to be alone.'

She walks to the driver's side of her car, acting all slow and robotic. It's weird as. She gets in and sits there, like Mum when she's about to drift away, staring through the windscreen at nothing.

He's lying next to Funda on the gym mats, breathing in the fruity smell of her hair. Her tits are swelling right beside him. She rolls over, pressing them against his firm pecs. Her tongue slides into his mouth as he cups her fat arse in his hands. He slips off her G-string and eases his cock in, squeezing her arse cheeks as he strokes away, finding the perfect rhythm. She's wet as, moaning his name. Fuck, Tyler! Oh, fu-uck . . .

The door crashes open as he's shooting his load.

'Sorry, bud,' says Barney, staring at Tyler's cock like he's never seen one before.

'Fuck off, you pedo!'

'No worries,' says the stupid prick, grinning.

The bowl's covered in Barney's curly grey pubes. Tyler rips off the last few squares of toilet paper and tries to clean himself up, but there's only enough to smear the jizz into his own thighs.

Barney bolts in the second he hears the toilet flush.

'Hey, Ty!' calls Mum as he's trying to sneak back into his bedroom. 'Come here a sec, will ya!'

She's always happy to chat when one of Barney's dodgy plans has worked. They better not have pawned the new hiking boots Ms Kelly gave him. He walks into the living room and sits up the other end of the couch, because he can still smell jizz on himself. Her eyes are all cloudy and pink around the edges.

'How was school?' she asks.

'Yeah, good.'

'What's this about a parent–teacher night?'

'Fucked if I know.'

'They sent us a letter the other day,' she says, looking around the room, confused, like it's someone else's place.

'It must've been a mistake.'

There's no way his teachers are meeting her. Ms Costello will just call DHS again and then he'll have to answer all of their messed-up questions.

'You look really handsome in a singlet, Ty,' she says. 'It reminds me of your father.'

Mum's eyes drift towards the telly. As she slumps back into the couch cushion, Tyler notices the dark roots showing in the middle of her hair. He can tell she would've been pretty when she was younger, when her hair was all yellow. He'll make sure that's how she looks in the tattoo.

'Bit pongy in here, ay,' says Barney, flicking Tyler a dopey grin. He wedges himself between them on the couch. 'Mind if I have a cheeky smoke?'

'You're gonna have one anyway.'

'Cheers, bud.' For once, Barney's smoking tailors. 'Got meself a bit of work.'

'Yeah, doing what?'

'Few of us are back loading trucks at the old woolshed. Pretty physical stuff,' says Barney, wincing as he inhales.

He's so full of shit.

They sit around, watching *Border Security*. There's nothing much for dinner, which is cool. Tyler's not that hungry. He can't remember the last time he saw Mum and Barney eating. It's sick how labradors can tell who's smuggling drugs just by sniffing people's luggage. A butch as Lebanese chick – who looks like a weightlifter – gets busted at the airport with vials of steroids in her shampoo bottles.

'Bet she's growing a pecker!' says Barney, nudging him.

Seeing him cackling away with half his ugly teeth missing makes Tyler wish that he could punch the rest out.

'Anita!' grunts Barney, lighting another dart. His pupils look like pinpricks. 'Hey, Neet!'

'Yeah, what?'

'Want a smoke?'

'Huh?'

'Smoke?' says Barney, tilting the deck at her.

She reaches over and takes one. Smoking's such a filthy habit. She never used to do it before Barney moved in.

All the people getting busted on *Border Security* have brown skin or darker. Big surprise. By the time they say what sentence the Lebanese chick got, Barney's drifted off. Mum's in her own place as well. Tyler plucks the unlit smoke from her lips before she drools all over it.

'What're-ya-doin?' she mumbles.

'Nothing.'

'How was school?'

'You already asked me that, Mum.'

'Did I?'

Her saliva soon starts bubbling again.

The new Army Reserve ad comes on, showing normal Aussies peeling open their shirts in slow motion to reveal khaki underneath, eyes full of pride.

He wouldn't expect Funda to understand. He just hopes that the war lasts long enough for him to get over to Iraq or Afghanistan, or wherever it ends up being, and drive around in some big Humvee on a long-range patrol, face covered in recon wrap, looking out for IEDs among collapsed shanties, burnt-out cars and goatherders who marry their sisters. Someday a sniper will open up on his convoy and soldiers will dive behind mud walls as rounds spit dust everywhere. They'll peg grenades to buy time. Tyler will quickly set up his mortar and fire at a compound full of terrorists – waiting . . . waiting . . . waiting – then watch as the earth rises and swallows every single one of them.

PAUL

0600 hrs.

Squats, press-ups, sit-ups, commando crawling through ditches, wading neck deep in leech-infested streams, shuttle runs with a mud man clinging to your back. Ninety per cent humidity. No water. No nothing.

'The sickener,' directing staff keep calling it.

Won't stop til four of the poor bastards drop.

0800 hrs.

Breakfast. Staff let candidates watch the butter melt into their toast. Your mouth can't help but start frothing. Then they take the grub away before anyone gets a bite.

Jog back into the National Park.

Start the whole thing from scratch . . .

Seven or eight hipsters are crammed onto the small stage, strings screeching as they tune their instruments. Davey's in a trance, watching the accordion expand and contract. He's taking it easy on the piss tonight. If he ever does hit it hard these days, it sure as hell isn't around Paul. Still, it's a relief to have the sober prick on board because without him, Paul'd feel uncomfortable in a bar like this. Tartan wallpaper and kids in skinny jeans, sipping ciders and boutique beers, hunched in on animated conversations.

The hipsters decide to give it a rest, laying into a few jugs of pale ale. Only one bloke left up on stage now, zig-zagging his bow along a fiddle, shaking his head at the sound tech.

'Come here often?' asks Paul.

'Only for open mic nights.'

'Interesting crowd.'

Davey lets it go through to the keeper. Sometimes it feels like he's got a thing or two on his mind that he doesn't want to come out and say. Especially not when he's sober. There's nothing wrong with raking in eighty K a year, owning your own apartment and working for the greater good. Better than being a student your whole life.

'How's uni going?'

'Alright,' says Davey. 'I'm thinking of staying out there next year to do a master's.'

'They pay you for that?'

Davey nods. 'It means I can teach down the track.'

'Is that what you wanna do?'

'Yeah, maybe.'

That's Davey in a nutshell. *Mister Maybe.*

'Have you told Dad yet?'

Wonder how much the folks have forked out for him over the years. Never shows any guilt, or appreciation. Genuine mystery what girls always see in him.

A bartender with a thick, waxed moustache brings over their grub.

'Cheers, mate,' says Paul. 'Aren't you forgetting the parrot on your shoulder?'

'Sorry, what?'

'Don't worry about it.'

The chicken parma actually tastes half decent. Not too cheesy. Paul wolfs it down. Oily salad, too. His appetite's been insane since he got serious about training. Davey picks away at his sloppy burrito – cheapest main on the menu – full of jalapeños and kidney beans.

'Sure you don't want another drink?' asks Paul. 'It's my shout.'

'Nah, I'm right.'

Bit awkward waiting at the bar for Captain Sparrow to mix the eternal cocktail, doing the cha-cha with his silver shaker, so Paul fires off a text to Anna:

How'd u pull up from training?

Boring as batshit question. Should throw in a joke:

Busted any more myths at work?

There's something different about her, even if she does make him feel like he's under cross-examination half the time. He'd love to get to the bottom of it. Maybe convince her to move in with him on the other side of Kokoda. She probably wouldn't have a bar of the Lean Cuisine meals.

Pity his phone hasn't pinged.

The hipster band kick off their sonic warfare, all of them going full throttle, strings competing with each other, producing jarring rhythms that you couldn't dance to if you tried. The old man would have a field day with this. Kids in their mid-twenties wearing marked-up rags from op shops, carrying on like they're poor Europeans living out of caravans. It's all just one big game of dress-up.

Hopefully Davey isn't buying it. The problem with these leftie arts student types is that they expect the world in funding, always rabbiting on about corporate greed, claiming the moral high ground, when none of them are any good at what *they* do. Or what they do is so obscure that no one gives a stuff. A community of airy-fairy intellectuals who'll be up shit creek in twenty years' time, blaming the system instead of their own lack of talent. Maybe the Liberals want to pour money into defence because it actually does some good in the long run.

He'd love to see everyone in this bar get put through the final seventy-two hours in the Special Forces selection course.

The stress positions don't look like much, but their backs would start to tickle pretty quickly with all that squatting. Tactical questioning would be a laugh once Captain Sparrow's gone a few days without his double-shot, free-range unicorn milk latte. Credit to the hipster band, though. They've certainly got the noise torture angle covered.

Astrid's next up on stage. She spends an eternity twisting the strings on her acoustic guitar, attaching a strange clamp to the frets. Blue eyes, curly blonde hair, broad, boyish shoulders.

'We're thinking of moving in together,' says Davey.

'Whereabouts?'

'Maybe somewhere round here.'

Astrid introduces herself into the mic. Few of her mates from the slums of Prague let out a big cheer.

'How's *your* love life?' asks Davey.

'Not bad, actually.'

'Yeah?'

'Early days.'

Still no ping in his pocket.

'Is she a cop?'

'Nope, bloody teacher!'

Astrid starts strumming. Legs spread, bracelets jangling against her guitar, which still doesn't sound too tuned. She takes it slow to begin with, before tucking into the melody. Davey's watching her real close as she belts out the lyrics. No doubt she's got pipes, even if the song isn't very catchy. Seeing her on the stool, eyes closed, face scrunched up, it's easy to imagine what it would be like: the tanned skin on her shoulders, hips rocking in slow figure eights . . .

'What do you reckon?' asks Davey.

'I reckon you're batting above your average, mate.'

'Of the song, I meant,' says the little bastard.

'Sorry if I'm a bit sweaty,' says Astrid, laying a hug on Paul. 'The lights get seriously hot up there.'

She extricates herself and plants a big smooch on Davey, swooping the front of his hair into a quiff. A lot more touchy-feely than the last one.

'Thanks for coming,' she says. Her eyes have that spacey, cult-like glow that the yoga types always have. 'It's nice to *finally* meet you. David's told me so much about you.'

'Talkative bastard, isn't he?'

Understands sarcasm. Promising.

'So, what did you think?' asks Astrid.

'Loved it, especially the first song.'

'Thanks,' she says, catching Davey grinning. 'What's so funny?'

'Paul isn't much of a music person.'

'Really?'

'Nothing personal,' he says, coming clean.

Davey and him have a good laugh.

'Why not?' asks Astrid, putting on some silly voice that's probably supposed to be cute.

'Just not my thing.'

'You're missing out.'

A few of the hipsters blow kisses at Astrid on their way past. Genuine fruit loops.

'Don't spose Davey's ever told you about the time he put me in hospital?'

'No, he *hasn't*,' says Astrid.

'This little troublemaker used to beg me to play cops and robbers in the backyard at Mum and Dad's place, years after it bored me shitless. Always wanted to be the copper. One time, we must've been, what, six and nine?'

'About that,' says Davey, knowing full well where it's all heading.

'I let him catch me outside Dad's shed. For some reason, Davey here got it into his thick skull that it was fair game to pelt a cricket ball at me. The seam nicked me right here,' says Paul, leaning across the table so Astrid can see the scar just above his left eyebrow. 'Split me all the way back to the white meat and ended up costing me twelve stitches.'

'That's awful!'

'I reckon he was more shaken up than me, especially once he saw the claret pissing out.'

'Yuck!' says Astrid, hiding her face on Davey's shoulder.

Paul feels his chinos vibrating.

'I hear you two might be moving out somewhere round here,' he says, fighting the urge to check his phone.

'If we can afford it,' says Astrid, flushed face reappearing, combing her fingers through Davey's hair again. Wouldn't be surprised if she's in love with the bastard. 'This area's got such a great vibe, you know.'

'And what do you do for a crust?' asks Paul.

'I work part-time at the museum.' Not quite a hospo job, but close enough. 'Obviously I play music, too.'

Bit rich calling music a job.

It's hard to know where to take the conversation from here. Davey's sitting there like a bloody mute. The whole thing would be running a shitload smoother if he were having a proper drink.

Paul sneaks a look at his phone under the table:

I don't mean to be presumptuous . . .

Sounds ominous.

'David tells me you're off to Kokoda in a few months,' says Astrid.

'Yep, every year we take a group of local kids over there to walk the trail,' says Paul. 'Some of the less fortunate ones.'

'That's so nice.'

He unlocks the screen and scrolls down:

but I'm not really in a position to
pursue anything at the moment

'How *is* everything going with the local kids?' asks Astrid, busting him as he looks back up from his phone. 'My friend who works at the Community Legal Centre told me that Africans in Flemington are two-and-a-half times more likely to be stopped and searched by the police than Caucasian people.'

'I wouldn't pay too much attention to those figures,' says Paul, feeling his cheeks burning. 'There're a lot of issues being distorted at the moment.'

'Didn't one kid's teeth get smashed in?'

'Bit more to that incident, from what I've heard.'

'And what about the boy they found in the Maribyrnong River last year? His family seem distraught.'

'Already been investigated.'

'Who by?'

Davey's staring at the empty stage, the gutless prick. It's nuts how everyone's always so hell-bent on seeing the coppers as the bad guys. If Astrid wants real corruption, she should go and live in one of those South American nose candy countries where cartels run the show. No such thing as the OPI over there.

Another vibration:

Sorry Paul, nothing personal

'Personal' is exactly what it is.

Condescending vego.

'Listen, I wasn't around for any of the Flemington stuff,' says Paul, making sure he looks Astrid square in the eyes, so she takes it all in. 'But you've gotta understand, if there's a group of kids rolling around the estate at two or three in the morning – which there often is – then of course we're gonna stop them for a friendly chat. It doesn't matter what colour their skin is. That's our job.'

'I understand,' she says, holding his gaze, 'but there's a difference between a friendly chat and a torch in the face.'

'Of course there is. No one's saying there isn't. Just remember, Astrid, these aren't all innocent kids. Most of them know exactly what they're doing. Trust me. They've got more prejudices against us than we do against them. We see them at point A here,' he says, sliding the salt and pepper shakers into the middle of the table to form a triangle with the sauce bottle, 'and point B over here a couple of hours later. Then, all of a sudden, they're at point C, then back to point A again, where they bloody started. None of them are ever actually going anywhere.'

'Why do they have to be *going* somewhere?'

'What do you think they're up to?'

'I wouldn't know,' says Astrid. 'Maybe they just don't want to go home.'

If only she could tag along in the divisional van and hear some of the lip they get, or have one of these wannabe gangsters right up in her grill, demanding everything she has. Bit different from playing dress-up.

'At the end of the day, you've gotta ask yourself these two questions,' says Paul, catching Davey's piss-weak eye. 'One: if a higher percentage of crimes are being committed by kids, or adults, of African descent, then shouldn't we be searching people who actually match that description? Would've thought that's a pretty obvious answer, but maybe it's just me. And two: if you're running away from the coppers in the first place, isn't there a fair chance you've got something to hide?'

Things go awfully quiet.

ANNA

A bongo stand capsizes, crashing into a row of djembes with a deafening thud. The kids go bananas as Tracy loses the plot.

Anna knows she's losing it, too, because among the commotion, she sees Paul dashing across the gym with a lanyard flailing around his neck. He helps Tracy retighten the screws and check the skins for rips, the purple G&T wash gradually draining from her cheeks.

It's definitely him.

Some of his police mates are leaning against the wooden wall bars, admiring the chaos.

Tracy weaves between music stands, trying to settle the percussion ensemble, aware that a dozen local primary school principals are watching on. They've got no idea how contrived this 'open day' is. Funny how Yassin's suspension just managed to cover it. And how the kids on Ritalin get to spend six periods tucked away in the student support office, playing *Minecraft* and creating avatars on *Second Life.*

Paul's finally spotted her.

Hopefully the texts she spent forty minutes drafting last night will make training less awkward. Maybe, in time, she'll even manage to show him that she's not a terrible person.

Rob Hunter emerges with his year elevens.

Absolute anarchy.

'Put that phone away, Funda!' snaps Jenny, draped in another one of her beautiful silk scarves. 'Final warning!'

Funda rests her head against Ali's shoulder as she scowls back at Jenny, sliding the phone into her jacket. The students fidgeting around them resemble a heaving black sea in their new winter uniforms. Last year there were barely enough kids at assemblies to cover the halfway line of the gym. Now it's almost three-quarters full.

'Have you submitted your application?' asks Jenny.

'Not yet,' says Anna, dreading the final grind of writing her key selection criteria. 'I've already resigned myself to the fact that he'll give it to Linda.'

'One of the aides told me Linda's still trying to get her year eights to use the Ultranet.'

'I don't think it'll make any difference.'

Having Jenny on the panel will at least give her one-third of a fair hearing. Not that she really cares anymore.

'How're you coping with Tyler?'

'We have our ups and –'

'I'LL TAKE THAT, THANKS!' yells Jenny, parting two rows of students to confiscate Funda's phone, putting terror in the eyes of the year sevens. Her heels pelt towards Anna. 'Sorry, love, where were we?' asks Jenny, slipping seamlessly back into friendship mode.

'Tyler Peirce.'

'Ah, that's right. He knocked on my door this morning and asked if he could keep his boots and his camping gear in my office.'

'Why?' asks Anna, feeling wounded.

'I know the mother's refusing to see her social worker again, so we can probably put two and two together.'

'Poor kid.'

God knows what he made of her meltdown yesterday, even if it *was* what he wanted.

'You're doing everything you can,' whispers Jenny, squeezing Anna's arm.

'Do you ever wish you could take a kid home for a night just to cook them a decent meal?' asks Anna, catching Paul staring at her across the black sea, not even pretending to be subtle.

'Every day of my life,' says Jenny, grinning wistfully.

* * *

Wild assembly

That music teacher's off her rocker!

Why don't we grab a feed some time
and have a chat, no strings attached?

* * *

The principal of Kensington Primary roams the room, uninvited, with her straightened, Shetland-pony hair, observing the kids as they write their persuasive language practice SACs. Walid raises his hand and asks her to read his introduction.

'This is a promising start,' Anna overhears her say, 'but it's a bit of a mouthful. You need to use more punctuation.'

Walid nods, wide-eyed. 'Where?'

'Your first sentence is five-and-a-half lines long,' says the principal of Kensington Primary. 'Think about when you'd like your reader to be able to take a breath.'

She leaves Walid stooped over his laptop, his nose inches from the screen as he mouths his essay and exhales.

'You're pissed off, yeah, miss?' says Musa to Anna.

'Sorry?'

'About this chick stepping on your turf.'

'Teaching's a collaborative profession, Musa.'

'I need you to lie like that to my mum at parent–teacher night,' he says, repositioning the Afro comb that's jutting out of his hair. 'You have to say nice things, you feel me?'

'I always tell the truth,' says Anna.

'What's the truth?'

'The truth is that you need to apply yourself more in class.'

'Please, you've gotta say it nicer than that. You don't understand African mums. If you don't say it nicer . . .'

Musa raises his hand and slaps his own cheek.

The principals from Flemington Primary and Ascot Vale West watch on, stone-faced, either side of Peter.

'Potential!' yells Musa. 'Say I've got potential.'

'You *do* have potential.'

'Yeah, then say that.'

'I will.'

'Thanks, miss, you're a sick bitch.'

'I'll assume that's a compliment,' says Anna, glancing up and seeing Peter's retinas burning with impatience. 'If you get back to work, I'll say even nicer things about you.'

'See!' says Musa, flashing his teeth at the jury of peeping toms behind him. 'She feels me.'

Once he starts typing, Anna finds her eyes drawn towards the dog-eared copy of *Macbeth* on top of her planner. The prospect of teaching it again, especially to this group, fills her with dread; having to translate all those archaic words into what's already a second or third language for the kids, just so some old bats at the Department of Education can feel smug for setting a text that's four hundred years old, seems like the height of absurdity.

Kadra's the only student not working. Sitting with her head bowed, she's staring at her own clasped hands. If nothing else, Anna's got to admire the determination. It's not over. The easy thing to do would be to exit her from every class, like Linda and all the other bigoted teachers who refuse to live in the real world.

'Mind if I sit here?' she asks. Kadra's gaze stays fixed on her lap. Anna pulls out the chair next to her. 'Do you understand what we're supposed to be doing, sweetie?'

Nothing.

Anna borrows a piece of paper from Walid and scribbles the acronym 'CDFASTCAT':

C – context
D – date
F – form
A – author
S – source
T – title
C – contention
A – audience
T – tone

Kadra refuses to look up. Anna can sense the judgement from the adults in the room, especially Peter, who's probably trawling through the sci-fi database of his brain, likening her to some incompetent *Star Wars* character.

'Careful, miss!' says Musa, fluffing his hair with the Afro comb. 'She's a spy for al-Shabaab.'

'Sorry if I've offended you, Kadra,' says Anna. She doesn't care who overhears. The kids know everything about her life now, anyway. 'I'm glad you're in my class, and that you and your sisters have come to this country. I really hope you start to feel welcome here soon.'

She slides the piece of paper towards Kadra.

'What're you gonna say to Kadra's mum?' asks Musa.

'She doesn't got no mum,' yells Jasmine.

Another missed call from Mum. The emotional energy required to call her back feels onerous. If she wants a visit, ringing every second day's going to have the reverse effect. Just like Paul's constant harassment:

Also happy to pop by your office this
arvo for a sneaky chat, if u tell me
where it is

This is what her life has come to: hiding in an overgrown laneway on her lunch break. Every single thing has been taken away. Even Ali spilling the beans about her ex. The kids were the last people left who didn't treat her with pity . . .

A twig snaps around the corner, followed by a spurt of

girlish giggling. Anna pokes her head out from her corrugated-iron refuge and sees Jasmine and a man with a smoothly shaved head leaning against someone's roller door, his hand cupping her arse as she teases his lips.

'Not *here*!' says Jasmine.

But there's a hint of playfulness in her tone. Anna sees her own hands stiffening as she tries to conceal herself against the cold, rippled iron. She stares at the berries that've dropped into the grooves between the cobblestones as the rustling of clothes escalates, paralysed by the need to make a decision. Slowly, she realises that her paralysis *is* her decision.

Her phone starts vibrating. She wraps it in her palms to smother the noise. When the electric waves stop, she inspects the screen and sees Zoe's name:

Impromptu idea

Want 2 c vaudeville smash tonight @
night cat?

Synth funk band good 4 a boogie

She feels the physical resistance forming and the shortlist of excuses being prepared. Exhaustion. Bacteria swarming in the leggings she hasn't washed in weeks. The character Zoe expects her to play – crass and outgoing, a sister in crime in a crush of vintage dresses, floral shirts and sweaty facial hair – no longer feels like it's in her repertoire. It's horrifying to think that Zoe's the last link between herself and fun. Without her, Anna might as well be dead.

WARNING: may be attractive men

Grunts quicken above the dull crunching of steel. All there is to do is focus on the spatter of berries – pink and purple pigments – and how vibrant the colours look against the canvas of the cobblestones. Almost, or maybe, hyperreal . . .

ALI

Kobe's strutting around the court in his Lakers tracksuit and his purple Adidas kicks, like Pac when he was coming out of prison for the last time, beefing with pretty much every reporter. This big I-don't-give-a-fuck-about-anything swagger. Kobe finishes the first round of the competition by launching into the air and doing a double-pump, reverse dunk.

'Not bad, not bad,' says Musa.

'Keep watching,' says Walid.

For the final, Kobe strips down to his Lakers singlet and tucks it into his shorts.

'What a boss,' says Ali.

Kobe hammers down a between-the-legs, over-the-top jam.

'TEN!' yells Musa, waving all his fingers at Ali's cracked computer screen. 'That shit is a ten for sure.'

Kobe's flexing and poking out his lips, playing up to the crowd. His girlfriend's going mental. So are the commentators.

'The boy got some rhythm,' says one of them.

Kobe bounces a ball to the corner, getting himself in the zone for his next dunk. All the photographers are squeezed together, sitting just outside the lines of the court, pointing their lenses up at him.

Musa's doing a drum roll on the lockers.

Just as Kobe loops the ball into the air, the screen freezes.

'THESE COMPUTERS ARE TRASH!' yells Musa, so everyone in the nearby classrooms can hear him.

'Fuck this school!' says Ali.

He looks around and tries a code on one of the year eight combination locks.

'This is like getting a lap dance,' says Musa, flicking at the screen where Kobe's frozen in time. 'Your dick gets hard and then nothing happens.'

'True,' says Ali, trying another lock.

'We should protest until they give us real computers.'

'Or call the news.'

'Look how you treat it, but,' says Walid.

Five keys are already missing from Ali's laptop, and some of the ones still there are sticky-taped on. It'll be lit seeing the principal have a heart attack at the end of the year when everyone has to give back their computers.

As Musa pounds the spacebar, trying to bring Kobe back to life, Ali spreads his KFC booklets on the floor to flick through them one last time. There's a crazy amount of information. It's like some of the forms are written in another language: ATO number, tax file number, bank branch. Getting paid is going to be basically impossible. They should just give you cash at the end of every shift.

He busts Musa drawing penises on his contract form.

'Don't do that,' says Ali. 'This is my chance.'

'*This is my chance*,' says Musa, pretending to be a girl.

He leaps up and struts around the corridor, combing his fro and poking out his lips like Kobe, trying to get the attention of the kids and the principals in the science labs.

'Yo, it's your police homies!' he yells.

Ali joins him by the window of the exam room. There's a circle of year nines with some of the police from Kokoda training talking to them: AJ, Athena and Paul, the cop who no one likes. He's standing by a whiteboard, making a list of ways to keep safe in the street. The things he's writing are obvious:

1) Don't talk to strangers
2) Never carry a weapon
3) Just walk away

They're the kind of things you'd say to kids in primary school, when you're pretending the world is simple.

'These skippies should learn to walk away themselves,' says Musa. 'You know two pigs just got busted for taking photos while they were torturing some cunt in his cell.'

'I heard that,' says Walid.

'Are they in trouble?' asks Ali.

'What do *you* think, man?' says Musa. 'It was probably the same pigs who whacked that G from Footscray, and now they know they can get away with anything. I'm telling you, they have no consequences. You shouldn't be tight with them.'

'We're not tight,' says Walid.

'Yeah, but they pretend you are,' says Musa, squishing his nose against the glass.

The first kid to get distracted by him, covering his teeth and pointing at the window, is Michael Garang, who's wrapped in a bulletproof vest. He must've just started at the school.

Paul's trying to get everyone in the circle to concentrate, but they can't because Musa's dropped his pants and is pressing his butt cheeks against the glass.

'You pigs can kiss my fat African arse,' he says, slowly rolling his cheeks from side to side.

Michael's bouncing on his knees with excitement.

'Fuck, Miss Costello's coming!' yells Ali.

Musa tries to quickly button up his pants. Ms Costello's shoes are echoing too fast, so he has to bolt down the stairs, kind of squatting and holding up his pants, like an extra-fat crab.

'Come back here, Musa!' yells Ms Costello.

But he keeps squatting and running.

You have to drain the chicken fillets, shake them, pour them into the flour and give them a massage, pat them down, shake them again and load all the pieces into the big silver fryer.

'Then we leave the fillets in the pressure cooker for ten minutes,' says the manager, who's got this crazy strong smell of perfume sprayed into an ashtray, similar to Kylie. So many things about the manager aren't real: her hair extensions, her eyelashes, maybe even her fingernails. 'Have you got that, Ali?'

'Yes, miss,' he says, realising, straight away, he's called her the wrong thing.

She glances at his cheeks. 'Before your next shift, make sure you shave, okay?'

'I will, sorry.'

'You should've already familiarised yourself with our personal hygiene standards. I can't put you on front of house today.'

She's on an even bigger power trip than Ms Costello when she took Funda's phone at assembly. Or maybe she's still mad about all the scribbled-out penises on his contract form.

Ali gets to have a go at making the chicken himself. He tries to put the same amount of flour on every fillet, but each one is a different size and some accidentally end up heaps doughier than others.

'Too slow!' says the manager, showing him how to do the butterfly presses again. It's like she's angry at all the dead chickens, scooping seasoning over the fillets and whacking them together with a psycho *thwap*. 'You only stir them through seven times. We do everything here *seven* times. That way it's easy to remember. Got it?'

'Yeah.'

'Go on, try again.'

Seven times, he reminds himself. Knowing she's watching makes it way harder. It feels like she wants him to stuff up. He's already sweating underneath his uniform and he can tell she'll get mad if his sweat drips into the seasoning tray, so he has to keep wiping his face with his gloves.

Eventually, the manager goes out to the car park and lets him breathe again. There's no way he'll ever be as fast as she expects him to be, or as fast as the other cooks. It's funny how they call them 'cooks' – like in an actual restaurant – when really all they're doing is putting meat in oil and letting a machine do the bubbling. Every time he runs out of chicken, he hurries across the slippery floor to the fridge, where there are hundreds of crates of legs, breasts, thighs, ribs and wings. Paradise for Musa. He's always bragging about how his cousin who works at KFC in Coburg spits in people's burgers, but it has to be bullshit. You don't have time to stop and spit in anything.

The only way to tell how much time is passing – and how much money he's making – is when the pressure cooker beeps. So far there've been five beeps, which equals fifty minutes, plus the time he's spent loading and unloading the frying racks. It's the kind of equation the tutor from homework club would help him solve. Her natural beauty is the opposite of the fake vibe of the manager at KFC. The tutor could easily show up again next week and prove Funda wrong. If she does, he'll let her know how he feels straight away. Even if he has to sing his love song in front of everyone.

Having a job and earning money is giving him more pride already. After he's released his EP and he sees *Towerz to tha Throne* in the Billboard Hot 100 chart for the first time, he'll make sure he remembers what it's like to cook chicken at KFC in F-Town, and he'll know that this is where it all started. As he's carrying a crate of wings, he imagines it's the last box of his clothes on the day he moves out of the towers, stepping out of the lift, walking through the foyer and bursting into the sunshine, knowing he's never coming back.

'So, you like it?' asks Najima.

'It's fast,' says Ali, tipping a rack of chicken tenders into the display window. 'I think the manager hates me.'

'Man, she hates everyone,' says Najima. She puffs her cheeks out and pretends she's smoking. '*Yalla, yalla!*'

Ali's too scared to laugh, in case the manager catches him on her way back from her latest cigarette break. His stomach grumbles, begging for dinner. But it's not like he thought. You can't eat balls of popcorn chicken whenever you're hungry, even if they've passed their use-by time.

'Boy, you got seasoning on your face,' says Najima.

He rubs above his eyes. 'Is it still there?'

'A bit, yeah.'

She covers her braces as she giggles. Now he's paranoid that he's had seasoning on his face the last two hours and none of the other cooks have said anything.

'How bout now?'

'Najiiiiiiiii!' shrieks Jasmine, dancing up to the counter in her school uniform.

As Jasmine orders, Najima pokes at the rainbow squares on the touchscreen and gives her a Twister with chips and a Pepsi all for the price of regular chips.

'Don't say nothing,' she whispers, filling a massive cup with ice. 'Everyone does it.'

'I'm not a fucking snitch.'

'Yeah, but your boy is.'

'I swear, there's no way Walid said that shit.'

'Then who did?'

'I don't know. Just not him.'

'Chill, man,' says Najima. 'I'm just saying, Yassin's gonna come at him. He *has* to.'

'The towers do my head in sometimes,' says Ali, hurrying back to the kitchen. He wraps the Twister, accidentally squeezing too much pepper mayonnaise onto it. When he brings it to the counter, Jasmine's pulling a dumb-arse face at him.

'Oh my God!' she says to Najima. 'Is that Sediment, the famous Turkish rapper?'

'Get stuffed, Jazzy!'

She hums the lyrics from his YouTube clip as she struts to her table, sucking on her free Pepsi.

'I'll tell you why I gave her a discount,' says Najima, busting Ali as he checks again for the manager. 'Do you know where Colonel Sanders secretly sends his money?'

'Nah.'

'The K-K-K!' she says. 'So it's like, revenge.'

'I thought the Colonel was dead or something.'

'Doesn't matter.'

Jasmine sits with a guy in a Death Row singlet who looks almost twice her age. His shoulders are massive. Even his neck has muscles, popping out from the glands.

'Who's she with?' asks Ali.

'That's her new boyfriend,' says Najima, covering her braces. 'You jealous, yeah?'

'As if.'

'Boy, you a bad liar.'

'I'd never be jealous of a girl from school. None of you have enough maturity.'

'Sure,' says Najima, still teasing him with her eyes.

Jasmine isn't really saying anything to her boyfriend. She just stares at the TV, nodding to some Katy Perry clip, as he leans back on his chair, acting like the whole joint belongs to him.

'I think I know him from somewhere,' says Ali.

'Yeah, that's Mukhtar.'

'For real?'

'Uh-huh.'

Ali remembers Mukhtar kicking it with Hassan at the half-court way back in the day – he had a sick jab step move – before everything went crazy with the cops.

'Didn't he, like, go away?'

'He's back now.'

'Far out, he looks different.'

'I know. Sexy, yeah. Jazzy says they're gonna get married and have babies. Like, ten babies. Enough for a hip-hop dance crew. Then they can busk in the city and have big crowds, go on *X Factor*, get rich, get famous . . .'

Mukhtar's slowly chewing his Twister, staring out the window with crocodile eyes. Babies look like the last thing in the world he could possibly be thinking about.

Ali cuts through the park, trying to find a bench near the oval to eat his apple pie, salivating at the thought of the hot, gluey sauce burning his tongue. His feet stab every time the spongy soles of his Air Force 1s sink into the grass. The first thing he's going to do when he gets paid is buy a new pair of kicks, with steel toecaps. Plus a packet of razors, so the manager doesn't hate him more than she already does. And pay off his uniform. It's unfair having to spend this much money before you even start making any. Saving up enough to record a whole EP – working part-time – is going to take forever.

Cars creep home from the city behind the trees, blinking lights, beneath the new zebra apartments that stare out at the four towers. Glowing glass worlds, displayed in the night. Some arsehole's bent the ring on the half-court. Now no one will be able to hoop for weeks. If the broken ring was on the other side of the road, outside the expensive apartments, the council would fix it straight away.

Yassin's crew are blazing near the soccer goals, listening to crackly old rap music. Wu-Tang or early Nas. Way before the game got ruined by autotune. The piano loop drops out and gunshots drill from the speakers. One of the Footscray City boys starts freestyling over the top of the beat, but his flow lags once the melody kicks back in.

'What the fuck are you staring at, fam?' yells a kid in yellow Air Jordans.

Fam. Ali's most hated word. It's just a dumb-arse way of making young'uns think someone's got their back, when they're even less safe than they'd be without the word.

'Nice uniform,' croaks Yassin.

His crew's laughter sounds more like hiccups.

'You wanna hit this?' asks the kid in Air Jordans, holding out a jay.

'Nah, man,' says Ali.

'Then keep walking, *bitch*!'

The hiccups laughter starts up again.

Ali heads towards the towers, getting another damp sniff of the skunk Yassin and his crew are putting in their lungs. Sitting around the oval isn't really an option now. By the time he reaches the foyer of the One Tweezy tower, the apple pie has gone cold in his hands.

TYLER

Warehouses, car dealers, tattoo parlours, tagged bus stops and dodgy little Vietnamese shops whiz by out the window. Trucks dominate the road, puffing out fumes and refusing to let anyone through on the inside lane. This suburb's even scummier than parts of Flemington. Shannon knows where pretty much all the meth labs and hydro houses are in this hood. Half of them have the pigs on their payroll, he reckons, giving them a cut of the profits, so only the other labs get busted.

Tyler has this weird feeling that him and Mum used to drive through here when they were visiting Dad in the prison with the mean guards – who were kind of like half-prisoners – and the boring Thomas the Tank Engine play equipment. Back when Mum had a car and Dad actually wanted visitors.

African kids are chilling around the rundown arcades, all of them looking shifty as. These ones have darker skin than the cocky Somali crews who think they own the high-rises. They're taking over the country. In fifty years' time, there'll probably be more African people than Aussie people, and more mosques than churches, unless some ballsy politician steps up and stops letting them all in.

'That's the park!' says the dude sitting next to Tyler, pointing at another depressing playground out the window. 'I swear, that's the one.'

'What park?' asks the driver.

'The one I was fucking telling you about, with the cops.'

'I remember,' says Shannon, not really interested.

'Me and my mate were shooting cans there a few years back,' says the dude in the sideways Yankees cap, turning to face Tyler, 'and this car's screeched off all of a sudden. We were so loose that we didn't even know it was there. Next thing a fucking helicopter's rocked up and I've gotta run back to get the roscoes we've stashed because the mildew's gonna rust them out . . .'

The driver keeps checking his rear-view mirror as he slowly nods his dreadlocks to the music. Eminem. He's always pissed off about something, even though he should have less to be mad about now that he's all rich and famous.

'And I've realised the trigger's still back. This thing's literally loaded in my pants, brah. My mate's lashed me, I've just started my three-year good behaviour bond, I'm about to blow my own balls off and this cop car's rolled up real slow, and I've gone; *I'm done*, yeah, *I'm fucking done!*'

'So what happened?' asks Tyler, even more bored than Shannon.

'Brah, they just kept driving. I couldn't believe it. After they left, I looked up at the sky and saw a shooting star. No word of a lie. A shooting star!'

He's almost as full of shit as Barney. Thinking about that dero, forcing Mum to get dopey with him every day, Tyler finds his knuckles clenching against the seatbelt buckle.

They turn off the main road, passing dry palm trees and mounds of gravel inside temporary fencing. The driver checks his rear-view mirror again before pulling up in front of a massive black-brick house in a dead-end street, killing the music.

'You right to wait here?' asks Shannon.

Tyler nods, acting cool.

Shannon grabs his backpack and pulls out a silver Nokia. The same phone Funda's got. 'My number's the only one,' he says, lobbing the phone to Tyler. 'Call me if you see anything.'

'For sure.'

'Keep your eyes open.'

Shannon and his two mates wait on the porch for about half a minute, looking up, before opening a side gate and going around to the backyard.

Tyler slumps so his head's only just above the window tube. It feels like he's on his first mission in the army. There's a trampoline on the front lawn and some toys – a tractor and maybe a bulldozer – lying across the driveway. All up, there must be six or seven bedrooms inside the house.

Someone peels back the curtain in the front room and quickly closes it. This might be the kind of thing Shannon was talking about. The problem is, if Tyler calls and it ends up being nothing, they'll think he's a pussy. Whoever owns this joint has probably got some muscle on the lookout as well. It's lit how the two of them are both keeping watch, trying not to let the other one know they're around.

A group of kids fang past on BMXs, towards the power lines at the end of the street, disappearing into the grasslands where they've stopped building houses.

If the pigs come, he'll have to bolt towards the grasslands or jump over one of the neighbours' fences and try to find somewhere to hide in their backyard, like a shed or a kennel. In the army, you'd have done your reconnaissance, so you'd know every escape route before you even started a mission. He's pretty much a sitting duck here. Surely it makes more sense to have a person who can actually drive keeping watch from the car, in case they need to make a getaway. From this mistake, he can already tell he's smarter than Shannon and his crew.

Lorikeets are screeching at each other from a tree in the next-door neighbour's yard.

Fuck knows how long it's been. He should've checked the time on the Nokia when they got out. Shannon didn't even say how long they were meant to take.

The curtain peels back again.

People get chopped up and stored in barrel drums, so no one ever finds their remains.

An engine roars behind him, rattling the windows in the car. He swings around and sees a white ute hurtling down the street, scattering the lorikeets. His brain's so hectic that he can't even remember if pigs make busts in Tritons. Those deadshit kids totally tipped them off. There isn't even time to run.

He tries to unlock the Nokia, but fumbles it onto the seat.

The ute swerves into the driveway opposite the black-brick house.

Just as Tyler's about to press the call button, he hears the side gate swing open. Shannon and his two mates walk out, past the trampoline, acting low-key.

A man in paint-covered overalls hops down from the ute and checks his mailbox, not even paying attention to them.

'All good?' asks Shannon.

'Yeah, easy,' says Tyler, slipping the phone back into his pocket, his heart throbbing.

'Your bro is the iceman,' says the dude who gets in beside him, putting on his annoying fake laugh as he offers the lamest whiteboy handshake ever.

'What happened with that frigid chick?' asks Shannon as he rolls a three-paper spliff in the front seat.

'Nothing yet,' says Tyler.

'Did you pussy out?'

'Nah, I just haven't had a chance to do anything.'

Tyler hates it how the other two dudes in the car are listening to his private business, probably imagining what Funda looks like, wanting to fuck her.

'If you hesitate, you masturbate,' says the poser next to him.

'It's all good,' says Tyler. 'I'm confident.'

Signs saying *FOR LEASE* are up everywhere in front of crummy apartment blocks. The last few places they've stopped at have been way more like what Tyler expected. Brick stumps where fences used to be. Rusty iron roofs and front yards with trailers and piles of rotting timber dumped on the grass. It's kind of disappointing that there are no more drop-offs to make.

Shannon sparks the spliff and sits on it for a minute or two before handing it to the driver. The car's starting to feel like a gas chamber. If Tyler knew the other dudes better, he'd make them open a window.

'Your turn,' says the driver, holding the spliff for him.

'Nah, I'm good.'

'Take it, man. I've gotta drive.'

The filter's sticky as with saliva. Tyler passes the spliff to the dude next to him, careful not to spill any ash.

'Hold up!' says the dude, trying to sound like Yassin and his dumb-arse crew, 'what's wrong with your bro, Shannon?'

'He likes to keep a clear head.' It's sick how Shannon's always sticking up for him. 'He's gotta stay fit for when he goes to the jungle. Tell them, man.'

'We're walking that trail where the Aussie soldiers shelled the Japs and chased them all into the sea.'

'Japan did some crazy shit in the war,' says the driver, croaking out his words, as if his nose is blocked.

'Yeah, I saw how they ate our intestines.'

'Not just that,' says the driver, finding Tyler's eyes in the rear-view mirror. 'They had a secret lab where they did all these messed-up experiments. They, like, amputated prisoners' arms and stuck them on the other side of their bodies, and put people in pressure chambers until their eyes –'

'Bullshit!' says the dude in the back.

'Seriously, man. They pulled all kinds of shit. Another one was deliberately giving people diseases and then cutting them open while they were still alive, so they could see how quickly the disease was killing them.'

Tyler wishes he'd known about this secret lab when Ms Kelly was crapping on about how nice Japanese people are.

'How come I've never heard of this?' asks Shannon.

'Coz they don't want you to.'

Eminem's rapping insanely fast now, going schizo about his

daughter, as the tree line next to the freeway thins out. Pickets for new estates are starting to appear in the kangaroo-coloured wasteland.

'What about Toy Soldiers for a name?' says the dude in the back, passing the spliff to Shannon.

'Huh?' croaks the driver.

'For a club. We could have model soldiers stuck on the walls and the bartenders could wear khaki crop tops, and every drink would have . . .'

When Tyler's on leave from the army, he'll get his own VIP lounge in the nightclub Shannon and his mates will own in the city. Plus free shots. It'll be way easier to score chicks. Not as easy as during World War II. Chicks went crazy for guys in uniform back then, especially Americans. But still, they'll respect what he's sacrificing, so they'll want to put out.

The haze inside the car is finally clearing. No one's talking anymore. Whenever people take drugs, they eventually go all quiet – like Mum and Barney – which is a boring as way to spend your life.

'Your bro needs to shut the fuck up,' says the dude in the back, doing his fake laugh again. 'He talks too much shit.'

Shannon's too ripped to defend him. Tyler doesn't know what to say back, but he wishes he could uppercut the dude in the jaw. A quick left. He could easily take the poser.

'You know not to talk about today with anyone, yeah?'

'Obviously,' says Tyler.

He catches the driver watching him in the mirror.

'Look at these cunts,' says the dude in the back, as they fly past five lanes of bumper-to-bumper traffic on the other side of the freeway. 'Working all day like suckers, brah.'

'True that,' mumbles Shannon.

They get onto the big concrete tongue of the West Gate Bridge and start rising towards the city, curving over the huge oil tankers and shipment boats on their way out of the docks. Tyler can't remember ever being on this bridge. When you stare above the grated barriers and the giant Aussie flag, rippling in the wind, it feels like you're floating in the sky, slowly making your way up to heaven.

The nervous Chinese man at the milk bar only hands over his mee goreng noodles when he sees Tyler's fifty-dollar note. For once, he'll get to have dinner. But if he buys anything else – even just a Fanta or a Big M – Mum and Barney will be suspicious. As he walks through the foyer of the Holland Court flats, he presses his hand against the scrunched-up notes in his pocket, making sure he acts normal. It's the first time he's ever properly had to worry about getting rolled in the lift.

PAUL

Hannah Gram • 20 April, 7:49am
Shock to see coroner siding w police over 'drowning' . . . not!

> **Visitor ➦ Hannah Gram** • 20 April, 7:57am
> *Is this seriously as far as this is going to go? Kid gets stopped 10–20 times a week for no reason, gets arrested then shows up dead a couple of hours later. Coincidence?????*

Ravi ➦ Hannah Gram • 20 April, 11:31am
No mention of trophy photo scandal either hmmm

Swagman • 20 April, 8:19pm
Everyone I speak to has lost all respect for the police. Obviously this blogs supposed to make them look good. Btw don't blame the kids family for rejecting findings, autopsy results, etc. Time for commissioner and his cronies to go, beyond a joke now

Absolute crackpots. Revising history as they whip each other up into a cyber-frenzy:

Baby Bombers 93 ➦ Swagman • 21 April, 6:22pm
FFS!!!!!!!!!! The coroners an independent body who comes to INDEPENDENT findings based on the FACTS. You could do with understanding a few of the facts yourself

Swagman ➦ Baby Bombers 93 • 21 April, 6:24pm
Free country mate

Baby Bombers 93 ➦ Swagman • 21 April, 6:25pm
Riddle me this: when was the last time you heard a grieving family say 'bang up job, coroner'?

Swagman ➦ Baby Bombers 93 • 21 April, 6:25pm
You're not a cop are ya?

Trading barbs with this muppet isn't going to get him anywhere. The ego of these trolls reminds him of Astrid and her hipster mates, regurgitating the same self-righteous nonsense that their parents drilled into them from the cot onwards:

> **Swagman** ↱ **Baby Bombers** 93 • 21 April, 6:28pm
> *Radio silence*
>
> **Swagman** ↱ **Baby Bombers 93** • 21 April, 6:29pm
> *The cap fits, constable bacon*

Paul checks his phone.

Still no reply from Anna.

The plunge in his gut reminds him of the delirious moment when the directing staff told him he didn't stack up to the Special Forces. At first he thought they were taking the piss. Another headfuck of a test – the final test, maybe – to see how he'd react. Six months of prep, three weeks in living hell, every single challenge met. And they wouldn't even give him a reason. As if, just like with Anna, he ought to know why.

It's impossible to find her on Google or Facebook. Her name's too generic. He types a Hail Mary: *anna kelly melbourne myspace*

'Eureka!'

Photos of her in her gawky teens and early twenties: pink hair, black hair, one side completely shaved, nose stud, bit of a weird plaid punk phase, dolled up at nightclubs, fruit picking with mates, posing in front of a bright blue museum, cartwheeling on a beach somewhere in South East Asia, in only a bikini . . .

Totally different vibe from the person who made him get out of bed and turn the lights off, and who tugged her knickers back on straight afterwards.

'Bugger me!' says AJ, squinting at a stooped figure who emerges in the left frame of the CCTV footage. It's a widish shot, but the resolution's just good enough to see everything.

'Know him?' asks Paul.

'I can't believe this prick's out already. We put him away last year, from memory.'

'What for?'

'Similar shit, café strip in Kensington.'

The old-timer shuffles past the Yaris a second time and ducks behind a station wagon. Brazen as hell, going for it outside the Newmarket shops in broad daylight.

'Few of his mob used to crash in the grandstand over at Arden Street, before they knocked it down,' says AJ, shaking his head at what's about to happen. 'Last time we picked him up – must've been March, maybe April a year back – he was roughing it on the creek trail.'

The old-timer peers through the window until the mum starts setting up her daughter's wheelchair, then he shuffles over and grabs everything right off the front seat. Wallet, phone, even takes her bloody keys.

The heavy-lidded prick barely registers what's going on as he's being cuffed, sweat shining off his blotchy forehead. Paul helps haul him out into the living room, where he sees Tyler from training waiting on what looks like an old Salvos couch, shooting daggers at the coppers.

'You okay, mate?' asks Paul, flicking him a friendly nod.

The little skinhead ignores him.

Woman slumped next to him on the musty cushions has got to be his mum. Same sharp cheekbones. Purple rings under the slits of her eyes and skin as white as a ghost, except for the pink craters on the inside of her arms.

'We're here to execute a search warrant,' says AJ, having to address Tyler, instead of the two drowsy adults.

'Huh?' slurs his mum.

'Before we search the premises, is there anything –'

'Youse-can't-do-that,' she says, eyelids flickering as her pupils adjust to the light. She tries to stand up, but her legs aren't all for it. Paul steadies her on her way back down. Arms like porcelain. 'Get ya filthy hands off me!'

Filthy. She can talk.

'I'll repeat,' says AJ, loud and clear. 'Is there anything you'd like to declare?'

'Yeah, your mate just assaulted me.'

AJ ploughs on. 'Once we've conducted the search, we're gonna take your fella down the station. Do you understand?'

'This is police harassment.'

'Can you please calm down, ma'am?'

'Don't fucken tell me what to do! Barn hasn't even done anything. We've been here together all day, haven't we?'

She looks at her bloke for support, but he's still off in la-la land, drool glued down his chin.

'This is all because of who *his* father is,' she says, pointing at Tyler, who's itching away at the back of his knees. 'Youse've been after us ever since you locked his dad up, instead of trying to catch real crooks. How bout them darkies selling drugs in the park every day? None of youse give a stuff about them.'

'I'll ask you one last time to calm down,' says AJ.

Tyler plucks a squashed ciggie from the couch and holds her wrist still as she lights it. Thankfully, it shuts her up.

There isn't much to search. Few foamy mattresses and dank-smelling clothes piled on the floor in the bedrooms. Urine-coloured pillows. The state of the carpet's something else, flecked with burns and brown bloodstains. Mould scaling the walls. They don't even have a fridge. Astrid would probably feel sorry for them. Reckon they've got no choice and all that pinko, progressive nonsense, which is a damn good way of letting them off scot-free. You've always got a choice. It's one thing to live like this. It's another to put a kid through it.

By the time AJ gives up on recovering anything, the mum's out cold again, the bounty already jabbed into that festy arm of hers.

'You right to look after her?' asks Paul, crouching in front of Tyler.

'I don't need your help.'

'Sure, mate.'

He's got to give it to the kid. Takes a shitload of effort to keep the act going. The problem is: if you keep it up long enough, it becomes who you are. Or what you are.

'I was really impressed with you at training. It's great to see someone pushing themselves to their limit.' Tyler avoids eye contact and pastes saliva across the rash on his left arm. 'Listen, if you ever need anyone to –'

'Whatever, pig!' He smirks like he wants to wear one right

between the ears, but there's no way Paul's giving him the satisfaction.

'Offer's always there.'

They lead the old-timer along the pisspot of a corridor, stupid grin splashed across his cheeks. Paul wishes he could slap it right off his face. Probably wouldn't even feel it.

'Stay with us, mate,' says AJ, nudging the clown into the lift, where someone's spray-painted over the security camera.

As they're jolting and squeaking down the shaft, staring at each other's key-scratched reflections, all Paul can think about is the waste of it; everything that poor mother from the Newmarket shops has been through, just for this prick and his missus to sit around, brain-dead, for a couple of days. He'll get in front of a judge and his Legal Aid do-gooder lawyer will find some intellectual disorder he's supposedly got and they'll crap on about how rough his upbringing was. Find the abuse in it. Then he'll get a slap on the wrist and the whole thing will start over again.

PAUL

'Fuck, man, it stinks in here!' moans Ali, stretching his loose-fitting Sixers singlet over his beak.

'How bout a bit of respect, mate?' says Paul. 'You know people live here.'

'Yeah, and those people should wear deodorant,' he says, directing his sledge at a bloke who's lingering by the window of the Holland Court foyer.

The bloke's sporting a red and black flannie and his grey hair's swooped back, like a washed-up rockabilly singer. In the time they've been waiting to start the stair climbs, he's already made three trips out to the car park to collect junkies and escort them into the lift. Paul would love to whip out his badge and give the stupid fucker the fright of his life.

'Let's start!' yells Ali.

'Has anyone heard from Binh?' asks Anna.

'I think he's working at the market,' says Walid.

'Yeah, chopping up dead dogs,' says Tyler. 'You know Vietnamese people eat dogs, miss?'

'Thanks for another fascinating insight into a foreign culture,' says Anna.

'They *really* like pugs.'

'Mm, sounds tasty.'

Bad play, taking his bait.

'Hey, miss, have you heard what Japan used to do to prisoners they didn't like?'

'No, and I don't want to, Tyler.'

He tells his Indigenous mate all about torture techniques, smirking as he tries to catch Anna's eye. Her cheeks are flushed, as if she's already tackled the twenty-odd flights of stairs.

'Stop staring at herrrrr,' hums Athena, frightening the bejesus out of Paul. 'You're getting a bit creepy.'

'Cheers.'

'Rule number one: never shit where you eat.'

'You're bloody enjoying this.'

'I am, actually.'

Washed-up rockabilly squints through the glass before smoothing back his hair and starting another trip out to the car park. Athena's all over it, too, pinching her chin beneath gritted teeth.

'Leave me alone!' yells a thickset girl, shoving Tyler in the chest. He keeps poking her in the side, grinning.

'You love it.'

'No, I *don't*,' she says, wriggling free.

He tries to prod her again and they start jostling, coaxing each other on just enough for Paul to figure they're flirting. She only extricates herself when she notices Ali watching.

There's muffled laughter as washed-up rockabilly brings back an emaciated couple who look like they're shuffling across a bed of hot coals as they enter the foyer. Once they get closer, Paul realises that it's Tyler's mum and the old-timer he and AJ arrested last night.

'Check out how fucked-up she is,' whispers foundation mummy.

Tyler's mum's even paler now, rubbing the sores on her cheeks. Imaginary pieces of glass, trapped beneath her skin. For a second Paul worries she might recognise him, but she's got no idea what planet she's on.

'Your mum's hot, Tyler,' says Ali, pissing himself.

'At least I've got a mum.'

'Never talk about her,' hisses the thickset girl.

'I'll talk about whoever I want,' says Tyler, before chasing after the three deadbeats. He catches up to them outside the lift.

'G'day bud,' says the old-timer, slapping him on the arm.

'Don't fucking touch me!'

The old-timer glances at Tyler's mum, who's still itching away at her hollowed-out cheeks. 'Righto, take it easy.'

One of the lifts pings open. Tyler blocks the entrance to it and folds his arms, towering over the old-timer.

'You're not coming up,' says Tyler.

'Hang on a sec –'

'Didn't you hear me, you dero?'

Athena sneaks towards the lifts, in case it all spills over.

'Please, Ty,' says his mum.

'Sorry, Mum, no way!'

Washed-up rockabilly realises a scene mightn't be his best play, so he ducks out the front for a smoko.

'You can fuck off as well!' says Tyler to the old-timer.

'Come on, bud –'

'I'm not your buddy.'

The silver doors slide shut.

'You heard me, piss off!' says Tyler, breaking into a psychotic smile. 'And don't come back!'

He releases his hands and clenches his fists, keeping his eyes glued on the old-timer, who looks shell-shocked.

'Stuff youse both then,' says the old-timer, sticking his rigid middle finger up at Tyler and his mum.

'No, Barn,' she whimpers.

'Your mum's a fucken whore anyway.'

'SAY THAT AGAIN!' yells Tyler, his torso stiffening. The old-timer takes a good look at him – weighing up the pros and cons – and decides to keep his mouth shut. 'Go on, I dare you to say it again!'

The old-timer shuffles out of the foyer, back over the hot coals. Tyler watches him every step of the way, puffing out his whole chest, looking almost disappointed.

ANNA

She avoids looking out for floor numbers as she slogs her way up the stairs, clutching the cold, germy rail and trying to ignore the stench of stale urine. Saliva lines her throat like hot tar, reducing each breath to a sickening splutter. It'd be enough of an ordeal without ten kilos of rice bags clogging her backpack, sending barbs of pain shooting into her lower vertebrae.

Relief floods through her when she sees Funda stopped at a concrete landing, unstrapping her backpack.

'This blows,' says Funda.

'I know,' says Anna.

She sets her backpack down with a thud, feeling her spine

uncoil. Funda slumps against the wall, propping her arms on her knees as she catches her breath.

'I heard what Ali said . . . about your boyfriend.'

'*Ex*-boyfriend,' says Anna, hoping it sounds jovial.

'He didn't mean it. He just says dumb shit sometimes.'

'You don't have to apologise for him.'

Sneakers squelch above them as Athena and Paul bark encouragement at the kids. Funda sighs, leading her fingers along the indentations in the concrete.

'Did you wanna fuck him up – your boyfriend – when you found out he was cheating?'

'I think I just felt numb, to be honest.'

Funda nods without looking up, still tracing her fingers over the concrete.

'Is everything okay, sweetie?'

'Uh-huh.'

Her eyebrows have been overplucked, making them lose their naturally thick arch.

'Can I ask something else?' says Funda.

'Of course.'

'How do you know when you're, like, *ready*?'

Anna almost bursts out laughing, remembering shards of clumsiness from her first time, down by the river at the local jazz festival, both shitfaced off UDL cans.

'I don't think it's as clear-cut as that.'

'Kylie lost hers in year seven.'

'That's irrelevant.'

Gradually, the echo of spiralling footsteps grows fainter, until they sound as though they're in another stratosphere.

'What age were you?'

It's hard to think of a compelling reason not to answer.

'Fourteen,' says Anna.

Funda looks up with glazed eyes.

'How much is it meant to hurt?'

'It's different for everyone, sweetie,' says Anna, feeling Funda flinch as she tries to pat her wrist. 'You know you don't have to do anything you don't want to, right?'

Funda nods, biting her lower lip.

'But if you *want* to do something . . . you can probably guess what I'm about to say.'

'Oh my God!' shrieks Funda, finally cracking it for a smile. 'It's not like I wanna have a baby or anything. Babies are disgusting.'

'They are a bit, aren't they?'

It feels great to share a laugh, even if it is on the falsest of false premises.

Wind buffets the trees below her as cars snake along the CityLink bypass, over the parted grass of the creek bed, towards the cranes and shipping containers that skirt Port Phillip Bay. Billboards rise from the jungle of factories and self-storage units, promoting soon-to-be-severed breakfast radio combinations. It all looks perfect with the overcast sky as the backdrop. Grey is the colour of this city. Give it long enough and it seeps into you.

The Melbourne Star. They talked about booking tickets to the observation wheel, once it reopened, only days before he stuck blue stickers over all his belongings.

He's stolen this city from her. All the places she used to

love, and the hopes she once had for herself in it. She doubts she even crosses his mind these days. People like him always get to move forward with their lives, leaving those with actual consciences to try to pick up the pieces. There's no justice. It's probably why billions of humans, worldwide, have convinced themselves to believe in an omniscient being. Admitting the sheer senselessness of it all is a far greater burden to bear.

Zoe rips into their shared plate of injera bread, unashamedly chewing with her mouth open. The air's thick with the smell of curries and marinated meats. Kate tries to put on a brave face as she eyes the tribal masks that hang from the vibrant orange walls of the restaurant. *Nothing too spicy* is a tough mantra to uphold when you're eating East African food.

'Any news on the doco, Zo?' asks Anna.

'There's an old smuggler we wanna interview in Jakarta,' says Zoe, swiping her bread through the sludge of lentils and chickpeas again, no doubt sending Kate's inner germophobe into meltdown mode. 'He's making some pretty explosive allegations about our customs ships.'

'What kind of allegations?'

'Sorry, I can't say yet.'

It's a wonder Zoe ever thought she could be content standing at the front of a classroom, feigning political objectivity.

'How are you supposed to get the interview then?'

'By scratching his back,' says Zoe. 'We're just waiting on some funds to come through, so we can get over there and have a proper chat with him. I think it's gonna be big.'

Her phone lights up and she starts frenetically typing.

'Met any Ryan Goslings lately?' Kate asks Anna.

'I don't want to talk about it.'

'Did you . . .?' says Kate, leaning closer to examine her features. 'You dirty little hornbag!'

'It's not like that.'

'Who was he?'

'Just a meathead from Kokoda training,' says Anna. 'It was a huge mistake.'

'How do you know?'

'Because he's one of those smug, sporty men whose idea of fun is holidaying in some poor Asian country and marvelling at how cheap everything is without stopping to wonder *why*.'

'Wow!' says Kate, grinning mischievously. 'You've really thought about it.'

'I haven't, trust me.'

'Yeah right, why don't you text him now?'

'I don't think that's a great idea,' says Anna. 'He's starting to freak me out, actually.'

She lays her phone next to the plate and shows Kate the string of texts Paul sent her during the open day. Zoe puts her own phone down to lean in and read the rectangular grey bubbles.

'Yikes,' says Kate. 'What did you write back?'

'Nothing, I just want him to go away.'

'Then be honest with him,' says Zoe, as if it's the simplest approach in the world. 'If you don't want him harassing you, tell him not to.'

'Or go to the cops,' adds Kate.

There's too much shame to admit that Paul's a cop. Anna gets her first proper look at Kate's engagement ring as she scrolls through Paul's supposedly playful messages again. Her guess is somewhere between six and eight grand's worth of genocidal diamonds. Hopefully it's enough bling to appease Kate.

'On a less creepy note,' says Anna, 'how's the planning for the big day going?'

'It's doing my head in,' says Kate, beaming with stress as she wipes her fingers, one at a time, on her serviette. 'Ryan's absolutely hopeless. All he cares about is what songs the band's going to play, and what beer they're going to have on tap . . .'

Anna fantasises about being overseas by then, exempting herself from a day of bridezilla-induced responsibilities and cocksure groomsmen.

'I know this sounds clichéd,' Kate's saying, 'but I've hired a personal trainer. My goal is to lose eight kilos. Nothing crazy. I'm going to look good, for once, in my wedding photos.'

'You don't need to lose weight,' says Zoe.

'No, I *want* to.'

Zoe flicks Anna a conspiratorial smile. She has to bite her cheeks to avoid wetting herself.

'Anyway, some of the teachers at my work read about your school last week,' says Kate. 'It seems like you've managed to turn things around.'

'Our new dictator has certainly created that impression.'

'So it's not true?'

'By my count he hasn't come up with one original idea yet,' says Anna. 'If rebranding constitutes change, then yes, he's turned things around. But we've also lost what little character we had in the first place.'

'What would you change?' asks Zoe.

'Me?' says Anna, trying to buy herself time. She glances at the enamel tray dolloped with meat at the table next to them. 'Think about what makes this restaurant so popular. They never compromise. If you don't like what they serve, or how they serve it, then you can go and eat somewhere else. On a long enough timeline, it gives them a point of difference from all the other bland restaurants in the area.'

'Yeah, but that's because it's financially viable.'

'Okay then, I'll tell you one thing I'd change,' says Anna, already regretting her previous analogy. 'This year *Macbeth* is on the year eleven EAL reading list, again.'

'I love *Macbeth*,' says Kate.

'Me too,' says Anna, 'but that's beside the point. Have you ever tried teaching it to kids whose first language isn't English?'

Kate gives her an obligatory shake of the head.

'It confuses the hell out of them. If anything, it's actually a hindrance to them learning the language.' She can see in their eyes that she's killing off any chance of going for a prosecco after dinner. 'So next term, I'm not teaching it.'

'What do you mean?' asks Kate.

'In my class, we're not studying *Macbeth*.'

'Have you told anyone?'

'No,' says Anna, hearing the childishness in her defiance, but knowing that her reasoning's sound. 'I care about these kids more than anyone at the Department of Education.'

'No one's saying you don't,' says Kate, 'but you can't just change the syllabus. You'll lose your job.'

'I can live with that,' says Anna, glaring at Kate.

Nothing too spicy, her eyes still say.

*

ALI

'I know,' hisses Najima, 'and why's that *sharmouta* always staring at us, yeah?'

'It's because she can't dance sexy herself,' says Jasmine.

'She probably dances like this . . .'

Najima crosses her eyes and wiggles around to 'Kush' on Channel V, deliberately out of time with the beat.

'Or like this . . .' says Jasmine, pretending to be Kadra as Najima covers her braces.

Dre puts on his angry flow, rapping around convertibles, private jets and wads of American money while everyone else in the clip stays frozen on the spot. Snoop raps his verse from a club with two women on either side of him, looking like a pimp, as blue lights sweep over their upper thighs.

'Yo, Sediment!' says Jasmine, pointing at the uneaten chicken wings Ali's supposed to be throwing out. 'I dare you to eat one.'

'I'm not *that* stupid.'

'The manager isn't even here.'

'Nah, no way.'

He tips the wings into a black rubbish bag and hobbles towards the back door.

'Why you walking so funny?' asks Najima.

'Coz Ms Kelly forced us to climb the towers three times this morning.'

'It looks like you need to shit, real bad.'

The bins outside don't smell much better than shit. All that wet, stinky cardboard and rotting chicken flesh makes him want to puke. When he gets back inside, Michael Garang and a crew of year nines are swarming the counter.

'We'll have two free Burger Boxes,' says Michael.

'Boy, you lucky I don't whoop your arse,' says Jasmine, shooing him away with her long, pink nails. 'I'll give you that for free.'

'Careful, fresh prince!' says one of his crew. 'She'll mess you up, man.'

'Okay, chill, we'll pay,' says Michael.

'I know you got money,' says Najima.

She's right. Somehow Michael does have money. Once he gets his Burger Boxes, him and his crew go and hang upstairs, laughing like hyenas.

'He's gonna get fucked up,' says Jasmine.

'Who, Michael?' asks Ali.

'The fresh prince, or whatever his name is. That boy's gonna get fucked up, for real.'

'How do you know?'

'Yassin and them took over his flat,' says Najima. 'Jazzy and Mukhtar was partying there last night.'

'What about, like, his sponsor?'

'They gone!' says Najima.

Familiar-sounding electronic bubbles are floating over a trap beat on Channel V.

'How come Mukhtar's getting lit with Yassin?' asks Ali.

'Who cares, man,' says Jasmine, rolling her shoulders then locking them as she dips her head to the beat. It's the track Chris Brown just dropped with Busta Rhymes and Lil Wayne, the rapper with actual diamonds in his teeth. 'I love this song!'

'Chris Brown's abs are sexy,' says Najima.

'Imagine, like, licking sweat off them.'

'Yeah, salty!' Najima slurps the imaginary sweat.

'You two are like stalkers or some shit,' says Ali, grabbing another rubbish bag to get away from them.

Michael's crew are the only customers left chilling on the second level, crowding around his stool as he plays them the voice of the female robot inside his iPhone.

'What do you, um, look like naked?' asks Michael.

'*Does my appearance matter to you?*' asks the robot.

'Let's fuck, yo!'

'*Michael, your language.*'

'Hear that? *Your language!*'

They all start yelling dirty things at the screen. Michael shakes his phone in the air, showing off his rusty front teeth. Ali notices the chicken bones and mashed potato, soaked with gravy, that they've tipped onto the table. When they bounce, he's going to have to clean it all up. For once, the thought of that – of how many times he'll have to do pretty much the exact same thing – is not something that winning a Grammy, or having hundreds of groupies, can immediately solve.

'Imagine being in the crowd, but,' says Musa, staring up at the screen through the haze of liquorice-smelling smoke. Wembley Stadium's packed. The pitch looks perfect – like the grass at the University of Melbourne – shaved into a green chessboard. 'Me and my cousin are gonna live in England for a year once we finish school, just to watch Arsenal.'

'Where would you stay?' asks Walid.

'I don't care, man. We'll crash wherever.'

'It snows in England, Musa.'

'Snow ain't shit!'

None of the players waiting in the tunnel are as big or as strong as the Chelsea striker, Didier Drogba. His glassy eyes glare straight ahead. You can tell he's ready for a huge match.

'Let's have a bet,' says Musa. 'If Tottenham wins, Walid has to do my English homework for the rest of the year.'

'Spurs have no chance,' says Walid.

'Make the bet, then.'

'What're you gonna do when Chelsea wins?' asks Ali.

'I'll do anything,' says Musa, rubbing his thighs, trying to get rid of his nervous energy.

'How bout you have to kiss a teacher or something?'

'Alright,' says Musa. 'I'm not scared.'

Him and Walid shake hands as the ref blows his whistle, pointing to the sky.

It's a careful start to the game. Both teams are afraid to concede an early goal. People in the lounge quickly get annoyed at the players for not taking enough risks. In the Africa Cup of Nations every country plays with flair, charging at defenders and trying to score goals, not always worrying about consequences.

Finally, Salomon Kalou steals the ball and bursts down the left flank on a counterattack. He crosses it into the box for Juan Mata, but he screws up the shot.

'SPANISH TRASH!' screams Musa. 'It's okay,' he says, patting Walid's shoulder. 'I only expect two hours of homework from you every night.'

'Hold tight,' says Ali. 'I'm gonna get you fools some tea.'

'I can't believe this dog,' says Musa, 'splashing his KFC slave money, man.'

'You eat there all the fucking time.'

'That's different. Chicken is, like, my girlfriend. I'm not allowed to cheat on her.'

On his way back from the bar, Ali spots Hassan watching the game, alone, from a leather couch near where the older men are playing cards.

'Sup, man?' says Ali, as Hassan wraps his lips around the mouthpiece of his hookah and slurps up bubbles.

'Not much,' says Hassan, refusing to slide his zombie eyes away from the screen.

'You think your boys will beat Chelsea in the final?'

'Easy,' says Hassan with slow confidence, as if soccer is the only truth he has left in the world.

Ali tries to remember how many years it's been since Hassan took him and Walid to the stall at the Vic Market where they sell every EPL team's shirt, extra cheap, to check out the new kits and sponsor's logos at the start of the season. Even the memory feels like it involves someone different from the person whose face is lit up in the purple blaze of the drinks fridge.

'You know Mukhtar got out?' says Ali.

'Yeah, I heard that.'

'Do you two still hang?'

Hassan shakes his fluffy chin, only stopping to slip an olive between his lips.

'Why not?'

'Listen!' croaks Hassan. 'I came here to watch this game, yeah.'

Nothing's happening in the game. Just obvious sideways passes that don't lead to anything.

'You wanna come watch with us?' asks Ali.

'I'm good,' says Hassan.

Ali stares at the rubble of ash in Hassan's hookah tray, two or three coals only just burning, and knows that it's time to leave him to it.

The score's still 0–0 when he brings the tea back to where Musa and Walid are standing.

'You know your bro's here?' he says to Walid.

'He's always here.'

'I asked him about Mukhtar,' says Ali, pretending to crack up. 'Big mistake, man.'

His lemon tea tastes like hot syrup, cleaning all the shisha smoke from his chest.

'So is Mukhtar part of the court case now?'

'Nah, not for a long time.'

'When's it even happening?'

'Soon,' says Walid, wincing as a Spurs shot flies narrowly wide. 'It's just slow. Our lawyers are good people. At the start, they warned us to be patient. People always want justice *now*, you know, like on TV. That's why they drop out.'

'Are you cunts even watching this?' snaps Musa.

'It's too boring,' says Ali.

'So's whatever you're talking about.'

Ali catches the attendant bringing Hassan a new bowl of olives and refilling his hookah tray with glowing cubes.

'Do the lawyers still think you can get a payment?'

'It's not about that,' says Walid. 'We want bigger things than money. We're gonna make the main policeman – the boss of everything – have to testify.'

'Is that the pig who never turns up to training?'

'Yeah.'

'What's *he* gonna say?'

'Maybe nothing,' says Walid. 'But it'll still be a bad look for him, having to be there.'

Frank Lampard plays a long ball to Didier Drogba, who steadies the ball with his back to the goal and flicks it by the final defender. He fires a left foot rocket, straight past the keeper, that cannons into the corner of the net.

Everyone's jumping up from the couches around Hassan and high-fiving, screaming, 'GOOOOAAAAAAAAAAL!'

Even Musa's excited, because something happened.

'Who're you gonna kiss?' asks Ali.

'I'll kiss Miss Kelly, man,' says Musa, slapping his tongue and his lips together. 'A big, black kiss!'

ALI

'WHERE THE FUCK ARE YOU?' yells one of the year seven nerds who's playing *Warcraft* in the library.

'Oh my God, are you blind?' squeaks his friend, his voice stuck between a man's and a boy's.

'Just tell me, Noah!'

Noah, Hunter, Bailey, Jackson. They keep screaming out names that sound more like people's surnames as they crowd around the desktops, making each other hyper.

'It moves just like him,' says Musa, watching a clip of the Tupac hologram, onstage with Snoop and Dre at Coachella.

Even Walid looks up from the website with the old Legal Studies exams on it, nodding along to the hologram of Pac with his pants sagging below his ripped abs. Ali whispers the lyrics to 'Hail Mary', nailing the flow, his punchy words lagging just behind the beat.

'NOOB!' yells the kid with the squeaky voice.

'Suck shit, Noah!'

'What's your problem?'

'You, bitch!'

'Listen to these skippies trying to sound gangsta,' says Musa, making sure they can hear him. 'They're, like, exactly who the principal wants at this school, instead of us, but all *they* wanna do is sound like us.'

'Maybe you should swap cribs then,' says Ali.

It's fine for the principal to say in the newspaper that he wants it to be a school 'for the community to be proud of', but if all he keeps doing is trying to get rich families to enrol their kids, then the place will end up no different from St. Bernard's, where the kids all have basically the same personality.

'Miss Kelly admitted this school's racist,' puffs Musa, grabbing his crotch just after Pac does.

'Are you really gonna kiss her today?'

'For sure,' says Musa. 'You should come watch.'

Ali reads the sample questions Walid's copying into his notebook: strengths and weaknesses of precedent, purpose of a committal hearing, effects of statutory interpretation. It's totally different from remembering lyrics. There's no way this information will be inside his brain at the end of the year.

'Check this out, Walid!' yells Musa.

'Give me a minute.'

'Nah, now!'

Walid leans over to look at the ugly, big-lipped fish with whiskers that's staring at them from an article on Musa's laptop screen. The skin between Walid's eyebrows tightens into an angry V. Next to the fish cartoon, there's a stubby holder with a crazy inscription:

My date of birth is 01/01/??

'Who made that?' asks Ali.

'The pigs,' says Musa.

'When?'

'They just got busted for it.'

Ali checks out the massive orange lips on the cartoon.

'What kind of fish is that, anyway?' he asks.

The nerdy year sevens won't stop screeching in their fake computer war as Walid sits, slumped, by the laptop.

'You all good, man?' asks Ali.

It's brutal seeing Walid so messed up that he can't move, or speak. Ali knows there's nothing he can say to make it better. Even in this country, after all this time, this is what the police still secretly think. All the handshakes, the footy lessons and the getting-to-know-each-other games they've forced Walid to play, expecting *him* to walk with a blindfold on, giving them his trust . . .

They mean nothing now.

Yassin brushes past Ali, who's peering through the shutters of the room, and sinks into the back row of Ms Kelly's EAL class. He refuses to take off his Weezy cap or his headphones, staring at the light purple sky out the window as he nods along to the album Kanye and Jay-Z teamed up on last year.

'I'm going to return your language analysis SACs now,' Ali hears Ms Kelly say. 'If you have any questions, I'm happy to answer them.'

As she searches through her folder, Jasmine and Najima start flicking balls of paper at the back of Kadra's head.

Walid barely flinches as Ms Kelly slaps Musa's test on the table, right next to him. Usually, the moment before getting a high mark on a test would be a proud one for Walid, but Ali can tell that he's in some whacked trance, still stressing about the fish cartoon.

'One hundred per cent,' yells Musa. 'Yeah boy!'

Ms Kelly doesn't have a test to give back to Kadra or Yassin, who's thumping his fist on the table as he raps Kanye's verse from 'No Church in the Wild', not giving a fuck how loud he's being.

'Excellent work,' says Ms Kelly, handing Walid his test and clenching her teeth into a smile. He turns over the stapled pieces of paper without looking at his score.

'What did you get?' asks Musa.

He tries to snatch the test out of Walid's hands, but only manages to rip off the bottom corner. Walid has to sit on top of the test to stop Musa from getting it.

'*Kol hawa!*' Ali hears Jasmine whisper, still trying to get Kadra's attention.

Musa's busy wobbling the legs of Walid's chair.

'Please remember,' says Ms Kelly, pretending she can't hear Yassin's terrible rapping, 'these grades are not the –'

'Hey, miss!' yells Musa. 'I need to talk to you about my test. I think you made a mistake.'

She exhales and walks over to his table, already muttering to herself. Musa winks at Ali through the window, wedging his knuckles between his teeth to stop himself from laughing.

'Come closer,' he says to Ms Kelly.

'I'm right where I am, thanks.'

'See this word . . . what does it mean?' asks Musa, pointing at his test. Ms Kelly squints at her own handwriting from upside down. As she leans in, Musa lunges across the table, his mouth wide open, and kisses her on the lips.

'What do you think you're doing?' she screams, trying to wipe his kiss off her lips.

'I was only joking, miss.'

'Get out!'

'Ali dared me.'

'OUT!'

Yassin's stopped rapping to stare at Ms Kelly's shivering hands, which are still frantically trying to wipe Musa's saliva off her face.

The principal waddles past Ali, straight into the room.

'Can you get rid of him?' yells Ms Kelly, her voice turning psycho.

'I'm going!' says Musa, standing up, booting his chair and stomping towards the roller door. 'Far out, some people can't take a *joke*.'

The principal tries to walk right next to him.

'FUCK OFF, YOU DUMB SKIPPY!'

'Musa, chill!' says Ali as he barges past, but it's like Musa doesn't even see him.

As Musa gets further down the corridor, his yelling gets angrier, until it becomes a lion's roar. There's a loud smash near the stairs. Glass tumbles from a classroom wall, shattering like layers of the thinnest ice.

TYLER

'Psst, what's-your-name!' whispers Tyler through the rusty school fence.

The girly-haired loner flinches, dropping his apple.

'It's cool,' says Tyler. 'Sorry, I forgot your name.'

'Ethan,' mumbles the year seven who he made friends with at the start of the year, too scared to look him in the eye.

'Has anyone been giving you shit?'

Ethan shakes his head as he checks to see if a teacher's watching.

'See that girl with curly hair?' says Tyler, pointing behind the dumpsters, where some year elevens and twelves are sneaking ciggies. 'I need you to get her for me.'

The loner stands there, his cheeks going pinker than the skin on his tanbark-covered apple.

'You won't get in trouble, I promise.'

'Okay,' says Ethan.

He takes forever to reach the dumpsters, finally tapping Funda on the arm and tilting his head in Tyler's direction. Tyler tries to look chill as she walks towards the fence, even though all he can think about is slipping off her skirt and her stockings, and tasting her.

'Why weren't you in class?' she says.

'Coz I didn't feel like it.'

Jasmine and Kylie are watching them, already gossiping.

'What's been happening?' he asks.

'Musa kissed Miss Kelly.'

'Seriously?'

'Yeah, Jazzy said she went mental afterwards.'

Tyler can imagine Ms Kelly losing her shit, acting like her life is harder than everyone else's.

'Did you miss me in PE?' he asks.

'Not really.'

'Fuck you, then.'

The recess bell rings. Everyone starts heading up to the lockers, except the kids playing soccer.

Funda turns to walk away.

'Hey, where're you going?'

'I've got IDM.'

'Fuck IDM!' says Tyler. 'Come hang with me.'

'I can't.'

'Yeah, you can. No one will even notice.'

Kylie's coming towards them, tracing her lips with a little pink tube. As always, she reeks of ciggies and Impulse.

'Hey, Kylie, can you get Funda marked off the roll?'

'Maybe,' she says, looking at Funda all funny. It's lame how chicks need to get each other's permission to do pretty much everything. They can't even go to the toilet by themselves.

'If I get busted, I'll be pissed,' says Funda.

'Whatever,' says Tyler, feeling inside his pocket to make sure the gum and the condoms are still in there.

Tyler checks out the newspaper on the table to avoid another awkward silence. The cover has a picture of a stubby holder with a cartoon of a fish that a bunch of pigs printed off. Somehow, people are saying it's racist.

'Where'd you get that fifty from?' asks Funda.

'Huh?' says Tyler.

'I saw you pay.'

'My mum gave it to me.'

'Okay,' she says, screwing her lips up. 'How's she going?'

'Good.'

There's no way he's telling her about the cramps and the

diarrhoea, or how Mum wailed like a baby when she was trying to sleep last night, begging him to make it all stop.

'Who was that guy she was with at training?'

'Barney,' says Tyler. 'He's gone now.'

'You were only pretending to go schizo at him, yeah?'

'What do you mean?'

'You wouldn't hurt him or anything?'

'It depends.'

Four dudes in hi-vis vests – the tradies who've been digging up the veggie garden at school – sit at the table next to them, wrapping their dirty fingers around footlong subs. One of them has a frizzy beard and an annoying Irish accent. The ginger dick keeps cackling at everything his mates say.

'Barney robbed a chick in a wheelchair.'

'Seriously?'

'Yeah, he's gotta go to court,' says Tyler. 'Hopefully they send him to jail and he becomes someone's bitch.'

Barney would make a perfect bitch with all the gaps in his mouth.

'So, like, do you ever see your dad?'

'Not anymore,' says Tyler.

'We don't have to talk about him, if you don't want.'

'Nah, I don't give a fuck.'

The rash on his left leg stings like a Chinese burn. Every jolt of his foot sends another stab of pain through his skin, deep into the muscle.

'Why don't you see him?'

'He's in a different unit,' says Tyler. 'We used to go heaps and you could tell he totally owned the joint. Him and his mates had FTP tats and none of them cared if they had to go to the slot or anything. The guards were all shitting themselves whenever he was around. You could actually see it. But now he just wants to pass his time without distractions.'

'That doesn't make sense.'

'What doesn't?'

'Why wouldn't he want you to visit?'

'He just doesn't,' says Tyler, acting bored.

If he tells her about the protection unit, then she'll tell Kylie, and then everyone at school will know.

'How long til he gets out?'

'I can't remember. They're always changing it.'

'Do you ever wonder, like, whether he meant to . . .' says Funda, scrunching her cookie wrapper into a ball.

'Yeah, meant what?'

'Forget it.'

'Listen, whatever you've heard, I promise it's bullshit,' he says, giving in and rubbing his burning leg. 'People have no idea what the fuck they're talking about.'

Needles of rain are hitting the window. The Irish dude's eyes dart to Funda's chest as he's cackling with his mates.

'What do you wanna do now?' she asks.

'I don't know,' says Tyler. 'What do *you* wanna do?'

'You're being weird today.'

She's the one being all weird.

'Ummm,' he says, watching as it starts to piss down on Racecourse Road. The trees are shaking so much that they could snap any second, and wet brown leaves are smeared over the tram tracks, like a squashed pile of dogshit.

'Where do you wanna go?' says Funda.

'Anywhere.'

'Hurry up and pick somewhere.'

'Fine, how bout your place?'

The tradies erupt. Funda gives Tyler an intense as look, twitching her uneven eyebrows.

'*What?*' he asks.

'Nothing.'

'Sure?'

'Yeah, nothing.'

'So it's cool if we go back to yours?'

'I don't care,' says Funda, acting like a total psycho. 'Can we please just leave?'

They bolt downhill, past drains that're gushing with stormwater, sploshing across the puddly concrete that's making the air smell fresh and icy. Funda looks unco as when she runs, shielding her eyes from the rain and clutching Tyler's arm, screeching right in his ear:

'I'm fucking drenched!'

'Me too.'

'Left here.'

The walk-ups on Victoria Street are even dodgier than the high-rises. Balconies crowded with couches, old mattresses and broken prams. Someone on the bottom level's had all their windows smashed, and the flat next to them is boarded up with wooden panels, every single one of them covered in Ali's lame-arse $EDIMENT tag.

Funda's place doesn't stink half as bad as Jai's. They've actually got some stuff in the kitchen – chairs, a table, a toaster, a microwave – and the tiles aren't covered in rust-coloured stains.

'Do you want a drink?' she asks. 'We've got Diet Coke.'

'I'm good.'

Her hair's wet and messy, but she still looks hot in a kind of vulnerable way, even with mascara dripping down her cheeks.

'Wanna hang in my room?'

'Yeah, whatever.'

He follows her to her room and lies on the bed, sliding a stick of gum onto his tongue. His t-shirt's got this soggy, sweaty smell, but there's jack shit he can do about it. Her room isn't like he imagined. The window's facing the wrong way and there are posters of Jason Derulo and Justin Bieber up everywhere.

'Block your eyes,' says Funda, before turning around to unbutton her school shirt.

Tyler peeks through the cracks in his fingers as she wipes the mascara off her cheeks. He can't really see anything, just her black bra strap and the way her hips start to curve out from the top of her stockings.

'Where's your dad?'

'At work,' she says, wriggling into a white Tommy Hilfiger jumper that kind of makes her look like a tomboy. 'You can look now.'

Tyler lowers his hands.

'He normally gets back at five,' says Funda.

'What does he do, again?'

'Him and my uncle – Ali's dad – share a taxi.'

'Cool.'

She checks to make sure the tag on her jumper's tucked in and curls up next to him on the bed. Her hair smells all wet and fruity.

'Does your dad get lots of pissed cunts in his taxi?'

'My uncle gets more coz he works at night. Sometimes they spew and he has to clean it up afterwards instead of, like, getting more customers. Then the taxi stinks like spew when my dad takes over in the morning.'

'That sucks balls,' says Tyler, wondering whether he should put his arm around her. He knows Shannon would.

Justin Bieber's got such a stupid haircut. It's seriously pathetic how chicks start screaming and crying like two-year-olds whenever they go to his concerts.

'So what are you gonna do if you don't get accepted into the army?' asks Funda.

'What?'

'Isn't there, like, a test?'

'Yeah, why the fuck wouldn't I get in?' says Tyler. He rolls up his t-shirt. 'Here, check out these abs.'

'Eew, gross!' she says, squirming away from him. It's not like *her* stomach's completely flat. 'I don't think they'll let you in if you've got eczema,' says Funda, still refusing to check out his sixpack.

'Bullshit!'

'I looked it up. You can't have skin problems.'

'You're just saying that coz you don't want me to go.'

'No, I'm not. If you wanna get killed, go ahead.'

He can hear pigeons gulping right outside the window, beneath the drizzle pattering on the concrete.

'You'd be totally devo if I died,' he says.

Funda rests her head against his shoulder. Her tits are right there, making a crease in her jumper. He can feel his cock going tingly as it starts to spread down the skin of his thigh.

'What're you doing on Wednesday?' she asks.

'What's on Wednesday?'

'Anzac Day. There's no school.'

'I haven't really thought about it.'

Hopefully they spend all Anzac Day fucking each other's brains out, trying every position.

'What're you thinking about?' asks Funda.

'I was just thinking it's weird. In Gallipoli, we were pretty much enemies and –'

'You mean Turks and Aussies.'

'Yeah, exactly.'

He wishes he could get the courage to start running his fingers through her hair, and make it seem casual.

'Except now the Aussie would win,' he says, flexing his left bicep.

'No way!'

'Do you seriously think you're stronger than me?'

'Um, yeah.'

Funda shoves him in the chest, but he grabs her wrist straight away. She tries to break free. He only releases her so he can sneak the gum back into his pocket. They wrestle on their sides. He lets it be an even fight until he pins both of her wrists and locks them together in his right hand.

'Let me *go*!' she shrieks, twisting her arms.

'Admit I'm stronger.'

'Never.'

Her teeth are chattering.

'Are you still cold?'

'No,' she says, softly. 'Just nervous, I think.'

He releases her wrists. They stare at each other, slowly

letting their noses come together. Her lips feel squishy. There's nowhere to put his left hand. She's making the weirdest sounds, all heavy and through her nostrils. Her lips finally open and their tongues spiral into each other's mouths. It's messy as, but it feels good, combining saliva and swallowing it. He reaches under her jumper and cups her tit over the padding of her bra, squeezing as hard as he can.

'Ow!' she says, panting. 'Be gentle.'

'Sorry.'

They go back to kissing. Saliva's pasted all over his lips and a strand of her hair's stuck on his tongue. There's no way he's stopping to pick it off. He runs his fingers underneath the padding and along her nipple, feeling it get hard. His cock feels like it's about to explode.

'You're so fucking hot,' he says, even though he doesn't mean to say it.

All he wants to do is get a condom on and find the right hole before he gacks all over his boxers. He creeps his fingers down her stomach, below her stockings – imagining how sticky she's going to be – until he feels the spikes of her pubic hair. She suddenly goes stiff and stops kissing him back.

'No, no, don't!'

'What's wrong?'

'Nothing,' she says, pulling away and straightening her bra. 'I just don't want to right now.'

He tugs his hand out of her stockings.

'Are you mad?' asks Funda.

Tyler drops his head to the pillow and stares at a Justin Bieber poster to try to make his cock go down.

'Sorry,' says Funda, sniffling.

'I don't get what I did wrong.'

'You didn't do anything wrong.'

'So why fucking stop?'

She's trying to say something else, but her rashy lips are wobbling too much. It makes him even more pissed off now that she's acting like a total sook.

'My uncle . . .' she says, stopping to wipe her nose on her sleeve.

'Yeah, what about him?'

Her hair's stuck in dark clumps down the side of her snotty face. She doesn't really look hot anymore.

'Forget it.'

'Nah, what about him?'

'When I was, like, really little . . .' is all she manages to say, before burying her head under the covers to muffle her sobbing.

Tyler doesn't have a clue whether she wants him to pat the covers or let her cry, or just get up and leave. He's never heard anything so raw, and brutal. The only thing he knows is that there has to be a punishment – the worst kind of punishment – for the person who caused this sobbing.

PAUL

Fucking Davey. They've never missed the opening bounce on Anzac Day. You'd think having no responsibilities would mean you're on time for everything – early even – but somehow the little bludger keeps rocking up later and later. And bugger the rest of them for indulging him. That's *why* this happens. At a set point, someone's got to cut the umbilical cord and call it for what it is: selfishness.

'The footy's about to start!' yells Paul.

'I don't think your father heard,' says Mum, poking her head out of the kitchen.

'DAD!'

'I keep telling him to have his hearing checked.'

Paul finds the old man out on the decking, tongs in one hand, stubby in the other. Fair stoop these days. His hair's more ragged. Silver wisps sprouting from his nose and his ears.

'What time's Davey getting here?'

'Half an hour ago,' mumbles the old man through the grey rat-tickler. 'Apparently they went pretty hard last night.'

'Astrid coming too?'

'I think so.' One of the few days every year when they get to spend some quality time as a family and she's got to bugger this up as well. 'Heard you and her had a bit of a blue?'

'I wouldn't say that. More a difference of opinion.'

'Astrid's very opinionated.'

'Jeez, you reckon!'

The old man's eyes stay fixed on the hotplate, giving diddly squat away.

'Davey told me the two of them are thinking of moving out,' says Paul.

'I'll believe it when I see it.'

'Me too.'

Paul inhales the fumes of the old man's lawnmower, wondering how much longer he'll be able to stay on top of the old backyard cricket pitch.

'How's he coming up with the coin?'

'Ask ya mother.'

'I'm asking *you*, Dad,' says Paul, trying to coax the old man's gaze away from the frothing steaks. 'I don't understand what the moral is here: sit on your arse, twiddle your thumbs for a decade, and everything will fall into your lap? It'll stand him in really good stead for the rest of his life.'

The old man starts stacking the sausages onto one of Mum's special china plates, brown juice sloshing everywhere.

'Look at him, keeping us all waiting like this. He never thinks about anyone but himself.'

'Some people need a nudge in the right direction.'

'Or a bit of tough love.'

Either way, the answer isn't written on the charcoaled hotplate that he keeps staring into.

'Those can go inside,' says the old man, pointing at the sausages with his tongs.

There's still a part of Paul that knows the repressed prick pulls rank and will do until the day he dies, grumpy and hollow-cheeked, with a catheter in his circumcised dick.

He ducks back into the living room to hear fifty thousand Bombers fans giving the umps a Bronx cheer.

'What's the score?' asks Mum.

'Pies are up by a goal.'

'Sugar!'

Paul lays the table to kill more time. Big bowl of potato salad in the middle, as always, plus a veggie lasagne. Hope Astrid appreciates the effort Mum's gone to and thanks her, maybe offers to pitch in a few bucks for ingredients.

'What's wrong?' asks Mum.

'Nothing.'

'Sure?'

'Yeah, I'm just hungry,' says Paul, eyeing the old man's burnt sausages. 'I haven't eaten since the dawn service.'

By the time they finish lunch, the first half of the footy will be over. Two people hit the piss and bugger up an entire day for everyone else. The worst thing is: no one except him seems to give a toss.

'How far away are they?'

'A couple of minutes, I think,' says Mum.

She's got no bloody idea. There's another roar from the crowd, followed by a chorus of boos.

'No point letting the meat go cold, is there?'

Paul shoves a sausage into his mouth and bites the head off the black snake, daring Mum to have a go at him.

* * *

U two even on your way?

Bit sick of your golden ticket routine with the folks, mate

They won't be here to bail u out forever

5 mins

You've got phone credit for once!

Gutsy effort from u, I take it all back

* * *

'Beer, Davey?' asks Paul.

'Get stuffed!'

'Be nice to your brother,' says Mum, even though the old man's having a chuckle.

You can still smell the turps on the little bastard. It takes a fair bit to get him to this point. Wonder how often they push it this far, or what else is in their systems.

'So, what did you two get up to last night?'

'We had a mate's going-away drinks,' says Davey.

'Loose night?'

Davey burps into his fist, croaks out a 'Yep.'

'That salad bowl's the old vomit bowl, isn't it, Mum?' says Paul, waving away the meaty stench of the burp. 'If you need to blow a few chunks, just let it rip, I reckon.'

'It's *not* the same bowl,' says Mum.

Even Astrid's having a decent laugh. There's something

different about her face this arvo. No eyeliner. It makes her look washed-out. She knows she's got to have a proper crack at the lasagne. That's one thing he'll enjoy: watching her struggle to get as much down the trap as she can.

Siren sounds for quarter time in the living room.

'Tell me, dear,' says Mum, as Paul's squinting to read the score, 'have you met any nice ladies at the station?'

'Don't know too many female coppers who'd wanna be called *nice ladies*, Mum.' It boils his blood, this stuff. The old man can see it, which is why he always leaves it alone. 'And even if there were any, I've seen it go tits-up between coppers too many times to think it's a clever idea.'

'Have you thought about online dating?' asks Astrid.

It's hard to tell if she's taking the piss or not.

'We've gotta stay pretty private.'

'There's no harm in trying,' says Mum.

'Why's this everyone's business?'

You'd swear it's the most pressing topic they've got to talk about. Christ, maybe it is.

'All I'm saying is, I wouldn't keep leaving it,' says Mum.

'Thanks for the vote of confidence.'

'She just wants grandkids to spoil,' grumbles the old man, sick to death of it himself.

Davey nudges his plate towards the middle of the table and burps into his fist again. Hasn't touched his spuds and isn't even halfway through his steak.

'That the best ya can do?' says the old man.

'For now, Dad.'

'Waste of food, if ya ask me.'

'You'll eat more later, won't you?' says Mum.

'Maybe.'

Mister Maybe looks like he's about to keel over. Still, difficult to have any sympathy for him.

'How's the househunting going?' asks Paul.

'No good,' says Davey.

'It's so corrupt,' says Astrid, as if it's a concrete bloody fact. 'Everyone says they'll pay over the asking price, and then the real estate agents don't even read people's applications. They just pick whoever's offered them the most money.'

Welcome to Capitalism 101.

'Hang in there, love,' says Mum, patting Astrid's bracelet-strangled hand. The gesture's got *daughter-in-law* written all over it. Should've guessed they'd be in cahoots by now.

Astrid's making a surprisingly good fist of her lasagne.

'Sounds like it's been an interesting few weeks out in Sunshine,' says Mum, terrified of letting any silence last longer than five seconds.

'I wouldn't know,' says Paul.

'Stuff like that probably happens all the time,' says Astrid. 'We just don't get to hear about it.'

'Jeez, that's a decent-sized assumption you're making,' says Paul. No point blowing up at her in front of the folks, which is probably what she wants. 'You ever told a joke that went down the wrong way?'

'Likening African kids to mudfish isn't a joke. Surely even you can see that.'

'*Even you*, what's that spose to mean?'

Not much diversity in her hipster friendship circle.

'Doesn't it concern you that the people you work with still

find this sort of thing funny? It's meant to be the twenty-first century.'

'Just because a few peanuts made a stupid decision, that doesn't make us all racist.'

'But it's not *one* stupid decision, Paul,' says Astrid. This is half the problem. Social justice warriors like her put every word you say under the microscope and the second you slip up, they think they've nailed you. 'What about the policemen who took the trophy photo of that poor South Sudanese man in custody? You'd swear we've learnt nothing from the Americans at Abu Ghraib.'

'Fair difference, I would've thought.'

'Have you seen the photo?'

'No.'

'Then how would you know?'

Got half a mind to pick up the rest of Davey's steak and swipe it across her veggie lasagne. This time next year, she'll have converted the little bastard to veganism and Krishna knows what else.

'And that's another thing I don't understand,' she says, as if Paul asked her for a list, 'how you all just close ranks whenever something like this happens. Are any of you actually allowed to have your own opinion?'

'Did you even hear what the Commissioner said?'

'Come on, that was only lip service.'

'Lip service, righto.'

'What's so funny?'

'Nothing,' says Paul, noticing her inflamed cheeks as he holds his bemused smile. 'Pretty easy to build a case when you're happy to ignore the other side of it.'

'Do you honestly think that's what I'm doing?'

'Yep.'

The Commissioner's the real loser in all of this. He can go as hard at the reckless pricks in Sunshine as he wants, but it isn't going to do his chances of getting the subpoena removed any good. Might as well skip Kokoda now, if it was meant to be a PR stunt.

'It does seem like there's still a problem,' says Mum, her voice quivering.

'Great insight, Mum!'

She hurts the most. His own flesh and blood. The way she's getting her knickers in a twist over a cartoon, you'd swear he was one of the numbskulls who had the stubby holders made in the first place.

The second quarter's started.

'Pretty quiet over there,' says Paul, glaring at Davey. 'What do you reckon, mate?'

Bit of brotherly support wouldn't go astray. Something similar about the silence coming from Davey and the old man, both staring at the floral tablecloth, always waiting for the storm to blow over.

Still nothing from Davey, the gutless prick.

'Fine then, if you've got nothing to say, I reckon I might as well head off.'

'Please don't!' says Mum. 'I made lamingtons.'

Bugger her lamingtons. And bugger the four of them. They're all a part of this, even the old man. Sucking on the teat of his stubby, swallowing his feelings. This is how the country's going to go from now on. Every generation gets more and more precious, bowing down to political correctness on steroids, until people are too afraid to express an actual opinion. A society of mutes. That'll suit Davey just fine.

'Enjoy the footy!' says Paul, getting up and storming out of the dining room. The TV screen's a blur of colour. No point the game even being on anymore.

ANNA

Nina Simone's got serious, serious chops. Singing along to 'Plain Gold Ring' is basically impossible, trying to stretch Nina's long, undulating notes over the crawling rhythm:

Boom, bah-bah, bah-bah, boom-boom-boom, bah-bah, bah-bah, boom-boom-boom . . .

What time's this song even in?

Bah-bah, bah-bah, boom-boom-boom, bah-bah, bah-bah . . .

There's no such thing as time anymore, determining her behaviour. Screw the smudged digits on the microwave, and the daylight forever fading over the racecourse out the window. Her eyes can close whenever they feel like closing. All there is left to do is to wince down another gulp of $2.99 Aldi chardonnay, and to ask herself the same question she asked herself maybe yesterday: *how far can I take this?*

Nina's wailing now. A volcano erupting and sucking its lava back inside.

The crisp sucking sound of Musa's lips, and her hysterical reaction – the hatred Jasmine accused her of straight afterwards – as if her own violation didn't count for anything. A racist person wouldn't spend this long stewing over it, wishing they could press rewind. That mightn't be the worst way to phrase it, if Jasmine or Musa ever talk to her again.

Couch cushion vibrating under buttock.
Stomach-less fart?
Mum.
Not in a million, billion years.
And Paul the stalker:

Whatever's up with u I honestly think
I can help u get thru it

Piss off Paul

She speaks!

Types

**She types*

So?

So nothing I'm drunk

How drunk?

Drunk enough to reply to you

I wish u got drunk more often

I have been

Not great for aerobic capacity

Meh

How's everything going?

Still hate my guts?

When the hell did the music stop?

Really got to go. That feeling when you try to stand up and suddenly your legs are made of jelly. 'Laughing legs', one of the Aussie soldiers called it. It *does* feel like your legs are laughing. But don't laugh, otherwise the embarrassing swimming pool thing will happen.

Sizing up the toilet seat, she finds herself speaking in a posh English accent:

'Now, Katie, never mind the toilet paper, or the faecal contamination. We don't have time for all that. Just. Let. It. Flow!'

Mercy.

'Good guuuuurl, Katie!'

U just get sick of communicating huh?

Amazing how Zoe always manages to sever these things so guiltlessly. What's it like being her; knowing you can fly into any city in the world and that night, if you feel like it, bring a stranger back to your hotel room?

A humid, pastel-coloured evening in Lisbon. Grilled fish on a terrace overlooking the water it was plucked from. Cherry brandy. The night bleeding from fado music into shoebox bars and onto sticky dance floors. Even more sloshed than this, her inhibitions melting away. Tanned Portuguese men whose sweat smells nice, and who don't try to talk during foreplay.

Not passed out in the bath or anything?

Attempted joke

I'm not the answer to your problems Paul

When did I say u were?

Sorry I'm blocking you

Perfect headspace to be ruthless in. What about *him*, too? She should've deleted his number the second she found out. And never have had to know the slow dagger of his silence.

Closure, finally.

If they'd met five or six years later, in their mid-twenties, he might've been ready to settle down. Not that 'settling down' is how she imagined it. But still. He wouldn't have had questions he needed answers to. Always wanting to kick on to Pony, The Retreat or Yah Yah's for one last gin and a boogie; anywhere but home, with her.

Everyone says it's not your fault, but it *is* your fault. You weren't enough, regardless of why. There's no other way to make sense of it. Total, unequivocal rejection.

ANNA

Two hours and twenty-six minutes to survive. Not quite enough time for another toilet run before her next appointment. She can feel a UTI coming on. Sugar injection required. There are only three Picnic bars left in the box of Kokoda fundraiser chocolates she's been pillaging all day, trying to restore her blood sugar levels. A stream of peanut, nougat and caramel saliva rusts away at her molars before oozing into the swamp of her stomach, making it gurgle in protest.

Hunger, for the first time in days. If she'd known the last two parents were going to be no-shows, she could've grabbed some pho up the street instead of compounding her headache by waiting inside this noisy, sweat-infested cauldron.

Funda's sitting at Rob's table in a hoodie, head bowed, picking away at her fingernails. Her dad – a heavy-set man with grey epaulettes on his shoulders – is listening to Rob try to sound teacherly, nodding solemnly, mumbling into the buttons on his chest every so often. Funda looks over, as if sensing she's being watched. Anna does her best to muster a smile, but Funda's expression barely changes.

Two hours and twenty-three minutes left. Anna uses her furry tongue to prise rice crisps from between her teeth.

An apple would be incredible right now.

Jenny strides into the library, ushering a curvy woman over to Anna's table. They're accompanied by a tall, thin man in a suit jacket that's several sizes too small, who Anna recognises as one of the Arabic interpreters from last year. She fights the urge to offer her hand to him.

'Anna, this is Mariam,' says Jenny in a condescendingly loud voice. 'Mariam is Musa's mother.'

'Lovely to meet you.'

Mariam sits down with a thud, exhaling involuntarily, before wriggling into a more comfortable position on her chair.

'Teaching your son is always interesting,' says Anna, making sure she looks Mariam in the eye as she speaks, instead of the interpreter.

She listens to her comment being relayed in tongue-heavy syllables, wondering whether the word 'interesting' has the same connotations in Arabic.

Mariam takes her time absorbing the comment, nodding slowly, before launching into a speech of her own. Small, dark splotches mark the skin just below the embers of her eyes, which feel like they're burning through Anna's veneer, exposing her aching skull and the sweet smell seeping from her pores.

'My son has caused a lot of trouble for me,' says the interpreter, shifting his gaze, diplomatically, between Mariam and Anna. 'All his teachers, they tell me he makes problems for his friends, and for other –'

'It's not so bad,' says Anna, finding herself adopting the interpreter's disjointed phrasing. 'If Musa can learn to apply himself, there's still time for him to pass.'

She waits for her words to contort into Arabic, fearing they'll sound even more helpless in translation.

Funda trudges behind her dad towards the library foyer, where Peter's schmoozing with parents and waving overenthusiastically at shy young siblings.

The interpreter begins to translate Mariam's reply, but produces a sharp smile as she cuts him off, compelled by another thought. This time he waits until he's certain she's finished. 'She is saying he should already know to apply himself. We have been hearing these things for so long. Musa, he doesn't understand . . .' says the interpreter, rubbing his sparse goatee as he tries to think of the most appropriate wording, 'how to control himself.'

'I know,' says Anna, horrified to catch herself using her hands to emphasise her words, 'but a lot of the students have issues with self-control. Musa isn't always the biggest problem for me. Most of the time, I enjoy teaching him. He can be very amusing.'

She softens her features into a smile, trying to anticipate when the interpreter's saying the word 'amusing'. Mariam doesn't flinch, delivering her response in the same firm tone.

'Musa, he must take everything too far,' says the interpreter, grimacing as if he's personally burdened by the information he's being forced to relay. 'The principal tells me this week about this thing he has done to you. Is it true?'

'Yes, it's true,' says Anna, wondering what, exactly, she's agreeing to. 'I think, maybe, Musa doesn't understand how serious his behaviour is sometimes.'

Mariam sits with her lips pursed, her cheekbones lost in swollen flesh, as she listens to the interpreter. She gazes above Anna, towards the buzzwords stuck high on the wall, no doubt making a scathing assessment of her fitness to teach. When Mariam finally decides to start talking, the two embers fix on Anna.

'If this thing is true,' says the interpreter, 'then it shows that he will never have control. I cannot trust him.'

'What do you mean *if*?' asks Anna.

A wince flashes across the face of the interpreter as he realises the impossibility of his situation.

'My apology,' he says, anxiously rubbing his goatee.

But there's no escaping the ferocity of the embers. You don't always need words to say *melodramatic white slut.*

•

How many casks of wine would it take to survive until the end of term?

Four litres would last around two days, so sixty-three days divided by two equals thirty-one-and-a-half shiny silver pillows. Plus a final-day binge/reward.

Thirty-three, to be safe.

This is madness, she knows. Amazing how methodical madness can feel. It might be the perfect state of mind to attack the leading teacher application and submit some sort of lucid, free-form selection criteria riff that simultaneously gets her the position and exposes Linda for the fraud that she is, without the need for an interview.

Cask wine not necessarily the friend of career-redefining riff, which may even be due tonight.

'Sorry,' she blurts to the stern Vietnamese woman behind the counter at FoodWorks, dumping her basket below the lollipop stands. 'I think I forgot my purse.'

Another place she can never come back to.

She stops in the street and digs out her planner from the levee of rice bags in her backpack, realising that the application was due last Friday.

Thank Christ.

No sign of Banjo or Pippa in the window at Hardimans. A group of grey-haired locals – a book club or historical society – are huddled by the fire in the dining room, trying to find meaning on the arthritic side of fifty.

It'll never be her problem.

Rusty iron ripples merge above the Maribyrnong River, giving the night sky an apocalyptic glow. The syrupy water could swallow her whole and freight trains would still unload at the grain silo tomorrow, pigeons lining their carriages, and conveyor belts would still drone in the surrounding factories. The thought of all this industry humming along without her produces a gush of calmness – or objectivity – that she hasn't felt in months.

Her weary form, slipping below the surface . . .

Even Zoe's grief would have its limits. Only her parents would really feel it.

She plucks out her phone and finds the voicemail from Mum yesterday, figuring she'll be able to cope with it in the clarity of this new state:

'Hi, darling daughter, is everything alright?'

Mum's familiar, eighties Aussie cinema twang.

'Listen . . . I didn't really wanna tell you like this, but since you haven't returned any of my calls . . . I just thought you should know that we had to have Sam put down two weeks ago . . .'

Cockatoos, squawking in the background.

'. . . been very sick . . .'

Dozens of different pitches, unbearably loud, morphing into a black ring of noise.

'. . . please call me back, so I know you're alright?'

Anna hurries into a side street, dragging her backpack by its straps, and manages to prop herself against someone's picket fence. She clenches her eyes to cope with the surge of heat that's already making her forehead feverishly wet. Blood curdles in her red-hot ears. Every click of her heart, amplified.

It's beating way too fast.

She tries to decelerate her breathing by searching for a point of focus . . .

The empty balcony of the terrace house across the street, framed by creeper plants, ready for months of winter neglect.

Life always ends in decay, whether it's mental or physical. She could've sworn Sam had another two or three years left in him. His beautiful soft coat and his triangle ears, tongue hanging out expectantly between bared bottom teeth. *Hah, hah, hah, hah, hah, hah, hah*. It kills her to think he hasn't been sleeping by the fire at night, next to Dad, as he guesses his way through the daily quiz: '*What do you reckon, Sam Boy?*' . . .

Suddenly, the perspiration on her temple is a lake, frozen over, making her jaw lock and her teeth kiss.

Everything's gone eerily quiet.

The distant clunk of train carriages.

Muted bullets.

Anna notices the indentations that the concrete has made in her hands. She could press her palms against the asphalt for hours, into the bone-chilling darkness of the morning, until the skin finally gives way. It'd be almost peaceful. She wouldn't even feel the moment that she started to bleed.

ALI

'Enough yapping!' says the manager, wobbling back towards the drive-thru window with her headset on.

'I swear her boyfriend dumped her or something,' says Ali, under his breath. 'She's full-on raging tonight.'

Jasmine grins as she scoops cold chips into Snack Boxes for the drive-thru order. 'If she got a boyfriend, I feel sorry for that man.'

'How's *your* boyfriend going?'

'Check this,' says Jasmine, yanking off one of her plastic gloves so she can tug a necklace out from beneath her collar. She pinches the gold locket on the end, opening it. 'Medusa, man, with snakes in her hair.'

'Do you care, like, about what Mukhtar does?'

'Fiends are gonna fiend,' says Jasmine. 'All he does is help them do it.'

'That's such a cooked way of –'

'I need those Snack Boxes,' yells the manager. Jasmine slips her necklace back under her shirt and packs the meals into a cardboard bag.

'What do *you* do that's so good, huh?'

'At least I don't do that,' says Ali.

'Yeah, coz you couldn't.'

She takes the bag to the manager and drops her shoulder into Ali on her way back to the register.

'See, you ain't gonna do nothing.'

Four students in ugly uni tops stumble up to the counter, completely wasted, like heaps of people from the Irish pub across the road do when they get hungry on their way home.

'Sup, girl?' says Ali, his heart leaping as he recognises the hot Malaysian tutor from homework club. White angel wings, printed on the chest of her jumper.

Her whole crew are looking at him funny.

'Sorry?' she says, in her sarcastic American accent, trying to focus her glazed eyes on him. She doesn't look as sexy wearing contacts instead of her geeky glasses.

'It's Ali . . . from homework club,' he says. 'You've been helping me and Walid with our maths work and shit.'

'Yeah,' she says, doing her cute, self-conscious smile.

Ali scrolls through his brain to remember the rhymes to the song he wrote her:

Prize (ta me)
Kiss me girl
Give ya life (ta me) . . .

One of the scruffy jocks with her has the dumbest rugby jumper on – black, red and yellow stripes – with the name of some stupid college over his pec. He's got no swag at all. It'd be lit to challenge him to a rap battle, right here, right now.

'I didn't see you the last few weeks,' says Ali, feeling his underarms sweating beneath the cotton of his shirt. 'What's been happening with you?'

'Sorry, uni's been hectic,' she says. Her eyes widen as the beeping from the drive-thru fills their silence. Jasmine's giggling, trying to psych him out. 'How've you and Walid been going?'

'Good. We're doing all this crazy training for the jungle,' he says, knowing it'll impress her, even if her friends are acting bored. 'I've also, like, been writing –'

'Ali!' says the manager, covering the microphone of her headset. 'Can I have a word?'

The tutor gives him her cute smile again as he follows the manager over to the Krusher machine. This is the worst cock block ever. Jasmine takes over serving the tutor and her friends. He's got to at least find a way of getting her number before they all bounce, in case her uni work stays hectic.

'You can't socialise with customers on the premises,' says the manager, wedging herself in front of him and forcing him to stare at her fake, fluttering eyelashes. 'If I catch you doing it again, I'll have to give you a performance warning.'

'I'm sorry,' says Ali, looking around her as Jasmine pokes away at the touchscreen.

'Are you listening to me?'

'Yeah, for sure.'

The scruffy jock knows he's got way less of a vibe going on with the tutor than Ali, so he gets psycho territorial, slinging his arm over her shoulder.

'Ali?' the manager's saying.

He ignores whatever else she's telling him off about, so he can see the tutor's reaction. She takes the jock's hand without looking away from the menu board and starts stroking his fingers, like she's done it hundreds and hundreds of times before.

*

Ali kicks the empty Coke bottle in front of Walid and lets him dribble it next, hearing the echoes of the plastic as they pass the torn music posters under Flemington Bridge.

'You were right about me and that tutor,' says Ali, feeling the crusty armpit of his uniform, where his sweat from earlier has dried. 'My bad, man.'

'Did you frighten her too much to come back?'

'I don't think she was coming back, anyway.'

There are at least four or five slashed posters under every new poster.

'How do you feel?' asks Walid.

'Depressed, or something,' says Ali. 'Her boyfriend is, like, the dumbest person ever.'

He sniffles and clears his throat, tasting the petrol-fumed air. The plastic bottle skids along the footpath in front of them, its cap flipping from end to end.

'How do *you* feel?'

'Depressed too, I think,' says Walid.

'Are we gonna get revenge on the pigs for that cartoon, or what?'

Walid exhales sharply, his breath steaming in the night.

'You think that'll end well for anyone?' he asks.

'Who cares, man. Someone's gotta pay.'

Ali boots the bottle into the darkness up ahead. They follow it behind the Community Centre – where they haven't played pool in months – and walk towards the four grainy towers that lurk above the empty park.

'Hey, let me ask you,' says Ali. 'Do you think my cousin and Tyler have been getting freaky?'

As Walid's answering, Ali catches the flicker of a shadow

against the back wall of the Community Centre. There's rustling among the tree trunks to the right of them. Sneakers shifting in tanbark. Some kind of whacked flanking movements.

'What the fu–'

Before he can spit out the sentence, four or five people rush at them and start grappling with Walid. Ali wraps his arms around Walid's waist, trying to drag him away.

'Get off me!' yells Walid.

There's a swarm of puffer jackets, reeking of cologne and hydro smoke. A blow ricochets through Walid's torso, strangling the air out of him. Ali knows that everything's hopeless, anyway, so he tries to shield Walid with his body, feeling almost relieved as knuckledusters drive into his own shoulder blade.

'Help!' he calls out, still clinging on.

An elbow cannons into his nose, snapping his head back with a loud crack. The earth disappears from underneath him. All of a sudden, the sky's upside down. Concrete pillars, blurred by the fuzzy outline of his nose.

There's a rip.

Buttons spill around his ears.

He tries to get back onto his feet, but his rubbery legs fold beneath him – not understanding the messages from his brain anymore – forcing him to prop himself on his knees.

'Walid?' he gargles, hearing the blood in the back of his mouth, drowning out his words.

A shoe connects with his ribs. He heaves for breath, his throat constricting. The noises he's making sound like they're coming from someone else's body. Thick globs leak from his nose. He covers it with his shirt, muffling his snotty breathing as he tries to wedge the bone back into position, squishing loose cartilage and swallowing a mouthful of warm, thick saliva.

He knows, from the lack of movement around him, that whatever's been going down is over. Another form's sprawled next to him among the paste of rubbish and gum leaves on the concrete, totally still, and the high-pitched cackles of laughter are slowly getting further away.

WINTER

LOST LITTLE RIVERS

PAUL

Courage, endurance, mateship and *sacrifice*. AJ's explaining what the words on the plaque mean to him as a copper, but Paul can see the fog of boredom on the kids' faces as they plod along in the mud behind AJ, resenting having to give up another Saturday morning to squeeze onto a bus and hike in the Dandenong Ranges.

More mossy plaques pop up as they climb the tourist trail, commemorating the key battlefronts of the Kokoda campaign – Imita Ridge, Eora Creek, Isurava Village – helping Paul picture what it was like with the actual trail spreading out over the mountains, clothes permanently drenched, flies, leeches, malaria parasites in your blood, blisters on your feet, holding the line with bayonets and beef tins as the earth trembled all around you. Some of the soldiers were the same age as these soft kids, huffing and puffing their way up the steps. Imagine them having to tough it out at Isurava. Or Davey. First hint of a shelling and he'd be off into the jungle, pants around his ankles, shit slopping down his legs, trying to ride the whole thing out.

Walid's the first kid to get spat out the back of the lead group, his slim torso collapsing under the weight of his back-pack. His mate, Ali, slows down to walk beside him.

Paul guzzles some water and waits for them, taking in the skinny mountain ash trees and the ferns swooping over the path up ahead, almost wishing that a group of Japs were crouched among the wash of green, faces smeared with paint, ready to rock and roll.

'Either of you fancy a quick breather?' he asks the boys.

'No thanks,' says Walid, hands curled around the padding of his straps, eyes never leaving the slippery steps.

Paul can hear the crunching in Ali's sinuses as he fights for saliva, puffing out little clouds. His nose still isn't looking too flash, even without the splint he had on for the best part of a month.

'Mind if I ask what happened to your schnoz, mate?'

'It was an accident,' says Ali.

'Don't spose this *accident* had anything to do with Walid here busting a few ribs?'

Both of them try to crank up the pace, but Paul slips in behind them, just like the directing staff used to when they were getting in his ear, urging him to do himself a favour and quit the selection course. Eventually Walid eases off and sheds his backpack on a bench by the side of the path. He's too knackered to object when Paul plants his arse down next to him, all three of them gulping the barky air into their lungs.

Anna hauls herself past them on the outside rail, gaiters swallowing her legs, still refusing to acknowledge his existence.

'Either of you know if that teacher of yours is okay?' asks Paul. 'Seems like she's going through the motions lately.'

'We're not gonna be your friend,' pants Ali.

'Righto, I hear you.'

It's all been a bit melodramatic, her blocking his number

and giving him the silent treatment ever since, as if he's a creep who hasn't got a clue where the line is.

'Let me ask you something else,' he says to Walid. 'We're holding an open day down at the station next week and we'd like to invite the people from your community to take over our mess hall and have a big cook-up for lunch, showing us how you make your food and whatnot. It'd be our shout, obviously. Hopefully it'll give all of us a chance to get to know each other, and to put some of this bad blood behind us.'

'Isn't that what *this* bullshit is about?' asks Ali.

'Fair play,' says Paul, feeling the dampness of the wood seep through to his arse crack. 'We're wanting to connect with the older generation, as well.'

He takes in Walid's furrowed expression as his brain ticks over, hunting for the worst possible angle ever since that stubby holder nonsense.

'So, what do you reckon?'

'It's not my decision.'

'I know, mate, I'm just asking what you *think*.'

Walid guides his boots over the roots that poke out like fossils in the mud.

'If you're only doing it to say you've done it, then people will know, and they won't wanna help you.' He blinks and wipes the sweat from the corners of his eyes. 'It's obvious when you're pretending.'

'Cheers for your honesty,' says Paul. 'I'll make sure we go about it the right way.'

'We'll see,' says Walid.

He hoists fifteen kilos of gear over his shoulder and sets off with Ali, the two of them morphing into the green wash of the forest. It's a pain in the sphincter now that Anna's up ahead, forcing Paul to dawdle along behind tourists, middle-aged dating-app couples and bouncy-bottomed women in Lycra.

Near the summit, he spots the glistening head of an old-timer, the Commissioner himself, waving people through with his hiking pole. Big sweat moons under his arms. About time he showed up to training. He's nowhere near as intimidating out of uniform – in a daggy grey t-shirt and navy footy shorts – without all those microphones jammed in his face. Poor bastard's been bleeding in the papers ever since the sacked coppers in Sunshine took it to the Review Board.

'How're you holding up, young man?' Paul asks him.

'Me?' huffs the Commissioner, his voice a loud whisper. 'I'm not feeling too young at the moment.'

'You'll be right,' says Paul, enjoying having the head honcho on the back foot. 'I heard a double amputee crawled the whole thing a couple of years ago.'

'The Thousand Steps or Kokoda?'

'Kokoda.'

'Don't tell me that!'

A fitness freak flies past them, fluoro pink sneakers and headphones, leaving a sharp punch of BO. The Commissioner shakes his head and breaks into a grin.

'Darryl,' he says, holding out his clammy hand.

'Paul Knowles.'

'You over at Flemington?'

'Yep, six months in.'

Darryl squints through his contacts, sizing him up. 'How you finding it?'

'No complaints,' says Paul. 'Interesting area.'

'Tell me about it.'

Athena emerges from the mist, coaxing a few of the less enthusiastic kids up the mountain. She nods at Darryl with her poker face firmly on and leaves them to it.

'Some of the stuff I've seen makes me thankful I come from good stock,' says Paul.

'That's a great way of looking at it,' says Darryl, taking in the next flight of sludge-lined steps with his steely gaze. 'We need more young blood like you.'

'Any pearls of wisdom?' asks Paul. 'If you were back on the beat, starting from scratch, what would you tell yourself?'

'Many of the estate kids trust you?'

'Probably not,' says Paul.

'Earn one kid's trust,' says Darryl, his voice still barely louder than a whisper. He digs his pole into the undergrowth and sets off slowly, joints already stiff, calves looking like drenched echidnas. 'Really earn it. The rest will sort itself out.'

* * *

Have a nice chat with the boss ya brown nose?

Ass(t) Commissioner Knowles

Bugger off Ath!

Seems like a decent bloke actually

Remains to be seen

* * *

'Only one power point,' says Paul, doing his gruff impression of the old man.

Davey's lip curls as he stares out the window. Best thing about the apartment is the view of the weatherboards across the street. No one's handing them over for rent.

A young couple squeeze into the bedroom and Paul gives them a wide berth – as wide as he can in this cramped shithole – because he hasn't showered since training this morning. You'd swear the place was designed for Oompa Loompas. It's amazing what all these hipsters are willing to put up with, just so they can have coffee and laksa on their doorstep, and spend their weekends sipping ten-dollar smoothies out of jam jars.

'It looked brighter in the photos,' says the woman as her fella guides his phone along the dusty skirting boards. 'We'd need to give it a serious clean.'

'And hang some plants up,' says Mister Grand Designs, as if the bedroom's already theirs.

The first thing Paul would do if he owned this dump would be to strip the carpet and lay new floorboards. Get rid of that wet-dog smell. White hairs everywhere. The ex-tenants haven't even bothered to steam clean the joint.

Davey drifts down the hallway and into the bathroom, probably fantasising about the life of procrastination that Astrid and him would lead. Leftie mates sharing cheese and crackers on the floor, drinking plonk, bouncing ideas off each other that'll never amount to anything. And they think *Paul*'s the one with his priorities back to front. He's surprised Astrid was willing to let him be her proxy after the whole Anzac Day debacle.

'How're the folks going?' he asks.

'Pretty cruisy.'

'They still think I'm a racist?'

'No one ever said that.'

'Didn't have to, mate.'

Paul runs the shower and opens his hand to test the piss-poor water pressure.

'They're pretty keen to bury the hatchet,' says Davey, patting his hair down as he eyes himself in the mirror.

'They've got my number.'

Paul wishes the two of them could've heard what the Commissioner said this morning. *More young blood like you.* It was nice to finally get some appreciation.

'What ended up happening with that teacher you were telling me about at the open mic night?'

'Cheers for reminding me,' says Paul. 'I've been trying not to think about her.'

'That bad, huh?'

'Totally ghosted me. No idea what I did wrong. I think she hits the turps pretty hard, to be honest.'

'Sounds like you dodged a bullet then.'

'Yeah, you're probably right,' says Paul, noticing the blue-green stains around the drain of the tub.

'What?'

'Nah, it's just . . . you know, for whatever stupid reason, sometimes you wanna show someone all the good that's in you, and it's a real fucker when they don't wanna see it.'

They peel back out into the living room. The suited-up prick from Nelson Alexander – the most popular crook in Flemington – is surrounded by new arrivals and is putting on that arrogant grin that real estate agents all have in spades, knowing he's got every single person by the cojones.

Two drop-dead-gorgeous, south-of-the-River sisters excuse themselves as they pass into the hallway. Total economy of movement, like spoilt Eastern bloc tennis players. The taller one gives Davey the eye.

'Jeez, you don't even have to work for it, do you?' says Paul, shaking his head at the little bastard.

'Work for what?'

'Fine, play dumb then. She's probably a bit hygienic for you, anyway.'

Mister Grand Designs paces over, dressed like he's in the bloody Wiggles, and starts airing his grievances with the prick from Nelson Alexander, who isn't too interested in listening.

'So, what do you think of the place?' asks Davey.

'Honestly?'

'Yeah, of course.'

'Living here would do my head in,' says Paul, catching a hit of his own pong. 'You won't wanna take too many of those tantric shits of yours with that draught in the bathroom. But never mind me. Do you reckon you two will apply?'

'We might as well. It's close to uni.'

A1 reasoning. If they think it'll be romantic shivering through winter in their Vinnies rags, then good luck to them.

'How much is this suit asking?'

'Three-seventy a week.'

'Jesus! And you're happy to pay that?'

'I guess so,' says Davey, shrugging. It makes Paul glad that he's chipping away at a mortgage that isn't much more than they'd be shelling out. 'Mum said we should put you down as a reference. She reckons it'll give us more street cred, or whatever, with the real estate agent.'

'Interesting,' says Paul. Suddenly everyone's happy for him to be a copper again. 'What does Astrid think?'

'She's cool with it.'

Bull fucking shit.

'You two gonna offer to pay overs?'

There's a hush when the youngsters notice Paul's police vest, but they quickly start gasbagging again, all hyped up on the green cordial that the volunteers are dishing out. The inside of the Youth Bus is like a nightclub: downlights, psychedelic graffiti and bright orange couches. Half a dozen boys are sprawled on the couches, feet up on cushions, watching *The Voice* on the plasma screen. One of them is Ali and Walid's mate, fat boy, who likes to flash his flabby arse at coppers.

'I could sing better than this skippy,' he boasts.

'Why'd that judge push her button then?'

'She can't sing neither,' says fat boy, letting a fart rip as he breaks into deafening vocal gymnastics.

Paul negotiates the swivel stools in the aisle, passing three kids who're camped around a desktop, yelling out soccer transfer rumours. Prints of Martin Luther King, Nelson Mandela and Cathy Freeman are splashed along the walls: the idols the Salvos wish these kids had, instead of the gangster rappers they're always listening to.

A few familiar-looking youngsters from the school are

braving the cold outside the Community Centre, joking around with volunteers as they queue for sausages.

Male volunteer in a fisherman's beanie's standing next to a boy who's playing basketball on an Xbox. The kid's roughing up the controller. A yellowish hue sweeps across his forehead, revealing rows of wavy, horizontal scarring.

'How's it going?' Paul asks the volunteer.

'Good, brother,' chirps the volunteer, as if they go back decades.

He smooths the chin of his designer stubble and resettles his beanie. Serious born-again vibe. Probably on the straight and narrow now, trying to atone for whatever's making him so jittery in Paul's presence.

The kid puts up a brick from three-quarter court.

'Any idea what you're doing?' asks born again, crouching down next to him.

'I'm good,' says the kid.

Born again stays crouched next to him, writhing in the aisle as he makes his own sound effects to the game.

'Who do you follow in the NBA?'

The kid stares into the glow of the screen, jamming the buttons, pretending he can't hear anything.

'Easy there,' jokes born again.

Paul leaves them to it, making his way to the crew on the couches. It doesn't take long for fat boy to thumb the tip of his nose and start oinking at him.

'Any of you know what *his* name is?' asks Paul, pointing to the kid who's mashing the buttons on the Xbox controller.

'That's Michael,' says fat boy, smirking to his mates. 'But he thinks he's the fresh prince.'

'And why's that?'

'*Wallah*, you don't know anything,' says fat boy. 'How'd you even pass your police test?'

'Lucky guesses, mate.'

Paul gets a sarcastic thumbs-up from fat boy, who makes a point of repositioning his Adidases on the cushion, daring him to have a crack. Hard to imagine a single sequence of events in this world that'd ever make fat boy trust him.

'GET OUTTA MY FUCKING FACE, MAN!' screams Michael, flinging the controller into the aisle.

Stools swivel as the other kids' eyes converge on the scene, hoping for some action.

'Watch your language!' snaps born again.

'Or what?'

Born again's back stiffens, ready for a dust-up. Some old street persona, clicking into gear.

'Zip it, you two!' yells Paul, quickly covering the distance between them as a couple of volunteers scurry up the steps to see what the commotion's about.

Born again's whispering something to Michael, scorn etched into his face as if something's snapped inside him.

'Quick word,' says Paul, ushering him away.

'Little cunt.'

'Let's give it a rest, I reckon,' says Paul, glancing back at Michael, who's got his arms crossed over his chest, his body in total lockdown.

'You need to learn some *manners*,' barks born again, over his shoulder. 'I was only trying to help you.'

Paul keeps him moving and hands him over to the other volunteers in the crisp air of the car park.

By the time he leaps up the steps and back inside the bus, Michael's just about catatonic on his stool. Hugging his ribs, jaw clenched, squinting into the glare of the screen.

ANNA

'I wasn't aware we were running Bikram yoga classes,' announces Jenny Costello as she enters the sauna-like staffroom, marching straight over to the thermostat.

'I thought I was the only one suffocating,' says Anna.

'How was your weekend?' asks Jenny, poking impatiently at the temperature button.

'Just another relaxing hike in the Dandenongs with fifteen kilos on my back. And yours?'

'Nonstop,' says Jenny, as if surprised – or affronted – by her own self-imposed busyness. She delves into the ribs of the fridge and locates her cup of low-fat yoghurt among the crush of foggy Tupperware. 'Not long now.'

'I know,' says Anna. 'I'd kill for a coffee.'

'Where would you start in this room?'

Anna finds her eyes sliding from Tracy to Linda, serviette balanced in her palm as she scoffs down gluggy Woolworth's mud cake.

'I suppose I should offer my congratulations,' says Jenny.

She clacks over to Linda, who greets her with a decaying, brown-crumbed smile.

Anna retreats to the framed light by the window and

watches them all, having the same stilted conversations they've had hundreds of times before, and will have hundreds of times again. It's frightening to think they spend more time in this environment than around the people they love, or are supposed to love.

'Apologies if today is a little difficult for you,' says Peter, plonking the pillow of his flesh on the seat next to her.

'It's fine. Linda deserves it.'

'That's nice of you to say.'

'No, I mean it,' says Anna, enjoying being the only uninhibited person in the room. 'I think we both know I wouldn't have been the most popular appointment.'

'I hope that didn't deter you from –'

'It didn't, trust me.'

This time next year, when she's overseas, burning her way through her old house deposit, all she has to do is remember the senselessness of interactions like this, how any alternative – no matter how impersonal – is healthier for the soul.

'You know I used to want to be a principal?'

'A noble endeavour,' says Peter, patronising her with one of his phoney smiles. 'And what would you like to be now?'

'I'm still trying to decide,' she says, glancing out the window and watching a dim shadow flit across the roof of the gymnasium. 'Maybe a bird?'

'Each to their own.' He combs his fingers through his hair and leans forwards, checking to make sure that his cloud-coloured shirt is still tucked in. 'I've been meaning to say, I really appreciate your enthusiasm with Tyler. He's lucky to have you on his team.'

'I don't think he has a team.'

Peter sighs and breaks into another phoney smile.

'Has anyone ever told you how difficult it is to give you a compliment?'

Anna lets the observation slowly wash over her, enjoying the ambiguity of her own silence. She can relate to why Tyler lashes out. That urge to send your life hurtling towards oblivion, burning everyone who believes in you, and how there's a strange, dark comfort in it. A comfort that the likes of Peter and Jenny will never understand.

'Miss, can I talk to you about something?' asks Najima, her body slanting against the doorframe of Anna's office.

'Of course, sweetie.'

Anna pulls out the wheelie chair from Linda's desk and offers it to Najima, who avoids leaning against the mesh of the ergonomic backrest.

'Is everything okay?'

'Kind of,' says Najima.

She slides closer to Anna's desk, bringing with her a rosy aroma that's infinitely nicer than the must of manila folders.

'What is it?'

'You know Kadra, yeah?'

Anna nods, feeling a pinch of dread.

'She's been watching some . . . I don't know how to say, like, some extreme videos.'

'What do you mean by *extreme*?'

'Like, really full-on.' Najima's pupils expand, two lenses snapping into focus.

'Are you sure she isn't just watching normal –'

'No, miss!' groans Najima. 'You don't understand. This guy, he says seriously evil stuff.'

'How do you know about all this?'

'Everyone knows. In computer club, we're always, like, kicking back, listening to music, yeah, and Kadra sits in the corner by herself with her headphones on,' says Najima, puffing out her hands and raising them to the ears of her hijab. 'She watches this guy on YouTube, like she's hypnotised. You can tell she's taking instructions in her head about what he wants her to do.'

Anna leans in, staring into Najima's resolute pupils. 'But have you actually heard this man telling her, or any of his viewers, to do anything wrong?'

'Pretty much, yeah,' says Najima. 'One of his things is, like, that it's a crime against God if you don't support Islam. So if you're in a country who's on America's side, then you have to do whatever you can.'

'I hope you know, these are very serious allegations that you're making.'

'You should tell the principal. Or the police.'

'Let's slow down a minute.'

A text chimes through on Najima's sequin-studded phone. She lowers her pupils to scan it.

'Remember when Kadra went schizo at Jazzy in the yard?' says Najima, slotting her phone into her purse. 'They weren't her opinions. She was just stealing this guy's opinions to get angry.'

'There's a difference between –'

'She doesn't even have any friends. Not one, in the whole school. Only her sisters.'

'Maybe you should've been more welcoming?'

'Oh my God. It's got nothing to do with that, miss. I'm trying to warn you. Some of these people, they're like, properly messed up. They do hateful things.'

'Which people?'

Linda barges into the office, unable to hide her disgust at seeing Najima swivelling on her chair.

'I don't get why you don't believe me,' says Najima.

'It's not that,' whispers Anna, peeling away a post-it note from her cluttered desktop. 'Do you know this man's name?'

'Why?'

'So I can have a look for myself.'

Najima scribbles down a long name as Linda lingers over them, reeking like a woollen ashtray.

'You won't understand anything,' says Najima.

She pulls out her phone and starts typing before she even reaches the door.

'What was that all about?' asks Linda, lip recoiling as she reclaims her chair.

'It's a long story.'

'Peter told me he didn't receive an application from you,' says Linda, unashamed of admitting that she's been prying. 'Do you mind if I ask why?'

'No, of course not,' says Anna. 'I decided I've got better things to do with my life.'

At least the look Linda gives her is no longer one of pity.

There's something comforting about the way he rolls his words on his tongue, each one bleeding into the next, as he tries to woo his viewers with his slow, cyclical rhythm. They're certainly not tuning in for the production values. His white hood melts into the upholstery of his armchair. Maybe it's supposed to give him an ethereal quality. God knows how many ASIO databases she'll be on after watching this. Najima was right. It's all gibberish to Anna, except that one word he keeps using – '*kafir*' – which she remembers Kadra spitting at her in the schoolyard.

ALI

Ali stares through the glass, over the floodlit football oval of St. Bernard's, as Walid reads the card with the sport questions on it under his breath, still paranoid that when he opens his mouth to speak, the words will forget to come out. Ali squints to see his own reflection, sliding his fingers along the bridge of his nose. The crookedness of the tip makes the rest of his face look like it's on the wrong angle, but maybe it'll give him street cred once his EP takes off. At least the headaches and the stabbing in his sinuses are happening less often now. He tries to block out another flash of the elbow snapping back into his septum by concentrating all his energy on Kylie's next question:

'What was the name of the first single ever released by Will Smith's daughter, Willow?' she asks, twirling the microphone away from her glossy lips.

Loud whispering spreads through the pavilion as people debate each other's memories.

'Sing some for us!' yells Athena, from the police table.

'Nuh-uh,' says Kylie. 'That song hurts my ears.'

Once the chuckling dies down, Ali listens in to some of the debates at the tables near them. It's amazing how confident people can be about a truth that isn't the real truth at all.

'Everything good?' asks Ali.

'Yeah,' says Walid, but his eyebrows frown into their V shape as he tries to read the card again.

'Screw these people, man.'

'You don't have to talk,' snaps Walid, shoving the card back into his pocket so his sweat doesn't leak through the words.

At the end of the popular culture round, Kylie and Funda collect the answer sheets from each table and start adding up the scores. The teachers' team – *Let Qui-Gons Be Qui-Gons* – sounds like the kind of joke the principal would come up with. He's wasted off sparkling wine, telling a story that's making everyone else at the table laugh, except Ms Kelly.

Two of the really ripped kids from St. Bernard's draw the winners of a raffle, then ask people to bid at something called a 'silent auction', to raise money for some school in Port Moresby that they'll be visiting. The prizes are these big, framed pictures of footy teams and jumpers graffitied in signatures. Adults queue up the front to write their offers, leaving Ali and Walid standing by the window, where they've spent almost the whole night.

'Howdy, strangers,' says Paul the policeman, slapping Ali on the shoulder and forcing Walid to shake his hand. 'You raring to go, mate?'

'I think I drank too much Coke,' says Walid.

'Don't enjoy public speaking much myself. Want a bit of free advice?'

'If you like.'

'Whenever I've gotta give a speech, the only thing I concentrate on is making sure I don't rush,' says Paul. Tyler and Jai are watching them, both mouthing 'snitch' at Walid. 'Doesn't matter how silly it makes you feel, start by talking as slowly as you can. If you do that, she'll be apples.'

Walid nods, trying his best to ignore Tyler and Jai.

'There's nothing worse than some clown racing through the questions while the rest of us have got no idea what they're on about.'

'Okay.'

'And don't look so bloody terrified, mate. In case you haven't noticed, half the people here are already trolleyed. They won't even remember it.'

'Thanks,' says Walid.

'While I've got you two,' says Paul, sneaking a look at Ali's nose, 'does either of you know a kid called Michael?'

'Michael who?' says Ali.

'The prince, or something like that.'

'What did he do?'

'Nothing,' says Paul. 'But you know him?'

'Kind of, yeah.'

'Reckon you could keep an eye on him for me, make sure he stays outta strife?'

'I can't really think about that now,' says Walid, his hand creeping back towards the card in his pocket.

'Fair enough, mate.'

Ms Kelly's having a full-on talk with the principal as he refills his glass with wine. She's the only teacher at the table who hasn't changed outfits since school finished.

'Have you got another minute?' Paul asks Walid, glancing at the police table. 'There's someone I want you to meet.'

'Who?'

'He's a good bloke, trust me.'

Ali follows Paul and Walid through the crowd, weaving between tables piled with glasses. Tyler catches sight of him and glares right into his eyes. They stop at a group of strangers at the back of the pavilion.

'Darryl, this is Ali and Walid,' says Paul, introducing them to the bald old guy with glasses who randomly rocked up to their last hike. 'Walid's the hotshot from training I was telling you about.'

'Pleased to meet you,' says the bald guy, pretty much only paying attention to Walid.

'Darryl's the Chief Commissioner,' says Paul. 'He'll be walking the trail with us.'

It's only now, wearing clothes without sweat stains, that Ali recognises the police boss from TV: the man Walid wants to put on the witness stand.

'You're welcome to pull up a seat,' says the police boss to Walid, looking at the scoreboard and smiling. 'As you can see, we need all the help we can get.'

It's obvious he's important by the way everyone cracks up at what he says, like he's the head of a major record label.

'Walid's hosting the next round,' says Paul. 'He's feeling a bit nervous.'

'Can you give us a few answers?' jokes the police boss.

'No, sorry.'

'Man of integrity, I respect that.'

Walid pats his pocket to make sure the card's still there.

'I'd love to have a chat some time about your experiences growing up in the public housing estate,' says the police boss, leaning closer to Walid and focusing his magnifying-glass eyes on him. 'If that'd be alright with you?'

Ali catches Walid wince and grab at his ribs, right where the crack is from the beatdown they copped.

'Excuse me, Darryl!' says one of the sponsors with pink-painted lips. 'Do you mind if I get a photo for my blog?'

She hands Paul her phone and poses next to the police boss, her whole body stinking of extra-sweet flowers. Paul rotates the phone to squeeze them both into the shot.

'Are you sure the flash went off?' she asks, holding her fake smile.

Ali overhears a conversation next to them where one of the police from training, AJ, is explaining to a woman why the Kokoda Project started:

'Long-term disengagement with local youth,' he says in his dumb Aussie accent.

Disengagement is one of those fake-arse political words that people only use because it sounds clever, but really it has no meaning. Or whatever meaning it has can't possibly be applied to what went down at the towers. Ali wishes the woman listening to AJ talk shit could hear some of the real stories, like how Musa says when you're in the back of a police van, they deliberately drive faster over speed bumps, or how a policeman cracked Mukhtar's front teeth with a torch, and how the only punishment for the policeman who did it was that he had to move to a different station, or how Hassan lost his entire personality in one night for a crime that never even happened . . .

'Jump in, Walid!' Paul's saying.

'Don't be shy,' says the sponsor, trying to wedge Walid between herself and the police boss.

Walid brushes her hand away and hurries past the queue of people writing bids at the silent auction. Ali can tell he doesn't want to be followed. If any of the people queuing up had seen what happened back in the day, they would realise that it was more than *disengagement*. But no one wants to know why they're really here, getting wasted and answering questions about celebrities. They just want to give away their money for jumpers and photographs that they don't even need, so they can drive home to their families feeling good about themselves.

ALI

'Slow down!' gasps Musa, rustling inside his oily paper bag. 'I'm trying to eat my breakfast.'

'You're making us late,' says Walid.

'Who gives a fuck?'

'Me!'

As Musa munches on his hash brown, he starts singing his favourite Kendrick track about being a crack baby, putting on a silly high-pitched voice like he's been sucking on one of those special gas balloons.

'You know you're a terrible rapper?' says Ali.

'Nah, my flow's just too real for you,' says Musa. He hums the second verse of the track because he doesn't know the lyrics. 'Anyway, I have some important news.'

'Yeah, what?'

'I'm getting deported.'

Young'uns in Debney Meadows uniforms are shrieking as they try to shove each other into puddles in the park.

'How can you get deported?' asks Walid.

'My mum organised it.'

'Where's she sending you?'

'Malaysia, man.'

'Who the fuck lives in Malaysia?' asks Ali.

'My uncle,' says Musa, letting his paper bag float away in the breeze. 'It's all good. You know what Malaysian bitches look like. They're crazy fit. Mm-hmm!'

'Why's your mum deporting you?'

'I think Miss Kelly said some fucked-up shit to her.'

The first bell's echoing beyond the brick terraces in the distance, but for once Walid doesn't seem worried by it.

'Did you argue with your mum?'

'You can't argue with her. Once she decides something, that's it. Conversation closed.'

'That's full-on,' says Ali.

'Yeah, I guess,' says Musa, as if he doesn't care about moving his life for the third time. He spots Jasmine, Najima and Kylie leaving Red Rooster and breaks into his Kobe strut. 'But the good news is: I don't have to try in school anymore.'

'When did you ever try?' asks Walid.

'Far out, you sound like my mum.'

Musa licks the crumbs off his fingers and puts on his silly gas balloon voice as they catch up to the girls, starting the Kendrick track all over again.

'Nah, man, they're normal clothes police,' says Jai, watching the two serious-as-fuck-looking women who're leaving Ms Costello's office. 'They're taking statements coz of that *loco* shit Kadra put on Facebook.'

'Immigration dress like that, too,' says Binh.

'Far out,' says Ali. 'Kadra's totally getting deported.'

'You'd know all about that,' says Jai.

'Piss off, man, I'm pure.'

'Not as pure as me,' says Jai, thumping his chest.

Ms Costello leads Kadra and her sisters past the line of staring students, pretending she doesn't notice, before hurrying them out the side exit of the building.

'Miss, can you just tell us what they did?' asks Ali.

'It's none of our business,' says Ms Kelly, calmly, turning her attention back to Funda, who's wiping her nose on the sleeve of her school jumper, staring at the nurse's office. 'It'll be over before you know it, sweetie, I promise.'

'Everything's all good, cuz,' says Ali, wrapping his arm around Funda.

'I hate needles,' she sniffles. 'I think I'm gonna spew.'

That's the last thing she needs to do. She's lost a crazy amount of weight lately. More than just from training. The deep, diagonal lines across her cheeks make her eyeballs seem always tired.

'What were you and Walid snitching to the pigs about last night?' asks Tyler, getting right in Ali's ear. 'I heard you're, like, police informers now.'

'Careful,' says Jai. 'He could be wearing a wire.'

'You cunts are bigger dogs than me,' says Ali.

Tyler runs his hand over the prickles on his scalp and puffs out his malnourished chest, like he did to his junkie stepdad in the foyer of the flats.

'There are more dogs in your family,' he whispers, a hint of amusement in his voice.

'What the fuck's *that* sposed to mean?'

Funda flicks Ali a psycho look, her eyeballs massive and bloodshot. She's got an even weirder vibe with Tyler lately.

To stop her panicking about them beefing, Ali turns around and faces the drawn blinds of the nurse's office, trying to block out whatever smack Tyler's still talking.

More dogs in your family . . .

It literally makes no sense.

Walid walks out of the nurse's office, peeling back a piece of fluff on his arm where there's a dark prick of blood.

'How much did it hurt?' asks Funda.

'Not that much,' says Walid.

Tyler's grinning, growling under his breath.

'Next, please!' calls the nurse.

She tells Ali to sit on the bed near her desk while she gets his Kokoda needle ready. Adrenaline starts to spread through his muscles as he unbuttons his shirt, making his heart thump against the cage of his chest.

'You'll feel a pinch, followed by a brief discomfort,' says the nurse, wetting his bicep, bored from saying the same thing so many times.

As she raises the needle, Ali turns his face towards the wall, concentrating on a chart of a purple human body: blood, bones and organs, all squished together. Suddenly, there's this intense pressure at the top of his arm, where it doesn't feel like there should be any pressure.

'Not long to go,' says the nurse.

Ali accidentally looks. The needle skewering his flesh is as thin as the sticks of lead that he feeds into his art pencils. His head starts racing. He squeezes his eyes shut, feeling like he's plunging into a dark, bottomless river . . .

Someone's saying his name, pressing their hand against his forehead.

The firmness of their fingers on his skin brings him back to the last time he ever saw his mum. Her expression when she briefly stopped cramming clothes into her wheelie bag to touch his face. Making time stand still. He sees the look clearly now, even though it meant nothing as it was happening. Panic is what she felt. For him to have a life, he understands, she had to give hers away.

Walid rattles his knuckles against the wire door that's already vibrating to the bass of the music. Ali recognises the mid-nineties beat with its tinny, electronic snare: 'Hit 'Em Up'. Tupac's going schizo, calling out Biggie, Mobb Deep and the whole Bad Boy crew, pretty much daring them to come at him.

'Maybe there's a special knock or something?' says Ali.

'Let's just wait,' says Walid, checking the corridor, where a pile of mattresses is blocking their escape down the stairs.

The only difference between this tower and the One Tweezy tower is that they have green paint peeling from the window frames here, instead of pink. The stale smell, the gaps in the walls, even the sloping corridors that make you feel like the whole building's sinking are all the same.

'This is the kind of stuff you should tell the police boss about,' says Ali.

'What?'

'Like, the stuff that happens in these kind of flats.'

'He already knows.'

Walid thumps his palm against the doorframe. This time someone stomps to the door, but they stay standing behind the wire, so Ali and Walid can't see them.

'Can I help you?' croaks a deep, Dre-like voice.

'We're here to see Michael,' says Walid.

'Who's Michael?'

'This is his crib, isn't it?'

The door gets nudged open. Mukhtar pokes his head out from the darkness. 'He's not home.'

'Do you know when –'

'What do you fucking want, man?'

A familiar sniff of cologne escapes through the wire as chicks' squealing echoes from deep within the flat.

'Is Jazzy partying with you?' asks Ali.

Mukhtar's crocodile eyes slide slowly across the logo of Ali's KFC uniform. He cracks his knuckles under his chin. 'You should go now, you feel me?'

'Tell Michael I wanna talk,' says Walid.

Mukhtar stares him down, biting his lip and giving Walid a glimpse of his chipped front teeth. Yassin's husky laughter erupts in a nearby bedroom. As the latch of the door clicks back into place, a girl moans in pleasure. Or maybe in pain.

TYLER

'Sup, bro?' grins Shannon, leaning against one of the palm trees out the front of the flats, wearing sunnies, even though the sky is grey. 'There're Obamas everywhere in your hood.'

'What's an Obama?' asks Jai.

Shannon ignores him. 'You good to hang?'

'We've got this dinner thing tonight,' says Tyler. 'We're meeting an Aussie soldier from Kokoda.'

'Where is it?'

'Some RSL,' says Jai.

'I'll drive you,' says Shannon, pretending not to notice that Jai's Aboriginal. 'Wanna chill with us?'

'Yeah, too easy.'

They follow Shannon to the Commodore he put a new body kit on last summer. It's sweet as cruising along Racecourse Road with the windows down, pumping Metallica, the guitar riff thrashing out of the speakers like an angry anaconda.

'The American army blast this on repeat whenever they wanna get confessions out of terrorists,' shouts Shannon.

'Serves those camel fuckers right,' says Tyler.

He sees Binh walking towards the North Melbourne flats and yells, 'WHAT'S UP, POWER POINT?'

Binh pretends not to hear him.

Shannon cuts through Kensington, swerving onto the wrong side of the road to overtake people driving like pussies, and parks behind the hill at the Arden Street footy oval.

'Ever had a compression session?' he asks, turning to Jai in the back seat.

'Yeah,' says Jai, 'with my stepmum.'

'You can go first then.'

Shannon pulls out his billy and a rusty little tin where you're supposed to keep fishing bait.

'Has Ty told you how we roll?' asks Shannon, packing a cone for Jai, pretending it's just a casual question.

'What do you mean?'

'Never mind,' says Shannon, winking at Tyler. There's no way he'd ever say shit to anyone about what they do.

Shannon finishes pressing the mix and hands Jai his billy.

'For fuck's sake!' he says. 'You've gotta cover the hole with your thumb.'

Jai lights the cone and slurps the smoke up the old bottle, making the murky water bubble like a spa. As he's exhaling, he has a massive coughing fit.

'Baby lungs,' says Shannon, shaking his head.

He grabs his billy and uses a bent safety pin to unblock the cone, emptying soot onto the cans of Woodstock and Red Bull around Tyler's feet.

'Man, that shit's potent,' croaks Jai, finally able to breathe again.

'Your turn, bro,' says Shannon.

'Nah, my throat hurts.'

'Don't be such a pussy.'

Shannon forces the billy into Tyler's hands.

'Come on, man!' says Jai, booting the back of his seat.

'Just one cone,' says Shannon. He takes off his sunnies and clutches Tyler's shoulder. 'You'll hardly feel anything, bro.'

'Fine,' says Tyler.

He snatches the rusty tin and packs a small cone, hoping it'll help him stop picturing what Funda's uncle looked like as he slobbered all over her body.

'More than *that*,' says Shannon.

Tyler sprinkles more of the mix in, trying to mostly pick hairs of tobacco. As long as he crunches out extra push-ups and sit-ups in the morning, the smoke will basically disappear from his lungs. He brings the flame up to the cone, watching as little pieces of bud darken.

'Pull harder!' says Shannon.

There's a tickle at the back of Tyler's throat.

'Nice one, bro, rip the whole cone!'

The smoke has nowhere to go. His lungs feel like they're about to explode, so he swallows and starts burping smoke back out. As Jai cracks up behind him, Tyler hears himself heaving for air, almost like he's outside his own head.

'Dude, where're you going?' yells Shannon, seeing him groping at the doorhandle.

Tyler manages to prise the door open and stumble to the bottom of the hill. He crouches over the grass, clenching his eyes shut so he doesn't have to see the acid that's surging up and out of his own throat. Blurry circles leap around in the darkness. A horn's blaring, stabbing into the side of his skull. Everything's spinning. Another surge of acid strangles his windpipe. Dying couldn't possibly be worse than this.

'TY, YA DICKHEAD!'

He opens his eyes and feels the breeze cool his sopping chin. Staring at the milky spatter on his hiking boots, he knows that whatever line there ever was that separated him from Mum is forever gone. And it might as well have never existed.

'Can you hear that?' asks Jai, his eyes all Chinese.

'What?'

'Shh, listen!'

Jai's right. Tingly sounds are pinging through the hallway of the RSL. It's like being trapped inside an arcade game.

'This way,' says Tyler.

He follows the sounds past posters of some fat-arsed singer with massive sideburns and glass cabinets full of war medals and photos of old farts. The black-and-white faces in the photos are freaky to look at, especially their eyes. Staring into your soul. As if they knew you'd someday be looking at them, thinking this exact thing.

Somehow, the old farts have all transported in time into the room where the tingly sounds are coming from. Slouched on stools in front of machines, constantly feeding coins in, clutching paper cups. Fluoro lights keep buzzing and zapping, releasing codes inside high frequencies that only the depressed old farts can understand. Pyramids, dingos, cherries. Every time you try to concentrate on the sounds coming from one machine, another one lets out a totally different burst of code.

'This is trippy,' says Jai.

'I know.'

'Whoa, check *that* out!'

Golden rainbows of coins are spewing on one woman's screen, sparkling and melting into each other in glitchy half-circles.

Real-life coins start pelting out of her machine.

Pup, pup, pup, pup, pup, pup, pup . . .

She isn't even amped.

Playing old-school Japanese games like *Double Dragon* or *Street Fighter II* right now would be lit.

'I've gotta get outta here,' says Jai.

'Whatever,' says Tyler, kind of relieved.

There are more depressed old farts in the bistro, eating rubbery-looking meat with their families. Their faces are purple and splotchy. Most of them probably have those bags you shit in when you can't shit by yourself anymore. Having to carry your own shit around with you all day would be embarrassing. It'd be better to just be dead.

'Where are they?'

'Who?' asks Tyler.

It's whacked. He keeps forgetting what's supposed to happen next. Dozens of knives and forks are trapped inside his head, scraping against the walls of his skull. You never even think about how loud cutlery is.

'People are staring at us, man.'

'Yeah, I know,' says Tyler. 'Chillax.'

He spots a group of tables that've been joined in the corner of the bistro. The sponsors, the pigs and the St. Bernard's yuppies are sitting together, pretending to be a happy family.

'Over there!'

They go on the end table to avoid the adults. Walid keeps tapping on the brown wood with his knuckles, trying to listen in to other people's conversations. Binh stares at his glass of Coke, watching bubbles race towards the ice cubes on the surface. It must be full-on for him to come to a place like this, knowing the horrible things that the old soldiers are thinking about him and his ancestors.

'Evening, boys,' says Athena, smiling from the corner of her mouth. Unlike at training, her hair's all spiky and shiny, like she just got out of the shower. 'Either of you want a drink?'

'Yeah, Fanta,' says Jai.

'I'm good,' says Tyler, trying to talk in his normal voice.

'You sure?' frowns Athena. 'It's on the house.'

'Uh-huh.'

She does her weird as smile again, thinking she's actually done something good with her life. Just imagining a drink makes it impossible to swallow. Hundreds of dry scales on the surface of his tongue, begging for only one drop of liquid. But you can't accept anything from a pig.

Jai cracks him on the arm. 'Are you listening?'

'Yeah, what?'

'That cop, man. She can tell.'

'What's she gonna do?'

'She could arrest us and your bro could get . . .'

Ali and Funda rock up, wedging themselves between the adults and the St. Bernard's dicks. It doesn't make sense how the two of them still hang out. Funda should never want to see Ali, or his sick fuck of a dad, again.

'Enjoy!' says Athena, leaving Jai's Fanta on the table.

Ms Kelly walks over to Ali and asks him to take off his Hornets cap. Ali laughs in her face.

'Come on, mate,' says the pig with initials instead of an actual name. 'You're representing all of us tonight.'

'Why does it matter?' says Ali.

'The rules are the rules,' says the pig.

Funda clutches the cotton ball on her arm and gives Tyler an intense as look that nearly makes him shit his pants.

'Ali, please!' says Ms Kelly.

'Far out,' he says, ripping off his cap.

'Thank you,' says the pig, obviously not meaning it.

Some seriously old couple have arrived, wearing clothes from five hundred years ago. The dude's face is basically halfway between a human and a zombie's, like a messed-up truth is stuck inside it. He must be the soldier that fought at Kokoda. Paul the pig keeps sucking up his arse, pretending to pay attention to every boring thing he says.

'She just winked at me, man,' says Jai.

'Who?'

'That cop who's into chicks.'

Athena's facing a totally different direction, checking out the zombie dude's war medals.

'You're paranoid.'

'Nah, she's totally fucking with me.'

'Whatever,' says Tyler, his throat all raspy. 'Wanna chill somewhere else then?'

'For sure.'

The darts room's the only place in the whole RSL that isn't packed with people who're nearly dead. They try to play a game, not that either of them have a clue what the rules are. It's pretty much impossible to throw a bullseye. Half the darts they peg don't even stick to the shitty old board.

'Watch this!' says Tyler.

He pitches one with his eyes closed and almost knocks a trophy off a ledge above the board. He grabs another dart and lets it rip at the ceiling, spearing right into the plaster. Jai clutches his crotch, his teeth covered in orange fur.

'Do you think they've . . .' says Jai, pausing to wipe his blazed eyes.

'Yeah, *what*, you dickhead?'

'They might have cameras.'

'Who cares?'

Tyler follows the ceiling dust sprinkling under the lights in slow motion. Tiny, never-ending grains, spiralling into his lungs.

'What's up with you guys?' asks Funda, startling him. He didn't even hear footsteps in the room.

'Nothing,' he says.

'Can we talk?'

'If you want.'

'Alone,' says Funda, tilting her straightened hair towards Jai, who's tripping out as he stares at the pixelated tiles. They're forming these insane, alien-headed patterns with eyes, noses and actual antennas. 'So?'

'Huh?'

'Oh my God,' says Funda. 'I need to talk to you.'

'Yeah, let's talk here.'

She looks at him the same way she did just before they started making out in her bed. Pupils dilating, searching for fuck knows what in his eyes. His throat starts tightening. Too much ceiling dust must've got in. He tries to clear it, but there isn't anywhere near enough saliva.

'Okay then,' says Funda. 'So, like, why don't you say hi to me anymore?'

Pressure's building behind his eye sockets. Electrodes, wired to his head, like some brutal interrogation technique. The image of Ali's dad – all fat and hairy-chested, lurking over Funda – keeps trying to creep into his mind.

'You can't just ignore me.'

Slot machines tingle away in the distance. Tyler's jealous of the old farts playing them, switching their brains off to live in a world where, at least for the night, there don't have to be any consequences for all the fucked-up shit they know.

'Please, Ty –'

'Don't . . .' is all he manages to choke out, knowing that if he tries to say anything else – even just one more word – his whole face will crumble.

*

PAUL

Kylie passes Paul two tiny metal discs over her bowl of barely touched chips, hardly pausing to look at them.

'Here,' he says, lowering the discs into Tyler's paws, 'take a gander at these.'

'What are they?'

'See that old-timer over there,' says Paul, pointing at the digger who's letting AJ chew his ear off, 'these were his dead meat tickets over in Kokoda. Every time a soldier was killed, his mates would leave one of these in the poor bugger's mouth, so the clean-up brigade could identify him.'

Tyler runs his thumb over the numbers that're engraved in the metal. The gravity of what's in his hand sweeps across his face, making him look almost sincere for once.

'You can see his blood type,' says Paul. 'In case he was injured and couldn't talk to the medical corps.'

'Hold up,' says Tyler's sleepy sidekick, 'that dude seriously fought in the war?'

'Affirmative.'

'How did he, like, survive?'

'Malaria,' says Paul. 'About a month in, he collapsed on the trail and they ended up carrying him to Owen's Corner. Took nearly two weeks. Once his fever broke, they popped him on the hospital ship back home.'

Tyler's red-webbed eyes are fixed on the digger, who's got piercing eyes himself. Almost the same grey as his suit jacket, dark veins snaking across his sagging cheeks.

'You're looking a bit pale, mate.'

'I've got a cold,' says Tyler.

'Bugger,' says Paul, sensing Tyler's finally on the cusp of dropping his act. In a weird way, the act is what gives him the perfect profile for the Special Forces; combativeness, that rogue element and a deadbeat family, which is where Paul figures his own chances bit the dust. They want you to fight as if you've got no one to come back to. 'Listen, I've been meaning to ask how everything's going on the home front?'

'Fine.'

'Don't know if I believe you.'

Tyler's too busy checking to see who's eavesdropping on them to hear him.

'Sure it's only a cold?'

'Yep.'

'Righto,' says Paul.

Kylie shrivels her powdery nose as she hands him the digger's emergency rations pack. Seventy years of rust eat into what was once a rich lick of green.

'What did he keep in that?' asks Tyler's sidekick.

'Nothing you boys would wanna eat,' says Paul, having a good chuckle as he surveys Kylie's bowl. 'There isn't much time for hot chips when you're getting hammered with artillery.'

'How come you know so much about war?' asks Tyler.

'I had a crack at enlisting about five years ago. Obviously didn't quite work out.'

Tyler squints at the smear of lights on the ceiling, digging his nails into the fold behind his elbow.

'Are you allowed in the army if you've got eczema?'

Won't dare take his eyes away from the lights, in case he accidentally shows that he gives a shit about something.

'Highly unlikely,' says Paul.

'Why?'

'Increased risk of infection.'

The colour's finally returning to Tyler's face. His nostrils flare and his freshly shaved head jolts, eyes sharpening into their familiar leer.

'Sorry, mate.'

'As if I give a fuck.'

Speakers crackle above them. A hush falls over the bistro as an old-timer recites the nightly Ode a pinch too close to a microphone. The digger bows his head, puffing out the sand-bags of his cheeks. He loses control of his lips and grabs his wife's hand, his bruised knuckles sinking into the quicksand of their entwined flesh.

A low growling starts up next to Paul.

He gives Tyler a nudge and raises his finger to his lips.

It doesn't do any good. He peers down and sees Tyler eyeballing Ali, baring his bottom teeth as he growls.

'Shh!' whispers Paul.

But Tyler's beyond giving a stuff, if ever he did.

'HEY, ALI . . .' he shouts, waiting for all eyes in the bistro to find him. Anna launches out of her chair, realising he's on a kamikaze mission. Her ungainly strides have got a snowball's hope in hell of stopping him. 'DO YOU KNOW WHAT THEY DO TO KID-FUCKERS IN PRISON?'

AJ helps Anna escort the pink-eyed punk out, as he grins for everyone who's still staring.

The digger's reaction is the worst. Barely a reaction at all. Just a nod, more to himself than anyone else. Almost as if he's figuring out, in real time, that this shitshow is the world that became of it all.

PAUL

'Everything okay, champ?' asks Paul.

'Not really,' whimpers a lanky red-headed kid, shielding his eyes from the early-morning drizzle as he looks up from the gutter. It's hard to reconcile him with the half-cut hipster from a few hours ago, full of bravado, thinking he was charming his way out of a noise complaint.

'Why don't we get you outta the rain?' says Athena.

Big red stands up and opens a heavy iron gate, leading them inside the house. Varnished floorboards and high, arched ceilings. It'd have to be worth at least a couple of million.

'I'm gonna get in so much shit,' says big red, his voice monotone with shock.

A handful of his mates are huddled in the study, looking up at Paul and Athena with drained, untrusting faces, as if they're being rescued from months in captivity.

'We'll need you all to come with us,' says Athena.

The kids silently slip into formation.

'Sorry, can I get either of you a drink?' asks big red as his mates funnel into the open-plan kitchen.

'We're right, thanks,' says Athena, lingering at the benchtop to inspect the jigsaw of glass where a huge frame's been smashed. 'Nice pad you've got here.'

'My parents own it,' says big red, staring at a naked nail that's jutting out of the wall. 'They're in Europe.'

Athena winces. 'So what happened?'

'Me and my sister were having a few drinks with our friends for the end of semester, and I guess . . . I'm not a hundred per cent sure, but I think someone must've left the front door open or, like, maybe . . .' says big red, crushing his freckly hands together as his voice trails off.

'I know, mate,' says Athena. 'Take your time.'

'It happened seriously fast. We were dancing and this group of, like, basically kids burst in here, singing over the top of our tunes. I thought they were joking. I just remember glass exploding everywhere, and screaming . . . then they lined us up over there,' he says, pointing towards the electric fireplace. 'They were threatening us with baseball bats, unless we gave them our phones and our wallets. I was trying not to make them get angrier, because they didn't have any fear.'

Paul starts scribbling the story into his notebook:

0645|drinking w uni friends, set upon by young group w baseball bats, paintings smashed, phones + wallets stolen

'And they stole some of our mum's jewellery,' says a girl with yellow-green eyes, who must've snuck up next to him. She rummages under the sink and pulls out a dustpan, determined to put their privileged puzzle back together.

'I'll get you to hold off on that,' says Athena, copping a

glare for her troubles. 'How many of them do you reckon there were?'

'Seven, that I saw,' says the girl.

'So you got a good look at them?'

'Yeah,' says big red, swaying on his stool as he watches storm clouds roll in through the retractable doors. 'They weren't wearing masks or anything.'

'Any idea who they were?'

'We used to go to school with one of them,' says the sister, who must be big red's twin. 'He was in the year below us, before he left. My friends thought he was hot.' She shifts the brush in her hand and turns her catlike glare on Paul. 'He was acting crazy tonight. Not like I remember him. But it was still him, for sure.'

'Either of you remember his name?' asks Athena.

Big red's stool could do with a squirt of WD-40. Seems more intent on watching heavy raindrops bruise the concrete of his folks' courtyard than answering Athena's question.

'Mukhtar,' says the sister, her eyes scrolling down Paul's notebook. 'I don't know his surname. He didn't recognise me, even when he was taking my phone. I didn't wanna say I knew him coz he kinda looked like he wanted to kill someone.'

Excruciating pain in his chest, like the black earth's going to erupt through it, as they commando crawl under barbed wire. Human slugs. Wriggling below the water's surface, taste of horse manure in his throat, directing staff simulating grazing fire. Sound dulling, elbows in quarter speed on the slimy puddle bed. The rush of oxygen and the splash of limbs all around him.

Swallowed whole again, rubber band lungs about to snap, and still that dull noise from above: thud, thud, thud, thud, thud, thud, thud . . .

She's bucketing down outside. Takes a few seconds for Paul to wrap his head around this reality. His phone's going berserk on the bedside table. It can't be the alarm already. Feels like he only just nodded off.

No Caller ID

If it's another Indian telemarketer, they're going to get a rocket and a half.

'Hello,' he grumbles, clearing the gunk from his eyes.

'Is this Paul Knowles?'

'Nah, it's the Pope.'

'I was hoping to speak –'

'Of course it's Paul Knowles.'

You'd swear it's ball bearings, pelting on the roof.

'My name's Rita,' she recites, in a husky voice. Few too many darts at corporate retreats over the years. 'I'm from Nelson Alexander. How are you this morning?'

'I'm intrigued.'

The little bastard must be in with a sneaky chance.

Another cyclist whistles along the path beside the old storm-water drain, dressed like he's in the Tour de France, and dings a few of the kids for playing chicken.

'None of that, boys!' yells Athena.

Fat lot of good it does. Ali forces the next cyclist to veer out of his way, almost colliding with an oncoming jogger. The smart-arse bounces in his boots as he high-fives Kylie.

Anna apologises to Athena, knowing full well what she's making of it.

'Want me to go and give him an earful?' asks Athena.

'I'll have a word with him later.'

Anna just doesn't want the two of them to be left alone. She sweeps the hair out of her eyes, still refusing to acknowledge Paul's existence. It hurts even more, knowing she spent so many years with that moustachioed poser who pops up in every second one of her MySpace snaps. Smiling sideways in his high-collared shirts and his old newsboy caps. The kind of bloke who'd let you know exactly how special he is, or thinks he is.

'Well, this is a barrel of laughs, isn't it?' says Athena.

A train blares past, like a horizontal rocket, heightening the awkward silence in its wake.

'No Tyler this arvo,' says Paul, pretending he's oblivious to being blacklisted.

'Tyler's no longer part of the program,' says Anna, her tone matching the gloom of the swampland up ahead, 'which is what he wanted, I suspect.'

'Blessing in disguise,' says Athena. 'You need team players over there.'

Paul catches an enraged twinge in Anna's eye – first flicker of life from her in weeks – before she sweeps her hair again and resets her expression.

'You okay with Tyler getting the chop?' asks Paul.

'It is what it is,' says Anna, shrugging.

Philosophy degree imminent.

The three of them plough on in the blustery silence. Paul keeps picturing Tyler grinning as he was being tugged out of the bistro, like he was happy he'd thrown it all away. Full of the fire that, for whatever reason, isn't inside Davey. Somehow, he feels more affinity for Tyler than his own kid brother.

'Great way to spend your winter,' says Athena, nodding as they approach a homeless camp under the rail bridge. Faceless figures are sprawled among mattresses and calico bags, braving the icy wind that's whistling in from the Bay.

A shabby-looking bloke hobbles out onto the bike path and goes up to Binh and Walid, cupping his hands. They manage to get past him, but Ali and a bunch of St. Bernard's boys crowd around the poor bugger, forcing him to backpedal, until he runs out of concrete. The little pricks stand there, pissing themselves, as he loses his footing and tumbles into the creek bed.

'Fucking parasites!' hisses Athena, chasing after the boys.

Paul slips off his backpack and shuffles down into the scrub by the water. Athena's letting the boys have it. The poor bugger looks more confused than anything else, lying on a bed of wet weeds, his whiskery jeans smeared with mud.

'I'm so sorry,' calls Anna.

As Paul's extending his hand to help the old-timer get to his feet, he realises who it is: Mister Wheelchair Bandit himself. All the sympathy he had goes straight out the window.

'Cheers, bud.'

'Reckon you're good to go?' asks Paul, looking the prick in the eyes without getting a hint of recognition back.

'No broken bones,' he cackles, showing off his missing chompers, breath like turpentine. He bends down gingerly, plucking at a litter of ciggie butts he must've spilt. Once he's done, Paul takes his scabby hand and hauls him back up onto the bike path, near where Anna's waiting. 'Don't spose either of you could spare any change?'

Anna digs a few coins out of her backpack and gives them to him.

'Thanks love, you're an angel.'

An angel, righto.

The old-timer hobbles back to his camp, dissolving into the darkness between pillars. Paul gets out his water bottle and rinses his hands. He feels the wind nipping at his wet skin. Even one night under the bridge would be a bloody ordeal. At a set point, the old-timer's way of life probably becomes its own punishment.

ANNA

'Did you get to interview the smuggler?' asks Anna.

'It was a fucking nightmare,' says Zoe, her cheeks even more tanned since her trip to Indonesia. 'He refused to talk until he got paid, and then what he did end up saying was basically unusable. We're pretty sure someone else got to him first.'

'So where does that leave you?'

'Back where we started.'

'Sorry, babe.'

A young, slick-haired waiter brings out a plate of charred flatbread with dips and a Cypriot superfood salad sprinkled with pomegranate seeds. He glances at Zoe, running his fingers along the logo of his navy-blue apron, before scurrying back towards the kitchen.

'Was there time for any sightseeing?' asks Kate.

'I wish,' says Zoe. 'All I did was yell at people. Or that's what it felt like.' She spoons the salad onto her plate, breaking their deadlock of politeness. 'Have you set a date yet, Katie?'

'We have,' says Kate, showing off the pale pink arches of her gums. 'That's one thing I wanted to talk to you about. The church is booked for March the ninth next year, so please put it in your diaries.'

Anna feels a rush of relief as she nods, knowing she won't be in the country then, or for the hens' night, where they'll probably end up drinking blushing bride cocktails while taking pole-dancing classes to be white, middle-class naughty.

'How's the personal trainer going?' asks Zoe.

'Very well, thank you. I'm under seventy kilos for the first time since high school, so no dessert for me tonight.'

'Is your trainer a hunk?'

'*She* is a hunk, yes.'

As if Ryan the Renovator would let her have one-on-one sessions with a man.

'And how about you?' asks Kate, accepting the salad bowl from Anna. 'You must be getting excited about your trip?'

'Excited isn't the right word.'

'What *is* then?'

'Terrified, maybe.'

'You'll be fine,' says Zoe, unable to hide her boredom with Anna's apprehension.

'I don't think I could do it,' says Kate.

Zoe slyly raises an eyebrow. The image of Kate trying to squat in the jungle, or bathe in a river with dozens of strangers, diligently covering her private parts, threatens the numb clarity Anna's felt ever since she resolved to quit.

'What's so funny, Zo?' asks Kate.

'Nothing.'

Anna surveys the restaurant to stop herself succumbing to laughter. It's such a *Kate* place. Couples in their late thirties and early forties who probably read a gushing review on *Broadsheet*, assuring themselves they're cultured because they're paying seventy dollars a head to take banal photographs of every single course of a celebrity chef's banquet.

'How's work?' asks Zoe.

'Complicated,' says Anna, feeling the silent emissions of their judgement.

'I thought everything was going well,' says Kate.

'It is, I guess.'

'So?'

Anna spoons in a mouthful of super salad, hating herself for enjoying the explosion of the pomegranate seeds. 'We've got a, ah . . . let's just call it a delicate situation.'

'Ooh, do tell!' says Kate.

'This stays between us, right?'

'Of course.'

Luckily, Zoe's baby-faced waiter – fine arts student vibe – has finally stopped circling.

'There are these three sisters originally from Somalia who enrolled at the school earlier this year. One of them, Kadra, is in my year eleven EAL class. We're not exactly on speaking terms at the moment, which is an entirely different story. She can be quite *firm* in her beliefs, if you follow my drift. An older cousin sponsored the girls out here, but I suspect she didn't have a clue what she was signing herself up for.'

Zoe's nodding ravenously, no doubt sensing a story she could screen at MIFF next year.

'I didn't find out until a few days ago, but apparently the cousin has been marching into the school lately, complaining to the principal that no one prepared her for any of this, and saying she doesn't know how to handle the –'

'Are they Sunni Muslims?' asks Zoe.

'Yeah, I mean, I think so. But one of the strange things is how much animosity there is between the girls and some of the other Muslim students, which is where this trouble started.'

'Wow!' says Zoe, her eyes glinting mischievously. 'Who would've thought religion would ever lead to conflict?'

'I know, right?' says Anna, using a triangle of flatbread to scoop up more super salad. 'Apparently a group of students – and I have a fair idea who – started a Facebook account in Kadra's name and posted a series of rather provocative comments. You can imagine the kind of rumours that went swirling around the school. When the rumours finally got back to the cousin, she decided it was all too much for her, so she packed up her stuff, left her unit and told the Department of Housing: *I can't deal with them anymore. Not my problem.* And the Department of Housing, in their infinite wisdom, sent the girls a letter saying they were getting evicted.'

'Can they even do that?' asks Kate.

'It turns out they can. And now shit's really hit the fan. Jenny, the student support coordinator, has spent days lobbying our local member, as well as the Department of Immigration, and beating Centrelink's door down, while the girls have sat in her office, having no idea where they're supposed to live, or whether they'll even be allowed to stay in the country.'

'Poor things.'

'Are the girls okay?' asks Zoe.

'To be honest, I wouldn't know,' says Anna. 'I'd hate to think what they make of life in this country.'

'Would you mind if I reached out to them?'

Before Anna can devise an answer, the waiter lays a plate of skewered wagyu tongues on the table. They look upsettingly appetising. Something about the way Zoe holds the waiter's gaze, encouraging his boyish enthusiasm while pretending to ridicule it, makes Anna just about pity her. For all Zoe's bravado, it's possible that she needs his attention as much as anyone else in the crowded restaurant.

'God,' whispers Zoe, unlocking her phone. 'It's a relief to finally get away from all those tossers.'

'I know,' says Anna, noticing the row of blue dots down the left side of Zoe's screen. 'Have you got plans now?'

'I said I'd meet this producer for a drink,' says Zoe, eyes devouring her new messages. 'We hooked up at Rainbow Serpent. It's more of a casual thing.'

'Does *he* know that?'

'Probably not.'

Zoe leans into a stranger's front garden and breaks off a stick of rosemary, running it under her nostrils. Kate's already waiting at her car, admonishing Zoe with a smile.

'Thank you both for a lovely evening,' says Kate.

As Zoe's hugging Kate goodbye, Anna becomes aware of a tall man striding towards them. He decelerates just as he should be slipping out of her periphery.

'Anna?'

She knows straight away.

'Hi,' she blurts out, unable to do anything other than smile moronically at the familiar herringbone pattern on his newsboy cap. It takes several seconds to register the rugged-up, marsupial appendage strapped to his torso.

'What're you doing here?' chirps Kate, trying to break the awkwardness, but only making it worse.

'Just going for a stroll,' he says, looking painfully natural with the bub conked out on his chest, its tiny form swelling ever so softly. 'We live around the corner now. Sometimes it's the only way to get this cheeky fella to nod off.'

'How's . . .?' asks Anna. 'Sorry, I don't know her name.'

'She's good,' he says, wide-eyed.

Her stomach's in knots already. All the marinated meats feel like they're about to rise to their acidic climax, burning her throat as they surge back out onto the footpath.

'How old is he?' asks Zoe, unconsciously shedding blades of rosemary.

'Little Finn is almost three months old,' he stammers, in an infantile voice, gazing tenderly at the sleeping child as he rocks from side to side on the balls of his feet. If this is even the slightest bit uncomfortable for him, he's not showing it. 'Are you still at the school?'

'Where else!' says Anna, forcing out a smile as she finishes doing the maths. 'I'm about to take a group of students to Papua New Guinea.'

'That sounds great,' he says.

You'd swear he means it.

The only consolation right now are the sleep-deprived lines spreading from the pillows of his eyelids.

'I've gotta go,' says Zoe.

'Yeah, I should too,' says Anna, thankful that someone has the sense to put an end to the interaction, even though it feels like she needs to get something more – something intangible – out of it.

'Nice seeing you,' he says, his lips curling as if it's still fathomable that he can escape from this as the good guy.

'You too,' says Anna, regretting it immediately.

She permits herself one last look at Little Finn. Pompom beanie on, burrowed into his daddy's concave chest throughout the whole ordeal; never knowing what his dad did, and the person whose life he tore apart.

ANNA

Purple-blue bullets twitch in the water, briefly disappearing behind rocks and flora before re-emerging in the centre of the tank. Artificial light pours down from above, lending the tank an ethereal glow. Imagining how large and distorted her face must seem to the fish, in their world of miniatures, is a beautifully impossible thing.

She glides her fingers along the glass, hoping to attract their attention. Watching triangles of light escape between her knuckles reminds her of how much she used to love interlocking fingers with him. The white scar tissue around his nails and his grimy, crosshatched skin, secured in her webbing.

It was too dark last night to notice his hands. There are so many things she should've said. Verbal blows she could've landed; retaliation for the hurt that he's heaped on her this past year. It would've wiped the pitying smile off his face. If he still thinks he has the right to dispense pity, cradling his little bundle of infidelity, then he can keep living his delusional life. He might never have come clean, if it weren't for Little Finn.

A hand brushes her forearm, causing her whole body to shudder.

'You're looking trim and terrific,' says Jenny.

'I don't believe you.'

Jenny steps back and surveys Anna's figure. 'No, I mean it. I think I'm jealous.'

'Don't be.'

They stare into the silence of the tank, which seems out of place in a school corridor. Anna tries to figure out what her purpose would be if she were shrunk into a fish and forced to spend the remainder of her existence inside the glass. More food than her fellow fish and a longer life, but surely a longer life would only lead to greater monotony, unless there was the hope that she could someday escape the tank . . .

'One of Peter's chums at Templestowe College came up with the idea,' says Jenny. 'He made the leadership team watch a TED Talk on it.'

'What else has he got in store for us?'

'He wants us to embrace vertical teaching next –'

'As in, no year levels?'

'Pretty much.'

'How's *that* going to work?'

'The older kids call the shots, as far as I can tell, and the rest of us sit back and drink piña coladas.'

Rob scuttles along the corridor, like a clothed rodent, barely able to contain his enthusiasm as he escorts the new Vietnamese CRT to the morning briefing. Jenny sharpens her features into a smile that becomes more wicked after they've passed by.

'Have you heard from Tyler?' asks Anna.

'Not since he informed me that I was an old hag and stormed out of my office yesterday,' says Jenny. 'I suspect he's off running with the wolves.'

Anna can tell, from the triumphant glint in Jenny's tone, that she knew Anna's efforts with Tyler were futile from the start and that she'd never have the strength to survive the perpetuity of the job, let alone embrace it.

'Any word on the Mohamed sisters?' asks Anna.

'Yes, actually,' says Jenny. 'I've made some of the more elaborate threats of my life in the past twenty-four hours.' Anna finds herself transfixed by the googly side-eye of a fish as it zips around the tank. 'The upshot is that I've managed to get the girls Centrelink funding, and the Department of Housing have agreed that they can stay in the unit and have their names on the lease because Kadra, lo and behold, is eighteen years old.'

'That's incredible.'

'It was quite the shit fight,' says Jenny. 'I've also managed to completely neglect my own children in the process.'

'How *are* the girls?'

'Obstinate, is the word that comes to mind. Catherine's interview's going to be on *One Plus One* this Thursday night. Hang on a sec, I think it's at eight thirty.' Jenny gets out her colossal Samsung and scrolls through it with her polished finger, beaming with the righteous pride of having raised a liberal celebrity. 'She said she was more nervous than on her wedding day . . . yep, here it is! Eight thirty, Thursday.'

'I won't miss it.'

Slitted gills. Eyes like a children's toy . . .

Jenny's heels pelt against the lino as she marches towards the staffroom, unable to endure the stillness of the water for a second longer.

*

'Big Moose in da house!' announces Musa, swaggering into the classroom and flopping down next to Walid.

'Quiet!' says Anna. 'This is supposed to be a test.'

Musa puffs out his cheeks and clicks his tongue, wiggling his shoulders to the salivary rhythm.

'Where's your pen?'

'The fuck do I need a pen for?' says Musa. 'It's my last day, then I'm outta this dump forever.' He resumes the rhythm, leaning across and slapping Walid's hand as he tries to write. 'Hey, can we have free time? I need to practise my stroke for the Malaysian bitches.'

'Sorry, not on my watch.'

'Whatever, miss, you can't make me do *shit* anyway.'

He starts thrusting his hips at Kadra, who maintains her vigil, staring at the table, as if it's going to reveal something more than a generic dotted pattern, printed thousands of times before.

'Musa, please grow up,' says Anna.

It's a relief, knowing that this will be the last time she has to contend with Kadra's refusal to write, and face the affront of collecting her uncreased paper afterwards. She wishes she had a way of finding out if Kadra is okay, or of letting her know that she does actually care, but pushing too hard feels the same as not pushing at all.

'Sorry we're late,' pants Najima as Jasmine and her dump their backpacks on the carpet. 'Mukhtar got arrested!'

'When?' asks Musa.

'Just then. He was coming down from the towers with Yassin, and the pigs all jumped on him. They were being rough and corrupt, like, hitting him with clipboards and stuff.'

'What was he arrested for?' asks Walid.

'Some bullshit,' says Jasmine. Anna notices the swell of skin under her chin. 'Pigs never have evidence.'

'They were getting it, but,' says Najima. 'There were, like, heaps of pigs going into the towers. I'm talking *heaps*,' she says, her eyes alive with the drama as gum snaps in her mouth. 'The detectives had suitcases and those special brown bags, yeah, like in *CSI*.'

'Kadra probably tipped them off,' says Jasmine.

The two girls growl at Kadra in sync, watching her for a response, but the yolk of her eyes never quivers.

'Leave her out of this,' says Anna.

'Why are you always on *her* side?' asks Jasmine.

'I don't see why there have to be sides.'

'*Wallah!*' sighs Najima, her braces on full display. 'There are always sides, miss. If you can't see them, that means you're on the side that's winning.'

ALI

They fall into another weird silence. It makes no sense why Kylie wanted them to come and hang at her flat, with all her grandma's dusty dolls piled on the TV unit.

'Does either of you wanna menthol ciggie?' she asks. 'I know where my nan keeps them.'

'Where's she at, anyway?' asks Ali.

'Playing pokies.'

'Does she ever win?' asks Funda.

'I guess,' says Kylie, standing up from one of the few patches of unused carpet in the whole flat. 'Ali, do you wanna share a ciggie?'

'I'm good,' he says, checking out the creepy little hats of the dolls crowded around the antenna. 'Why does your gran have a thing for dolls, anyway?'

'She says they're antiques.'

Kylie dodges the stale-smelling bags that're piled, chest-high, in the living room and opens a bedroom door.

'We should totally give that doll a haircut,' whispers Ali, pointing at a knotty-haired bride doll that looks like something that would get possessed in a dumb horror movie. Funda gives him a bitchy glare from the other end of the couch. 'Come on, cuz, it's funny.'

'It's sad,' says Funda.

'You're the one who's sad.'

She doesn't even bother to defend herself. A window rattles in the bedroom. Through the open door, Ali catches sight of even more dolls on top of an overflowing wardrobe. Some of them are naked and others are babies, dressed in faded onesies.

'What was up with that crazy shit Tyler said at the RSL?' asks Ali. 'I swear, man, he's been trying to fuck with my head or something.'

'He was just being random,' says Funda.

'Did you guys actually hook up, or what?'

Funda flattens the itchy gold fabric on the armrest of the couch, unsmoothing it, then smoothing it again. Refusing to look up. It's like hanging out with Dad. Someone can be right next to you, but not there at all.

'This place is more of a dump than where *I* grew up,' says Ali, just to say something.

'You know they're knocking down the walk-ups?'

'Seriously?'

'Yeah, Jai told me. Him and his dad got a letter saying they have to move out, like, next year,' says Funda, finally looking up to whisper, 'Kylie, too.'

Even though Yassin's crew basically destroyed Ali's old crib – and Musa booted the kitchen cupboard in – this is somehow worse; knowing that the first four years of his life will only ever exist in his own head.

'Do you remember when my mum left?' asks Ali.

The smoke wafting in from the bedroom smells fresher than the actual flat.

'Cuz?'

'Not really,' says Funda.

'I asked Dad.'

'What did he say?'

'Nothing.'

Kylie tiptoes back into the room, avoiding all the gross plastic bags, and settles on the same unused patch of carpet.

'Did you two have a fight?' she asks.

'Nah,' says Funda.

'She's being weird coz she thinks I don't know about her and Tyler,' says Ali.

'There's nothing *to* know,' says Funda.

'Yeah, right.'

She unsmooths the couch hair, holding her palm flat on the armrest with her whole head kind of swaying.

'I've gotta go,' sniffles Funda to Kylie, stumbling into a wooden coat rack on her way towards the front door.

'Cuz!' calls Ali.

But she's already gone.

'What did I do wrong?'

Kylie shrugs, twisting her silver nose stud. Her cheeks look even more ghost-like than usual. There's no way she'll be able to carry all her goth make-up on the trail next week.

'How's your album going?' she asks.

'Slow,' says Ali, losing concentration from how intensely Kylie's pupils are suddenly staring into his. 'My manager makes me work basically every day after school, but it's kinda good coz it'll help me afford more studio time.'

'Funda showed me the song you did on YouTube.'

'Did you dig it?'

'Yeah, it was lit.'

'The next clip's gonna be off tap, trust me.'

'I can't wait to see it.'

No one's ever looked at him so intensely.

'It'll drop next year,' says Ali, feeling his pecs tightening, 'once I've, like, mixed and released the whole EP.'

'That's amazing.'

'Here,' he says, shoving his hand into his backpack and pulling out his lyric book. 'Wanna read my rhymes? Every track's pretty much written.'

Kylie joins him on the couch, leaning in so she can see his notes:

[Jazzy Flow harmonies over fast funk beat, overlapping cars & trains & five-o sirens to give that f-town feel, drop in with spoken werd]

Yall know me as prince ali
Shout out to all my afro soldiers (what up!)

Pigs be sayin thats all water under tha bridge
Aint no water under flemington bridge
Creek bed 2 dry fo that
We got blazers bitches boosters whateva
But no H-2-O no H-B-O down there
Maybe if they eva shine they torches
Stead o crackin them thru peoples teeth
They see that?

[Sirens, radios, sounds of someone being cuffed]

Sediment on tha mic
Check it!

'Can you sing some to me?' asks Kylie, her warm breath smelling of ash, but somehow not of menthol.

Musa's posing on the red carpet with Beyoncé, holding Grammys and smiling with all his teeth:

If anyone ows me $$$$$ meet me at flem bridge station at 10 tonite if anyone wants to give me one last blowjob meet me at flem bridge station at 10 tonite

'No one will show up,' says Ali.

'Yeah, they will,' says Musa, snatching back his phone as terracotta roofs flash by out the window of the train. 'And I'll be like: *Chill out, ladies, one at a time!*'

*

Every customer has this look of desperation as they hunt through old movies and PlayStation games, most of them stolen by fiends and sold to get high. The store reeks of sweat and stale carpet, kind of like Kylie's flat. Imagining her face, with her cute nose stud and her shiny lips, makes Ali want to add one last track to the EP. Some crazy wordplay about dolls.

'How much do you cunts think they'll give me?' asks Musa, balancing his laptop on a thirty-nine-dollar amplifier.

'Fifty bucks,' says Walid.

'Way higher, man.'

The attendants at the back of the store are watching Musa and Walid with the same look they always get at 7-Eleven.

'You know the easiest way to make money?' says Musa, pretending he doesn't notice the attendants. 'Selling rhino horns. They give you, like, sixty thousand bucks on the black market, just for one.'

'That's not very nice to the rhinos,' says Ali.

'Man, fuck the rhinos! I swear, once I saw off five rhino horns, I'm starting my own label.'

He picks up a microphone with no wires and bursts into the opening verse of Kendrick's latest track, chopping the sweaty air with his hand as he sings about how he's going to be buried with twenty million dollars when he dies.

Ali can see the attendants trying to decide if they should ask him to stop distracting the other customers.

In a way, this hurts even more than seeing Musa in cuffs, getting scraped along the concrete. You can never tell all of the little rivers that history might've split into if it hadn't happened. The crazy thing about Walid's case against the police is: that's kind of what they're asking the judge to do, and then they're asking the judge to put a price on every lost little river.

'*Dooooo, do-do-do-do, da-do-do-dooooo!*' toots Musa, squeezing his lips into his fist as he plays the trumpet intro from Kendrick's video clip . . .

It's horrible feeling the minutes escaping, knowing they'll be the last minutes they ever get to spend together. There are so many things Ali wants to say, but will never be able to.

'Is your uncle a nice guy?' he asks.

'I've never met him,' says Musa, eyeing off a pair of fat headphones inside a locked cabinet. 'My mum says he's strict as fuck, like the Arsenal manager.'

'What if he has a temper at you?' asks Walid.

'I swear, man, if he even tries to step up to me, he'll be sorry,' says Musa, rattling the plastic.

'What language do they talk in Malaysia?'

'Malaysian, you dumb-arse.'

'So how are you, like, gonna *do* anything?'

'With my charm,' says Musa, controlling his smile with an imaginary piece of string, making it get bigger and smaller by yanking his fingers up and down. 'It sucks that I'm getting deported, but. I would've become a politician and totally bossed this country.'

'As if,' says Ali.

'I'm serious! I would've made all these sick changes to the law, like forcing our school to have an African principal, like Obama or Jamie Foxx – someone with swag – so we could come late in the morning. And, wait, wait, you'll like this one, Walid,' he says, pausing to yank the imaginary string again. 'Only African kids get MacBooks . . . to make it even for the slave ships, instead of giving us this cheap-arse *khara*!' says Musa, pimp-slapping his laptop, which finally convinces one of the attendants to stomp over to them.

'You should be gentle to that computer,' says Walid, 'or they won't buy it from you.'

'True,' says Musa, patting the laptop and lowering his voice to a whisper. 'I'm so sorry, baby. I didn't mean to slap you around. I get angry sometimes because I have lots of emotional trauma.'

Emotional trauma.

It's the first time Ali's ever heard him say those words.

The attendant arrives as Musa's vibrating his tongue on the lid of his laptop.

'You like that, don't you baby?' he whispers.

'Can I help you boys?' asks the attendant.

'I'm donating this computer to you homies for a special price,' says Musa.

It's obvious that the attendant doesn't want to touch the laptop now that it's covered in saliva, so Musa has to open it for him. As the screen lights up, Ali feels his eyes sliding towards the marks where they peeled off the school stickers.

'Only two hundred dollars,' says Musa, yanking the string to create another smile, pretending he can't see the look of disgust on the attendant's face.

ALI

'Have you got *any* idea where Jasmine and Najima are?' asks the manager, even more pissed off than usual because she hasn't got time to smoke.

'Nah, sorry,' says Ali.

'So unreliable,' she mutters, wobbling angrily back to her office to call them again.

The line for the drive-thru is stretching all the way to the entrance of the car park. People are honking their horns. But being this understaffed is good, in a way, because you never have time to get bored.

'Next customer, please,' says Ali.

He looks up and sees Yassin standing at the front of the queue, staring at the menu board as he runs his fingers along the rows of scalp between his braids. It's like he's acting deliberately slow to challenge the other customers to get mad at him, knowing he'll never have to fight his own fights.

'You all good?' asks Ali.

'I'll have three Family Feasts,' says Yassin, sliding a green hundred-dollar note from his money clip.

As Ali pokes the order into the touchscreen, he hears the cooks getting blamed by the manager for how long everything's taking. For all her yelling, she isn't actually doing anything to help the drive-thru line get shorter.

'Far out,' croaks Yassin, smirking at Ali while a car horn stays held down. 'You need to sort your shit out.'

His crew are grabbing extra chairs from the dining room so they can sit by the front window, where Ali, Musa and Walid always used to hang.

'CHANGE THE CHANNEL!' squeaks a high-pitched voice from within the crew.

It's Michael Garang, in a white t-shirt that's two or three sizes too big, swallowing half his legs.

On the TV above him, a family of lions are circling a massive buffalo. The old English dude who knows pretty much everything about animals is commentating, explaining how the lions always pick on the weakest buffalo.

'This shit is *boring*!' squeaks Michael.

Finally, the lions get the courage to take down the buffalo and crowd around its carcass.

'Michael grinds with you, yeah?' asks Ali.

'Huh?'

'I'm not trying to dog on you guys, or anything, but you can't let him stay involved.'

Yassin flicks his nostril with his knuckles.

'Why do *you* give a fuck?'

'Just . . . this is a favour,' says Ali, realising, from Yassin's hard eyes, that the word means nothing to him. 'You don't even need Michael.'

The lions are jerking their heads, ripping away at the buffalo's chewy skin. They're more relaxed now because there's enough meat for the whole family to sink their teeth into.

'I tell you what,' says Ali, hearing the bitching from other customers who want to order, 'if you let Michael do his thing and, like, be free, you can have my vintage Sixers singlet. The black one I was rocking at your party, yeah?'

All Yassin does is twitch his nostril, looking bored.

Eventually, one of the cooks shoves his Family Feasts through the kitchen window and Ali puts them on a tray.

'Think about what I said,' he reminds Yassin, who grabs the tray and slowly struts back to his crew, like he's walking through imaginary water.

'Finally!' shrieks the manager.

Ali spins around, thinking he's in shit, but the manager's already going mental at Najima near the deep fryers, not even caring if customers can hear her. There's more than just disappointment in her voice.

The Footscray City boys from Yassin's crew are staring into the kitchen, doing their dumb hiccups laughter.

'Fine,' snaps Najima. 'I'm sorry.'

Michael Garang lets out a loud whistle, grinning over a piece of original recipe chicken.

'*Doqon*,' hisses Najima, when she finally gets to open the register next to Ali, bringing with her a breeze of fresh flowers.

'Why were you so late?' asks Ali.

'I was at Jasmine's place.'

'Yeah, where's she at?'

Najima checks to see if the manager's watching.

'I've got the best news,' she says, forgetting to cover her braces as she smiles. 'Jazzy's having a baby!'

*

TYLER

Ali's deadshit dad looks exactly how he imagined. Fat, bald and ugly. Watching him waddle out of the flats, hauling his saggy arse through the car park, makes Tyler want to catch up and deck the fat fuck on the bonnet of his taxi. Slimy kid-fucker. Acting like he never took someone's life away.

'Where've you been?' asks Mum, pacing over to him.

'Just out,' says Tyler.

'I've been waiting here all day.'

Her anger's already going away because she knows what him coming home means.

'What's this?' he asks, poking his new Chuck Taylor at a ball of paper near the front door.

'I think someone left a note for you,' she says, still pacing.

'You better not have fucking read it.'

'Why would I do that?'

He picks up the note and gets a burst of fruit – a smell too fresh for this scummy den – so he slips it into his pocket for later.

'Everything good, Ty?'

'Yeah, chill out for a minute,' he says, dodging her to get to his bedroom. It's been turned inside out, his stuff scattered everywhere, just like it was after the pigs arrested Barney. She's even found the fiver of bud he'd stashed in his old Volleys at the back of the wardrobe. Fuck knows how she smoked it without papers. 'Jesus, Mum!'

'What?'

'You *know* what.'

In her messed-up head, it's his fault that she had to boost it, for making her wait. He can already hear her creeping towards the door, wanting to see if he's stashing anything else.

'I know you're out there,' he yells.

The door swings open, but he's ready with a fifty-dollar note, sliding it straight into her shaky palm.

'Is that all?' she asks.

'Yeah, that's fucking heaps.'

Seeing the red vessels overlapping in the corners of her eyes does his head in, knowing he's kind of causing them. But watching her suffer was a million times worse.

'This is all I've got,' he says, trying to hold her palm still as he gives her another fifty. He isn't ready for how frail her hand feels. The loose, squishy skin around her knuckles barely shields her sinking veins. If he presses even the tiniest bit harder, her bones will crumble like a handful of chalk.

Blood swirls out of Mum's eye. Knowing she's going to be part of him forever is the only thing making this pain worth it. It feels like the tattoo gun's drilling up his spine, shredding his flesh as it plants the ink under his skin. The needle kills every time it slices into the muscles around his armpit, where there's already less definition now that he's stopped doing push-ups every day.

He tries to concentrate on all the different smells in the kitchen to take his mind off the pain: the lemony disinfectant that the dude with stretchy earlobe piercings keeps spraying and wiping into his arm to stop the bleeding, and the burnt plasticky stench of whatever his girlfriend's smoking in her pipe – the stuff Shannon brought them in exchange for the tat – plus the whole joint reeks of unchanged kitty litter.

'Stop moving!' says the dude with earlobe piercings, pressing deliberately hard because he's pissed off that his girlfriend's more into Shannon than him.

'Then I worked on the Goldie for a few years . . .' she's saying, even though Shannon's barely listening.

He should've warned Tyler that it'd burn way worse than eczema. There's still heaps of shading in left to do. Asking how long it's going to take isn't an option, so he sits there, watching his own elbow vibrate on the table. Just like in a fight, you can't show any pain, because pain is weakness.

Shannon sparks up a spliff as one of the kittens tiptoes into the kitchen and starts meowing.

'Here, give us a drag,' says Tyler.

'Nah, bro, it'll hurt more.'

As if that's even possible.

The dude's girlfriend keeps crapping on about some ex-boyfriend who was a massive cokehead, not even noticing the kitten brushing against her shins.

Tyler feels his elbow stop vibrating.

'Are you gonna feed that fucking thing?' yells the dude with earlobe piercings, shooing the kitten away with his foot.

Shannon passes him the spliff and he rests it between his lips, squinting through the smoke as he stabs the needle back into Tyler's bicep. From upside down, it's hard to tell how much the features even look like Mum's. Especially on his swollen, sliced up skin.

'I can't find the can,' moans the dude's girlfriend, flinging open cupboard doors as the kitten's meowing gets more and more desperate.

Tyler steals a convertible off some yuppie skank in a bikini and upgrades the paint job to orange, adding bumpers and a rear spoiler. Doing actual missions is boring as, so he floors it around the hills at sunset, going for crazy burnouts and trying to land backflips on the highway. The graphics on *GTA* are so realistic now – the way light flashes off his bonnet as he twists in the air – that it's basically the same as real life.

Once he's back in the city streets, he decides to only run over non-white people. Shannon's mates quickly figure out what he's doing, cracking up whenever he mows someone down.

'Your bro's fucking *loco*.'

'I know,' says Shannon, staring at the screen with his sunburnt eyes. 'He just got suspended.'

Sirens are cutting sick as more units join the chase. A wall of cop cars are waiting for Tyler at an overpass. He sprints towards them with a pump-action and gets wasted, dropping to the concrete in slow motion.

'That was hectic, brah,' says the annoying dude with the fake laugh, passing Tyler the bong.

Shannon grabs the controller and selects a mission.

After ripping a few quick cones, Tyler's chest starts to relax. It doesn't matter that there's THC in his system now. Fuck the army. If they seriously think having itchy skin will stop him from dishing out justice, then they're in for a surprise.

He shoves his hands into his pockets to warm them up and finds the fruity-smelling note from earlier, recognising Funda's girly handwriting from her pencil case. He makes sure no one's watching as he unravels it:

> *Hi Tyler!*
> *I wish you were still coming on the trip with us, but I guess you didn't really want to? What you said to Ali in front of everyone was risky for me. If you still care about me, I need you to not let anything happen with you and him. Ok?*

Even just thinking about Ali's butt-ugly face, with its crooked, tomatoey nose, makes him want to cave it back in, but technically, nothing *will* happen between the two of them.

'I was bumping coke with this Lebo at Revs last night,' says the dude with the fake laugh, packing himself a cone, 'and it turns out he's some massive promoter.'

'For real?' croaks the dude with dreads.

'Yeah, he gave me his card. I looked him up. He's done nights everywhere. Billboard, Eve, Chasers, Love Machine.'

'Sweet.'

Marley prances over and tries to settle against Tyler's leg, but he can't get comfortable, even with heaps of belly rubbing.

'This cunt was fully legit. You should've heard some of the stories he was telling me about DJs and their riders, brah. I'm talking, like, freaky –'

'Give us the billy!' says Tyler, sick of the story already.

He packs a cone and sparks it up, pulling until he feels the burn in the back of his throat.

'Where was I up to?' asks the dude, doing his fake laugh.

Everyone's too munted to answer.

'Fuck, anyway, he was going on about how he used to be

tight with these schizo Middle Eastern cunts,' says the dude with the fake laugh. 'You know, the boys who ran the north-west crew before they got busted . . .'

Shannon parks his Hummer outside a streetball court to break up a beatdown and take on two jacked Albanians.

'They'd go on these epic pseudo runs with, like, twenty different identities . . .' the dick's saying, pretty much talking to himself now, as Shannon chases one of the Albanians up the fire escape of a sugar factory. He catches the dude and shanks him, sending him plunging into the river below.

Ali's dad doesn't deserve a quick punishment like that. It'd be sick to try some of the fucked-up shit that Japan pulled during World War II, or to waterboard him like the CIA does to camel fuckers who take on America. The best ancient torture technique he could use would be the one they do on the fat-arsed detective in *2 Fast 2 Furious*, where you strap a cage full of rats on someone's stomach, so the rats have nowhere to escape. Then you light charcoal on top of the cage to force the rats to gnaw their way through the person's intestines.

Tyler packs another bong and holds the smoke in his lungs for as long as he can, before exhaling. He finds his pupils breaking the graphics down into little brown, green and gold pixels, reassembling thousands of times every single second. It makes his eyes sting. He lets them slide shut as he sinks back onto the couch pillows, so he can float around in the middle of the surround sound system, listening to boots trample grass, ammo clicking and the squelching of flesh . . .

He jolts awake, hearing Shannon's mates cackling at another lame joke. This disgusting rotting taste is in his mouth, like a possum has crawled in there and died. His tummy's going crazy. Tyler straightens himself on the couch, opening his eyes to see the dude with dreads hovering over Marley, blowing smoke in his face.

'Check it out, he's already got the munchies,' says the dick with the fake laugh, tipping salt and vinegar crumbs onto the carpet. 'Have some chips, brah.'

Marley bumps into the leg of the coffee table and lets out a scared yelp.

'What the fuck are you doing?' yells Tyler.

'Whoa, chill!'

'Dogs can't eat that,' says Tyler, covering the crumbs with his foot.

'It's cool,' says Shannon, pausing the game.

'Nah, fuck that! What did Marley ever do to them?'

'You better check yourself!' says the dude with dreads.

'Or what?'

'Calm down,' says Shannon. 'They didn't mean nothing.'

'Yeah they did,' says Tyler, watching Marley wheeze as he bares his side gums. 'Torturing animals is messed up.'

'You better get your bro into line.'

'As if I'm scared of you two try-hards.'

'Here, come with me,' says Shannon, leading Tyler out of the bedroom. Marley shuffles next to them, forgetting how to use his back paws.

It's blustery as on the decking outside, but the fresh air feels good on Tyler's face, making him instantly more awake.

'Seriously, if they ever pull that shit again,' he says, staring Shannon down, 'I'll fucking kill them.'

'They won't,' says Shannon, lighting a ciggie. 'What's up with you, anyway?'

'Nothing.'

'Dude, that wasn't nothing. You went properly psycho in there,' says Shannon. 'No offence, bro, but you sounded like me when I was young . . . before I learnt to control my anger.' He does this proud smile, balancing the ciggie between his lips, so he can unload a three-punch combo into Tyler's abs. 'It's good to get mad, yeah, but you've gotta use it in the right way. No one fights well when they lose their head.'

The two dicks are cackling again in the bedroom. There's no way Tyler's ever forgiving them for this.

'Let it go,' says Shannon. 'They're just being dumb cunts.'

'Make sure you fucking tell them –'

'Yeah, yeah, I know.'

Shannon throws a jab into the guts of the punching bag, watching it vibrate on its hinges in the sensor light.

'Are we sweet?'

'I guess.'

Marley finally makes it outside and tries to settle on the grass next to his kennel.

'You coming back in?' asks Shannon.

'Give us a minute.'

'All good, bro, take your time.'

Shannon flicks the ciggie onto the dewy grass and slaps him on the back, sending a stab of pain down his right arm.

The Glad Wrap feels like it's cutting off his circulation, creating these trapped grids of blood that remind him of fish scales. He peels back the plastic to check out the tat. Mum's face is shining with baby cream and practically leaping away from his skin, looking all young and pretty again.

Marley lets out another scared yelp, still struggling to get comfortable. Tyler walks over and gathers him in his arms. He settles on the decking and rests Marley in his lap, trying to slow down the dog's short, panicky breathing.

'Everything's gonna be cool,' whispers Tyler, stroking behind Marley's ears.

He stares into the windy night sky, watching the violence of the darkness. The neighbour's extension looks like it's almost finished. Not that he'll ever get to see it.

PAUL

He slides the rope back under the roof racks, taking up the slack and securing the futon. The amount of dirty hippy sex that these two have probably had on it makes him wish he'd disinfected the disgusting thing beforehand.

'You got a couch yet?' he asks.

'We're going to the Salvos this arvo,' says Davey, yellow gunk still in his eyes from having to wake up this side of nine in the morning. 'Astrid reckons we'll get a cheap one there.'

'They sell second-hand jocks, too?'

Davey grins, zipping up his overflowing backpack.

'I go commando these days.'

'Of course you fucking do, you grot.'

Astrid's clutching Mum's elbows to try to stop her from weeping on the front porch.

'That everything?' asks Paul.

'I think so.'

'Oh, come here,' blubbers Astrid, giving Mum a big hug and getting swallowed in the waves of her woollen scarf. 'Now you're making *me* feel sad.'

'Give it a rest, Mum!' yells Paul, bounding up the steps. 'It's not like he's off to the trenches.'

'I'm allowed to be emotional,' she bites back.

Paul ducks inside to give them some space and finds the old man at the kitchen table, dressing-gown on, hunched over his morning paper. The grumpy bastard's oozing that familiar pong of coffee breath and dried night sweat.

'She making a scene of it out there?'

'What do *you* reckon?' says Paul. 'They'll probably get evicted in a month or two, anyway.'

'They better bloody not.'

The old man has a few cracks at hocking up a ball of phlegm, revving the rusty old motor in his chest, and spits the residue into his hankie.

'Listen, Dad, about Anzac Day –'

'Don't waste ya breath.'

'Nah, I was outta line storming off like that. It never solves anything.'

'Forget it.'

'You reckon Mum will?'

'She's just terrified something's gonna happen to ya,' says the old man, dabbing at the grey rat-tickler with his hankie. 'Too much time on her hands.'

She'll have even more now with Davey in Fallujah.

'Think you'll manage without the little bastard?'

'Happiest day of my life,' says the old man, deadpan as ever, his pupils sinking to the editorial section of the paper.

Back in the brisk morning air, Paul sees Davey leaning against the passenger side of the Kluger, waiting out the eternal goodbye between Mum and Astrid.

'These fell outta your backpack,' says Paul, tossing him a bottle of serotonin pills that he plucked off the nature strip a few minutes ago. 'They yours or hers?'

Davey pockets the bottle and thinks it over.

'Mine,' he says, dryly, as if impersonating the old man.

'How long you been guzzling them for?'

'Guzzling them,' snorts Davey, shaking his noggin as air whistles out of his nostrils.

Staring at the brick veneer they grew up in, moss eating away at the crocodile skin of the roof tiles, it feels like the slow death of a simpler way of life; where you could pile into a station wagon every summer, drive to the beach and not have to worry about melanomas.

'You don't have to answer,' says Paul.

'Since my last year at high school,' says Davey, stiffening his spine so that it's no longer resting on the window.

'Sorry, mate,' says Paul. 'I honestly didn't have a clue.'

'I know.'

Astrid and Mum finally wrap up the affection-fest on the front porch with a smooch on the lips.

'Dad found me out in the shed,' says Davey, soft and detached, as if it's just another sentence.

'You right there, muscles?'

'I think so,' says Davey, letting his end of the futon drag along the corridor.

'What's wrong?'

'It's just my back.'

'Let go then,' says Paul, taking on the extra weight and hauling the lumpy mattress into the bedroom. 'Where do you want this?'

'Anywhere,' says Davey, clutching his side.

Paul plonks the futon next to a pile of their junk – dreamcatcher, salt lamp, candleholders and paperbacks – that've all probably been plucked from hard rubbish collections.

Davey grimaces.

'Come on, mate, it can't be *that* bad.'

They squeak back along the mouldy carpet, past the interrogation cell that the real estate agent reckons is a second bedroom. Astrid's whistling to herself as she untangles fairy lights in the kitchen. Davey slumps onto the floorboards, still probing at his lower back.

'We've got a casualty,' announces Paul.

Astrid's lips stretch into a sympathetic pout. 'Would you like some water, Paul? It's all we've got.'

'Cheers.'

She fills the old man's *'93 Premiers* mug and hands it to him, her face beaming with sweat, like she's onstage.

'Dad give you this, did he?'

'It's on loan.'

There's nowhere to sit in this squat, so Paul wanders over to the fridge and studies the polaroids that they've blu-tacked to it: in the backyard at the folks' place last Father's Day, a group of friends sinking Coronas at a house party, Astrid and Davey on a hill at some music festival, Davey wearing a fluoro-green singlet and a pair of Ray-Bans, poking out his ugly tongue.

'Taken any photos of this?' asks Paul, inspecting the salty stains that're eroding the plaster around the fridge.

'We just moved in,' says Astrid.

'Should get onto it today and email them to the agent, in case they try to slug you some of your bond at the other end.'

'You know who you sound like?' says Davey.

'I don't give a stuff,' says Paul. 'I'm just trying to look out for you two hippies.'

'*Hippies!*' shrieks Astrid, hamming it up.

'If the shoe fits,' says Paul, nodding at the knotted ball of fairy lights in front of her. He gulps down his dusty water. 'Need a hand with anything else,' he asks, flexing, 'while you've got these two weapons at your disposal?'

Astrid rolls her eyes and has a giggle.

'I think we've got it from here,' says Davey. 'Thanks for everything.'

'And for putting in a good word for us,' says Astrid.

'No worries,' says Paul, opening the flyscreen door. 'You two lovebirds are in my patch now, so behave yourselves.'

Next-door neighbour's cooking a serious-smelling curry.

Once Paul gets to the car, he realises that he's left his keys on the kitchen bench. As he hurries back up the stairs, he hears Astrid singing in that big, beefy voice of hers:

'*My poor, poor bay-bee!*'

He holds off on knocking, peering into the apartment through the rusty aluminium mesh. Davey's still sprawled on the floorboards with his hand massaging his own spine, goofy grin splashed across his face as he watches Astrid strum a ukulele and sway her hips above him.

'*What're we gonna do-ooo with you-ooo?*' she croons, kicking her legs up like a Vegas showgirl.

Been two decades since Paul's seen the little bastard smile like this.

*

'No, no, no!' gasps a woman in a bright orange shawl, who must be Walid's mum, waving her forefinger at Paul.

She points at the peeled banana in his hand and shows him how the imaginary pieces are supposed to mix with his beef and yellow rice.

'Righto, gotcha,' says Paul, laying the banana back on his plastic plate. 'This smells delicious, by the way.'

'Thank you.'

'What do you call it?'

'*Suqaar*,' she says, using a pair of tongs to rearrange the chunks of meat and potatoes on the tray in front of her.

He has a crack at pronouncing the name, hearing his own cheery voice rise above the whispers of foreign languages inside the crowded station.

'You know your son's gonna go a long way in life,' says Paul, winking at Walid, who's serving flatbread next to her. 'I reckon I'll be taking orders from him someday.'

'Let's wait,' says Walid.

'He's also too modest,' says Paul, getting a whiff of garlic from his steaming pile of grub. 'Nicest meal we'll be eating in a while, hey?'

'Yeah, I know.'

Walid hands him a serviette, flinching as their fingers touch.

'Anyway, cheers for being a part of this, mate.'

Paul ducks out of the mess hall into the courtyard where AJ's letting little tackers take it in turns to sit on top of a police motorbike.

'When you grow up,' he overhears AJ say to one of the honorary constables, 'do you wanna be a policeman?'

Paul hops into the driver's side of the '62 Studebaker Lark that they've been showing off to the kids, so he can have a few minutes to eat in peace. The grub's not too dissimilar to some of the Italian dishes you pay thirty bucks a pop for in the city, sans banana. Chilli certainly packs a decent enough punch.

He watches AJ and a few of the regulars from the Youth Bus pose for a photo next to an old VL Commodore Turbo, overlapping their middle and ring fingers to form a W.

Something more authentic about Athena's demeanour, chowing down on a stuffed pastry, using her spare hand as a plate, while one of the fruit loops from the Flemington Theatre Group chews her ear off. No qualms about answering back with her mouth full of mince.

'Wanna hop in, lads?' yells Paul, poking his head out of the Studebaker as Ali and Walid emerge in the courtyard.

'We have to go back to school,' says Walid.

'Just for a couple of minutes.'

'Come on, man,' says Ali, nudging him. 'Let's check out his crazy-arse car.'

Walid eventually permits himself to sink onto the leather seat next to Paul. He drums his fingers on the ashtray lid between them, staring out the windscreen at the yellow monstrosity where AJ's still posing for photos.

'Can you believe we used to roll around in those thirty years ago?' asks Paul.

'I guess,' says Walid. 'I wasn't born then.'

The detachment in his voice isn't too dissimilar to Davey when he's giving you doughnuts. It's like Walid figures the slant of the whole event's resting on him, and if he dishes out even a sliver of trust, he'll never get it back.

'Any word on Michael?'

'I hollered at his crew,' says Ali from the back seat, always trying to sound tougher than he is. 'We'll see.'

'Thanks, mate, fingers crossed.'

Paul shovels in a mouthful of beef and banana, between lips that're already tingling.

'Far out,' grumbles Ali, feigning a cough. 'Is there, like, a petrol leak in here or something?'

'Nah, it's just the unburnt fuel in the motor.'

'That shit stinks.'

'I don't mind it,' says Paul, feeling his nose leaking from the onslaught of chilli. He doesn't dare use his only serviette to stem the flow. 'Big day tomorrow.'

'I hope so,' says Walid, his fingers still twitching on the ashtray. 'What's your boss gonna say when he testifies?'

'That's the million-dollar question, isn't it?'

Paul's tummy rumbles in the silence.

'At the quiz night, he said he wanted to talk to me about where we live,' says Walid. 'Do you think he still wants that?'

'Honestly,' says Paul, 'I wouldn't know.'

'That means *no*, right?'

'Jeez, you're really tightening the screws on me.'

His tummy lets out another long, hydraulic rumble, as if the air's being strangled out of his intestine.

'Do you like the food?' asks Walid.

'I do, actually,' says Paul, peering down at the plate that's been keeping his thigh warm. He bites the bullet and uses the serviette to blow his nose. Snot surges into the textured wings of the paper. 'Sorry, mate, no offence intended.'

'You don't have to be sorry,' says Walid, twisting in his seat to watch Paul mop his nostrils. 'You just have to get used to it.'

ANNA

'Miss Kelly!' chirps Peter, his fleshy face spreading into a phoney smile as he looks up from his desktop. 'To what do I owe the rare pleasure?'

'Have you got time to talk?'

'Anything, for one of our young guns.'

She takes the seat opposite him, feeling like a student awaiting punishment. There's a Jedi figurine on his desk and a framed photo on the wall of Peter with his wife and his two adult sons, standing in front of the Big Pineapple.

'I'm quitting,' says Anna, enjoying seeing him finally drop the façade.

'Right now?'

'After Kokoda.'

In the photo, Peter's wearing thongs, boardshorts and an unflattering tropical shirt, as though he's designed his outfit to match the ridiculous oversized tourist attraction.

'May I ask why?'

'I'm burnt out,' says Anna. 'Isn't it obvious?'

'No, it isn't,' he says, his fingers swallowing the plastic shell of his mouse. 'Why didn't you come to me sooner?'

'You're always busy.'

A jackhammer starts blasting through concrete outside the window, continuing the school's everlasting facelift.

'I'm sorry you feel that way,' says Peter, raising his voice to be heard above the drilling. 'I'd like to think that the wellbeing of my staff always comes first, but I apologise if you've felt uncomfortable about approaching me.'

It's as if there's a direct line running from the compressor into the sockets of her skull, bringing on an excruciating tightness behind her eyes.

'Do you ever feel like you're incapable of doing it any longer?' asks Anna. 'I mean, of doing it for one more day. That's how I feel every single night before work. This . . . I guess you'd call it a looming dread. I lie in bed, and I can't begin to imagine how I'm going to survive the next day without curling up into a ball and howling in front of the students.'

The folds on Peter's cheeks melt into a smile.

'Try teaching for four decades.'

'But that's what I'm trying to say. I don't think I *could* imagine it.'

'Sure you could. You're fantastic at your job.'

'Linda must've . . .' whimpers Anna, feeling her lower lip starting to tremble. 'Someone's told you what happened last year, right?'

'It wouldn't be any of my business if they had.'

The matter-of-fact tone of his voice makes the tightness behind her eyes give way. She overhears a spasm of wet sounds choking out of her upper body. For once, surrendering in front of someone else doesn't feel like a taboo.

Peter stands up creakily and draws the blinds.

'Thanks,' she rasps, hearing the disgusting crackling of her own mucus. Peter nudges a box of tissues towards her, smiling with more benevolence than she deserves. 'You should probably know, I didn't teach the prescribed text to my year elevens this term.'

'What did you teach them?'

'I don't think I taught them anything,' says Anna, yelping out a laugh. 'Every one of them hates my guts. And if I wasn't a complete mess all the time, I might've been able to handle it.'

'I doubt it's your fault,' says Peter.

'It's *all* my fault,' says Anna, surprising herself with her sudden resolve. 'They deserve so much more.'

A group of girls are screeching with delight in the yard.

'There might still be ways around this,' says Peter, settling his buttocks back onto his seat. 'If you want there to be.'

'Honestly, I think I'm beyond caring.'

She studies the photo on the wall again as she blows her nose. The eldest of Peter's sons is looking sideways at him, bursting into an embarrassed smile. The beauty of the photo is the involuntary love in his expression.

'So, what's the plan after Kokoda?' asks Peter.

'Fly to Europe, drink some sangria, lie beside a pool with a book . . . and figure out the rest from there.'

Just thinking about that first moment when she realises she's free – not understanding a word being spoken from the deckchair next to her – helps her lungs fill with air.

'And what're you planning on doing after that?'

'I've got no idea,' says Anna. 'It feels a long way off.'

'Well, we'd love you to come back, if it's an option that you'd consider.'

'Seriously?'

'Of course,' he says, cheeks melting again. 'I'd rather you take a leave of absence than abandon us.'

'But what about –'

'I suspect you're forgetting, in this job I have to deal with a lot of . . . how shall I say it? . . . dead wood. You've probably got a fair idea who I'm alluding to. The last thing I want to do, if I can help it, is lose one of the people who genuinely cares.'

At some point in the past few minutes, the convulsions outside the window must've stopped.

'Am I allowed to think about it?'

'I'd encourage you to think,' says Peter, spreading his hands above a tacky blue lightsaber, pretending there's an adoring audience in his office. 'That's what we're here to do, isn't it?'

It's the kind of elaborate gesture that's always made him come across as insincere in his briefings. But seeing how self-deprecating his performance is – the olive branch of another failed attempt at humour – the gesture suddenly seems no different from the hideous tropical shirt he's sporting in the family photograph.

The muscular torsos of the plane trees, the slush of leaves in the gutters and the black-splotched exteriors of terraces, all wrapped in a wet winter's blanket. Anna savours every detail – even the stench of adolescent sweat – knowing it'll be the last time she gets to experience this walk in at least twelve months.

She sees the silhouettes of the Mohamed sisters up ahead and slows down, unable to bear the thought of their eyes being trained on her as she overtakes them. There's a discipline to the way the girls walk, spread across the footpath in silent formation. They turn left at a roundabout, heading towards the four cloud-cuddled pillars, which feel like the hub of everything she'll never understand.

The youngest sister suddenly skips ahead, forgetting to check for cars, and leaps over a puddle around a blocked drain, skidding to a stop on the concrete.

Within seconds, Kadra's scolding her, the ferociousness of her pitch no different from the day in the yard when she screamed at Jasmine. All the venom in the world, rolling off her tongue; a teenager already more exhausted of youth than Anna, through no fault of her own.

'My mother's always been a hard worker,' says Jenny's daughter, Catherine, holding all of her tension in her exposed shoulders. The studio-lit freckles on them look eerily similar to Jenny's. 'From a young age, she instilled a sense of determination in my sister and me. She'd hate me for saying this, but I remember when I was about nine, arguing with her over whether I was going to church or not. We had this huge tug-of-war out in the street, which –'

'I have to ask,' interrupts the host, 'given your position, do you think science and faith are mutually exclusive?'

'Not at all,' says Catherine, leaning back on her stool and finally releasing her shoulders. 'If you read the Bible, it *does* say that we have dominion – and I would interpret that as meaning a responsibility – over the planet . . .'

Total psycho

Easy, Zo

You asked 4 my opinion babe

Anna lays her phone down and stares at the pill packets sprawled on top of her self-inflating mattress. The sight of her two-hundred-dollar water purifier, its tube twisting behind her quick-dry towel, makes the trip feel inescapably real for the first time.

Corporatespeak alert!

'As well as the digital environment, which allows our messages to be significantly amplified.'

'Have you received much online abuse?'

'I don't think I'd be allowed to repeat some of it on air,' says Catherine, her jaw sharpening at whatever memories are rising to the surface.

Commencing charm offensive

How long til she runs for parliament?

Greens or alp?

Good question

ALP more likely

Once morals succumb to personal ambition

Lol

'One of the things we've noticed is that people connect with a sense of agency, especially young people,' says Catherine, pausing just long enough to allow a cutaway of the host nodding her assent. 'They're the ones who stand to lose the most. Future generations are going to judge us for the way that we acted, or didn't act . . .'

Even though the point is valid, Anna finds it difficult to stomach coming from someone so assured of their standing in life. It feels like the fundamental quality that her students – the 'young people' Catherine assumes she's advocating for – are missing. For all of their bravado, they can't see how the world will ever open up for them, no matter how much determination they have. Whereas people like Catherine, from the day they were old enough to dream of a future, have never doubted that they'd be fitted with a smooth-sounding lapel mic, and that their voice would be heard.

ALI

A kid in a soaked school uniform glides by on a BMX, leaning back and doing a mono on Racecourse Road.

'Fresh prince, hold up!' yells Ali.

Michael Garang bunny-hops onto the footpath, standing up in the pedals as he rides towards them.

'Yo, snitch!' he says when he recognises Walid, grinning with his rusty teeth.

'You've got no idea what you're saying,' says Walid, checking out Michael's shirt while he wheels around and pulls in beside them. 'I thought you don't go to school anymore.'

'I was bored today.'

'What about your job?'

'Man, what job?'

'You don't have to lie to us,' says Ali, watching Michael roll past the Holland Court tower, high in his pedals, bubblegum popping in his mouth.

'Yassin says he doesn't need me no more.'

'You're lucky he says that.'

'No way, man. That job's got swag.'

'It's not a job,' says Ali, noticing Tyler standing in the Telstra booth with $EDIMENT tags fading on the glass, pressing the phone against his ear. Tyler keeps rubbing his shaved head, hardly listening to whoever's talking to him.

'Where are we going?' asks Michael, springing off his bike so he can follow them through a gap in the walk-ups, where the concrete's covered in pigeon shit.

'Home,' says Ali.

'Yassin and them are still in your flat, yeah?' asks Walid.

'I think so,' says Michael.

'So where are you staying?'

'Just around, man.'

Michael shields his eyes from the drizzle as his fat BMX tyres fizz across the weakly lit car park.

'We're going away for ten days,' says Ali, 'but we can help you when we get back, yeah? You just have to stay busy while we're gone.'

Ten days feels like a whole lifetime.

'Make sure you keep going to school,' says Walid.

'The teachers hate me, man.'

'It's not like that,' says Walid, glaring into Michael's eyes, which are wet with chemicals. 'They just don't understand where you've been.'

'Do you have much money?' asks Ali.

Michael shakes his head, releasing another loud pop.

'Here, only use this for food,' says Ali, handing him two twenty-dollar notes from his work pants. He knows where the money's probably going, but if he doesn't show faith in the fresh prince now, no one ever will.

'Can you last until we come back?' asks Walid.

Michael squints at the deserted half-court, unable to stay in the conversation any longer.

His eyes look a lifetime sadder than when Musa sang 'Lemon Tree' to him at the Community Centre. The crazy thing about the lyrics is: some people don't even get to have lemons that they can turn into lemonade.

ALI

Reporters and cameramen are blocking the path to wherever it is that Walid and the lawyers are trying to go, but the lawyers keep walking. And the crowd magically clears. Seeing Walid getting treated as important all of a sudden, after years and years when no one wanted to know he existed, is whacked. Now the same people who ignored him have decided that he *did* exist the whole time, and being treated like he didn't exist was the biggest crime that could've been committed against him.

'This shit's hectic,' says Hassan, staying close to Ali, his hands hiding in the pockets of his puffer jacket. 'I don't get what happened in there.'

'I think you guys won,' says Ali, still trying to figure out how a trial can only last fifteen minutes.

'Do we get money now?'

'I don't know.'

A group of Hassan's old friends – the 'applicants', as the judge called them – and their lawyers stop in the shade of a shiny glass building, holding folders full of documents that prove the police have prejudices.

'We should move,' says Hassan, hurrying over to a pond by the side of the group, so they're further out of the way.

The main lawyer ignores the questions being yelled at her by the reporters and starts her speech for the fluffy microphones, talking about the courage of the complainants to stay strong.

'Is she the one who bought you lunch at that expensive restaurant?' asks Ali.

'We had bolognaise,' says Hassan, watching her.

As the lawyer speaks, the photographers pan their lenses to the complainants. Seeing Walid's face framed in the screens of TV cameras, as if he's Kanye or Jay-Z, makes it basically impossible not to be jealous.

'Check this dog out,' whispers Hassan.

The police boss is making his way through the crowd of reporters, wearing his special shirt with dark-blue patches on the shoulders, holding a piece of paper.

'Why the fuck is she shaking his hand?' asks Hassan.

'To show respect,' says Ali.

'He doesn't deserve respect.'

The lawyer steps out of the shot as the police boss gets ready to speak, his tie flapping like a donkey's tail in the wind.

'Let me begin by saying that today's settlement marks a crisis in confidence,' he reads, putting on the same concerned face he always has when there are cameras around, 'and a fresh start for all of us . . .'

'He should talk from his heart,' says Hassan. 'It doesn't mean anything when it's off a bit of paper.'

'They're too scared to talk from their heart.'

'Yeah, probably because they don't have them.'

It sounds like the police boss kind of wants to take responsibility for the messed-up things that've happened around the towers over the years, but he doesn't want to admit that kids have been stopped hundreds of times and beaten up, just because of the colour of their skin.

'Everyone knows he's talking shit, right?' says Hassan.

'I can't tell.'

'If you guys go away with him, it's like you're helping him prove his own lies.'

'But if we don't, what does *that* prove?'

The half-circles underneath Hassan's eyes look even more swollen in the daylight, when he's not slumped in darkness, dominating *FIFA*.

'Walid's different than you,' says Ali.

'What does that mean?'

'He hasn't, like, given up.'

'Is that honestly what you think?'

'Yeah, pretty much,' says Ali, pointing at Hassan's padded belly. 'That's what everyone thinks.'

'You don't understand anything,' says Hassan. He itches at the collar of his Magic Hand Carwash uniform, which is poking out the top of his jacket. 'This isn't giving up,' he says in his slow, lazy voice. 'This is keeping going.'

He shakes his head as he stares down the police boss, who's listing all the changes he's going to make now that they've been busted:

'A review of stop and search policies, cultural awareness training, employing multicultural liaison officers . . .'

Walid's listening to the fake political words coming out of the police boss's mouth while he looks beyond the cameras, towards the beautiful park on the other side of the tram tracks. City workers are racing along the paths that wind through the blanket of yellow leaves so they can eat their lunch in the sunshine. None of them probably has a clue what it's like to have knees digging into their spine as their neck is locked off, cheeks driven into the concrete by people high on hatred. Even just watching it was horrible enough.

Somehow, after everything that's happened to Walid, he seems calmer than Ali's ever seen him. Knowing he finally has his chance to speak. The police boss stops crapping on and steps aside, gesturing to Walid. In the hush of the reporters, where the clicking of pedestrian signals takes over, the one thing Walid has, more than anyone around him, is dignity.

THE SKY IS FALLING

ANNA

Clouds of cotton wrap around the mountains beyond the airstrip, below orange and violet vapours that're lingering from the late-afternoon thunderstorm. Anna can feel the mugginess plastering knotty hair across her forehead. She must look like shit. You go five days without a mirror and your fixations about the physical form gradually dissolve, reducing you to what you are inside; every psychological thread ribboning out in front of you, like the trail itself, beckoning to be explored.

Once again, she finds herself imagining this lush, tropical terrain subjected to warfare. The wild pumpkins, the giant brown knuckles of the tree roots, the slippery log crossings and the mud-sucking trail, which must've felt like the final gruelling frontier for Japanese soldiers before the bounty of the Australian mainland. She's surprised by how much it affects her. Not in the moments when the police want it to – during Paul's patriotic drivel at the Isurava Memorial, or while laying poppies at Brigade Hill – but in the hum when human voices cease and insects take over. When she's able to conceive that what she *does* conceive is less than one one-millionth of the actual story.

A cleft of light is spearing through the clouds, gushing over the ranges they've somehow managed to scale. The duality of terror and raw physical beauty must've been impossible to endure. Every crystal-clear stream, heightened for the soldiers because their own mortality was staring them right in the face. It feels only natural that no life beyond this – no love in a partner or child's eyes – could ever compare to the gravity of it, even if the physical vessel survives.

ALI

He does his best not to swallow any stream water as he lets out another silent groan of pleasure. None of the people washing clothes around them seem to be noticing what Kylie's doing with her hand below the waterline while she hums to herself, pretending she's only lying beside him, staring at the wall of green and purple vegetation before them.

Ali checks over his shoulder to see if Funda's watching, but she's bathing behind a giant rock where one of the sponsor's thermals are laid out drying, not wanting anyone to see her in a singlet.

Clear water flows over Kylie's pale, flickering body. The slickness of her hair, swooped back on her skull, makes her whole face look different. Natural and healthy. Skin smooth without so much foundation. She hasn't even looked at him once. Just lying there, peacefully, massaging the head of his cock, letting her fist collapse every few seconds and stretch back his foreskin, as if she knows exactly how he wants her to do it.

Another groan escapes from deep within Ali's chest. He can already tell that the bravado hip-hop's taught him – dissing your enemies, pretending you're invincible – won't help him as he clenches his abs, trying to fight whatever's rising up from within them. Giving in this quickly, his breath trembling as a drop of water trickles into his throat, feels like defeat.

TYLER

Ali's dad's breathing is slow and wheezy as he holds the steering wheel, his tummy expanding in the corner of Tyler's eye. This must be how soldiers feel, right before they go into combat for the first time. Palms damp and legs light and tingly, every muscle alive. It takes all the concentration he has to make sure his feet stay still on the rubber mat. He can feel the knife handle pressing against his calf, shifting around in his sock with every little jolt of the taxi.

Familiar sights keep sliding by, somehow more intense tonight: the massive green, white and orange flag flowing above the Irish pub, African cafés that only Africans go to, glazed ducks hanging in the windows of Chinese restaurants, dumpling joints, pho, kebabs, rotten grocers, bottle shops, deros talking shit on the bench outside the stinky musical toilet, bitching because the world didn't turn out the way they wanted it to. Tonight at least, for him, it will.

Tyler tilts his head slightly and marks the spot where he's going to jam the blade in. Just above Ali's dad's belly. A quick shank in the lungs, or any vital organ, should work. He'll have to pull the knife out straight away, in case the fat fuck tries to grab it. If the first shank doesn't go deep enough, he'll happily stab the kid-fucker again.

*

PAUL

'Jesus Christ!' says Athena as Paul folds up the portable pump, watching the nuggety village kids get stuck into the soccer balls that VicPol have donated. 'It hurts my head to see people with so much energy.'

'How's the knee?' asks Paul.

'Completely buggered,' she says with a wry grin, her cheeks already starting to hollow out. 'Inflamed tendon, maybe cartilage damage, the medico reckons.'

'You gonna let the porters spot you, like a geriatric, on the downhills tomorrow?'

'Don't stir the pot, Knowlesy.'

He lets his chuckling fizzle out and give way to the hum of cicadas. Soccer balls skim around, picking up smears of the beautiful brown earth. They cheer the kids on, watching them scuff up mud between the raised, thatched huts of the village.

All the huts look identical to the one in the background of the famous photo of the 39th Battalion, every soldier as haggard as an insomniac – making Athena look like a beauty queen – after five weeks of continuous action. Waves of Japs pouring out of the jungle, outnumbering them three to one, hammering them with artillery, shells bursting in the trees and showering the poor bastards with shrapnel.

Seeing the slit trenches they had to deal with for himself has only increased his gratitude to the Aussie diggers for what they went through; the eeriness of camping out all night in one of those small, slimy pits, clothes sopping, ciggie papers turning to mush, shivering through to dawn, as well as the corroding mortars and grenades that still pop up along the trail, gives

Paul an even greater appreciation of the depths of the thing, and why missing out on the Special Forces all those years ago might've been dodging an almighty bullet.

ANNA

Shrieks of laughter echo from the village behind her, where a game of sport has broken out. A few police are encouraging the local kids in that ultra-enthusiastic, slightly patronising manner they all seem to have perfected.

As she leans forward to slap more dried mud from her gaiters, her stomach lurches, craving the two-minute noodles that now constitute dinner. The thought of the salty sachets of flavour makes her mouth start frothing. But she isn't quite ready to trade in the view for it yet.

The Commissioner isn't, either. Sprawled on the itchy grass of the airstrip in his sweat-stained Nike gear, staring at the clouds below them, taking in what must be a rare allotment of solitude for him. No matter what spin he ends up putting on this experience, surely, in this moment, he understands that he's nothing more than anyone else in the group. As much as it's about the kids from the estate seeing him swabbing his feet with antiseptic cream and powdering his crusty toes every morning, he also needs to see the same vulnerability in them, so he can finally comprehend that they're nothing less than him.

ALI

Wild chickens flutter out from the stilts of huts, not sure what to do among the chaos. It's kind of like the crazy games of barefoot soccer that Walid's described from when he was growing up in the camps, where hundreds of kids ran around with no boundary markings, only hoping to touch the ball once.

Every time Ali changes direction, the blisters on his heels sting, like lemon juice in an open wound. But the pain's totally worth it. The local kids have serious moves, sidestepping adults who're twice their height and scampering away with the ball, laughing their arses off, happy, even though none of them have any electricity to watch the Premier League.

AJ gets the ball and ignores Binh's run so he can try to cross it to Walid, still pretending they're friends, even after what the police boss admitted outside court. Ali easily intercepts the ball and rolls it into the path of the square-jawed St. Bernard's school captain. Paul reaches out and pats Walid on the back of his Didier Drogba shirt, cracking himself up, always acting like he's the hero of his own life.

TYLER

They glide under the railway bridge, past the bright blue glow of the plaza. In his head, it's always happened at the next set of traffic lights, but if they get a green, he'll have to do it somewhere around the ugly apartment blocks at Kensington Banks, or out near the Maribyrnong River, where the pigs drowned that African kid and got away with it.

In five minutes, it'll be over. Just thinking about doing it makes the blood vessels pound against his temples. *No one fights well when they lose their head.* Shannon would be ashamed of how much of a pussy he's being, worrying about the tingles that're spreading along his arms to the tips of his fingers. He rubs them against his skin to try to dry the sweat off, but it feels like they're acting on their own now, picking up all this crazy electricity.

'Who's she?'

'Huh?' grunts Tyler. He looks down and realises that he's tracing his fingers over the raised skin on his bicep, scraping at the scab of Mum's face. 'No one.'

They get another green light and race by the semi-trailers and four-wheel drives that're being filled with petrol at Shell.

'How old are you?' grunts the fat fuck.

'Eighteen.'

'You don't look eighteen.'

Talking is seriously messing with his concentration. Next red light, even if they're still talking shit, he'll do it.

PAUL

Almost impossible to get a touch of the soccer ball with the way it's pinging around. Especially with his legs feeling like the hefty logs they crossed swamps on today. No acceleration left, calves as tight as drumskins.

He catches sight of Anna making her way towards the campsite with the watercolours of the sky behind her. There's an air to her these past couple of days, like the history of it all – which she probably used to shit all over – is finally sinking in.

She flicks him a fatigued 'hi' and he salutes her back, army-style. Enough warmth in her puffy-cheeked smile to know that he's no longer public enemy number one.

Jai calls out and sends the ball his way. Paul has a crack

at trapping it, but his feet are too heavy to cooperate with his brain, accidentally allowing the ball to dribble through to Walid. He sets off to the far end of the field in his sopping Chelsea top and nutmegs Athena in goals, side-footing the ball between backpacks.

Walid spreads his arms into an aeroplane celebration, tilting his imaginary wings as he skirts the palm trees on the edge of the village. On his way back to his own team, it's not so much that he even acknowledges Paul, but at least as he whizzes past, for once, his smile doesn't break.

ANNA

She squelches past pawpaw trees and damp khaki clothes that're hanging between banana plants, towards the dark mass of forms huddled around the fire. The falsettos of the porters reach her in waves, their unfamiliar melodies allowing her to enjoy the infinity of language. As she makes her way up the final thigh-stabbing climb of the day, glimpsing the leafy roofs of traditional huts on the outskirts of the village, she marvels at how measured her own breathing sounds, the steamy air cleansing her lungs. It's been hours since *he* crossed her mind. Guilt is the last thing she owes him. He's the one who put her on this walk, in this remote village, in this changed body. A body still somehow pulsing. At least the steady beating in her chest, whatever it does or doesn't amount to, is a feeling that she can finally trust.

*

ALI

Pretty much everyone huddled around the fire's swaying to the strumming of acoustic guitars, ukuleles and the porters' high-pitched harmonies. The unknown words make the back of Ali's neck tingle – even more than when he listens to 'Changes' by Pac – forcing him to feel the craziness that's happened in this jungle, and to understand why the old dude from the RSL couldn't keep his lips still anymore.

Funda's the only person not digging the music. Sitting beside Ali with her head drooped, itching, almost violently, at the ant bites on her legs. He wraps his arm around her, already smelling sweat from his damp armpits.

'How can you, like, *do* that in front of people?' she asks.

'Do what?'

'I saw you and Kylie in the creek. It's disgusting.'

'You should be happy for us,' he says, giving her a cheeky grin that would normally crack her up. 'You alright, cuz?'

The scent of smoky, freshly cooked fish drifts into his nostrils from one of the nearby huts. He can taste the mix of flesh and stream water in the air.

'I wanna go home.'

'What're you talking about?' says Ali. 'This is *way* better than home.'

Her frizzy hair dips even lower until her face is hidden between her own legs.

'Seriously,' he whispers. 'What's going on?'

'Nothing.'

'Just tell me, cuz.'

Her bare shoulders tremble the same way they used to

whenever she was pissing herself laughing at a joke he'd made.

'You remember what Tyler said at the RSL?' she says, her voice muffled.

'For sure.'

'He was talking about your dad.'

Ali stares into the flames, feeling the heat reach for his cheeks, just about singeing them, as he tries to wrap his brain around whatever the hell she's talking about.

'So how do you . . .' he says, pausing as he scrapes sweat and insect repellent from his right arm, grime collecting beneath his fingernails. 'Did Dad, like . . . hurt you?'

Funda nods, her hair a knotty blanket of darkness.

'Fuck,' is all Ali can say, forcing his fingers to stop clawing at his own skin. The smell of fish flesh is getting even stronger, making his tummy churn. Or maybe it's from swallowing stream water. Every single thing about Mum – and his life – suddenly makes sense. He wishes he could see her, right now, and say sorry. But he can't even bring himself to say the word to Funda.

Splintery logs crackle below a billycan in the heart of the fire. Ali's eyes water as he remembers the glee on Tyler's face as he shouted 'KID-FUCKERS' in front of the whole restaurant, as if he knew a secret joke.

'Hold up, why would Tyler know that?'

Funda refuses to answer, or look up.

'Cuz?'

'I told him,' she whimpers. 'It was an accident.'

'How could you?' croaks Ali, his voice breaking up as he realises there's nothing he can do to stop the consequences of her telling Tyler. Funda's shoulders start shaking again, the rest of her body rocking, as she lets out a howl that's almost the same pitch as the porters' singing.

TYLER

He forces himself to remember what he felt when Funda was hiding her head under the covers in her bedroom, and the sounds that wouldn't stop – more animal than human – which seemed like they were coming from deeper in her body than any sounds he'd ever heard anyone make . . .

The taxi thumps over a pothole, shifting the knife in his sock. It feels like the blade's pricking his anklebone. Adjusting it would be too obvious, so he presses all his weight into the ball of his foot to stop his leg from moving.

The whistling coming from the fat fuck's nostrils, above his ugly moustache, is getting even more annoying. It's like his lungs are filled with dust that keeps rising, trying to escape, and then resettling.

The meter clicks, startling Tyler.

'You okay, kid?'

'Yep.'

His thigh's vibrating so much that he can't even read the rectangular yellow digits that say how much it's all supposed to cost. Blood's definitely leaking out of his ankle, forming a warm clot where the skin's sticking to the fabric of his sock.

'Do you have enough money to pay?'

'Uh-huh,' says Tyler.

Tyres rumble right in his ears as dotted lines disappear in front of him. He can feel the fat fuck watching him with those sleazy eyes that've already seen a shitload more than they deserve to. Electricity surges through his body. He knows Dad's felt this electricity before. Nothing beyond it matters.

'Tell me if you're gonna be sick.'

'I will,' he says, calmly.

Up ahead, the last light before the river pulses from green to orange, and – like it always does – from orange to red.

Acknowledgements

Lester Freamon, who's painted his share of dollhouse miniatures, once said, 'All the pieces matter.' This was a novel of (too) many pieces; an absurd narrative undertaking that I could never have completed on my own.

Huge thanks to everyone I've interviewed in the past eight years. Most of you – dealers, users, police, teachers, former students of mine – don't wish to be acknowledged by name, but please know that the reality of the world portrayed in this book is because of your generosity. I have tried to do your worlds justice and to represent them as realistically, and unflinchingly, as I can, with scrupulous sensitivity.

To Abdulaahi in purgatory, thank you for our candid chats. No matter what has happened, I believe you never stood a chance.

On a professional level, I must thank my agent, Sarah McKenzie from the 'Wick, for enthusiastically getting back to me four days after I first submitted work to her. It's lovely to have a(n albeit polite) skull-cracker on my side.

The eloquent Geordie Williamson wrote back to us only two days after our submission. His soft voice and guidance throughout this process/ordeal have helped me breathe easier.

Seriously. Having a publisher who believes in you is a privilege.

Thanks to editors Belinda Huang and Brianne Collins, who both contributed a shitload in the final slog to get this white whale over the line. Forever grateful to you two for dignifying my creative efforts. And apologies to Brianne for stubbornly insisting on the grammatical errors in dialogue throughout this novel. Whatever happens, it's on me.

Much gratitude to Peter FitzSimons for researching and writing *Kokoda*, which helped me flesh out the war passages in this novel, and to Matt Kilfoyle, who kindly described the Kokoda Trail to me at (probably excruciating) length. Gratitude also to writers Zadie Smith and George Saunders – neither of whom I've met – for their ambitious, original and fearless fiction.

Many friends have helped, in different ways, along the way. Thanks for your encouragement in the early stages of the manuscript, Chris, Mirra, Richie, Tim, Ben and Carla. Special thanks to Will and Pip, for putting me up in the Top End while I drafted the second act of this novel, its most fluid part.

I only have one writer who I call a friend, and that is the always odd-socked Miles Allinson. Cheers for being broke like me, buddy, and for keeping on going . . . out of sheer rage.

Deepest thanks to the night owls that are the Middleton/Gartner family – Anne, Kent and Lexi – for showing constant interest in my endeavours, but for also respecting my dislike of talking about them. I couldn't ask for a luckier life to be born into. Thanks also to the Barnes family, for welcoming a Saint into tribal council.

Finally, and above all, thanks to my own family, which

increased in number over the course of this novel. We have a very small home with a large amount of love, which, I imagine, is a lot better than the opposite. Eternal love to Jess and Lenny. Two beautiful people with beautiful hearts and beautiful eyes. With you both, my life has peace.

–MM